All heads around th⎯⎯⎯ Ormont expectantly. A strange silence descended.

Ormont leaned forward to the console and drew the microphone closer on its flexible support. He had thought a lot about what he would say to those who were about to follow him when this moment arrived. In the end, he decided to dispense with written notes altogether and let his thoughts speak themselves naturally, which accorded more with his style. He nodded to the bridge communications officer, who put out an announcement that the director in chief would address the ship. Ormont's console camera lamp came on, indicating that his image was going out to all parts of the *Aurora*.

He began, "This is your director in chief speaking. Very soon now, in a matter of minutes, we will depart on what will possibly be the most stupendous, exciting, and fantastic adventure ever undertaken by members of the human race. One day in the distant future, our descendants will be the seed out of which will grow a new world of our kind. For that world to preserve all the variety, richness, and potential that our kind has come to represent through its millennia of history, we go not just as the Builders from Sofi, but as unique individuals bringing talents of every kind from remote regions of Earth, its nations, races, cultures, and peoples...."

Books by James P. Hogan

MIGRATION

—⚡—

JAMES P. HOGAN

MIGRATION

This is a work of fiction. All the characters and events portrayed in this book are fictional, and any resemblance to real people or incidents is purely coincidental.

A Baen Books Original

Baen Publishing Enterprises
P.O. Box 1403
Riverdale, NY 10471
www.baen.com

ISBN: 978-1-4391-3447-4

Cover art by Alan Pollack

First paperback printing, June 2011

Library of Congress Control Number: 2010005096

Distributed by Simon & Schuster
1230 Avenue of the Americas
New York, NY 10020

Pages by Joy Freeman (www.pagesbyjoy.com)
Printed in the United States of America

MIGRATION

PART ONE
Breaking Ties

– ONE –

Nobody that Korshak had met in his thirty-one years of mostly traveling, nor any of the preserved writings that he knew of, had been able to tell him precisely how long ago the old world had destroyed itself in the Great Conflagration. Some put it at two or three generations; others said centuries; a few thought as much as a thousand years. Different schools of history had different ways of estimating, and no two seemed able to produce the same result. The ruins of cities that had once extended for miles decayed away under weather, weeds, and encroaching sands, and the machines that had animated them corroded back into the earth without divulging their secrets.

He stood looking down over the site of one of those old cities now, from a stance among the rocks on the hill where they had camped the night before. It was called Escalos, in the land known as Arigane. Little appeared to have changed significantly since the last time they were here. The outer parts of what had been the original city had long turned into mounds of overgrown rubble rising above jumbled streets of clay-brick and wooden hovels, although in places the lines could still be discerned of broad avenues made to carry thousands of vehicles that now existed only as rare, faded pictures or piles of unearthed rust. Farther in toward the center, thrusting here and there above the roofs of the state offices and court building, and the domes of Shandrahl's palace, the skeletal remnants of towering structures stood in mute testament to arts that existed here no more. But elsewhere they had been revived. And one day Korshak would learn them.

"The cabinet is ready." Ronti's voice came from below.

Korshak turned. "How about the stew?" he called back.

"That's ready, too. And we still have half a bottle of wine."

"Ah, right! First things first, eh?" Korshak picked his way back down to where the wagon stood in a glade among the trees, by a pool formed from a widening of the stream. Sprung high on its axles, it was enclosed under a barrel roof and painted bright red with elaborate designs and mystical symbols along the sides, and a driver's bench up front, behind which a flap door opened from the interior. The two horses were tethered a short distance away, where there was water and plenty of grass. The descent down into Escalos would be an easy haul for them.

Ronti was behind the wagon, squatting on a box by the fire as he ladled from the hanging pot into a couple of earthenware bowls. He was slight and wiry in build, with a mat of black hair, pointed mustachios adorning a mobile, sun-darkened countenance, and dark, beady eyes that never seemed quite able to take the world seriously, but saw more than they pretended to. Korshak had first encountered him five years previously in the seaport town of Belamon, working as a street acrobat and contortionist. Such talents were exactly the kind of thing needed for an assistant in a new routine that Korshak had devised, and he offered the position on the spot. Ronti turned out to be the most capable partner that Korshak had ever worked with, and they had remained together ever since.

Korshak sat down on a folded blanket placed over one of the rocks, took the bowl that Ronti proffered, and broke some bread off the loaf lying on a board by the fire. On the far side, Sultan gnawed at a bone of mutton chop nestled protectively between his paws. Ronti poured wine into a couple of earthenware mugs. "Anything of note?" he inquired as he handed one to Korshak.

"They've been rebuilding where they had that fire near the market. Otherwise, everything looks much the same. There are what look like gibbets outside the main gate. Shandrahl must be having another of his purges."

Ronti made a face. "Let's hope there aren't any hitches with the act tomorrow, then," he said.

"I'd be more concerned about anything going wrong with what happens afterward," Korshak replied.

"Thanks, but I'd prefer not to think about that."

"Then think about longer after still—what it will all be for," Korshak suggested. "Do you know what Masumichi told me one time when I talked to him in the window that sees across vast distances? The stars, where we will be going, are all suns, but just farther away. Do you know how far, Ronti?"

Ronti stirred the food together in his bowl for a few seconds and shrugged. "If the world were the size of my hand, then, say, the distance to the middle of Escalos?" he guessed. He thought while he continued chewing, and then added, "But since I don't really know how big the world is, I suppose that doesn't mean very much."

"I'm not sure I do, either," Korshak confessed. "But Masumichi gave me a different example that I did understand, which will amaze you."

"Go on, amaze me," Ronti invited.

Korshak looked around, then touched the end of a finger on a sliver of charred wood that had fallen outside the hearthstones. "The whole world would fit inside the Sun thousands of times," he said. "Now imagine the Sun reduced to the size of one of those specks of black there on my finger. Well, have you any idea what the distance would be to the *nearest* other star? About four miles!"

Ronti stopped chewing and stared. "I'm amazed."

"And where we're going is thousands of times farther even than that."

It took Ronti a while longer, of breaking and oiling bread, more munching in silence, and then a draft from his wine mug, to absorb the information. "And did Masumichi tell you how this is possible?" he asked at last. "Since I, for one, cannot conceive it. To fly through the sky and talk over huge distances—that I can grasp, even if I don't understand how it's done. But what kind of old-world magic is this?"

"*Real* magic!" Korshak answered. "Except that it isn't magic. Magic without tricks. We'll know wonders that we never dreamed of, and that's what makes the risks worthwhile. Without some risks, life is not a life at all—no more than eating and sleeping and existing from one day to the next, all of them the same, until you live out your spell. Is that how you want it to be? That's what you should be thinking about, Ronti."

Ronti mopped his bowl with the last of his bread, and finished his wine. "Well, I say life is to be dealt with a day at a time," he said. "And right now that means making sure that our own, this-worldly kind of magic, modest as it may be, will work. Otherwise we'll never get to what you're talking about anyway. Do you want to check the cabinet?"

Korshak tossed a remnant of meat to Sultan and stood up. "Yes, let's see it."

Ronti had assembled the cabinet on the lowered tailboard of the wagon beneath the rear shutter, which hinged upward to form an overhead shade. It was as high as a man, wide enough to accommodate two standing side by side, and the same in depth. Its front consisted of a pair of doors ornamented with designs that were echoed on the sides. The doors were open, revealing a pole with a lamp at the top standing in the center, but the details beyond were in shadow. Ronti sprung up the step onto the tailboard and produced a matchbook from a pocket of his jacket. He leaned into the cabinet to light the lamp, and then stepped aside. The light showed the two sides and rear of the interior lined uniformly in quilted maroon silk, and a dark, matted floor. Korshak ran his eye over it critically. There were no telltale stains, blotches, or other irregularities whose reflection would give the secret away. The hidden edges blended into the pattern of the lining invisibly.

"Fine," he pronounced. Then, letting his voice rise to a showman's tone, he went on, "As you can see, a perfectly ordinary box in every way, as deep as it is wide," which Ronti demonstrated by turning the cabinet around on casters fitted beneath its corners. He opened the rear wall, which could now be seen as also comprising two doors, enabling a view right through, while Korshak continued, directing his words and gestures at Sultan since there was nobody else. "No false back or hidden compartments. Would anyone care to inspect the inside and satisfy themselves before we proceed further?" Sultan was following alertly but remained with his bone.

Up on the wagon, Ronti turned the cabinet to face forward again, still with both sets of doors open, and stepped into it through the front and then out through the back. Closing the rear doors behind him, he then walked back around to the front.

"Good," Korshak told him. "Carry on. I want to see the effect from here."

Ronti stepped into the front of the cabinet once more, but this time he turned and closed the doors. Korshak listened for any giveaway squeaks or clicks, but detected nothing. Inside the cabinet, Ronti would be opening the two top-to-floor panels that hinged out at the rear corners from shallow recesses in the side walls to meet at the central pole. Thus, they partitioned off a triangular space at the back of the cabinet, between the pole and the two rear corners, large enough to hold a man standing, or with a squeeze, two. Normally, Korshak would open the front doors at this point, but since he was down on the ground, playing the part of a spectator, Ronti let himself out the back of the cabinet, came around again, and did it for him.

The reverse surfaces of the two hinged panels—the surfaces that faced inward when the panels were in their recesses—consisted of high-quality mirrors. In the opened position, each mirror reflected an image of a silk-lined side wall, which to an observer looking in the front appeared to be the rear wall. Korshak checked carefully for correct alignments and continuity of hue. The illusion of the cabinet's being empty was perfect. It could be used to make a person vanish, or if the preliminary see-through demonstration were omitted, to have one person walk in and a different one step out. As was his custom with all his creations, Korshak had inscribed his name cryptically into the ornamental patterning.

Mechanical illusions were Korshak's specialty. The disappearing cabinet was his latest invention, into which he had invested his greatest skill and care. The performance would need to be his most compelling ever. He intended to steal a princess from under the eyes of her tyrannical father and a man she despised, to whom she had been promised as a bride, before an audience of courtiers and officers in the center of the royal palace. One of the problems with life tended to be that it didn't permit any rehearsal.

Later, when they were preparing to depart, Korshak dismantled the cabinet and stowed the parts away, while Ronti attended to packing the cooking ware and harnessing the horses. By the time Korshak climbed down to close up the rear, Ronti was already up on the driver's bench, waiting with the reins. As Korshak bolted the tailboard, a light low in the sky to the east caught his eye. It moved discernibly even as he watched, and he smiled. *Aurora* was passing over. Before very much longer now, they would be up there, too. Then he would learn real magic.

- TWO -

In the female quarters facing the inner court and garden of Shandrahl's palace in the center of Escalos, Vaydien arched her back defiantly against the wall of her private chambers. "*Never!* My father can force me to marry you, yes—through fear for my life, in the same way that he threatens all who would defy him. But don't expect me to declare subservience to the House of Erendred. Let nobody believe that this was by my choice."

Zileg, crown prince and heir to lordship over the neighboring land of Urst, regarded her in the amused way that one might have shown to a hissing kitten. He was tall and powerful in build, and with his dark eyes, rich mane of black hair, and tapered mustache, handsome too in terms of looks; but his vanity and arrogance repelled her, and in cruelty he could equal either of the two rulers.

"A spirited child. I like that. But do you seriously believe that anyone is interested in *your* preferences? Your place is to serve a purpose in a greater scheme of things than your understanding of the world could grasp. Don't ever forget it."

Vaydien shook her head despairingly. "My role is to create an illusion of trust between your people and mine until Shandrahl has prepared his ground, and it suits him to betray you. Just as it suited him to get rid of my mother when she had served her purpose. Are you really too blind to see it?"

Anger flashed in Zileg's eyes. He moved a step forward, his hand rising reflexively. "Be careful how you speak to your future sovereign. I see that a proper sense of respect and decorum is also something that you need to learn."

Vaydien presented her cheek. "Go on! Today I am still Shandrahl's daughter. Strike her if you dare."

Zileg hesitated, then drew back with a snort. "A week from now you will be mine. Then we'll see. I shall take pleasure in breaking that insolence of yours."

"Is that your idea of sport? Abusing women. A man worthy of the name would find greater contest."

Zileg's face whitened, and for a moment Vaydien thought he would be unable to restrain himself further. Then he turned away abruptly, and seeing the vase of flowers that she had been working on when he entered, crushed several of the heads savagely in his hand. "There will be no time for such idle distractions when you become part of Erendred's household," he told her. "You will be at my side at the banquet tonight. I would advise you to use the time until then profitably by reflecting on the wisdom of your ways." With that, he strode darkly from the room.

Vaydien waited until she heard the outer door to her chambers close, and only then closed her eyes and allowed herself to exhale shakily. While the pounding in her chest gradually abated, she removed the mangled blooms and leaves from the vase and did her best to repair the arrangement.

Zileg had arrived from Urst three days previously with a cavalry troop from the regiment that he commanded, to take his bride-to-be back for the wedding. His intention was to be seen bringing her back to his future realm in a style befitting their rank, riding to drums and trumpets in a carriage provided by the ruler of Arigane, led and flanked by a picked escort bearing his own colors. As custom dictated, Shandrahl would not be present to contest Erendred's status at the ceremony, but would arrive to join in the celebrations in the days following. In the meantime, he would be hosting a banquet and entertainments in Zileg's honor that evening, before sending the couple on their way tomorrow. He had no compunction about using his daughter as a bargaining chip to buy stability in the shorter term where politically expedient. Vaydien shuddered at the images that ran through her mind of the kind of life which that would portend. But there could be no escape from it now.

Unless . . .

Unless she could believe the things that Korshak had told her. . . . But no. That had been long ago. Time had run out. Things like that had no place in her thoughts now.

A slight sound from the outer room of her chambers caught her ear—as if made by someone moving stealthily. Vaydien stopped what she was doing and crossed warily to the open doorway. Leetha, her younger half-sister, was poised at the outer door, in the act of turning the handle to let herself out.

"*Brat!*" Vaydien exploded. "What are you doing in here? Have you been spying on me?"

Leetha responded by brazening things out. "Do you know what, Vaydien? You're stupid! I have more common sense and know more about reality than you ever will. Even at my age I'd make Zileg a better wife, because I can recognize a good thing when I see it."

Vaydien was too exhausted after her confrontation with Zileg to be up to taking on another one. "You don't understand. . . ."

Leetha shook her head incredulously, golden curls swirling above her pale green gown. "I don't understand *you*. What kind of woman would spoil a future like that? To be the wife of a dashing, fine-looking military officer, who could one day be the most powerful ruler in the entire region. If you weren't the first in line . . . It isn't fair. Ugh! It makes me so angry."

Vaydien sighed tiredly. Leetha was as blind as Zileg, but at least she had the excuse of being young. If the truth were known, Leetha very likely *was* destined to become a powerful lady in the land one day—but not as the wife of Zileg. If Vaydien guessed their father's designs correctly, Zileg would be discarded when Erendred's domain was overrun to become a part of Arigane, which was why he was being set up now with a wife who would be expendable. Leetha's mother would have no argument with that. Getting Vaydien out of the way to clear the way for her own daughter's future would suit her very well indeed.

But talk along such lines would be shameful and unbecoming—as well as futile. Before Vaydien could respond, a soft knock sounded on the door. She turned her head toward it. "Yes?"

"Mirsto."

"Yes, of course."

The door opened to admit a portly, aging, white-haired, bearded figure, clad in a blue robe. As the court physician, Mirsto was one of the few males permitted free access to this part of the palace. Even Zileg had overstepped protocol in entering—but Vaydien had expected nothing better. Mirsto gave Leetha an admonishing look.

"Do you need to be here right now? Your sister has a lot to do today, preparing for tonight and then leaving tomorrow. She should be getting some rest."

"She doesn't deserve—" Leetha began, but Vaydien cut in.

"We were just talking. Leetha was about to leave anyway." Vaydien shifted her eyes. "Weren't you?"

A moment passed. Leetha seemed reluctant to move. "Vaydien and I do have private matters to discuss," Mirsto told her pointedly. She took in the look on his face, sniffed, and let herself out with a haughty toss of her curls. Mirsto moved to close the door behind her.

Vaydien let several seconds pass, releasing her tension in a long, drawn-out breath. Mirsto reached out and squeezed her shoulder reassuringly. The gesture was well-meant, Vaydien knew, but it felt empty. "I saw her follow Zileg in," Mirsto explained. "It seemed better to wait until he'd left."

Vaydien could feel her eyes moistening with tears of frustration and helplessness. "I'm being sacrificed to Shandrahl's ambitions, just as my mother was. Nothing but evil rules the world. Is that what ended the last one?" Then she saw that Mirsto's eyes, still sharp and bright despite his years, were twinkling. "Why do you look like that? What place can there be for mirth, on today of all days?"

"Oh, I don't know that it's *all* evil," he replied. "I seem to remember a certain young gentleman who entertained the court here some time ago, who displayed fine manners and principles. He knew of wondrous people who talked of building a new world. And he promised one day to come back, I do recall."

Vaydien stared at him searchingly, as if fearing a poor joke. "At this late hour. How could it be?"

"There is talk of surprise entertainment at the banquet tonight. And he was extremely well-received the last time."

"You really believe it could be possible?" Vaydien whispered. Mirsto led the way through to the rear room where she had been before, with the large windows opening out to the garden of the inner court. His voice took on a more serious and confidential tone.

"I've had reports from the town. His wagon arrived in the hills above Escalos the day before yesterday."

Just when Vaydien had given up hope. She found herself trying to laugh, but it wouldn't come. Her head was a whirl of feelings and emotions jostling to try and form themselves into something coherent. "It seems impossible. And yet, everything he did seemed impossible...." Coming back into the room, she stopped suddenly, staring at the empty table.

"What?" Mirsto asked her.

Vaydien gestured. "There was a vase of flowers right here only a moment ago. I was working on it." She looked from side to side, at a loss.

Mirsto's countenance wrinkled into a smile. "I rather think I feel magical influences at work already." He moved forward and peered around. "Ah!" Vaydien followed his gaze. The vase was a short distance away

outside, standing on a rock amid the shrubbery bordering the pool. Several bright red flowers that hadn't
been there before filled the gaps left by the damaged
ones. Vaydien stared incredulously.

"You'd better go and investigate," Mirsto advised.
"It seems he's found the one place where your father's
agents won't be watching. I'll stand guard for you
in the other room. If anyone comes, I'll tell them
you're resting."

– THREE –

Besides being a part of Korshak's stock-in-trade, finding out things that people were not supposed to know formed an irrepressible side to his nature. Investigations pursued in the course of earlier visits had revealed the tunnel built beneath Shandrahl's palace to provide a way out in the event of an emergency. It seemed that fears of danger and treachery came as constant companions with lives dedicated to amassing wealth and power. The tunnel gave access to the inner court and royal quarters, and had a side passage connecting to the servants' quarters, where Korshak and Ronti had been directed on their arrival. As well as providing its intended means of escape, therefore, the tunnel also afforded a convenient way in.

Korshak crouched in the shrubbery by the pool outside the windows, and smiled to himself at the consternation visible within over the vanished vase of flowers. A more conventional way of announcing himself wouldn't have been consistent with his style. He watched as eventually Mirsto spotted the vase on its rock near to where Korshak was hidden, said something to Vaydien and pointed, and then left the

19

room. Looking mystified, while at the same time rapt in wonder, Vaydien moved to the windows, opened one of them, and emerged. She came forward slowly, searching from side to side with her eyes, not moving her head too visibly, and followed a narrow path to a bower screened by the shrubbery, where a seat faced out toward the pool.

"Korshak?" she murmured in a low, cautious voice. He rose, smiling, just a few feet away from her, stepped forward, and clasped her hands. She stared for a moment in delighted disbelief and kissed him impulsively, but her expression changed to one of alarm. "You must be insane, coming here like this."

"Did you ever doubt it?"

"But how did you get in?"

"I have no need of doors. Didn't you know?"

"Oh, you're impossible! Do you even know how to be serious about anything? My father has eyes everywhere. Have you any idea what would happen if you were caught?"

"Eyes look outward. Never back inside their own heads."

Vaydien sighed despairingly; but she was happy. Korshak lowered himself onto the seat and drew her down next to him. "I was beginning not to believe you'd be back," she said.

"Then you need to get to know me better," he answered. "I always keep promises."

She looked at him hesitantly. "And does that mean you'll take me with you? That was also a promise."

"Of course."

"When?"

"Tonight."

Vaydien choked weakly. Just as she had been finding her strength.... "Now I think you are serious," she managed.

"I always tell the truth, too."

Vaydien took in a long breath while she fought to maintain her composure. "You ... also seem to have a way of keeping surprises until the last moment," she said finally.

Korshak shrugged. "Otherwise, they wouldn't be surprises. Besides, the worst way I know of guarding a secret is to make it known too soon."

"What, even to me?" Vaydien looked shocked. "Who would I tell, apart from Mirsto? And I know that you trust him."

"You don't have to tell anyone. People have other ways of communicating themselves, that they're unaware of, but which those who make it their business to be suspicious are very good at reading.... In any case, Mirsto already knows."

Vaydien gave a satisfied nod. "I *knew* there was something odd afoot the moment he walked in. He talks with his eyes." She looked mildly reproachful. "He could have just told me, without you risking your neck like this."

"Send an old man to speak for me, while I hide like a rabbit?" Korshak shook his head. "That's not my way."

"I know it isn't. And that's why I want to go with you—to a new world." She snuggled more closely against him, resting a hand on his shoulder. "Tell me more about it. Another world that turns about a distant star that's another sun. The light that moves across the sky is the great ship that will take us there."

"Yes," Korshak replied. It was another subject about which he had refrained from divulging too much.

"But how are we to get to it?"

"The builders of the ship will bring us there. They are the ones whose images I have seen and talked with in my travels."

Vaydien shook her head distantly and dreamily. "What manner of arts can build a ship that travels across the sky, large enough to carry thousands, you say, yet so high that it appears as a speck? Can one sail to the stars?"

Korshak took her hand, admired it, and lifted it to his lips while he considered the question. "Shandrahl has metalsmiths who work in the forge and armory to shape weapons for his soldiers," he said.

"Ye-es," Vaydien looked at him uncertainly.

"And in schools and craft shops out in the city, there are those who cut and polish lenses for spyglasses and magnifiers, and others whose artifice enables steam to turn engines that move mills and other ingenious devices."

"Secrets that only the specially gifted can know," Vaydien said, voicing the generally held belief.

"Those are just a few, isolated techniques that have been preserved without understanding from a far vaster trove of knowledge that once existed, that enabled feats beyond our comprehension."

"You mean greater magic than that which you persuade people you command?"

Korshak snorted and grinned. "If you like." He had already made it clear to Vaydien that the things he did were accomplished through trickery—although at times he wasn't sure if she completely believed him.

"I have seen strange, intricately fashioned parts of

metals and other materials that were unearthed, that could serve no discernible purpose," Vaydien said slowly. "And once, a decayed device with studs that I was told would let its owner talk instantly to anyone, anywhere. But I was never sure whether to believe it."

"Oh, such things were once commonplace," Korshak assured her.

"And was it that knowledge that destroyed the old world?" she asked.

"Yes. But it didn't have to. The world then was not like the one that you know today—divided into many regions like Arigane and Urst, that are cut off from other places and communicate little. The knowledge that existed then was available to all people, everywhere. There are places in the world today where that knowledge has been resurrected, and the ancient wonders have been created again. But those who have rediscovered that knowledge will not, this time, give it freely to the world to be misused again. It is shared only with selected adepts. To be accepted, they must show themselves worthy in spirit and disposition, as well as aptitude of mind."

"And is that how you were chosen?"

Korshak nodded. "But the same patterns of evil have been arising again in the nations taking shape across the world. So the Builders decided that they would go away and begin a new world of their own, where their knowledge will be used wisely. And so they constructed the great ship that you see traveling across the sky as a light. Its name is *Aurora*."

Vaydien was listening, spellbound, her deep brown eyes watching Korshak's face unwaveringly. "And we depart tonight?" she repeated.

"Tonight. You, and I, and Mirsto, with Ronti."

"What must I do?"

"That is what I have come to tell you. Now, listen carefully. . . ."

At a table in the kitchens at the rear of the palace, Ronti was eating soup and bread with some of the household staff.

"The same magician that astounded them before," one of the cooks informed the table over her shoulder, from where she was stirring the contents of a large pot on a stove. "What's his secret, Mr. Ronti? Everyone has a secret. His must be a special one."

"You don't think he'd tell you, do you?" one of the scullery maids said scornfully.

Ronti sat back and treated them to a look of one imparting a rare confidence. Part of his function was to take on the hat of Korshak's agent when the opportunity presented itself. "It's the bloodline," he told them. "Korshak is from a family that has produced generations of adepts. His mother could see into the future. She said when he was young that he would one day visit a land far from the sea, where the first daughter would marry a warrior chief and become queen of a great nation."

"Lady Vaydien and Prince Zileg!" an upstairs servant girl exclaimed in an awed voice. "Just as is happening. She foretold it!"

"Master Predger told me once that he thinks it's all trickery," the cook said. "Isn't that so, Master?"

A man seated at the table head, who was evidently the one referred to, finished a mouthful of food and cleared his throat. He was older than the average of the others, erectly poised and dressed more formally, and could have been a head butler. "All I'll say is that I'm not convinced. I heed the words of Mirsto, who says that we should be cautious in belief of all things, and demand evidence."

"But we all 'eard 'ow 'is mother knew about Lady Vaydien and Prince Zileg years ago," a man in rough outdoor garb put in from the far side. "'Ow could that 'ave been trickery?"

"You see," the servant girl invited triumphantly.

A young man who looked like a stable hand, sitting next to the one who had just spoken, looked up. "I hear Prince Zileg doesn't have much time for ideas of magic, either. He says that properly argued reason can reveal natural, everyday causes for all things. In Urst they're making a better quality of steel by adding burned bones to the melt."

"Where did you hear that?" the head butler demanded.

"Jarsind the smith talked to one of Zileg's guards while we were shoeing their horses. Prince Zileg takes a great interest in the work of artisans."

"Did you hear that, Nastra?" the scullery maid called to the cook. "You'd better start keeping the bones for Jarsind." Ronti had been watching the scullery maid. Her name was Eena. Although lacking in refinement, she was sharp-eyed, intelligent, the kind who would rise to a challenge. Born into a different background, she could have gone far. Also, Ronti's instinct told him she had a mischievous streak, which would suit his purpose.

The cook eyed Eena derisively. "Jarsind? The only thing he'd know to do with them would be throw them to the dogs." Laughter greeted the remark.

Ronti listened intently as he continued eating. He had observed Zileg's hostility toward Korshak, and read that it was rooted in more than just skepticism toward magic. Zileg was shrewd and missed little. Such was human nature that a penchant for cruelty and vanity didn't preclude intelligence. That could be a dangerous combination.

"More bread, Mr. Ronti?" the maid next to him asked.

"Please." Ronti took a piece from the dish and looked around the table. "We noticed from our camp in the hills yesterday that there's some rebuilding going on near the marketplace," he said. "What's the story?"

"Oh, there was a big fire about half a year ago now," the stable hand answered. "It started in the rooms at the back of the inn. . . ." He went on to elaborate, letting Ronti lead them away from Shandrahl's smith and the new steel being developed in Urst. Five minutes from now, Ronti doubted if any of them would remember that the subject had been broached at all. But Ronti would report every detail back to Korshak.

From such seemingly trivial snippets, were many wondrous miracles and prophecies born.

Later, Ronti just happened to be passing along the passage to the door opening from the yard, when Eena came out of a pantry, carrying an oil jar.

"Still here?" she said playfully. "I thought you'd gone back to your wagon outside."

Ronti kept his voice low. "I stayed back to have a word with you, Eena—when the others were out of the way."

"Really?" The tone of her voice asked, now where had she heard this before? But her eyes were saying she could be interested.

"No, it's nothing like that. I need to recruit an accomplice. I think you're the right kind of person."

Eena studied him, puzzled but curious. "Accomplice? What for?"

Ronti glanced behind him, then steered her back into the pantry doorway and moved closer. "It's for our act tonight. We just want to add a harmless little joke into the routine...."

− FOUR −

High above the surface of Earth, Masumichi Shikoba headed back toward the two-level suite, now in the final stages of being fitted out, that would be his personal quarters in the three-miles-long, six-miles-around orbiting *Aurora*. His first premonition that something was amiss came when he emerged from an elevator into the gallery running through the complex of residential units and saw the scattering of twigs and leaves forming a trail along a side corridor to end at his front door. He turned his face toward the lens in the panel alongside, opened the door with a voiced command, entered warily . . . and stopped, stunned.

To facilitate free expression and cater to individual preferences, the *Aurora*'s design made extensive use of modular constructions that could be configured into whatever style of space the occupants desired. Masumichi had specified a simple layout of sleeping and living space above and a personal working area for his robotics research below, with a spiral stairway connecting the two. Instead, a circular opening eight feet or so across had appeared in the ceiling, making way for the trunk and branches of what, from the leaves that he could see above, appeared to be a young sycamore tree. Its base was encased in some kind of temporary structure covered by plastic sheeting. The two robots that he was developing as general-purpose prototypes and assigning various construction tasks as test projects regarded him dutifully. They had universally pivoting heads with wide-angle and narrow-focus lenses for all-around viewing, and bulky torsos sprouting slender, bi-tubular limbs with bulbous joints, giving them somewhat the appearance of metallic stick men with mantis heads. Masumichi had left them with a decorating job, evidenced by their generous splattering of paint.

"What's this?" he inquired, gesturing at the tree.

"That's the tree," GPP-1/B informed him.

"What tree?"

"You told us to paint a tree in the lower level. There wasn't a tree there, so we got one from the Bot and Ag Conservatory. What color do you want it?" The robot seemed to register the sinking feeling that Masumichi was trying not to show. "Er, we weren't sure about going through to upstairs. It didn't seem right to cut it and just use half.... We could get a shorter one if you like."

"Bot and Ag people very cooperative," GPP-1/A put in. "Like having plant things grow anywhere possible."

Masumichi could see his mistake. "I meant a *picture* of one—a mural, after you'd done the walls," he said resignedly.

"Oh."

1/B and 1/A looked at each other with what could have passed as mutual recrimination, but Masumichi dismissed the impression as subjective. Whatever electronic exchanges might have flowed between them were lost on him. While he was still grappling in befuddlement with how best to handle things, voices sounded in the open doorway behind.

"Ah yes, he's back."

"Masumichi, what's all the mess on the floor out here? Are you planting a forest?"

It was Helmut Goben, whose work lay in mapping biological molecular machinery, and his partner, Sonja Taag, a teacher. With them was a slim, fair-haired girl in her twenties that Masumichi didn't know. Before he could stop them or say anything, they had come on in.

"We stopped by earlier, but you were out," Helmut went on. "We're looking for some ideas on..." His voice trailed off as they stopped, staring in astonishment. Masumichi, too embarrassed to speak, showed his teeth in a parody of a smile. The two robot geniuses stood motionless.

Sonja walked slowly around the base of the tree, turned to assess the proportions of the space that it was standing in, then looked up at the terrace that the upper floor had become, encircling the upper parts. Helmut moved to the bottom of the spiral stairs to contemplate the effect from there.

"It's *brilliant*!" Sonja breathed wonderingly. "The harmonizing of life's natural rhythms with personal growth and spiritual space. Oh, Helmut, we must do something like this!"

"You, ah...like it?" Masumichi checked uncertainly.

"I take it that the living area will be above, embracing the leafage from all sides as an integral part of the mood," Helmut observed. "While the trunk down here in the lab area symbolizes the constant thrust and direction of our work toward higher things and a richer understanding of life. Truly inspired, Masumichi. However did you think of it?"

"Ah, hum, as you say, just an inspiration, I guess," was all that Masumichi could muster by way of return just at that instant. To one side, GPP-1/B shuffled its feet in a way that could have meant anything.

"And the way it brings together the two extremes of . . ." Helmut checked himself and glanced at the fair-haired girl, who had followed them in. "But we're forgetting our manners. Masumichi, we'd like you to meet Fave, who only came up in the last few days. She's from the Breeton islands." They were located to the west of the main northern land mass, which still went by its old-word name of "Asia." The western fringe was a region where significant amounts of old-world learning and technological abilities were beginning to reappear.

"Our privilege to have you with us," Masumichi said, giving the normal form of welcome to a newcomer aboard.

"Mine entirely," Fave responded.

"So, will Fave be working with you?" Masumichi asked Helmut.

"Oh, no. We just met her by chance at the game yesterday."

Masumichi interrogated Fave with his eyes for a moment. "Something medical," he pronounced. "Herbs and plant remedies, or pharmaceuticals."

She shook her head and laughed. "Nothing like that. Singing and dance."

Well, that was a good thing, too, Masumichi thought to himself. He had been involved with the *Aurora* program since the early days and had always favored a population made up from as wide a variety of knowledge, talents, and points of view as possible. He thought that many of the scheme's architects tended to focus too narrowly on recruiting individuals from backgrounds offering immediate material benefit to the enterprise, which he feared would result in a society that was overly pragmatic and utilitarian, losing much of the richness of what it meant to be human. Creative originality couldn't be commanded by planning committees. Fortunately, those who shared this view had prevailed.

"So, you are the one who works with robots," Fave went on. "Helmut tells me you designed the lattice-crawlers and manipulator pods that assembled the ship."

"Well, I was one of the people involved," Masumichi agreed.

"And those are yours, too?" Fave indicated the two GPPs looking on silently.

"In the experimental stage at present," Masumichi told her. "The aim is general-purpose helpers that can be directed via natural language. They're fitting out and decorating the suite, as you can no doubt tell."

"How about ones that can dance?" Fave suggested.

"Now, there's a thought," Masumichi said. "But the dynamics involved are a lot more complicated than you probably think."

"But even young children can do it."

Masumichi smiled. "Many of the most complex things in life give an illusion of being simple because they are done unconsciously. But it's precisely *because* we do them unconsciously that makes it so difficult to understand how we do them. Decoding natural language is another example."

"If you let him get started on this, we'll be here all day," Helmut warned Fave.

"But I'm interested," Fave said.

"We have years ahead of us," Sonja reminded her.

A tone sounded from Masumichi's phone. He pulled it from his jacket pocket and answered. The caller was Iver, an operator in an observation section in the Surface Operations branch of the *Aurora*'s Command Directorate, which was where Masumichi had just returned from. Surface Operations was responsible for communications and liaison with the ground bases, and maintained a network of control rooms and facilities through the ship.

"The identification that you were looking for just came in," Iver informed Masumichi. "Location confirmed and situation appears stable. Shall I send through the details?"

Masumichi thought for several seconds. "I'd rather come back there and see for myself," he said finally. "Just a moment, Iver." He turned to the others, who were watching. "Something's come up that I've been waiting for. I really need to go and check. Would you excuse me? As Sonja says, we've got years to talk about robots."

"Not at all," Helmut said. "We're the ones who showed up unannounced."

"You can stay on and look around some more if you wish," Masumichi offered."

"I'd love to," Sonja said. "We might pick up some more ideas. You're sure you wouldn't mind?"

Masumichi waved an arm around in the way of a host giving them free run of the place. "Go ahead. It's not as if I've moved in yet. These are GPP-1/A and 1/B.

They can help with any questions. It will be a good test
for their language processors, too." And then, into the
phone, "I'm on my way back. See you in a few minutes."

"Check," Iver acknowledged, and hung up.

As far as Masumichi had been able to make out
from legends of old and the records that had sur-
vived, the world had never seen anything quite like
the *Aurora* project. He tried to picture what it meant
as he sat with several others in a capsule speeding
noiselessly through one of the communications transit
tubes running to every part of the ship.

Undertakings on such a scale had once been coordinated by governments able to command the resources
of vast territories, or by organizations, sometimes global
in extent, devoted to accumulating wealth through
industry and commerce. But nothing of such a nature
existed in the emerging post-Conflagration world. The
thousands of individuals who had been involved in
making *Aurora* a reality did so out of belief in an
idea and personal dedication, with no dependency
on concentrated sources of wealth at all. Out of all
the diverse drives, visions, challenges, and dreams, a
single-minded purposefulness had coalesced from the
wreckage of the order that had destroyed itself. Some
described it as the nearest thing to a godless religion.
And the common factor that bound everyone together
did indeed exhibit a religious quality in the form of
faith that diligence and devotion could earn a better
future, and a common cause to defend against evils that
would work to prevent it from happening. The faith
was in the potential of the unfettered human intellect
and soul to achieve a higher level of existence than

one limited by considerations of survival and material security. The threat lay in the danger of allowing the power thus realized to be subjugated to serving the baser ambitions that had led to ruin instead of wisdom when humankind confronted the same choice before.

Hence, little of the scientific rediscovery that was occurring owed anything to the patronage of conquerors or money cartels in the patchwork of princedoms, city states, tribal domains, and embryonic nations that were taking shape in the present world. Instead, those who sought the higher learning, and others that chance delivered, who were judged worthy, came to Sofi, the land of those who had come to be known as the Builders. Sofi was situated on the western side of the northern part of the immense double continent that old-world maps showed as the "Americas," now known as "Merka" and "Amazonia." Secure along a coast facing a broad ocean, and protected by mountain and desert barriers from the miscellany of less-developed territories farther inland, Sofi was where the arts that had culminated in *Aurora* were consolidated and guarded. Soon now, the Builders and those who had been chosen to join them would leave to build a new world elsewhere, away from the menace of the same rising tides of rivalry and unreason that had engulfed all before. Yes, the organizational politics and logistics were complex. But capable people inspired by a common vision could work wonders.

Masumichi got off at a transit point in the lower levels and took an elevator up to emerge into surroundings of office and instrumentation cubicles, and control rooms. He found Iver at his station in an area overlooked by a large display of part of Earth that *Aurora* was currently passing over. It showed the snow-covered island region of Merka's far north, outlined indistinctly beneath whorls and banks of cloud.

Iver used one of his screens to bring up an image that had been captured earlier. It showed a view looking obliquely down over a city standing astride a river, with hilly country to the south and flatter terrain broken by patches of forest to the north. A map of the south-central region of the eastern part of Asia was inset in one corner, with a highlighted rectangle framing part of the territory known locally as Arigane.

"Taken eighteen minutes ago," Iver said. "Some false color added for enhancement."

Masumichi identified the larger bulk of the palace and citadel in the central part of the city. He had been having the area watched for the last few days, ever since a sizeable column of what looked like mounted soldiers arrived from somewhere to the west. "You say he's there now?" he queried, turning his head.

In reply, Iver zoomed in to a closer view that resolved the palace into two adjoining hexagons, one consisting of larger official buildings, the other to the rear, domestic and private quarters surrounding an inner retreat of courts and gardens. Standing on one side of what appeared to be a stable yard between the outer wall and the kitchens and servants' quarters was a barrel-roofed wagon, painted bright red.

"That's it—what you were looking for?" Iver checked.

"That's it. We've been waiting weeks to see if he'd show up."

Iver swung his seat around and leaned back curiously. "So who is he? What's the story?" he asked.

"A potential recruit, who ran into one of the crabs a while ago," Masumichi replied. He was referring to the remote-directed surveyors put down at out-of-the-way spots on the surface for various reasons, so called on account of their all-terrain articulated legs and manipulators. They were also equipped to support two-way visual conversations between the operators aboard *Aurora* and anyone of interest who might be encountered. "His name is Korshak. He has set himself an intriguing and difficult task of extricating the lady he's decided he loves from an impossible situation. If he pulls it off, he'll have proved himself."

"What is he, in that horse and cart? Some kind of trader?" Iver asked.

"A traveling illusionist. Intelligent, imaginative, innovative, and eager to learn. One who sees what others don't see, with a unique perspective on everything. I got him accepted as ideal for the kind of mix that we need."

Iver nodded and returned a faint smile. "He sounds as if he could bring us some entertaining moments," he agreed.

"More than just entertainment, I would hope," Masumichi replied vaguely.

One of the reasons why Masumichi had gotten involved in recruitment was that it gave him access to the people in charge of Sofi's limited fleet of aircraft, which typically numbered one to two hundred machines. With nowhere else to fly regular services to, its only needs were for travel within Sofi and occasional special-purpose missions farther abroad. Sometimes, individuals destined to join *Aurora* were flown from inaccessible faraway locations to Sofi, to be shuttled up to the ship. That was what interested Masumichi.

Not all of the various political, military, and other interests coming together in some shape or form around the world were happy about the *Aurora* venture. In particular, those who were themselves at various stages of technological rediscovery, and harboring ambitions of dominance, were infuriated at losing the best of their innovators to Sofi. The rulers of Masumichi's original island homeland off the east of Asia had promised him wealth and prestige if he agreed to stay put. When he refused, things had turned ugly, with intimations that members of his family might not fare so well if he didn't change his mind. His inclination in response was to bring the closer of them with him. But even though his father had been one of the pioneer figures in the *Aurora* project, understandable constraints made it difficult to justify such requests beyond immediate spouses and children.

He looked again at the image of the red wagon in the stable yard, still frozen on the screen. If Korshak pulled it off, he and his companions would still face a long and perilous journey to reach Sofi. And time was getting short. *Aurora* was scheduled to lift out of Earth orbit in a little over two months. Four places were allotted to them, which in all probability would never be used. But as of the moment, Masumichi had no clear idea how he intended exploiting the situation.

~ FIVE ~

Korshak's performance was given in a large salon opening off from the palace banqueting hall. It was typically used for assembling and entertaining guests prior to a major function, or as a sitting room when dances were held. Double doors from the main hall opened through to the rear of the salon's major part, which was where the audience was seated. This included Shandrahl and his consort, Doriet, along with a retinue of nobles and ladies from their court; Prince Zileg with staff officers and officials who had accompanied him from Urst; and an assortment of palace functionaries and other notables invited for the occasion. Vaydien sat beside Zileg as his bride-to-be. Her younger half-sister, Leetha, was with her mother. The hall behind the doors at the rear was undergoing finishing touches for the banquet that would follow.

At the other end of the salon, in front of the audience, a smaller space defined by two sections of wall projecting a short distance inward provided a convenient proscenium. The areas screened by the walls on either side afforded wings where equipment could be kept out of sight until needed, or other preparations

effected that might be required during an act. Black
drapes at the rear curtained off a narrow space running the full width of the wall, while a door from the
wing to stage left gave access to a corridor connecting
serving rooms on one side of the banqueting hall to
the kitchens and cellars.

Korshak stood facing the assembly, clad in a blue
tunic and loose white trousers, his dark, curly hair
flowing down over the collar of a scarlet cloak emblazoned with gold stars and moons that projected the
appropriate mood and image; it also provided concealment for many objects and handy pouches. His
hands grasped the two brightly patterned cylinders
standing on end a short distance apart on the table
in front of him. The routine was going well, with the
onlookers into the spirit of things and eager for more.
He raised the cylinders from the table to reveal a
bottle that had been covered by one, and under the
other, a glass. The bottle and glass were identical in
appearance to the ones that had occupied opposite
positions when he covered them a moment ago, giving the effect of their having changed places. Cries of
astonishment, laughter, and applause greeted the feat.
Korshak lowered the cylinders back onto the table,
then raised them again to show the objects returned
to their original sides.

The trick was common among street performers,
and the company was virtually certain to include some
who knew, or would guess, that the normal technique
used bottomless bottles which the performer could
lower over either glass at will by applying pressure
through thumb holes in the cylinders, or by making
the cylinders flexible enough for the bottles to be

gripped through them. The liquid that Korshak had poured from one of the bottles at the start had been held in a compartment contained in the upper part.

But Korshak's system was not of the kind used by street entertainers. It was a variant of his own invention, bearing his signature on a side of the table, that made use of hidden recesses below the tabletop where items could be received from above or from which they could be delivered back again, according to the manipulations of spring catches operated by levers from behind. Thus, instead of raising a bottle along with its cylinder to uncover the glass that had been hidden under it—which was the normal way—with Korshak's system the bottle was carried down below the tabletop, and the opening filled by a disk of matching material previously held in the cylinder space above the bottle, on top of which rested another glass. This left the cylinder empty.

Korshak lifted the cylinders to show bottle and glass having apparently changed places again. He gazed slowly around the attentive faces, waiting for the knowing nods being exchanged here and there to subside, and let his smile broaden in a way that seemed to say, *Yes, I know what some of you are thinking.* Then he leveled the cylinder that he was holding above the glass—the one that by the usual method should be concealing a bottle—and swept it around to one side, then the other, letting everyone see that it was empty. Exclamations of surprise greeted the revelation. Without losing momentum, Korshak lowered the cylinders and moved the lever back to restore the bottle; at the same time, he caused the bottle and glass on the other side to be taken up into their cylinder together and replaced by a new item consigned from below the tabletop. When he raised the cylinders again, the bottle was apparently back where it had been, but the glass on the other side had become a bowl of swimming fish.

As a new wave of applause filled the room, he picked up the bowl in both hands and came around the table, while behind him Ronti, who had been standing back just outside the left wing, moved in to wheel the table away. The bowl was divided by a vertical glass partition that kept the fish in one half. The other half contained a chemical solution that emitted light when a mixture of certain salts was added. As he continued moving forward, Korshak turned the bowl around to bring the prepared half toward the audience, at the same time releasing the pellet that had been secured by wax at the rim. Silence descended as the space between his hands transformed into an eerie white glow. This was also the cue for servants who had been briefed earlier to dim the lamps at the back of the room, ostensibly to enhance the effect; but it would serve other purposes later.

"As fish swim through the oceans that connect the lands, so impressions swim through the ocean that connects minds," Korshak intoned, staring down into the glow. Actually, on his side he was looking at the fish, but the effect was the same. "I see thoughts that are present now, here in this room." He paused as if to let an image clarify. "This very day the hound of the night is given young ones." Then, looking up and about, "Can anyone here tell us the meaning?"

There was a pause, heads turning this way and that. Then Leetha piped up from beside her mother,

"One of the dogs had puppies this morning. And she's black. Her name is Ebony."

One or two people laughed, but then another said, "You never know. He could be right."

"Couldn't be a coincidence," someone else agreed.

"Amazing!"

"Very good, dear," Doriet complimented.

Then Zileg's voice came in disdainfully over the top of them. "Nonsense. It's the kind of servant gossip that anyone could have picked up." Exactly so. But Korshak had expected as much and used it as a lead in.

He resumed, "Now I see something else . . . from a land to the west, over mountain and plain. . . ." The officers and officials from Urst became suddenly very still and attentive. Korshak went on, "A strange riddle that I am unable to explain. An old saying has it that there is steel in the bones of the lion. But I am reading now that there are bones in the steel. How to interpret this, I don't know." Korshak looked around invitingly again. "Does it mean anything to anyone?"

Silence fell for several seconds. Then heads among Zileg's company began turning toward him questioningly. Finally, one of them exclaimed, "The burned bones that harden and temper! No one here knows of it yet."

"How can it be?" another demanded.

Zileg had no answer. Having made his point, Korshak turned the bowl back as the glow faded, showing the fish swimming around unharmed and unconcerned. Another round of applause ensued, though somewhat more subdued this time as many in the room lapsed into thought or glanced at each other ominously. Moving on before the mood could take root, Korshak handed the bowl to Ronti, who had been moving the cabinet out to the center-stage area and was now waiting behind, and turned to gesture at his latest accomplishment. At a nod from Ronti, servants on both sides uncovered additional lamps to illuminate it, further enhancing the contrast in lighting between the rear of the room and the front.

"I obtained this from a caravan of merchants far to the east," Korshak announced. "They told me it was crafted by masters in distant Sofi, who have revived techniques of magic thought to have died with the old world." As he spoke, he approached the cabinet and opened the doors to show the interior apparently empty. He closed the doors and continued speaking while he and Ronti turned the cabinet through a complete circle, exhibiting all four sides. "It is said that distance was no impediment then—that travel from anyplace to anywhere could be effected in an instant. There are many today who do not believe such things to be possible. However, I will now bring back for you a glimpse of the arts that were lost."

Ronti retrieved one of several folded garments, fashioned from a dark gray material, from a small table that he had set to one side, and came forward with it draped over his arm. Korshak took it and opened it out, revealing it to be a long robe with an enveloping cowl. "Behold, the shroud of translocation, which embodies the power to carry the wearer beyond the constraints of space and time," he informed the audience.

An air of expectancy came over the room as Korshak placed the robe over Ronti's shoulders and then moved past him to open the cabinet doors. Ronti pulled the cowl around his face, gathered the robe about him, stepped inside, and then turned to stand while Korshak closed the doors in front of him.

They had positioned the cabinet well forward in the stage area. Korshak stepped back and then walked around to the space between it and the black drapes at the rear. "Note that there's no possibility of another exit at the back." He turned and called to the people seated at the front on the audience's extreme left-hand side. "Watch me and confirm that I remain in sight." He moved behind the cabinet to stand against the drapes, and addressed those sitting to the right. "And I am visible to you on that side?"

"Yes," a uniformed officer answered.

Turning back toward the first group, "And still to you on that side?" Several ladies sitting together nodded vigorously. Korshak emerged on the other side to complete a circuit of the cabinet, and drew up to take in the room for a moment. "Now," he pronounced simply, and with that moved forward and threw the doors open to show the interior once again devoid of any sign of occupancy. The audience was more intrigued than surprised now, and sensed that more was to come. Korshak took another of the folded robes from the side table and came forward to within a few feet of the front row of seats.

"No doubt there are those among you who suspect some kind of trick mechanism that depends on the knowledge of my assistant to operate. But I shall demonstrate that it is not so. Any one of you can avail yourself of this ability. There is no risk attached, of any kind. Would anyone care to step forward?" A moment of stillness followed as he had anticipated, while he cast his gaze around. When he saw one or two people starting to stiffen or hesitate, he looked toward where Zileg was sitting and said before any could respond, "I would confidently consign our noblest and fairest to the experience. Would Your Highness, the prince, consent to my borrowing his lovely bride-to-be?" Korshak added hastily, to a scattering of chuckles, "I promise to bring her back before the big day."

Zileg was clearly not pleased, but not even he could summon the ill grace to object. In any case, before he had a chance to, Vaydien had risen to her feet and was coming forward to an accompaniment of encouraging cheers and hand clapping. She caught Korshak's eye for an instant as she turned for him to drape the robe around her, and then let him lead her by the hand into the cabinet. He closed the doors and faced the room again.

"Distance is no barrier, time an illusion. Where are they at this instant? To the north, to the south? Over land, over sea? Maybe even drawn by some mystical force back to the wondrous land of Sofi itself." He paused to survey the room. The air was serious now.

When he opened the doors again, the hooded figure was still there. Puzzled looks appeared. Somebody groaned. Had it gone wrong after all? But when the figure stepped out and threw back its cowl, it turned out to be Ronti, back again. While the audience was mulling and coming to terms with this unexpected development, Korshak and Ronti turned the cabinet around through a circle again, ostensibly to show nothing amiss. But this time they left it farther back—practically against the drapes. Nobody registered the fact.

Korshak lifted a slate that had been lying with the folded robes, set it up vertically on the table where all could see it, and resumed. "We have glimpsed the Ancients' mastery over space. Now we will reenact a rendition of their command over time itself." He raised his head a fraction to call to a servant at the rear, who was awaiting the cue. "The light, if you please." All heads turned as a lamp was turned up above a small alcove by the doors leading to the main hall. In the alcove was a high-backed chair with carved arms, standing behind a footstool. While the audience was still taking in this new turn, Ronti walked back through the center aisle and took his place in the chair. In the comparative darkness at the back of the room, the light from the lamp above highlighted the form of his head and shoulders, enveloped in the cowl and robe. Korshak drew attention back to the front of the room.

"Does someone here have the time of day at this moment?"

After some fumbling in different places, a man near the center announced, "Almost a quarter past the eighteenth hour." Korshak chalked the information onto the slate. People all around were looking mystified. Nobody had any idea where this could be leading.

"Note that my assistant is here in this room at this moment," Korshak instructed. "But before proceeding further with him, we must bring back Princess Vaydien." He crossed to the cabinet and opened it to reveal a second hooded figure returned from beyond. But something about it didn't seem right. The figure was turning its head from side to side as if trying to get its bearings, and acting in a generally agitated manner—not suggestive of royalty at all. Korshak took the figure's hand and led it out. Looking perplexed, he lifted back the cowl. It wasn't Vaydien—who by that time had already exited from the cabinet's secret compartment behind the mirrors, through a divide in the black drapes, and from there along the space behind them to the side exit from the wings.

Laughter erupted among some of the court and palace staff, who recognized the face and took it as a joke that Korshak had thrown in. "Who are you?" Korshak demanded.

"My name is Eena, sir," the scullery maid answered, seemingly bewildered, playing well the part that Ronti had rehearsed her in. She had been inside the cabinet when it was wheeled in from the wings.

Korshak threw the audience a grimace that looked like a sick attempt at a smile, drawing more laughter as others caught on. "Where are you from?"

"If you please, sir, I work in the kitchens."

"Here, in the palace of Shandrahl?"

"Why, yes, sir. I was there just a moment ago."

"How did you get here?"

"I . . . don't know."

Even Shandrahl was unable to suppress a smile. Korshak turned and looked toward the rear of the room as if suddenly remembering something else. "But time moves on! Nothing can arrest it, not even the powers of the Ancients. Observe." He pointed. Everyone in the room turned to regard the solemn, hooded shape still sitting in the light of the lamp above the alcove, its lower part lost in shadow behind the footstool. What none of them knew was that the cowl and shoulder portion of the robe that Ronti had worn contained stiffening strips of cane that would preserve its shape when lifted from the wearer. With it, during the distraction afforded by Korshak's clowning, Ronti had shed the top part of his tunic, uncovering the jacket of an Urst cavalry officer that he had been wearing underneath, and slipped out through the rear doors into the banqueting hall. By now he would be on his way through the corridor to the kitchen area and cellars to join Vaydien.

Every eye in the room watched in awe and trepidation as ghostly white vapors rose around the motionless form in the alcove. They thickened to obscure it completely for a moment or two, and then thinned; but the form was still there. Attention remained riveted on it, the room breathless and silent, waiting for something to happen. But nothing did. Finally, Zileg turned back impatiently, his expression demanding an explanation. Others followed suit in quick succession.

But by then the front of the room was deserted, with no trace of Korshak to be seen.

Korshak caught up with Vaydien and Ronti where the side passage from the kitchens joined the palace's escape tunnel. They emerged at a landing place on the riverbank, where Mirsto had opened the concealed gate and was waiting with a boat. They followed the river for a little over a mile downstream to a copse just outside the city, where four fast horses, watched over by Sultan, were hitched among the trees—saddled, provisioned for lightweight travel, and ready to go.

~ SIX ~

Tranth City, with the surrounding region that it dominated, which extended a couple of hundred miles or so in each direction, was located on the opposite side of Merka from Sofi. From a descending surface lander launched fifteen minutes previously by a mother craft from *Aurora* cruising in the upper stratosphere, Lois Iles contemplated the scene enlarging gradually below. At the far end of the cabin behind her, looking bored and indifferent in a baggy suit, his mouth working absently on a piece of chewing root, Quentago sat between two hefty escorts from the ship. Although Lois's principal field was optical physics—she had played a major part in working out the functions of devices found in the ruins of several old-world astronomical observatories preserved in Sofi's central mountain range—she was also active in recruiting for the mission, which meant being on the lookout for exceptional individuals. People like Quentago, with the contempt they displayed for every kind of principle in their pursuit of self-gratification, repulsed her. Not only did they debase everything it meant to be human; they bragged about it.

Tranth was ruled by a gangster faction that had come to power through violence and made law as expedient. They had rebuilt a hydrocarbon-based technology of sorts and were putting all else second to expanding their industrial base to achieve military dominance in the region. Mills, mine heads, and factory buildings disgorging smoke cluttered the outlying areas, with grimy houses growing denser farther in to become a belt of ugliness choking the urban center. After the open, airy townships of Sofi, the narrow streets hemmed in by tall, austere buildings looked airless and cramped.

From their earliest days, the Sofians had progressed quickly in deciphering old-world scientific texts, enabling rapid advances in physics that had resulted in a decision to move directly to nuclear techniques for power generation and supplying process heat for materials extraction, manufacture, and other needs. Such boldness of innovation was characteristic of the Sofian way of going about things, leading them through a succession of breakthroughs in the furthering of knowledge and its application to practical matters. This, and their policy of not making their discoveries widely available, had given them uncontested technical supremacy and made possible its culmination in *Aurora*.

The lander came down as directed in an open space behind a line of high, solid-looking stone buildings. It looked like a site being cleared for new construction, walled on either side and enclosed at the front by a chain-link fence with a wide gate. Maybe a dozen armed guards, who could have been police or soldiers, were stationed at the gate and outside in the street. A vehicle with two figures waiting in front of it was standing inside, clear of the touchdown area. As the lander's power died, Lois picked up the document wallet containing her notes, unbuckled her seat restraint, and rose to her feet. The exit was forward from the passenger cabin, through a bulkhead door and behind the crew stations. Farther back, Quentago remained seated with his two escorts.

"Nice flight down," Lois complimented as the pilot got up from his seat and moved back to unlatch the door.

"We try to please," he acknowledged as he operated the control to open the door and lower the access steps. One of Masumichi Shikoba's robots was sitting in the copilot's seat, taking in the view outside. It had come down from the ship as an observer. A still-unsolved problem with trying to develop artificial intelligences was finding an effective way to equip them with the "world knowledge" that came naturally to humans as a consequence of growing up and living in it. One of Masumichi's strategies was to expose them to as wide a range of experiences as possible as a way of getting them to form the conceptual associations necessary for inferential reasoning.

The pilot glanced back at the cabin through the open door behind Lois, winked at her, and said to the robot in a carrying voice, "You did real well. Ten out of ten. Now let's see how you handle docking when we take her back up."

That got Quentago's attention. "*What?!*" came his strangled voice from the rear. "*That* was flying us? I don't care how the talks go. I'm not going back up."

"Easy," one of the escorts cautioned.

The robot turned its head to look at the pilot.

"Please explain reason for asserting as true what must be known to be false," it requested.

"I see they haven't programmed you for getting a joke yet," the pilot said, grinning.

"Please explain 'joke.'"

"Catch you later," Lois said and left them to it.

The air outside as she descended the steps was cool with a touch of dampness. It carried a whiff of sulfurous odor from somewhere, probably an industrial emission. The vehicle was some kind of oil- or gasoline-powered passenger car, shiny black, heavy, and boxy, with three doors on each side, large wheels with what looked like internally sprung tires, and a motor compartment at the rear. The Tranthians had a trading arrangement with oil producers to the south, on the neck connecting Merka to the southern half of the continent. They operated their own mines for coal, ores, and other minerals, most of them reopened workings from the old-world era.

One of the two men standing in front of the car approached. Lois assumed him to be Gratz. She hadn't been given all the details of the Directorate's prior dealings with Tranth, but apparently he was a state attorney. He struck her more as a hired bruiser or political policeman, with his blockish build, long coat of gray rubberized material, brimmed hat set squarely above craglike features, and expression of studied opacity. He drew up without offering a hand or other form of salutation.

"Lois Iles?"

"Attorney Gratz."

"Quentago is not with you?"

"He will remain aboard the lander until I've met

Clure and can verify the deal—as was agreed. I take it that Clure is elsewhere."

"Not far from here. We will drive, yes?"

Gratz turned and let her follow him back. The other man, wearing an olive tunic with a black leather cap, held the door for them and then went around to the rear. The interior was quilted, with leather seats, the dash panel in front of the driver's seat cut from wood or an imitation. Noises that sounded like a hand crank being turned came from behind, and the motor started, settling down after a few seconds to a steady clickety-clack chugging. Moments later, the driver reappeared, climbed in at the front, and engaged gear.

They drove out through the gate, past a gaggle of onlookers who had seen the lander come down and stayed to gawk despite shouts from the guards to move on. As they turned onto the street of drab stone frontages to what looked like official buildings, an escort car that had been waiting a short distance back moved out to follow them. The few people about were also drab, wrapped in dark, enveloping garb that insulated them from the world and conferred anonymity, their eyes turned toward the ground or trained straight ahead, avoiding contact that might invite attention. From ground level, the indifferent quality of architecture and the poor state of repairs on every side was obvious. Projecting the state's power abroad took priority.

"This Clure, I have worked hard to protect him," Gratz said. The tone sounded mechanical, as dispassionate as the countenance. "It is not easy. He has dangerous ideas that he does not keep to himself. It makes powerful enemies."

Lois took it as an artless ploy to pre-settle the issue, regardless of what impressions she might form. Marney Clure had somehow come to the attention of certain people in *Aurora* as a person fired by the kind of vision, and with a flare for imparting it to others, that would enrich the venture. However—probably for the same reasons—Clure had fallen foul of the Tranthian authorities and was being held under detention as an agitator and subversive. Getting the Tranthians to part with him should have been an easy enough matter. But their ways of doing business meant that they never gave away anything that someone else wanted without getting some kind of return, even if it would cost them nothing to do so.

Quentago was a Tranthian thug who had been apprehended in Sofi, where he had come in pursuit of a fugitive math genius whom the Tranthian authorities considered to be state property and had explicitly prohibited from leaving. Quentago had connections among people who mattered in Tranth, and eliciting agreement from them for an exchange had not proved difficult.

"Well, let's just hope that what I've heard was a fair assessment," Lois replied. In fact, from the Aurorans' point of view, there was little to deliberate over, since it was a convenient way to rid themselves of an unsavory customer. But Gratz needed to be made to feel that he was working for his deal.

"You realize that there are limits to how much I can do?" Gratz said. In other words, *What happens to him is in your hands*.

"Are you asking me to take responsibility for decisions that your government might make concerning its own internal matter?" Lois answered. Two figures in uniforms similar to those worn by the guards posted at the gate were swaggering along the sidewalk outside. An old man stepped into the gutter to get out of their way.

"Why put him to the risk? What is it to you?"

"The work I do is judged according to certain standards."

Gratz raised his eyebrows and looked away. "As you wish."

They turned into a narrow street with sooty row houses on one side and a high, windowless wall with metal barbs along the top lining the other. It ended at a pair of heavy wooden gates in an arch overlooked by a watchtower, with a guardhouse on one side. An officer came out and waved the car through as the gates were opened by guards on the inside. The arch opened into a cobbled yard enclosed by the wall on one side, and on the others by outbuildings in the shadow of a large, foreboding structure with small barred windows and steep gables.

An officer accompanied by a guard came out of an entrance to receive them as the driver opened the car door, and Lois and Gratz climbed out. No words were exchanged. The officer led them back in and through a lobby area of plain, yellow-painted walls, with a counter desk on one side, behind which was some kind of office room, visible through a window. A hallway at the rear of the lobby brought them to a stairway, which they ascended to a landing with corridors leading away on both sides. They followed the one to the right, and after a short distance the officer stopped at one of the doors and rapped sharply on it with a key ring. A guard within opened it, and the officer led the two visitors through to a bare room with a table in the center below a single hanging lamp. The only other occupant, sitting at one of the three chairs drawn up to the table, clad in a two-piece garment of light green, was presumably Marney Clure. The officer sent a perfunctory wave in his direction and withdrew, followed by the guard who had been posted inside the room. As the door closed behind them, Gratz lowered himself onto one of the empty chairs at the table. Lois took the remaining one, opposite Clure, laid her document wallet down in front of her, and opened it in readiness.

Marney Clure was younger than Lois had imagined, probably in his early thirties, or even late twenties. He had a fresh, boyish face with color in his complexion, straight yellow hair falling into a loose mop over his forehead, and a blond fuzz of several days' growth softening his cheeks and chin. His eyes were a clear blue-gray, quick and shrewd, returning her gaze steadily with the depth and self-assurance of one twice his years. At the same time, there was a hint of mirth in them that told of an irrepressibility of spirit that even his present surroundings and circumstances couldn't overcome.

"This is Ms. Iles," Gratz began, addressing Clure. "She is sent by people who want to make you an offer. This is the best deal I have for you." Clure shifted his eyes to her curiously, but more in a way that seemed to be weighing her up than asking what. It was as if he were looking for a measure of her first as a person, before getting into details of what she was selling.

"A new future, Mr. Clure," Lois said. "A different *kind* of future."

"Here, you have no future," Gratz threw in.

Clure kept his eyes on her. "If it's military, or some kind of troublemaking to provide an excuse for protective intervention somewhere, the answer's no." His voice was calm and deliberate, leaving no room for doubts. Then he cocked his head to one side. "But you don't look like a military recruiter."

"Why would you be so adamant, if I were?" she asked.

He shrugged. "It doesn't solve anything. Just causes a lot of hate and reasons for revenge, and makes problems worse. The wrong people get rich."

"Who do you think should get rich?"

Clure took a moment to reflect. This probably wasn't going in any of the directions he had expected, but he seemed happy enough follow it through. "Well, the way I see it is, nobody's born with anything. So whatever they get on top of what they produce themselves must come from other people. And the only way other people are going to give it to them is if they get something worthwhile back in return. So the ones who should end up with a lot to show are the ones who can do things better when it comes to providing what other people need." He rubbed his nose with a knuckle for a moment. "And when you look at it, most people who are rich never do much with the stuff they've got. It's just a token to let people know who you are. But if you really had anything of value to offer, you wouldn't need it. They'd know who you are."

The line of conversation suited Lois perfectly. Far

from having come to sell anything, her prime concern was evaluating what *Aurora* stood to gain. From what she had heard so far, Clure could have been one of the program's founders. "So, what are you doing here?" she couldn't help asking, gesturing at the room. She glanced at Gratz. He nodded at Clure to go ahead.

Clure smiled, as if at an inner joke. "I'm a subversive, don't you see? A threat to the security of the state. Actually, the charge was of being a member of a banned political organization that I've never had any connection with. But that was just a frame-up to—" He caught the beginnings of an objection from Gratz. "Oh, come on, Borgio, you know I was framed. No, I didn't expect you to dig too deeply into it as my defense. You had your orders." He looked back at Lois before Gratz could take them off track. "To keep me out of circulation because too many people were listening to the things I was saying, and thinking about them. I guess I'm not very, what you'd call . . . 'tactful' in these matters. The thought of organized opposition doesn't go down well with the people who run things around here."

"What kind of things were you saying?" Lois asked.

"The kinds of thing we were talking about a moment ago. The people who do the work and produce all the real value deserve better. But they're kept down and exploited by parasites who rule through violence and fear, and have stolen enough to buy protection for themselves." Clure tossed Gratz a look that said he could think anything he wanted. "There has to be a better way. This way was how the old world ran, and look what happened."

Lois held his eye, but her expression remained

enigmatic. "Do you think there could be a better way, Mr. Clure?"

"Maybe, if enough people believed in it, and were capable of organizing themselves to meet force with force if they had to, to protect it. Someone has to try. Look at the way things are starting to go again already. But the ones who make it that way are not as invincible as people think. They have to lie. Inside, they're cowards, and they scare easily. Why else do you think I'm here?"

Gratz was breathing heavily, but he managed to contain himself. A silence fell for several seconds while Lois stared at Clure fixedly. Finally, she said in a curious voice, "Suppose I told you that there are people who have resolved to build just such a world as you describe. A new world, elsewhere, far from the reemerging forces that would destroy it. How would you feel about playing a part?"

Gratz seized the chance to get back onto the track that he understood. "I would advise you to go while you still can," he told Clure. "Right now, you are regarded as a nuisance. If you ever looked like becoming a serious threat, there would be no way out for you, ever."

Clure looked at him searchingly, across at Lois, clearly intrigued now, and then back at Gratz. "Exactly what are we talking about? How soon could this be arranged?"

"The papers are prepared now, in the main office downstairs," Gratz replied. "Ms. Iles has transport waiting. You can leave with her."

They talked for maybe another half hour, but there was already no doubt as to Clure's decision. He drove with Lois and Gratz back to the lander, where Quentago was produced and the exchange concluded. The lander took off shortly afterward to rejoin the mother craft from the *Aurora*. Lois was more than happy with the day's business. It was the best trade she had seen made in a long time.

- SEVEN -

The reasons for Sofi's enormous technological lead over the assortment of disconnected states, provinces, and tribal lands that made up the rest of the world went back to the times immediately following the Conflagration. One of the foremost was the concentration of extraordinarily capable people in the population that arose there out of the ruins of the old world. Some believed that the old world had never fully died in that region, and its inhabitants were a remnant of essentially pre-Conflagration stock who had kept their genetic and cultural identity intact, along with much of their skills and aptitudes. Such a notion was certainly in keeping with the readiness with which they were able to absorb and apply the repositories of old-world knowledge that they found around themselves or sent expeditions to recover from elsewhere—lost, for the most part, on the populations of other areas. In this way, Sofi became a legendary sanctuary, spoken of with awe, that the talented and gifted would give up their old lives and journey across the world to join. The resulting one-way diffusion of ability and learning translated into a superiority that as a matter of policy was kept firmly within Sofi's borders.

This inevitably gave rise to envy and ambitions of rivalry both in neighboring areas and farther abroad, among those whose preferred way of procuring the necessaries of life was to take them by force from whoever produced or otherwise possessed them. In response, the Sofians had, over the years, developed a numerically small but effective military capability. It didn't have to be large, because the superiority of Sofi's weaponry to anything that a potential opponent could bring to bear rendered a credible threat nonexistent. One of the principal rationales for Sofi's isolationist stance was to keep things that way.

A consequence of this was the lack of any incentive to create a global trading and communications infrastructure of the kind that had existed before—there wasn't much out there to trade or communicate with. So, instead of being broad-based and universal, Sofian technologies evolved to be narrow-focused and intensive.

In place of tens of thousands of airliners, they produced a few high-performance aircraft, some experimental space probes, and finally a starship. As the uniqueness of Sofia's situation consolidated, two opposed movements developed within the political leadership regarding the future course to which they should direct themselves.

The "Traditionalists" kept to the original Sofian position that saw expansionism and the desire to impose one's own ways as the root of the conflicts that had ended the old world through an endless cycle of resentment, resistance, retaliation, and revenge.

Instead, they believed that staying out of the affairs of others, while maintaining an impregnable position at home and setting an example by their own quality of life, would demonstrate the superiority of peaceful and prosperous cooperation. In the same way that the more enlightened and capable individuals came to Sofi of their own accord when they were ready, so would other nations and peoples move to become part of a widening community of like minds. Yes, it would take time and patience, but look what had happened to the world that had tried to rush things.

The other position, that of the "Progressives," had found its voice later, when Sofi's pre-eminence was past dispute. It saw an opportunity to unify the world under one system of thought and ideals that would never come again, and should be seized while no force existed that could stop it. The self-immolation of the old world had resulted from a virtually equal power balance between vast political-economic groupings, each believing in its own invincibility, which had guaranteed the escalation of violence to global dimensions. No such obstacle existed to prevent Sofi from asserting its hegemony everywhere today, and establishing a worldwide order of stability that would last. Boldness and resolve had brought the Sofians to where they were. The same qualities would ensure they remained there permanently.

If a division this deep was appearing within Sofi itself, did it mean the beginnings of the same pattern as before, that would spread over the world once again, inexorably and unstoppably, anyway? That was when the Traditionalists, who had originated the starship program as a mission of exploration and discovery, broadened the concept to one of creating their own world elsewhere based on the ideals that they championed.

From records that remained, it was known that, at an undetermined time before the Conflagration ended their interest in such matters, a consortium of scientific groups from the old world—some of them enigmatically sponsored by political blocs that seemed to be rivals—had launched an unmanned star probe to investigate an interesting planetary system revealed by astronomical observations. The information sent back by the probe began arriving during the recovery period, when Sofi was coming together as a nation and gaining experience with fledgling astronomical and computer-communications capabilities of its own. Successful decoding of the data provided an additional stimulus for the Sofians to go ahead with the venture they had been considering—to build a starship inspired by an old-world follow-up design study that had never been taken further. As the plans and charts gave way to the physical reality of the immense structure taking shape in orbit, the concept was expanded to become Sofian Traditionalists' means of realizing their ideal of the future on a world of another star. The world their descendants would arrive at was a planet of the system that the old-world robot probe had traveled to long ago, where it was still in orbit, waiting. The planet's name had not been changed from the one the ancient builders of the probe had given it: Hera.

The task of defending the state would become more demanding after the *Aurora*'s departure, while Sofi adjusted to its changed situation. In anticipation, the past six months had seen a stepping up of military recruiting, accompanied by intensified training and regular practice maneuvers. Much of this activity was staged in the vicinity of the launch bases serving the *Aurora* program where the forces involved could be called in quickly if needed. Opposition to the venture existed in various forms and for various reasons both abroad and within Sofi itself, and the launch bases would be the obvious targets of any attempt to disrupt operations.

As an officer with the Internal Security Office of the Sofian military, Andri Lubanov had a duty to protect *Aurora* as part of the official policy enacted by the Traditionalist-dominated Sofian government. However, he didn't agree with the philosophy that it reflected. If people wanted to found a colony somewhere else, that was fine; and getting away from tyranny had probably played a major part in shaping human history. But for a group who belonged to a potentially world-dominating culture to be talking about emigrating to another star to be able to live the way they wished made no sense. To Lubanov's way of thinking, they were letting themselves be chased out by inferiors. The Sofians had the ability to create whatever kind of society they wanted right here on Earth, to extend it as far as they chose, and there was nothing out there to prevent them.

But Lubanov went beyond the stated Progressive position by privately expressing the opinion that the mission as currently planned constituted a defection on the debt owed to Sofi for making it possible at all. This brought his name to the attention of what had begun as a clandestine circle within the Sofian military, that felt likewise and were resolved not to let the debt just fly away without some kind of settlement. Lubanov was approached, evaluated, cautiously introduced to their plans, and eventually became one of them.

As the day scheduled for *Aurora*'s liftout from orbit drew nearer, the number of Progressives harboring similar resentments swelled to become an effective but officially unrecognized opposition voice within the Sofian administration. Its position was basically that all of Sofi had contributed to *Aurora*'s becoming a reality, and therefore all of Sofi should be acknowledged as having rights of ownership. Departure should be postponed while the terms under which the two factions would part were renegotiated. These would cover the redirecting of some of *Aurora*'s concentration of resources to leaving Sofi better prepared to face its own future, inducements for certain key figures to change their minds about leaving, and suchlike.

It went without saying that the reactions of the Traditionalists were not expected to be exactly enthusiastic, and therefore a bargaining position would need to be secured. This would take the form of a swift move to occupy and take control of the launch bases before the last shuttle-loads of personnel and supplies were sent up to the ship. The operation was designated Torus. It would be set in motion by the issuing of the code words "Winter Rain."

Lubanov met Dreese for lunch in the usual place, the outside terrace of a waterside café on the east side of the Frisc peninsula, looking out over the bay that opened to the ocean via a narrow neck of water. A sprawl of connected metropolitan centers had grown on the northern part of the peninsula, over the ruins of a former city, with space-engineering complexes and launch facilities situated farther south. Some of the better-preserved structures of the old city had been restored as museums or historical exhibits. The bridge crossing the bay to the east was built on the piers of an old-world bridge that had stood in the same place; sections of it had endured sufficiently to be incorporated into the newer construction. The channel connecting the bay to the ocean in the west had been spanned by an even more spectacular bridge, but it had collapsed or been destroyed, and the Sofians had replaced it with a tunnel.

Dreese was on the intelligence staff, and also involved in Torus. The officer that he reported to, referred to as Actor and never named directly, would be directing the planned coup. Lubanov's position with Internal Security involved regular contact with the *Aurora* project administration, making him ideally placed to monitor their progress and keep the Torus group informed. His meeting with Dreese was in connection with a report that Lubanov had supplied several days previously on the latest developments.

"So would you say that the program is about on schedule?" Dreese asked after they had gone over some of the details. "We're still looking at lifting out from orbit six weeks from now?" He was squat and solidly built, with a swarthy complexion and full black beard. While he claimed Sofian birth and a military pedigree, Lubanov's sources indicated him to be from a mining background in the desert region on the far side of the eastern mountains, having originated somewhere in the interior. Not that it mattered very much. But Lubanov had worked in intelligence and security for many years in his distant native region before coming to Sofi, and liking to know the real story behind things had become part of his nature.

"It might be delayed," Lubanov replied. "They're still rounding up last-minute recruits from remote locations. That's taking longer than expected."

"The guy that makes robots, who wants to bring his whole family?"

"Among others."

"I can't see that affecting things substantially," Dreese said. "If it became urgent, they could be flown here in a matter of days."

"Probably so," Lubanov agreed. "But in addition to that, the latest test data is necessitating some adjustments to the drive sequencing. Getting that right could take them longer."

This was in reference to bringing the *Aurora* up to final flight readiness. In its earlier stages of construction, as key structural components and system functions were completed, the ship had made several test runs to distances ranging from translunar to halfway to the orbit of Mars. But trials of limited range and duration could reveal only so much. The only way to fully learn the performance envelope of a starship and know the conditions it might encounter would be in the final, one-way mission. As a next-best thing, over the years leading up to final launch, a series of scaled-down test platforms had been dispatched to investigate various design concepts, and the information they returned had helped guide the engineering of the *Aurora*'s final form. Lubanov was talking about changes being made as a result of the latest data to come in.

"Are we talking about anything major?" Dreese asked.

"Not from what I gather."

"So, perhaps a modest extension of the launch date. Not any significant change."

"That would be the safest way to bet."

"Could it happen sooner than six weeks?"

Lubanov shook his head. "From the stockpiles of materials and equipment that are still to be sent up from the ground bases, I can't see it."

Dreese nodded as if that was what he had been wanting to hear. He regarded Lubanov silently for several seconds, then shifted his eyes unconsciously to emphasize confidentiality. "That is what we have concluded also. I am to inform you that there will be a meeting with Actor for a detailed briefing two days from now. You will be informed of the specifics. It would be good if you can find out more about these drive-sequencing adjustments and what they are likely to involve."

"The engineering assessment has already been prepared," Lubanov said. "I've requested a copy."

"How long would you expect it to take?"

"It could be when I get back, if I press for it. Say, tomorrow at the latest. I'll have it summarized in time for the meeting."

Dreese nodded. "Good."

Lubanov allowed a pause and regarded him meaningfully. "Do you think it's *Winter Rain*?"

Dreese said nothing, but held Lubanov's eye for a long moment. Then he nodded almost imperceptibly.

It was no coincidence that the military units that had been moved closest to the ground bases were all commanded by officers who had been recruited to Torus.

– EIGHT –

After Dreese left, Lubanov sat finishing his drink for a while, and then rose to walk slowly along the waterfront. He walked for a long time, deep in thought, taking in the bay, its bridge, and the far shore. The day was sunny and clear, the water blue from the reflected sky. A mild breeze was blowing from the west, bringing freshness from the hills fringing the ocean. At one point he stopped to lean his elbows on the rail above an embankment built upon concrete footings that once formed part of a vast system of docks, from which ships had carried commerce to the far reaches of the world. Some miles farther south along the same shore of the peninsula was an aircraft base serving mainly other places around Sofi and accommodating typically twenty or so machines at any time. Remains could still be seen there of what had been one of hundreds of hubs between which huge air fleets had traversed a global network. Maybe the world would one day know such things again. But if so, Lubanov would never see them. His time for gazing at mountains, bays, and distant shores, feeling natural sunshine and ocean breezes, would soon be over. In a mere few days now, his would be an artificial world in miniature, voyaging toward another star that wouldn't be reached in his lifetime. He would die out there somewhere, and Earth would be just a memory.

Lubanov's placement in the Sofian military internal-security apparatus had been arranged some years earlier, when it became apparent that opposition to *Aurora* was growing, and a need for close inside intelligence became crucial. The precaution was well-taken. The original case put forward by the disaffected Progressives was not unreasonable in some ways, and could maybe have been open to deliberation even without occupation of the launch bases. But as time went by and more extreme views added themselves to the movement, its mood became uglier. Now there was talk of stopping the project permanently, to be claimed as a national resource, with some advocating the open use of force to achieve it. This was exactly what some of *Aurora*'s strategists had prophesied would happen. The final weeks of preparation were critical, and there could be no question of allowing the project to be jeopardized by the risk of rogue military units with access to space-capable vessels and Sofian weaponry taking matters into their own hands. Lubanov's disagreement with the Traditionalist philosophy made him an obvious candidate to be approached by the Torus conspirators as a sympathizer and potential inside informer. That his objections were genuine and not a cover story helped camouflage the direction in which his true commitment lay.

If that was how he felt, why, then, was he going with *Aurora* at all? Why not work for the success of Torus, in precisely the way its planners believed him to be doing, and if better terms were negotiated as a consequence, remain on Earth in the stronger and more stable Sofi that he would have helped bring about?

It was a question of weighing up odds, and Lubanov was, if anything, a pragmatist. He had fled to Sofi and changed his name to escape a revenge vendetta that had arisen from his previous work, and even though that had been long ago, he knew there were still people looking for him who wouldn't give up. The thug that his department had picked up in Sofi, who had tracked a runaway mathematician all the way from Tranth and just been deported back there again, showed how close they could get. And the people that Lubanov had to worry about were a lot more efficient at what they did than anything that would come out of Tranth.

He had lived long enough with such fellow travelers as fear, mistrust, deception, and treachery. Yes, the sun was warm and the scenery of Earth stirring. But the beckoning stars offered tranquility and inner peace. Having reaffirmed his decision to himself, Lubanov turned and walked away from the shoreline at a quicker pace to take care of the final matters outstanding.

He returned to the Internal Security section of the military administration center on the south side of the city, and went through his normal routine of checking for messages and updating himself on the day's more crucial activities. An adjutant reminded him of several appointments for tomorrow. Lubanov told him to cancel them, saying he would be away for the next day and maybe more on something urgent that had just come up. Then he went to his office and spent some time going through his files to remove anything suspicious that might trigger an alert in the next forty-eight hours. After that it wouldn't matter. Finally, he used the monitor on his desk to call Chel. She was the kind of person who loved hikes through the forests and swimming off beaches, the bustle of the town, and the solitude of the desert. Also, she was a dedicated Progressive. She would never have gone with the *Aurora*.

Her face appeared on the screen moments later, pointy and angular, black hair sweeping down one side of her face, almost over her eye. Surprise flickered for an instant—Lubanov didn't usually call when she was working. "Hey. What's happening?" she greeted.

Lubanov had to bite his lip before replying. He had been rehearsing the words to himself. "Look, something's come up. I have to leave for somewhere down south in a hurry. It might be a day or two."

"Oh. You won't be back tonight?"

He shook his head. "As I said, it just came up. I should know more tomorrow."

"Want to tell me what it's about?"

"Uh-uh. You know how it is."

She made a visible effort not to look too disappointed. "Well...I hope it doesn't involve some kind of trouble, anyway—you know, with nasty people. Maybe it'll make me start some of the things I've been meaning to do. Call me when you're coming back?"

Something seemed to swell in Lubanov's throat. He nodded mechanically but couldn't voice the promise. He detested moments like this, detested himself—feeling that he should say more, but at the same time just wanting to get it wrapped up. This was the last time he would say anything to her. She noticed the ambivalence on his face and narrowed her eyes questioningly. Large, dark eyes, deep and sensitive.

"Are you sure everything's all right? You look kind of strange."

"Oh, it's just . . . I have a lot of things going around in my mind right now." A stab of resentment at being in this position came out of nowhere, almost causing him to say something sharp, but he suppressed it. "But right now, I have to go."

"Oka-ay." The eyes moved searchingly, still showing doubt. "Be careful, Andri, whatever it is. I'll see you whenever, then."

"Good-bye, Chel."

After leaving the building, he walked across the forecourt to the motor pool, booked out a minisize staff car on a three-day requisition, and shortly afterward, drove out through the main gate of the administration center for the last time. His first stop was at a shipping office in the air-travel terminal south of the city, where he had reserved space a week previously to store some bags of personal effects in anticipation of this day. From there he headed on south for the launch facility at Yaquinta, about three hours' drive away, where a shuttle for the *Aurora* was scheduled to leave shortly after midnight.

Not generally known was that the ground staff at Yaquinta had been reduced to a skeleton crew. Neither was the fact that the daily shipping volumes over the last couple of months had been quietly increased, and as a result Yaquinta's quota of materials for the *Aurora* was already up in orbit and aboard. The same was true for the quotas assigned to the other launch bases.

On arriving at the gate, Lubanov supplied the

pseudonym and password that he had been issued, and was admitted. His first act after entering was to have the operations supervisor transmit a coded message to the *Aurora* confirming that "Redman" had terminated ground work and was on his way. The shuttle lifted off on time, balanced on a lengthening column of plasma glow, several hours later.

Aboard the *Aurora*, Lubanov was met by two officers from the ship's Police Arm and conducted directly to a room in the Council Center, where a representation of the Command Directorate and its advisors had convened and were waiting. Lubanov reported that the situation on the surface pointed to military intervention, and that the order to move could be given in as soon as two days. The mission's director in chief was notified, duly arrived, and summoned more of his senior staff and the ruling Council to join the assembly. Shortly afterward, orders went out to the captain and Flight Engineering to prepare for flight readiness within twenty-four hours.

What Lubanov had said to Dreese about delays likely to be incurred over the drive sequencing wasn't quite accurate. The last data calling for changes had come in from the outward-bound test craft some time ago, and the necessary adjustments were already completed.

– NINE –

Masumichi Shikoba was still awaiting the arrival of some equipment to be installed in the lower-level lab area of his unique apartment-cum-arboretum, and in the meantime had been given the use of working space in an engineering research section of the *Aurora*'s college system. Nath Borden, who attended the Council as the representative of the Recruitment Board, which Masumichi dealt with extensively, called while Masumichi was alone in the office, studying a student paper on algorithms for resolving ambiguities in robotic vision. Humans just "knew," for example, that the top of a lamppost seen protruding above the roof of a house probably wasn't a part of the house, but to machines such things weren't always so obvious. One of Masumichi's experimental models had recently demolished a small maze of mirrors that it had tried to negotiate with its sonar ranging turned off.

"Are you alone?" Borden asked from the screen. His voice was oddly low and confidential.

"One moment." Masumichi got up, went to close the office door, and returned. "What's up?"

"There's just been a special meeting. Things have

started moving quickly, so there isn't a lot of time right now. I'll give you the full story later. It will be general knowledge very soon, in any case. Basically, news from the surface is that they might be planning to move against the bases in the next two or three days. The chief has started the countdown to flight readiness. Everything on the ground is being wrapped up. The last of our people down there should be aboard within twenty-four hours. This is it, Masumichi! We're on our way!"

"Oh."

Borden looked out of the screen searchingly for a few seconds, as if he had been expecting more of a reaction.

"That's nice," Masumichi obliged.

"There's a piece of unfinished business that I'd like to try and take care of," Borden went on. "One catch of fish out there that we haven't netted."

"The magician," Masumichi guessed. He was the one who had nominated Korshak for recruitment, maintained contact with him, and then instigated the party's escape. As far as Masumichi knew, they were the only ones left. The other late recruits from various places had all been brought in already and shuttled up to the ship as part of the precautionary planning for an early liftout.

"We had to wait for the wedding," Masumichi said. "It was the only way."

"I know," Borden answered. "But I don't like leaving loose ends. We can still get them here. I'd like you to handle it."

In fact, Masumichi had been worried about Korshak and his companions, and meaning to raise the matter. But what could they do in this kind of time? He frowned. "Twenty-four hours? To get an aircraft assigned, fly it out there, and bring them back to Sofi? Would there even be shuttles leaving any of the ground bases by then?"

"Forget the bases," Borden said. "As soon as the news goes out publicly up here, there'll be a blackout on ground communications anyway. The carrier won't be brought back up for another twelve hours." He meant the *Aurora*'s mother craft for surface landers. They were smaller than the heavy-lift shuttles, more versatile, but without the range to make the *Aurora*'s orbital altitude. "We can use one of the landers again. They're all being recalled to the carrier. I've already requisitioned one for you. Copying details." A window appeared in a corner of the screen, showing the reference and a contact name in Surface Operations control.

"Got it," Masumichi confirmed.

"Can I leave it with you, Masumichi? All of a sudden I've got a million things to take care of."

"Sure. . . ." Even as Masumichi said it, a distant, thoughtful look came into his eyes. His mind was racing ahead. This could have possibilities, he told himself. "Sure," he said again, not noticing that the screen had already blanked out.

Masumichi had still been grappling with the problem of getting the rest of his family away after the threats if he didn't change his mind about leaving. This could be the answer. It would be short notice for them, of course. But there were times in life when the chances that presented themselves had to be seized. Yes, this had possibilities indeed. . . .

He addressed the screen in a louder tone. "Voice

on. Tell 2D to step in here for a moment, please."
GPT-2D was the General Purpose Test robot that he
had sent down to Tranth with Lois Iles, when she had
been unable to obtain an aircraft for a time-critical
mission and used a surface lander instead. The robot
appeared in the doorway a few moments later from
the lab area outside.

"Yes, chief?"

"The surface lander that you flew down to Tranth
in not long ago."

"Yes?"

Masumichi tilted his head curiously. "How many
humans would you say you could get inside it?"

"Should I presume you mean of adult size? Not
infants?"

A flicker of impatience crossed Masumichi's face.
"Yes, of course."

"Hm. Let me see." 2D rubbed its equivalent of a
chin. The robots were programmed to mimic human
mannerisms. People dealing with them found the familiarity reassuring. "Taking the average adult weight as
82 kilograms, and assuming a density for body tissue
of 0.95 that of water, the indicated volume is 0.086
cubic meters. From the design specifications held in
the ship's databank, the volume of the passenger cabin
works out at 33.3 cubic meters. So you'd be able to
fit in 387 humans, rounded to the nearest integer. . . . I
assume you didn't want to include fractions of humans."
There was an expectant pause. "That was a joke."

Masumichi sighed. "Forget it. Carry on with whatever you were doing."

"Right, Chief."

Masumichi waited until 2D had clumped out again,

and then called Lois Iles, who was in another part of the ship, analyzing images from the observatory. "Lois, about that trip you made down to Tranth recently," he said.

"Okay."

"How many passengers could that surface lander take?"

"That's an odd question that I'd never have won a prize for guessing."

"You know me."

She thought for a moment. "Well, I didn't exactly count the seats, but there were two on each side of the aisle, six or seven rows . . . let's say six. That would give you twenty-four."

This could work, Masumichi thought to himself. Allowing four for Korshak's party, twenty would more than cover the short list that he'd drawn up. A few more could probably sit on the floor in the aisle and the door space if need be. "Thanks, Lois. Thank you *very* much," he acknowledged.

She gave him a puzzled look. "Can I ask why you want to know?"

"Later, if you don't mind. I'm pushed for time just at the moment. But all will be revealed in good time."

"Well, okay. . . . Glad I was able to help."

Masumichi cut the connection and brought back the details of the contact in Surface Operations that Borden had given him. Yes, this could work, he told himself again.

- TEN -

They were getting near the coast now, entering country that Korshak knew well. The hill track that they had been following descended to join a road that brought them to a stone bridge crossing a neck of water where a river entered a valley containing a long lake. Past the bridge, the road ran along the shore of the lake, now lying to their left, with grasslands and marsh extending away on the right. On the far side of the lake on one side, and beyond the flats on the other, the valley was hemmed in by steep slopes rising to rocky ridges. At the bottom end of the lake ahead of them, the valley narrowed to a steep-sided defile passing between two summits. From there on, the terrain opened out into the land of the Shengshoans, and Korshak estimated that by late tomorrow they should reach the port of Belamon.

The Shengshoans were a seafaring people, and their tall, four-masted ships were the swiftest ocean-goers of which Korshak had heard tell. He was known and liked among them, and he was gambling on there being an eastbound sailing to Merka that would take them to Sofi or land them close enough to get there within the two months that he had been given. If they found themselves facing a wait at Belamon, things could be tight. But Korshak had seen no reason to burden the others with such concerns.

The ruts that had forced them to ride in single file since the bridge petered out as the ground became firmer, and Vaydien moved up to ride alongside him. Ronti was ahead, with Sultan running tirelessly this way and that to investigate some scent picked up in the wind, or to chase a bird or small creature hidden in the grass. Mirsto was in the rear, patiently following for hour after hour and saying little. Korshak had observed the signs of tiredness but not commented, and Mirsto didn't complain. They were maintaining a slow but steady pace, sufficient to cover a reasonable day's distance while at the same time sparing the horses. With no extra mount to fall back on, they couldn't afford to exhaust any of them or run the risk of one going lame.

"Have you noticed that mountain ahead?" Vaydien waved an arm to indicate the left-hand summit at the end of the lake. "I thought that was a funny black cloud behind it. But now I think it's smoke coming up from the top."

"Yes, I've been watching it," Korshak answered.

"What do you think it means?"

Korshak shrugged. "It's too localized to be a scrub fire or anything like that. Looks more like some kind of beacon."

"It couldn't be a volcano, could it?"

"Ha-ha!" Korshak shook his head. "There would be lava flumes and sheets—a whole different appearance. That's just a pile of old rock and rubble. Probably someone's signaling to somewhere on the other side that he'll be home tomorrow."

Vaydien looked at the peak for a few moments longer, and then a solemn look came over her face. She turned her head down and stared unseeingly at the easy rise and fall of the horse's head in front of her, her mind distant.

Korshak watched her and nodded. "Yes, it's true. Very soon now, we won't be seeing mountains and valleys again. But places like that are dry and dusty. They make you sweat and your back ache. We'll have a world of more wondrous things, one filled with people who are as gods."

Vaydien looked at him and forced a smile. "How did you know what I was thinking?" she asked.

"Oh, come. You know me well enough by now. Do you think I don't really read minds?"

"I'm beginning to know when not to take you seriously. *And* I know that your magic is all trickery and mirrors."

He looked at her keenly. "Well, take me seriously now, Vaydien. It isn't too late if you're having second thoughts. I have many friends among the Shengshoans who would get you safely back to Arigane. You have no regrets? You're still sure about this?"

"Arigane." Vaydien repeated the word with a shudder. "To be given as a chattel to a man I despise, in deceit until it pleases my father to betray him? A sacrifice to his vanity, as my mother was?" She reached out to lay a hand on Korshak's arm and nodded decisively. "You need have no worries on that account. I am sure."

"That's good."

Vaydien's manner brightened. "So, tell me more

about these wonders. What do you think the ship that crosses the sky might look like?"

"I don't have to think. I can tell you. Imagine a giant wheel mounted in the center of an axle that tapers like the Pyramid Tower of Escalos, except that it's round. But it holds a whole city within itself, and parks, and farms. Nay—cities!"

"How can you know this, Korshak?"

"The iron beast of which I have told you." Korshak had described the strange artificial walking creature of the Builders that he had encountered almost two years previously in a remote region. "Through the window in which faces appeared, I was also able to see places inside the ship. They have palaces built from crystal and light; rooms that travel between floors of buildings; objects that move of their own accord. The center of Escalos would not compare to it as the rudest shanty hamlet in outermost Arigane compares to Escalos. And I have seen what our world looks like from . . . What's this now?"

In front, Ronti had stopped and was peering ahead, with Sultan standing rigidly, ears pricked. Korshak and Vaydien drew up alongside him. A body of mounted figures had appeared in the distance, coming along the road in the opposite direction.

Zileg had waited many days for this moment. As he and his cavalry tracked the four fugitives through villages, over hills, and down valleys, he had planned in his mind the deaths by slow torment that he would devise for the whore, the charlatan who had bewitched her, his accomplice, and the addle-headed physician, when he brought them back to Urst. And if Shandrahl saw fit to make war over it, then so be it. It would only have been a matter of time anyway. Had the fool really imagined that Zileg wouldn't see through his attempt at a subterfuge to buy time? Better now, while Zileg was of a temper for it.

The headman of a township they passed through had produced a map of the country bordering the Shengshoan lands, where the four were clearly heading— doubtless intending to take a ship from somewhere like Belamon. For several miles the road ran beside a lake through a narrow valley enclosed by steep ridges on both sides, with access only at the ends. The feature formed a natural trap. Zileg had slackened the pace of pursuit as they drew near, and sent a fast detachment of light horse circling around and ahead to cut off the exit. The column of black smoke, uninterrupted by infusions of white, above one of the peaks guarding the gorge at the far end of the lake told him that they had arrived, and the fugitives had been sighted. As he came with his main body of troops to the top of a rise from where the road led down to the stone bridge at the entrance to the valley, he called a halt to survey the way ahead.

His lieutenant, Ullatari, scanned the road beyond the bridge with a spyglass and reported. "No sign of them yet, sir." Which meant that the fugitives were inside the valley, somewhere between the two forces. Exactly as planned.

"And no sign of any flying ship, either, I do believe," Zileg said, looking up and about, his voice light with sarcasm. The younger half-sister, Leetha, had overheard Vaydien say something to Mirsto about a flying ship that the magician had told them they would escape in.

"Perhaps his magic is running out today," Ullatari suggested.

"Along with his luck," Zileg replied grimly. "Give the order to advance at canter."

With the bridge secured, there would be no way out. He had them now!

Korshak lowered the glasses from his eyes. "Urst cavalry," he announced shortly. On one side of him, Vaydien emitted a cry of dismay.

"It can only mean Zileg," Ronti said. "He's tracked us."

"Worse," Korshak answered. "If some have managed to get ahead of us, there are sure to be more behind. We have to get back over the bridge before they catch up." Vaydien was shaking her head in protest and about to say something, but he stayed her with a wave. "Not now. Save your breath and just ride." Mirsto had drawn up behind them, his eyes dull, without even the energy to ask what was happening. Korshak turned his horse about and gripped the old man's elbow. "One more effort," he urged. "We're cut off forward. We have to make a run for the bridge. There will be more following." Mirsto nodded. Ronti was already away at full gallop. Korshak waved for Vaydien to follow and shepherded Mirsto up to speed behind her. Then, after pausing to take in one more view of the approaching horsemen behind, he returned the glasses to his saddle pouch and spurred his horse forward again. Sultan, who had stopped and waited, bounded alongside.

Ahead, Vaydien was hunched low, all her concentration now on maintaining the pace. Korshak's worry was with Mirsto, who was swaying unsteadily in his saddle and would slow them down even if they made it to the open country beyond the bridge. What kind of decision might Korshak be forced to make if their pursuers stayed with them and were seen to be gaining? He didn't want to think about it.

They came to the softer part of the road, where the ruts reappeared, and were forced to slacken the pace. But on checking the road behind again, Korshak saw that the horsemen had, if anything, fallen back. It was impossible for them not to have seen Korshak and his companions, yet they were in no hurry. The meaning of the smoke column was now painfully clear.

The reason for their pursuers' confidence became evident when they came back within sight of the bridge and saw the cavalry waiting on the far side, pennants flying, formed up as a main unit blocking the road with flanking detachments standing to the sides. Ronti stopped, and looked back, hope gone from his face. Vaydien could only sit, frozen in horror, while Mirsto stared ahead blankly. They seemed to be waiting for Korshak to concede that it was over.

But Korshak was not looking at them, or at the bridge. Something else, above and beyond in the sky, had caught his eye. At first he had thought it was a bird, but it didn't fly like any bird he'd ever seen— and it was growing larger at a rate faster than any bird could have. It didn't seem to be a living thing at all, for it didn't flap or flutter, but moved more like a ship, seen far from a shore. It was closer now, seemingly heading directly toward them as it came lower, as if it knew they were there.... Could it be possible? Surely not, Korshak told himself.

But already he was crossing and uncrossing his arms wildly above his head to attract attention. *"Here! We're right here!"* he heard himself shouting. *"That's right! Just like that! Straight on down!"*

Zileg, stationed in front of the center, smiled to himself as he watched. Alongside him, Ullatari frowned as he used his spyglass. "What's come over him?" Ullatari murmured. "He seems to be signaling something urgent. I can hear him shouting."

"Or making mystical passes and spells," Zileg said. "Maybe he's trying to summon his flying ship." His mouth twisted into a sneer as he continued taking in the spectacle through his own glass. He evidently wanted to enjoy this for as long as possible. Then Ullatari became aware of the sounds of growing agitation among the troopers formed up behind them. At the same time, a low but steadily growing droning noise registered on his senses. The men were staring upward and gesturing. Ullatari raised his eyes to follow their gaze, and sent a startled look back at Zileg.

"Sir..."

The noise swelled to a roar as the object came down right over them. Its lines were smooth and rounded like the body of a fish, its skin white and gleaming in the sun, and it had short wings too small to have fitted any bird, and not moving like those of a bird. Cries of alarm were coming up from the soldiers, with some cringing in fear, others struggling to control their protesting mounts.

"Steady in the ranks!" Zileg roared, unsheathing his sword.

The vehicle, creature—whatever it was—landed a

short distance from the far side of the bridge, on an open, grassy expanse beside the road. The magician had already turned his horse toward it and was calling to the others and waving them in the same direction.

"Order the archers forward," Zileg snarled. "They'll not escape me now. Magic or not, I'll have their heads or die in the attempt."

"Archers to the fore!" Ullatari relayed.

Zileg turned in his saddle and called to the whole company. "Are you warriors of Urst, or children who cower at goblins? A dukedom to any man who brings me a head. If their magic would protect them, why do they flee like mice? He who will not follow me now is not worthy of the flag we ride under. Across the bridge and at them! Trumpeters, sound the charge. *Forward!*"

The scientist hadn't been sure exactly how many of his relatives they might have to pick up, so Control had bent the rules and told Ferl to free up an extra seat by flying the lander solo. But somehow the orders had gotten tangled, or somebody forgot to cancel something from the earlier mission, and the same crazy robot that had accompanied him on the Tranth mission showed up in the copilot's seat. By that time the whole ship was in a tizzy over the news of liftout in under twenty-four hours, and the carrier was expecting to be recalled at any moment, so Ferl had decided to not argue but just go with it. All of a sudden he was grateful for having some help there on the flight deck rather than none.

"Lander to Carrier, yeah, we've found them and we're down," he barked into his mike. "But I don't know what's going on. There's some kind of a war out

there, coming this way fast." He turned his head to
GPT-2D long enough to snap, "Go back there, open
up the door, and get all of them inside. Fast!"

The robot hastened to unbuckle and comply. Just
as Ferl was about to resume talking into the mike,
it said, "The horses won't fit in."

Ferl groaned. "Oh shit.... Forget the horses. Just
the people, okay?"

The robot lurched back and operated the control
to open the door and lower the access steps. Sounds
of trumpets and battle cries rising to a crescendo
came from outside. Armored horsemen brandishing
swords, spears, axes, and bows were streaming onto
the bridge, while in front of the lander the four people
it had come to collect were dismounting in haste and
running toward it. The girl was the first to enter. She
stopped in the entrance space, as bewildered by the
robot's appearance as were the faces of the people
crammed into the passenger cabin behind. It touched
her lightly on the arm with a fingertip and motioned
with the other hand. "Must hurry. Sorry, no horses."

Two men were approaching the steps as fast as they
were able while they helped an older one, heavily
built and white-haired, clad in a hooded riding cloak.
They still had some distance to go. A large black dog
was growling and had positioned itself between them
and the oncoming horsemen.

"What about the dog?" GPT-2D asked Ferl.

"What?" Ferl jerked his head around again. "Yeah,
sure. The dog's okay." Then, back into his mike, "I'm
telling ya, we've got an emergency situation here. I've
got a full load of people and three outside who look
like touch and go. What do you want..."

A rack by the door carried the painted label FLARE
PISTOL. The robot stared at it and consulted its
network of definitions and associations. Flares were
pyrotechnic devices used in emergencies. The captain
had just said this was an emergency. A "pistol" was
a weapon, usually a firearm, that was discharged at
enemies. "Enemy" described a relationship between
humans in which harm was effected or threatened.
The howling horde coming across the bridge waving
objects that a quick check of the database showed to
be implements specifically designed for the purpose of
inflicting homicide and mayhem had all the appearances
of harboring intentions that were anything but friendly.
The logical inferences were clear enough. GPT-2D
took down the flare pistol, descended the steps, and
marched out to the center of the roadway to do its
duty with the first arrows clattering off its casing.

Streaming a trail of incandescent crimson smoke, the
flare tore through the leading ranks and exploded in a
blaze of light and starbursts among the close-packed
throng in the middle of the bridge behind. The front
of the assault broke up amid screams of terror, rearing
horses, and unseated bodies, while the panic farther
back sent riders colliding in all directions, with men
and mounts tumbling into the water on both sides.
When GPT-2D looked back at the lander, the older
man had reached the steps and was being helped up
by one of the others, while the third bundled the
dog inside. The robot stood, unsure of whether the
pandemonium that it had created constituted an end
to the emergency or not. The old man was inside;
the doorway stood empty.

Then Ferl's voice called over the loudhailer from

inside. "Hey, Rocketeer, are you gonna stand there all day? Let's go."

"Yes, chief." GPT-2D hurried back and clambered up the steps. The newcomers had found seats and were settling the dog in the aisle. They were looking about strangely at the surroundings, as had the others that had been picked up earlier. GPT-2D closed up the door and steps, and moved back to snap their harnesses for them, which people from these parts didn't seem to understand. Then it went forward and settled back into the copilot's seat. The look on Ferl's face was unlike any human expression that it had seen before. Slipping on a set of phones, it caught the last part of the message coming in from Control.

"...we have recall orders from the ship up here. How much longer are you going to need?"

"Everything's fine," Ferl replied in the captain's seat. "They're all aboard now. Emergency over. We're on our way."

− ELEVEN −

So, finally, the time had come. The decision that would mean spending the rest of one's lifetime in a way never experienced by any human beings in history was about to be made permanent. And it would be irreversible.

Solemn-faced and brooding, his hair steel-gray, Lund Ormont, director in chief of the *Aurora* mission, sat at his station behind the window of the bridge overlooking the Control Deck. All of the consoles and crew positions were manned. The carrier had returned and been taken on board. The last shuttles had delivered the remaining personnel from the ground bases and attached externally as auxiliary craft. Along with Ormont on the bridge, the ship's captain and chief of flight engineering were confirming the final countdown details being reported by their staffs.

The position implied far more than ship's commander, director in chief of a space mission, or even mayor of a large city. The vast enterprise that he was heading would become a nation-state in flight. The role ahead called not just for ability in command and management, but for political leadership. And failure to come up to the challenges and demands that could be expected had destroyed a much larger and more robust world than the microcosm contained in the *Aurora*.

The dominant method of selecting political leaders in the old world had been through a kind of popularity contest in which the citizenry was expected to judge and choose their rulers directly. Such mass-endorsed adulation seemed bound to create inflated self-images and delusions of greatness that would inevitably result in immense power and authority being vested in hands superbly unfit to wield them. Doctors, architects, engineers, and other professionals were appraised and certified by bodies of peers who were expert in the field in question. How much more important was the supreme profession of running a country?

The procedure that had given Ormont his position was modeled on the way the government was formed in Sofi. Eligible candidates had to meet some of the highest educational standards required by any profession, and in addition have demonstrated practical competence in a progression of public offices of increasing responsibility. The final choice was made by an appointing body of individuals in turn elected by the people, who were responsible to them for their decision in the same way that the Highways Department was responsible for the performance of the engineers entrusted with the design and construction of the country's bridges. The system conferred full authority and demanded acceptance of total responsibility, which suited Ormont perfectly. He believed such conditions were essential to running an operation of any importance effectively, and felt contempt for those who hid behind collective anonymity by attributing their pronouncements to such faceless originators as "The Committee." A leader not prepared to put his name to his decisions and stand by them was not worthy of the name.

His own background had been with the military, which he had played a part in shaping in earlier years, when Sofi found it necessary to organize more comprehensive defenses. People often expressed surprise that he wasn't staying on as a Progressive to further develop Sofi's interests and extend its influence. But he had spent enough time in the thick of Sofian politics to see the way things were heading. Too many strong minds with diametrically opposed ideas were vying with each other, dissipating their energies fruitlessly in mutual obstructionism and achieving little. Ormont liked to see things getting done—and getting done his way.

By temperament he was a commander first and a politician second, and that was the role that the mission required. As was true with most, his reasons for leaving were varied and complex, but high among them was the appeal of the unique form of directorship that the position entailed. *Aurora*'s population was made up to a large degree of intellectuals and idealists—bright and creative people, yes, and sometimes surprisingly obstinate; but in Ormont's experience they tended to be too trusting in their expectations of human nature, and politically naive. Ormont had long ago made it a first rule never to totally trust anybody.

It was he who had insisted years ago on having eyes and ears inside Sofian military intelligence that would remain loyal to the *Aurora* planners, and found the ideal person in the form of Lubanov. Intellectuals were brilliant when it came to designing starships and making robots, but they would never think of such things or consider them necessary. But had it not been for those precautions, the entire future of the mission might even now have been in question. Sofi was still hidden by Earth's curvature, but ground observation on the previous orbital pass had shown military units converging on the shuttle bases and support facilities. Electronic intercepts had revealed little more, but that was to be expected.

The captain reported from his station. "Final interlocks at ready and holding." It meant they were ready to go.

A short distance away on Ormont's other side, the chief of flight engineering scanned his summary displays. "Drive main and subs confirming. Compensators synched and responding."

All heads around the bridge turned toward Ormont expectantly. A strange silence descended.

Ormont leaned forward to the console and drew the microphone closer on its flexible support. He had thought a lot about what he would say to those who were about to follow him when this moment arrived. Some of the sentiments and phrases that he had written down seemed, on rereading, too grandiose and lyrical, and when he tried to tone them down, pompous and pretentious. When he tried boiling things down to bare facts, the result carried all the human color and warmth of a military briefing. In the end, he decided to dispense with written notes altogether and let his thoughts speak themselves naturally, which accorded more with his style. He nodded to the bridge communications officer, who put out an announcement that the director in chief would address the ship. Ormont's console camera lamp came on, indicating that his image was going out to all parts of the *Aurora*.

He began, "This is your director in chief speaking. Very soon now, in a matter of minutes, we will depart on what will possibly be the most stupendous, exciting, and fantastic adventure ever undertaken by members of the human race. One day in the distant future, our descendants will be the seed out of which will grow a new world of our kind. For that world to preserve all the variety, richness, and potential that our kind has come to represent through its millennia of history, we go not just as the Builders from Sofi, but as unique individuals bringing talents of every kind from remote regions of Earth, its nations, races, cultures, and peoples...."

"While we must never forget those to whom we owe our heritage, from this day onward the most important truth that should guide our thinking and our lives is that we are all united as Aurorans."

Korshak and his companions sat listening in a room built of metal and strange-colored materials that they and the others already inside the white, smooth-skinned bird had been brought to after it arrived at the island flying high above the world. He had thought at first that the island was the ship that crossed the sky. But then the island had begun climbing higher, until the forests and mountains beneath were lost and the clouds themselves reduced to smears painted on a surface that shrank to reveal its curved edge, while above, the sky turned black, and stars appeared. And up there, the island had brought them to the Great Ship that Korshak had seen in the window carried by the metal beast that he had first met long ago. The wheel and its tapering axle grew larger as they approached, awesome in grandeur and line, vaster than any city, until the island was swallowed up in a cavern that opened to just a small part of it.

They were inside it now, moored between metal towers hung with pipes and cables, and constructions the like of which Korshak had never seen, behind huge doors that had closed behind them. It seemed that the ship was at that moment preparing to begin its voyage to another world, and disembarking from the island would be delayed until they were under way. Korshak was stunned. He and his party could never have reached Sofi in time. Yet the Builders had sent their white bird to bring them. Who were these beings of such power and magnanimity that a vagabond trickster, his accomplice, and two fugitives from a petty tyrant could be worth such effort? Masumichi, whose face had been the first to appear in the window of the metal beast, and others who had spoken from it since, had shown interest in Korshak's magical and other arts. He confessed to himself that he was at a loss. Did they believe that *they* had something to learn from *him*?

He looked down at Vaydien, who was sitting close, one hand clasping his, her head resting against his shoulder. She seemed in a daze and had hardly spoken. Korshak slipped an arm across her shoulders and squeezed reassuringly.

"Are we really here?" she murmured. "All this around me is real?"

"Oh, yes, very real," Korshak told her.

Vaydien was silent for a while. "Then I've woken up from a nightmare," she said.

Meanwhile, an image of the Great Ship's king continued speaking from the window on the wall at the far end of the room. Along with the others, Korshak had been given a box small enough to carry in a pocket or clip to a belt or the edge of a tunic, connected by a cord to a plug that the wearer placed in an ear. From the plug, a voice repeated the king's words in whatever tongue was selected by turning a wheel on the box.

"I know the thought sits heavily with some of you that we will never see nor set foot on Earth again. But is that really such a tragedy? The forces and passions appearing there are the same as those that destroyed it before. Let me share with you some of the things I've observed in recent years, and where I think they will lead before very much longer...."

"Does the thought sit heavily with you?" Korshak asked Mirsto, who was sitting on the far side of a small table from them, his cloak draped over the adjacent seat. Sultan was lying alongside Mirsto's feet, ears erect and eyes shifting constantly, taking in the strange new world.

"Oh, I think I've seen as much of it as I care to," Mirsto replied. He seemed to be recovering from his exertions down on the surface. "A world this size from now on should suit me just fine. Gallivanting around in all that space down there was beginning to be somewhat taxing."

Ronti was sitting a short distance from them, near the people who had also been brought up in the white bird. They were dressed in all manner of garb and carried an assortment of bags and other objects that looked as if they had been grabbed in haste at short notice. Their speech was different from that of the Arigane and Shengshoan regions, but like Korshak, Ronti had picked up a smattering of it in their travels. What intrigued Ronti most of all was the talking, manlike metal creature that had single-handedly routed an entire troop of Zileg's cavalry with exploding lights and streaming fiery smoke. If the Builders so chose, they could surely have vanquished the world. But to rule over a world of the vanquished was not what they desired. So what depths of wisdom and insight were there to be learned here?

The creature was sitting beside the captain of the white bird, as it had during the brief journey up to the flying island. Less than two hours before, it had performed a feat greater than that of any hero that Ronti had heard sung of in ballad or told in legend; yet it showed no more emotion than would a house servant after driving away a pack of noisy dogs who were being a nuisance on the street. What manner of creature was it? Did it live, or had the Builders made it, as they had the craft that sailed in the skies and everything else that made up this world of miracles that they were now in?

All the same, Ronti's natural cockiness hadn't deserted him entirely. He was pretty certain that he could show it a thing or two when it came to acrobatics, he told himself as he eyed it up and down.

"One thing I can promise you all is that the things we are saying farewell to will fade into insignificance

compared to the wonders that lie ahead. Aurora represents the greatest concentration of human creativity and inventiveness that has ever been brought together in a single place at one time...."

In the leafy upper level of his abode, Masumichi Shikoba had Ormont's address playing on the wall screen in the living area. At the same time, he was using a viewpad hooked into the visual system of GPT-2D, still aboard the recently docked carrier, to check over the group of close family and other relatives that the lander had brought up. It turned out there were seven rows of seats in the lander, not six as Lois Iles had conservatively guessed, which gave twenty-eight places, or twenty-four available after allowing four for Korshak's party. Of these, he had filled twenty—not bad at all, considering the instant decisions that they had been forced to make. Eight had declined to go, as Masumichi had assumed some inevitably would. He supposed that he would now have to explain and justify his actions to the Recruitment Board, whom he hadn't so much as notified, let alone consulted. However, the fact remained that had it not been for his robot, the lander's entire mission—which Nath Borden, who sat on the Board, had expressly requested Masumichi to take care of—would almost certainly have been aborted. So all in all, he felt that he had a pretty strong case and could stand his ground. In any case, what were they going to do about it now—throw him overboard?

While the carrier was returning to the *Aurora*, Masumichi had replayed the sequence that GPT-2D had recorded of its extraordinary stunt at the bridge. He'd had no idea that his robots would be capable of such initiative in circumstances so complex and demanding, and he was eager to analyze the associative-matrix audit trail to see what he could make of what had happened. He was beginning to suspect that perhaps he had been underestimating his creations for a long time. It seemed they could be surprisingly resourceful.

"And let's not forget the new generation that will be appearing and growing up in the years ahead. Aurora is the only world that they will ever know. Their trust in and dependence on the future that we build will be total. We owe every one of those yet unborn a unique debt, now, to make sure of..."

Sonja Taag sat out on the patio of the duplex apartment that she would be sharing with Helmut Goben, and listened to Ormont's words coming through the open glass door from where Helmut was watching on the screen inside. They were on the topmost level of a structural module called Evergreen, devoted primarily to intensive cultivation, with an upper area of simulated outdoor recreational parkland containing a sprinkling of residences. The apartment looked out at a miniature landscape where streams tumbled into grass-banked ponds, and hiking trails wound their way through trees beneath an artificial, variable-weather sky lit by arc discharge and mirror optics. The richness of light and variety of colors brought together in the confined space produced an intensity unrivaled anywhere on Earth, and with the peculiar curvatures of the underlying geometry resulted in an effect that could have come out of a fairy tale. Yes, Sonja thought to herself, the children growing up in such surroundings might be deprived in some ways, as a few people maintained. But they would surely gain in others.

"He's talking about you, Sonja," Helmut's voice called from inside.

"Yes, I heard it."

Since she was a teacher, children were her special interest. She saw *Aurora* as a chance to help make real the kind of teaching environment that she had always dreamed of—to uncover and develop the potential that every human mind was capable of and meant for, free from the baggage of defensive polities, institutionalized prejudices, and obligatory deceptions that came with having to survive amid a patchwork of hostile and competing interests as part of Earth's legacy. What would arrive one day at the planet Hera could represent a leap forward in the advancement of human culture that would take Earth another thousand years.

She leaned back in her chair and gazed over the treetops to where the starfield was visible through a section of roof low down where the sky ended.

To devote one's life to something meaningful that was bigger than they were, and which would endure for long after they were gone. Wasn't that what fulfillment in living was all about?

"Our world will see a new system of relationships and values. No more can it be divided between producers and takers. In the environment into which we will be heading, every one of us will depend utterly on the skills and dedication of everyone else. The worth of every individual will be judged not by what they own, or by the means they have acquired to compel others, but by what they can contribute...."

In the graphics laboratory of the observatory located in the *Aurora*'s Hub section, Lois Iles had routed the audio to the speaker of the terminal where she was working. The main screen on the terminal was showing a reconstruction of an image transmitted from Hera by the probe that had left the old world long ago, before the time of the Conflagration. In a chair at the worktop behind her, Marney Clure, whose exchange she had mediated from Tranth, was using another screen to browse through the archive of images. He had asked to come to the observatory and see the kind of work she did.

Even after enhancement processing, the scenes were of low resolution and poor quality, and much of the instrument data had been corrupted after traveling an immense distance under noisy conditions. To have decoded anything at all that had originated from ancient, partially understood technology was an impressive enough feat in itself. The Sofian test platforms sent ahead in more recent years as part of the *Aurora* program were programmed to carry on all the way to Hera, but the mission would be well on its way before it could expect to receive anything back from there.

In the meantime, the information available about Hera was restricted to what could be gleaned from orbital observation by the single old-world probe. It indicated a planet that was Earthlike in its physical and chemical makeup, with oceans, a breathable, friendly atmosphere, and climatic zones extending between possibly greater extremes than on Earth. The atmospheric composition and surface appearance confirmed the presence of life, though of what kind and progressed to what degree could not be ascertained. There had been no sign of major artificial works or electronic activity that would suggest an advanced civilization.

"I never realized that anything like this existed," Clure murmured, keeping his eyes on the screen. He was listening to Ormont, but had been too enthralled by the things he was seeing to stop when the announcement came on. "And this was all achieved just by Sofi. What could the whole world do if it could only learn to live together?"

"A lot," Lois agreed. "But it's heading the wrong way. You know how things were in Tranth. People who think the way you do were never heard."

"Do you really believe things can be different?" Clure asked. "Even Sofi was starting to get divided within itself."

"Finding out is what *Aurora* is all about," Lois replied.

He learned fast, she thought. When she brought him up from Tranth, it had been simply as a duty that she had been assigned. But now she was beginning to appreciate more the qualities that made him stand out, which had attracted attention beyond Tranth. And now he would be able to help build the kind of world for all that he believed in. Ormont had just said that the worth of individuals would be judged not by what they possessed or the power they held over others, but by what they contributed. If Marney Clure's kind of world became reality in the course of the mission, and if that set the pattern for a new branch of the human race that would one day spread across Hera, then, Lois told herself, she could say that she had already made her contribution to it.

Something was wrong. Andri Lubanov, who was supposed to be Torus's prime inside intelligence source on *Aurora*, had said that liftout was six weeks away at least, and possibly longer. Now he had disappeared suddenly, after destroying sensitive records and giving his mistress what was obviously a storyline to delay suspicions, and communications from the ship had gone silent. None of the ground personnel associated with the mission could be raised, shuttle traffic from the bases had ceased, and radar evaluations during the *Aurora*'s last pass overhead had failed to show the usual pattern of attendant-craft activity in the vicinity. Actor had issued the code *Winter Rain* without further delay, and operation Torus was in motion.

Dreese had flown down in a military chopper to accompany the force detailed to occupy the sprawling logistics base at Yaquinta. It was still night, and the column of vehicles had drawn up before the main gates, which stood chained and locked in the illumination of searchlights. Detachments taking other routes had sealed the other entrances around the perimeter. The stipulated five minutes since the issuing of an ultimatum by loudhailer to open up and refrain from offering resistance had elapsed. There had been no response, either directly or by radio, and no sign of movement beyond the fence. Dreese nodded to the commander standing with him beside the open staff car.

"Okay, take it out."

The commander gave an order, and the cordon of infantry around the gate area opened up to allow passage for the earth mover that had been waiting behind them. It rolled forward into the searchlight glare on its huge wheels, and used its front bucket to demolish the gates in a crash of rending metal.

"Follow on through. Secure all objectives according to plan," Dreese instructed.

✧   ✧   ✧

"The last links are broken. The ties are cut. There can be no going back to the past. So let us all look as one to the future, and the new life that is about to begin."

Andri Lubanov listened to Ormont's final words from a seat in a communications room opening off from the *Aurora*'s bridge. A screen dominating the room showed a view of the ship's Hub structure and the base of one of the support booms connecting to the outer Ring. Observing from a place this close to the nerve center of the operation was a privilege earned by his undercover work inside the Sofian Internal Security Office. Ormont held the mission to be permanently in his debt, and would always be a friend. They thought alike.

If Lubanov's personal views conflicted with the mission's ideals, he would have to learn to live with them or resolve them, he reflected. There could be no going back now. But whichever way that worked out, from now on he would be able to breathe and sleep easily, free from the threat of revenge vendettas catching up with him from the far side of the world. And the days of double-dealing and deception, which had never left him savoring the best of tastes, were over.

Years ago, back in his own country, he had believed in the martial tradition of duty and honor, but been disillusioned by the realities of experience. From what he had seen of human nature, the time would come when the values that *Aurora* stood for would have to be defended, and his kind would be needed. The difference this time would be that there was something worth defending.

The view on the screen changed to show Ormont and his two principal senior officers on the raised dais at the forward end of the bridge. Around Lubanov in the communications room, figures turned in their seats, and faces looked up from consoles expectantly. Ormont pushed away the microphone that he had been using and looked to one side.

"Disengage final overrides. Confirm exit vector."

"Vector confirmed on all, sir."

"Initiate main and hold."

"Positive function, holding at intermediate." It meant they were lifting from orbit. *Aurora* was straining to go.

"Bring her up to full power."

There was nobody left in the base, anywhere. . . . Dreese stood, nonplused, in the staff car outside the main office building as the officer who had gone inside with a squad reappeared at the doors and came over at a crisp pace. "Nothing, sir. It's deserted."

Soldiers were breaking open the coverings of what looked like cargo loads, stacked in rows awaiting transfer to the pad area. They were dummies, consisting only of wooden frames, piles of rock and sand, and empty crates. The materiel to be shuttled up was gone. Inside the opened doors of a storage shed to one side, the lights came on to show it cleared out. Beside the driver in the front seats of the car, an adjutant who was talking to an officer with the forward unit looked up from his phone. "It's the same everywhere. Nobody around the pad area. The control center is empty."

And then, light coming suddenly from above caused Dreese to look up. A column of white was glowing high overhead, lengthening as he watched, until it extended across half the sky. Around him, the other officers squinted and shielded their eyes as the brightness intensified, revealing the buildings of the base with the gantries and shuttles behind in an eerie, artificial day.

Dreese stared, his hand covering the peak of his cap. And despite himself, a smile spread slowly across his face, and his lips curled back to show his teeth as the realization came to him of what it all meant.

"Go, baby, go!" he breathed. "Good luck, guys!"

PART TWO
The Void

~ TWELVE ~

Sofi's uniqueness attracted the talented and gifted from far and wide, many of whom, for that reason, had been misfits in the various circumstances that they came from. As a consequence, Sofi became a meeting ground for a multitude of views concerning the principles a society should be based on and how it should be organized to reflect them. Since coercion was anathema to the kinds of people that typified the cultural mix, and its eventual ineffectiveness in any case evident to most, the system that emerged was pluralistic, tolerant, and firm in respecting such freedoms as the right to dissent and individual self-determination.

This social foundation had become established by the time the *Aurora* project was conceived, and raised the question of how the society-in-miniature that would make up the mission itself was to be structured and organized. Since the answer to this would influence the architecture and functional layout of much of the ship in many ways, it was an issue that had to be addressed in the earlier years, when Sofi's achievements were already unparalleled anywhere, and its commitment to idealism was at its height.

119

Disagreements quickly broke out among the mission planners over the philosophy that should govern the ship's design. Should residential units be zoned together as such, or distributed across areas that mixed different kinds of use? If zoned, should they be segregated by type? To what degree should they be customizable? Would services and amenities be better centralized or localized? At what point would conformity become stifling to the point of provoking antisocial behavior, while at the other extreme, at what point would opportunity for endless variety begin to dissipate energies uselessly in nonsensical competition and displays of status? On more significant scales, what would be the psychological effects of large interior vistas and outside panoramas of stars, compared to the sense of security imparted by more restricted and enclosed spaces? Would giving high visibility to the offices and presence of the Directorate, and the ultimate authority over ship's affairs that it embodied, serve as a source of reassurance? Or should it be kept discreetly backstage to avoid reminding the inhabitants of so much that had been left behind forever?

Then some began to see the problem as lying not in the choice of which of the contending plans to go with, but in the zealousness that was being shown over wanting to plan everything in the first place. Everyone was trying to promote their vision of the ideal society—and in the process, reflecting the practically universal but seldom-acknowledged human conviction that the world would be a better place if more people were like themselves. Whichever version of utopia was considered, the question arose of what to do about those who didn't share the ideals that the vision presumed. And for a society that sought to accommodate a spectrum of values embracing the full variability of human nature, this was no small matter. In short, what was to be done about the social dissidents and misfits that would always exist, no matter what the planners came up with?

Proposals for screening prospective migrants against an approved set of psychological and other standards were rejected. Such procedures worked for creating specialized military units or recruiting teams for demanding work such as the space ventures that had taken place in recent years, but *Aurora* was a one-way ticket and fully self-contained. A choice that turned out to be wrong couldn't be relieved from duty or transferred out when the tour was over. And beyond that, having to set special standards would be equivalent to admitting that the community didn't reflect the real human condition to begin with, which would have been in conflict with the policy of preserving a broad representation of human diversity. In any case, even with an ideal initial population, aberrants would inevitably be born later, who didn't conform to the original selection criteria, so the criteria would become irrelevant.

Imposing a mandated order that would brook no dissenters was out of the question. Besides going against every principle that Sofi had been founded on, enforcing conformity over generations would surely destroy the very capacities for creativity and innovation that had made *Aurora* possible. The descendants who would one day arrive at Hera would need the resourcefulness and abilities to open up and settle an unknown world—faculties that would have been long stifled in a population conditioned to passive obedience and turned into a human sheep pen.

Reasons could always be found for requiring people to live the way others thought they should, in the name of serving a greater common good. Once the "common good" had been identified, then any questioning of it automatically became the mark of the common enemy. In an artificial space habitat, safety and security considerations afforded ready-made justification for sacrificing individual freedom to authoritarian demands. The importance of efficiently managing its limited physical resources provided another. It would have been ironic if, after making such an investment of talent and effort to escape from the oppressive forces that were threatening once again to engulf Earth, the mission found it had, at the end of it all, to resort to precisely such measures in order to survive. Or had it to conclude that the way of life that it had been conceived to preserve wasn't suitable for exporting into space at all?

In short, there would be those who objected to whatever the designers came up with, and there seemed to be no universally acceptable way of dealing with them. The question therefore reduced to finding a way to avoid confronting them with any set-piece plan that it was possible to disagree with. Or put another way, how to design a society whose one, overriding attribute would be that of not being designed?

The solution that the designers' thinking finally converged upon was not to try. Instead, they decided to let the eventual form of the mission design itself. Arguing over how people should live, work, and play, what sort of social order they should exist under, and how they should think, for generations who were not even born yet, in a situation that nobody had ever experienced before, was probably futile anyway. For the simple fact was that nobody knew, or probably could even imagine, what the conditions might be of such an expedition ten, twenty, thirty years out, or what kind of stresses might arise to challenge its resourcefulness. Quite possibly, even the natures of the people who would have come into being by that time could be completely alien to the comprehension of anyone shaped by planet-bound perspectives.

The correct approach, then, was surely to try to anticipate nothing, but to build in the flexibility that would enable the people concerned to create their own style of society as they went. And since, from the disagreements that had precipitated the whole debate in the first place, one form of society would never suit everyone, this would have to mean "societies." There was no need for ideologues or experts to specify in advance what kind of geometry the descendants in years hence would inhabit, the way their society would be organized, or how they would function in it. Because, as the unpredictable factors that time would bring began to unfold, and different groups emerged with their own ideas about the kind of world that they thought they wanted to live in, they would be able, simply, to *go out and build their own.*

So the idea took root—inspired in some ways by biological genetics—of an "organism" being sent into a new and unknown environment, carrying with it the seeds of its subsequent evolution in response to the cues that an unpredictable future might provide. A difference, of course, was that biological organisms could build themselves from materials supplied by the surroundings, whereas a starship conceived to spawn embryonic communities would have to carry its own with it. Hence, the final form of *Aurora* came to include large repositories of extra materials and equipment of the kind used for the craft's construction.

In the years while the main ship was taking shape, the stockpile that it carried was supplemented by making some of the test platforms launched ahead serve also as freight rafts, to be overtaken and consolidated in the course of the voyage. Their prime purpose was to investigate propulsion systems intended to drive a starship, and realistic results required stretching performance to the limits. This meant giving them realistic loads to haul, with the result that the amount of mass distributed along the course ahead—even after some losses due to the inevitable failures—eventually came to total several times that used for the construction of *Aurora* itself.

All of the rival schools of thought, weary from arguing their own pet theory, warmed to the idea. What better way could there be to allay the disgruntlements that were bound to surface among any human community shut up for a long period in a limited space, and provide an outlet for surplus energies than getting involved in creating a new world? Tired of seeing the same mall-like concourses and residential decks every day, with the same patches of hydroponic greens overhead, interspersed with star-filled sky windows? Fine. Get a like-minded group together and design yourselves a world that looks like a town on Earth, one made up of village-scapes and smallholdings, or maybe a collection of bright lights and amusement parks ... or anything else you want. Those who didn't agree with the form of government inherited from Sofi could set up a monarchy or political system patterned on one of the nations back on Earth; a sect devoted to some emergent cult figure; or even an experiment in collective ownership and living if it appealed to them.

And the nice thing about it was that none of the attachments to a social formula or lifestyle had to be permanent. The changes and contrasts of moving from one to another could provide a source of variety that could well prove essential to a healthy life. It could be an invaluable means of education, too. For what more effective way could there be of revealing the realities of someone else's ideal than shuttling across a few miles of space and trying it for a while? And what better preparation could those distant descendants have for dealing with the conflicts that go to make up real human existence than to have lived with them all their lives?

So, what mix of objects would eventually drop into orbit above Hera? A variety of thriving, mutually supportive communities, ready to extend the pattern across a new world? Or mutually distrustful armed fortresses, seeking only their own territory to enclose and defend? Nobody knew. At the beginning of such a venture, nobody could.

That was the whole point.

- THIRTEEN -

The six-mile-circumference Ring surrounding the *Aurora*'s central hull like a wheel on an axle was attached by two immense pillars extending in opposite directions from an annular supporting structure set forward of midships, known as the Hub. Sofian science had established that gravity resulted from the electrical nature of matter, which had led to the development of techniques whereby the effect could be synthesized and controlled. When the ship was experiencing acceleration under the main drive, normal weight perpendicular to the internal decks was achieved by adjusting the angle of the simulated component vector. The vessel's circular architecture about a central axle had been adopted as a fallback to enable g simulation by rotation in the event of the electrical system—a comparatively recent conception, still to be thoroughly proven—failing during the voyage.

The Ring was made up of twelve modules connected by isolating locks that could be closed in an emergency, and were built to varying shapes and designs, depending on function. Some housed multilevel conglomerations of architecture providing high-density living and working space, along with essential services and amenities—in effect, the "towns." Others, such as Evergreen, contained agricultural levels and expanses of parkland to supplement the more intensive hydroponic and aeroponic cultivation carried out in the industrial complexes, and to offer a semblance of the open air. There was a sports and recreation center that included an artificial beach with waves; a zoo that did a good job of re-creating a representative sample of Earth's natural habitats; a college system offering courses in arts, crafts, and sciences; and a museum with departments dedicated to just about everything.

All in all, Korshak thought, surely a sufficient variety of interest and distractions to satisfy a lively and curious eleven-year-old boy. It mystified him that Mirsto Junior's greatest source of fascination seemed to lie in the hidden underworld of machinery and its associated labyrinths of pipework, power lines, and ducting upon which the visible day-to-day existence depended. For somebody of that age to be attuned to the significance of such things was unusual. Korshak read it as a sign of some exceptional quality of insight that would one day find mature expression. As would any proud father harboring high hopes of the future for his son.

Vaydien had insisted on the name, after the Mirsto who had come with them from Arigane consented to being their firstborn's godfather. The original Mirsto had died less than a year afterward. Korshak had long ago guessed that the reason for including an elderly contingent in the *Aurora*'s population had been to make room for the young who would soon start appearing. Korshak and Mirsto Junior were on their way from

Astropolis, the Ring module in which their residence
was located, to the one called Jakka, where Masumichi
still occupied his original apartment-laboratory duplex.
Masumichi had called Korshak to say that he wanted
to discuss something confidential, and Junior never
missed a chance to visit Masumichi's and see the
robots. That meant that instead of one of the regular
transit tubes that ran aboveground and through the
public concourses, they were taking a maintenance
line buried beneath the normally frequented levels.
The world that it served was a gloomy, somber place
of structural anchors, ladders, catwalks, cables and
pipe mazes, and galleries filled with metal housings,
control gear, and machines.

Immensity came cheaply to objects constructed
in space. To somebody who had known the size and
strength of the load-bearing members that had been
needed to hold up large structures under their weight
back on Earth, *Aurora*'s underpinnings appeared
unnaturally slender and light. Korshak now knew this
was because the "weight" experienced in the higher,
inhabited levels was an artificial effect created locally
for comfort and convenience, which manifested itself as
a force between generators embedded in the decks and
the objects they affected. Since the generators down
here operated at a lower level—resulting in a light-
headed, floating sensation inside the capsule—there
wasn't the same weight-compounding effect transmitted downward as happened when the attraction came
from below. It was derived from the electrical forces
that were the source of so many other miracles that
Sofians took for granted, but quite how, Korshak still
didn't fully understand.

He paid less attention these days to his magic of old. He marveled that there should be such popular demand for his talents among people surrounded by real magic in which he was still discovering new wonders. The mechanical and physical concepts of Sofian science were familiar enough by now, but an intuitive grasp of the more abstract forms of theory and their mathematical expression eluded him. He had come to the conclusion that while some individuals seemed to be born with minds that naturally worked that way, his did not.

He had found that the most valuable contribution he could make stemmed from his knowledge of human behavior. As the population increased and diversified, a gaggle of sister worlds had begun to appear around *Aurora* in the way the mission planners had envisaged, the whole assembly being known by the collective name "Constellation." It seemed to be a fact of nature that some people would always disagree over fundamentals that others considered obvious. The motives and long-term intentions of the founding groups were not always clear, and the Directorate's advisors welcomed help in better understanding how two individuals could look at the same thing and each see something completely different. Some things that the psychologists couldn't explain came easily to an illusionist.

A little over ten months previously, Constellation had caught up with the first of the cargo rafts sent on ahead before *Aurora*'s launch from Earth. It meant that a lot of additional construction materials had become available, and agitators and activists were campaigning for support to build various kinds of new habitats. One program that had gone ahead without delay was the conversion of the raft's propulsion unit into a fast reconnaissance probe to be sent ahead to Hera, carrying a mixed robot survey and workforce. The information they would transmit back would surpass anything sent by the simple instruments that the old-world probe had carried. Conversion involved replacing the raft's fusion drive with a baryonic-annihilation system of the kind developed by the Sofians in later years and used to power the *Aurora*. Korshak still had some learning to do when it came to this level of physics, but his understanding was that the baryonic-annihilation process yielded the total energy equivalent of the mass involved, making it somewhere around a thousand times more powerful than fusion. The new probe, designated *Envoy*, was scheduled to depart in a little over a month.

"Do you know what this makes me think of?" Mirsto Junior asked without taking his eyes from the window. They were in a six-seat capsule riding on a wave of magnetic flux through the transparent-walled transit tube.

"What?" Korshak asked.

"Being underneath one of the old cities back on Earth. Is this what it was like?"

"I honestly couldn't tell you. I wasn't from that time. The world I knew came a lot later." Without the light and life that existed only a short distance above them, it certainly felt more like some lost and forgotten part of the old world, Korshak had to agree. Away from the airiness and the views of the stars, it was easy to forget that a fragile shell was all that separated them from the unimaginable vastness of space extending away in every direction outside. "Do you feel safer?" he asked curiously. "More enclosed and protected. Is that why you like it down here?"

Mirsto screwed his face up as he watched a bay of transformers and insulating supports pass by, illuminated briefly by the light from the capsule. "I don't know. I'd never really thought about it like that. What's there not to feel safe about?"

"Oh, the way things are out here. Just thin walls and radiation barriers between us and everything that's out there. It's not the same as having a few thousand miles of solid planet, and then a hundred miles of atmosphere outside that. People who lived on Earth talk about it sometimes."

Mirsto shrugged vaguely. He had no concept of such things. For him, life was simply the way it had always been. "I like all the machines and tunnels and things down here that people never see," he said. "It's more real. The same as with magic."

"Magic?" Korshak smiled in genuine surprise. "How do you mean?"

"Well . . . with a magic trick, there's the bit that everyone sees, that they think is all of it. But there's really another part, too, that they don't see. What they see isn't really what happens. It only seems that way because of what they don't see. So what they don't see is really real." Mirsto gestured briefly at the surroundings they were passing through. "It's the same with the world. People up there act as if what they see around them is all there is. But none of it could happen without what's down here. So this has to be more real." He fell silent as a new thought struck him, then resumed. "Did they have machines like this everywhere underneath Earth as well? I suppose they had to. But Earth went on and on for thousands of miles. How could anybody ever have made all those machines?"

Jakka was a rectangular, urban-style Ring module measuring roughly a half mile along a side. Masumichi's place was in the center, which consisted mostly of high-density, multilevel construction surrounding pedestrian precincts and communication corridors. It housed a large residential population from mixed social and occupational backgrounds, giving it something of a cosmopolitan flavor, and much of the academic and research work associated with the sciences was concentrated there. The uppermost levels were fashioned in the manner of buildings set among open terraces and plazas below a roof of shutters that could present artificial sunlight in a daytime sky, or be opened to reveal the stars. It was named after a long-dead hero from Sofi's founding years.

Korshak and Mirsto were met at the door by Kog, one of Masumichi's new robots. The robots looked less like assemblages of plumbing these days, and possessed more versatile joints than earlier models—a result of new, self-regenerating materials that combined the toughness of metals with the flexibility of plastic. Another of Masumichi's innovations was a photo-active facial coating that could be made to display variable patterns simulating human expressions. In addition, Kog featured a small panel in the upper chest that functioned as a screen to display graphical constructions or video clips, which proved a great aid to communication. Despite the years of ongoing research, there were still times when the ambiguities of natural human language could lead to unexpected interpretations and consequences.

"Hello," Kog greeted. Its voice was lofty and a shade distant, as if it were addressing someone in the next room. Getting the finer graduations of intonation right was another subject still being worked on. The screen on its chest showed Hori, one of Masumichi's innumerable relatives, grinning and waving excitedly from somewhere inside, with part of the famous sycamore tree visible in the background. Evidently, he was also visiting. He and Mirsto were about the same age, notorious partners in mischief and crime, and inseparable for most of the time. Hori fascinated Mirsto with snippets of science picked up from Masumichi, and strange rites and customs preserved by others in the family. Mirsto taught Hori magic tricks.

"Hi, Kog," Mirsto returned; then, to the screen, "I thought you said you were going to the Hub with Aya and Rensh."

"The low-gee court's closed today," Hori replied. "So we decided to go next week instead. Hey, guess what my dad says we're doing for Calley's birthday."

"What?"

"He's taking us to Plantation for three days. It's over *fifty* miles away! Can you imagine that? There's no town or tubes or ground cars at all. They grow stuff everywhere, and there are animals running loose. And you get to ride a real horse to go anywhere, or else you have to walk."

"Yes, I've been there." Mirsto turned the inevitable look toward his father. "Can we go again sometime?"

"We'll see," Korshak told him. "Maybe when your new sister's a few months older. Your mother has her hands pretty full just now." For convenience, *Aurora* preserved Earth's traditional ways of dividing time, even though they no longer had any celestial significance.

"*Months!*"

Kog was leading them up the spiral staircase to the living area on the higher level, above which the tree was pruned to stop it engulfing the apartment completely. Masumichi's living space was divided into annular sections around the central opening like parts of a pineapple ring, each with its own inner terrace open to the greenery. A year or so previously, several pairs of birds had mysteriously appeared and made nests in the branches, and from there proceeded to make free use of the surroundings as their adopted territory. The resulting distractions made it impossible for Masumichi to concentrate, not to mention the hygienic effects, and evicting them turned out to be a major operation. The accepted explanation was that the birds must have somehow found their way through the connecting locks from one of the agricultural or animal rearing modules, and thence through the ducting system. However, there were rumors among younger elements of Masumichi's extended family that Hori and Mirsto had had a hand in it after visiting the zoo and learning that birds had lived free and unconstrained back on Earth.

Masumichi, wearing a loose multicolored robe and sandals, was waiting in the sitting room adjacent to the kitchen and dining area, where it seemed he had been relaxing. A viewpad displaying text was set down alongside a glass on the side table by the recliner, and the room was playing music that Korshak recognized as reconstructed from old-world sources. Would the long-dead composer ever have guessed that his work would one day be heard in a place like this? Korshak wondered. Hori had probably been amusing himself downstairs in the lab.

"You're looking well," Masumichi commented as he came across to usher the arrivals in. "And young master Mirsto. How is your mother?"

"Fine, thank you, sir. And my new sister, Kilea, too."

"I'm glad to hear it."

"Sleeping through the night, finally," Korshak put in.

"So you're getting some rest again yourselves, eh?" Masumichi nodded and smiled briefly. "How's Ronti?"

"Never better. He says that teaching acrobatics again has made him ten years younger. But I never did think he'd ever age anyway. Today he's at Beach, organizing a show that they want us to put on there."

"Hmph. More likely making time with that artist lady he was with last time, if I know Ronti," Masumichi said. He turned toward Hori. "Mirsto was hoping to see the neural coupler while he's here. Why don't you and Kog take him down to the lab and let him try it?"—a hardly subtle hint that he and Korshak wanted to be alone.

"Yes, can we?" Mirsto said. "Dad told me about it. He says it's a thing that you strap around your head like a hood, and you can see and hear what a robot's seeing and hearing. You think you are the robot. It sounds really great."

"Can Kog show them the trick I taught it first?" Hori asked. Masumichi raised his eyes momentarily at Korshak and gestured for Hori to go ahead. Hori felt in one of his pockets, then another, and produced a white ball, maybe an inch across, made of some soft, rubbery material. Few people would have caught it, but Korshak registered a surreptitious movement of

Kog's hand hanging nonchalantly down by its side as it moved forward to take the ball from Hori.

Smooth, Korshak thought approvingly. Hori's fumbling in his pockets had been deliberate, a distraction to draw attention from Kog while it retrieved a duplicate ball from where it had been concealed—probably somewhere in the robot's attachment belt. Clearly, the two of them had set it up beforehand.

Kog held the ball aloft between thumb and forefinger, made a show of solemnly turning back the cuff of a sleeve it didn't have, and let the ball fall into its palm while turning its hand to show the back with fingers spread, apparently empty. Then, under cover of a quick pass made with the other hand, it turned its hand palm-forward, showing it to be hiding nothing. Korshak knew the move, of course, because he had taught it to Mirsto. It involved pushing the palmed ball through between the fingers at the precise instant that it was covered by the pass, and then holding it out of sight behind the closed fingers by pinching the material between two of them. That was why something soft was used. It was a tricky sleight to master, requiring lots of practice and confidence. With their smaller hands, even the boys were seldom able to execute it as well as Kog had just demonstrated.

"Excellent!" Korshak pronounced—and meant it.

"Wow!" Mirsto supplied.

In conclusion, Kog, managing to look quite pleased with itself, directed attention to its other hand by extending it and looking at it, and opened the fingers slowly one by one to reveal the duplicate ball that had been there all the time. That was when Hori moved a little nearer, as if following, in the process just happening to brush close to Kog's side. Once again, only Korshak caught the slight movement of Kog slipping the "vanished" ball to its accomplice in order to be able to show a genuinely empty hand if challenged.

"Great stuff, Kog," Korshak complimented. "Maybe we should give you a slot in the show at Beach, too."

"The subject exposes some curious anomalies in human reasoning," Kog commented.

"So, can we go and see the neural coupler now?" Mirsto asked.

"Sure. That's what my uncle was telling us," Hori said. The term was used freely. Just about all of the younger element of the Shikoba clan referred to Masumichi as "uncle."

"Is that okay?" Mirsto asked, looking at Korshak.

"You heard Mr. Shikoba."

"Let's go, Kog," Hori said.

"And don't touch anything else down there," Masumichi told them as the two boys and the robot began moving toward the doorway.

"We won't."

"Kog, keep an eye on them. Call me if they do."

"Yes, boss."

Masumichi waited until they had gone, then sighed, shook his head, and turned to gesture at his partly-filled glass, "Can I get you something, Korshak?"

"Oh, a small *tashi* would go down well. Maybe with a touch of lime." Korshak settled down on the couch near the recliner, while Masumichi went through to the dining area.

"You seemed suitably impressed with Kog's performance just now," Masamuchi's voice called through the connecting archway over the clink of glassware.

"It was good," Korshak agreed. "You've been improving them."

"We had to refine the faculty of intuitive spatial awareness right down at the level of subconscious basics," Masumichi replied. "That was what made the difference. They have to know instinctually that what they think they're seeing doesn't make sense. Logical ability alone isn't enough. It was pretty much as you guessed."

"So they don't think seeing is believing anymore. Is that what you're saying?"

"Not so easily as before, anyway."

"A pity you can't do the same for some people," Korshak remarked.

Korshak's familiarity with illusions, and the insights it gave to human psychology, had helped Masumichi greatly in his work. The earlier robots had remained unimpressed when shown examples of objects "magically" disappearing from one place and reappearing in another. Similarly, they hadn't displayed any surprise at something apparently broken into pieces only moments before being produced restored and intact. On being quizzed by Masumichi after a demonstration of the latter kind, one of them had answered that the parts must have been put together to make the object in the first place, so what was so strange about seeing them put together to make the same thing again?

"But you didn't see anyone putting them back together the second time," Masumichi had persisted.

"I didn't see anyone put them together the first time, either," the robot responded.

It was always the same pattern: eminently logical, but missing the whole point.

Behavioral research on human infants had shown that by even a few months of age, they formed the notion that a physical object continued to exist when it was out of sight. For example, when a ball was rolled into a tunnel, they would shift their gaze to the far end in anticipation of its emerging there. Such intuitions arose from the experience of existing and moving as an object in three-dimensional space, which was something shared by all human beings, and enabled them to communicate easily by means of commonly understood metaphors. (Unlike the ball in the tunnel, in "getting an idea through" to someone else, nothing physically moved "through" anything—but everyone knew what was meant.) But the necessary preadaptation at the fundamental level of human neural wiring had to be there for it to work. This was what had been missing in Masumichi's robots. From what Masumichi had just said, it sounded as if an intuitive "feel" for the effect that a magic trick was supposed to produce was necessary in order to create it proficiently—the attempts of the earlier robots had been hopeless. This came as no surprise to Korshak. He didn't try to pretend that he understood why.

Masumichi came back in from the dining area, handed a glass to Korshak, and went over to resume his place in the recliner.

"So, what is the latest on the coupler?" Korshak asked, sitting back and crossing a leg over his other knee. "It sounds as if you've moved on to a new model."

The neural coupler was a new concept in interfacing that Masumichi was developing for better control of telebots—robots that were remote-directed by human operators for things like space construction and work in hazardous environments, as opposed to autonomous types like Kog, which were still considered experimental. Information received from the robot was injected directly into the sensory centers of the operator's brain, while key voluntary motor-control commands were interpreted and transmitted back the other way, bypassing all the messiness of interfacing helmets and body harnesses.

Masumichi confirmed with a nod. "Kog is the first to have it built in from scratch. I've got the bandwidth problem straightened out. We're pretty much ready to begin practical trials." The last time Korshak was involved, Masumichi had been testing a prototype design added on to a predecessor of Kog's, called Tek.

"Not too soon, either. There's going to be plenty of work for them with all the proposals for new constructions that are going around," Korshak said. "Everybody seems to be having ideas about how governments ought to be run."

"Marney Clure says the problem with all of them is that they create inequality by definition," Masumichi said. "He wants to start a colony that doesn't have any. An anarchy. Do you know anything about it?"

Korshak shook his head. "I never had much time for ideas about how other people ought to live. Taking care of one life is enough."

"He seems to be getting attention. A lot of young people like what he's saying. But they're always the ones who rebel the most against being kept in line, I suppose."

Korshak took a taste from his glass and looked skeptical. "So, whose rules decide? Everyone ends up in a free-for-all. How could it work? It would end up like Tranth—all the way back to what he came from years ago."

Masumichi shrugged. "It's Marney's idea, not mine."

Silence fell. Korshak studied the window-framing sycamore boughs at the far end of the room, and then looked back. "Anyway, I'm sure that wasn't what you wanted to talk about," he said.

"Yes, er... well." Masumichi fidgeted in his chair. "I could use some help with something, Korshak. It's kind of personal and confidential, and needs to be handled discreetly. You'd be the right person."

"Okay."

Masumichi made a face and rubbed his nose awkwardly. He had obviously known this moment would come, yet seemed to have been putting it off. Finally he gestured downward in a vague way that failed to communicate anything specific. "The truth is, I've lost one."

"One what?"

"An AI vehicle. One of the robots."

Korshak realized that the gesture was at the laboratory area below. "That... sounds like something that would take some doing," was all that he could manage by way of reply just at that moment.

"It's not always easy, living alone, you know," Masumichi said. "You have that charming former princess as a wife.... And especially for someone involved in work as intensive and demanding as mine, with long hours of concentration..." The suddenly defensive-sounding tone and the apparent change of subject left Korshak at a loss. He could only knit his brow and show an empty palm in total incomprehension. Masumichi continued. "All right, so every once in a while I take a few hours off to unwind with some company on Istella. It's not uncommon among single professionals, you know. I don't know why it gets to be socially frowned upon. Human nature is what it is. People only create problems for themselves when they try to deny it."

Now it was making more sense. Korshak had to bite his lip to prevent himself from smiling. Istella was the name of the off-ship pleasure resort that had been one of the first of the *Aurora's* companion worlds to be built. The mission's original planners had been generous in their provision for healthy and wholesome sports and entertainments, recreations that were culturally elevating as well as physically beneficial, and other such activities conducive to the improvement of body, mind, and character. But either through a sensed need for propriety that came with the job, or because they genuinely lived in blissful remoteness from such matters, there was no concession to such things as the gaudier bars and show houses, casinos, and other attractions that characterized parts of just about any town in Sofi or anywhere else, that real flesh-and-blood people liked to spend time in every now and then.

The Directorate had expressed surprise and some confusion when the proposal was put forward to remedy the situation by creating such a facility outside their range of jurisdiction. Probably spurred by feelings of civic duty, they had voiced misgivings and attempted to discourage the venture, but it all proved to no avail when a referendum carried the decision with a majority that was overwhelming. An interesting conclusion from polls carried out before and afterward was that the way people voted anonymously could be directly opposite to the position they adopted publicly. The project went through, and Istella had done a flourishing business ever since.

Masumichi still hadn't explained what this had to do with a missing robot, but Korshak thought he already had a good idea of what had probably happened. The biggest problem in getting the robots to communicate reliably in natural language was their lack of commonly shared "world knowledge," which humans acquired as a result of growing up in the same physical, cultural, and experiential world. For years, going back to the time when GPT-2D had routed Zileg's cavalry on the road to Belamon and before, one of Masumichi's principal strategies for remedying this had been to broaden his robots' horizons of concept and association by exposing them to as wide a range of experiences as possible.

"Let me guess," Korshak offered. "You took one there to let it see more of life—a new side to the world that it hadn't come across previously. Right?"

Masumichi stared for a second, then nodded shortly. "It was Tek." Masumichi paused morosely, and then sighed. "I had been under extreme pressure of work. As I mentioned, to ease the stress I occasionally indulge in certain . . ." Korshak nodded and waved away any need to elaborate. Masumichi went on. "I told Tek to walk around Istella, see the place, and talk to people. I'd meet it later in a bar called the Rainbow." He shrugged, indicating that there wasn't much else to add. "It never showed up, and I haven't seen it since."

"And that's it?"

"It's enough, Korshak. *Envoy* is due to go in a month. Its tasks when it arrives at Hera will depend almost totally on autonomous robots. If word got around that Tek has gone astray, it could raise questions about the reliability of robots generally and result in the whole program being set back. It would be just the kind of ammunition that the opposition needs." In the unique circumstances of Constellation's existence, physical materials took on inestimable value. Agitators and activist groups were objecting that to send a portion of the newly acquired stock away again in the form of *Envoy* represented a reckless waste of resources that would better serve future generations by being kept here, where they would one day be needed more.

Korshak hesitated, not wanting to contradict by stating the obvious. The line of models like Tek and Kog that Masumichi had produced for general cognitive and behavioral research were in a different class from the robots developed for *Envoy*, which were adaptive to a degree but designed essentially to carry out a limited range of specialized tasks. There was no reason why any decision concerning them should be influenced by an unanticipated quirk in Tek's makeup.

Masumichi sensed Korshak's reservation and shifted uncomfortably in his chair.

"All right, there's more. I'd just rather not make this official. Some of the people I depend on for backing and cooperation can be a bit stuffy about Istella. . . . And, yes, I'll be frank, it would be personally embarrassing. You know Tek, and you have a flare for getting to the bottom of the strange and perplexing. How would you like to take a crack at this?"

"Hm." Korshak contemplated the remainder of his

drink, swirling it one way, then the other. "Don't they have a tracking device that would locate it?" he asked, looking up. "I'd have thought you'd make them with something like that."

"It never seemed necessary," Masumichi replied. "It's not as if they have somewhere the size of Earth to get lost in—and in any case, I never anticipated a situation like this. They do have two-way communication, which I thought would be sufficient if I ever needed to know where one was. But that isn't a lot of good if it's switched off."

"How long ago did this happen?" Korshak asked.

"Nearly two weeks. I've been making discreet inquiries, but without result."

Korshak shook his head wonderingly. "It's hard to believe. As you said, it isn't as if there was somewhere the size of Earth for it to get lost in. Yet nobody's seen a hint of it?"

"It just seems to have evaporated." Masumichi picked up his own glass at last and emptied it in a gulp. "You're pretty good at making things vanish and bringing them back again, Korshak. I'm hoping you can make it work here, too."

– FOURTEEN –

Istella was also popularly known as the Christmas Tree, something mentioned widely in surviving old-world writings, although nobody was quite sure what kind of tree it had referred to. For reasons that were obscure, the term had also meant a collection of multicolored lights, and it was in this sense that it was applied to Istella.

From *Aurora* it looked like a cluster of gemstones glittering in the blackness of space. A night sky lent atmosphere to the miniworld's style of attractions, and the consequent extensive use of window roofing in its construction gave effect to its lavish internal illuminations. Constellation—the configuration of *Aurora* and its daughter worlds—did not maintain a constant orientation with respect to the fixed distant stars, but rotated slowly about the common center of gravity, causing the background to turn. Once every twenty-two minutes, the lights of Istella passed in front of a particularly brilliant nebula, giving the appearance of jewels set in a crown.

Closer up, Istella resolved into a squat dumbbell composed of two wheels connected by a short, thick cylinder. The cylinder housed such support functions as power generation and environmental control, as well as carrying the docking ports for the ferries. The nightlife that Istella had been built to provide took place in the wheels, which were named Haydon and Bruso, after the project's two leading instigators and architects from years back. Haydon's plazas and arcades were dominated by a central domed structure containing a number of restaurants and bars, a casino, and a theater. The dome was floodlit in rich blue and known as the Blue Palace. This was the end of Istella that featured shows and clubs catering to most people's ideas of a night out that was "exciting," "different," and even acceptably "daring"—but observing unspoken, yet generally recognized limits. The raunchier stuff was to be found in Bruso.

That was the direction in which Korshak and Ronti headed after disembarking from the *Aurora* ferry and clearing the docking bay. The name blazed as a hologram, repeating and moving above one of the two illuminated archways on opposite sides of the reception concourse. The promenade beyond led to Bruso's central "Square" and was lined on both sides by bars, a variety of eateries and shops, and animated signs advertising everything from current shows and attractions to specialty clubs and sex partners given to various penchants.

Plenty of people were about, the regular numbers of browsers and sidewalk-table patrons swollen by the new arrivals from the ferry and others on their way to catch it before it departed. There were colorfully dressed groups, here to party and have fun; guys checking the scene; girls doing their best to get checked;

and the inevitable sprinkling of loners keeping to the background behind the anonymity of pulled-down hats, enveloping clothes, and a proliferation of beards that challenged the statistical norm of the population.

"I guess the Happy Feet must have walked," Ronti commented as they strolled through the throng, looking around and taking in the sights. That had been the name of a dance studio that doubled as a popular party venue. In its place had appeared an establishment billing itself as the "Oyster Bar," its interior dark, with blue lighting and aquarium tanks in the walls. Marine-related names and decorative themes were widespread, reflecting a commonly felt nostalgia for the oceans of Earth. Nobody aged twelve or under had ever seen one.

"That's probably a better place for a bar anyway," Korshak said. "Good spot for meeting people when they come off the ferries. And maybe a last drink on the way home if they've got time to kill."

"So at least we don't have to wonder if Tek decided to take up dancing," Ronti joked.

"Oh, I don't know. If I ran the Feet, I'd have moved it closer to the Square."

"We'll see."

Of all the unlikely situations that Korshak had found himself in through his varied and colorful life, looking for a lost robot was perhaps the strangest. Agreeing to take on the task had been more than simply helping a friend in need, or choosing the easier between accepting and refusing. True, he was compulsively curious by nature, and attraction to anything out of the ordinary had been ingrained into him long enough to qualify as an instinct. But beyond that, he and Masumichi had developed a strong professional working relationship, in which each was able to benefit from the specialized knowledge and experience of the other.

It had to do with communication. In many ways, the art of the illusionist depended on subtly communicating the suggestion of something being seen that in fact was not seen, which equated to defining the conceptual framework within which a spectacle would be judged. Or, put another way, setting the assumptions by which a communicated message would be interpreted. And assumptions were all-important in communicating. Because of the world knowledge that all humans shared, humans communicating with each other tended to supply only the information that they didn't assume the other already had. And the amount they assumed was enormous. In one of their discussions on the subject, Masumichi had illustrated the point with the simple dialog:

"I'm leaving you."

"Who is she?"

Just six words in total, but capturing a panorama of emotions, tragedy, conflict, and drama that any human would understand immediately. An artificial mind, however, not grounded in the same reality by experience, would have either to be given explicitly every fact about human existence that was necessary to comprehend the exchange in all its depth and shades of meaning, or alternatively, some set of rules for inferring them from more general principles. Masumichi had finally conceded that the first was not practical; whatever approach was tried, the amount of data that needed to be supplied exploded exponentially with increasing complexity of the situation being addressed. The

only other way, then, was to build into the software
a process for integrating new items of knowledge into
a network of associations that would grow and modify
itself as experience directed—in a way, attempting
to mimic the uncanny, universal learning ability that
every human baby was born with. Masumichi's earlier attempts had run into difficulties because of his
failure to appreciate the extent to which associations
are formed unconsciously through suggestion, and it
was in this area that Korshak's insights had proved
invaluable.

On the other hand, Masumichi's analytical methods were frequently able to provide Korshak with a
more precise understanding of what was happening
to produce effects which he knew from long practice
worked, but until now had never tried to discover
exactly why. Indeed, without the introduction to the
ways of Sofian science that Masumichi more than
anyone had given him, Korshak wouldn't have known
where to begin looking to discover such things, even
if he had wanted to.

They emerged into the bustle and life of the Square,
with its lights and color and music on every side.
Terrace bars and restaurants overlooked the scene
against a background of show houses and storefronts,
while above, the grandeur of space and stars unfolded
beyond the enclosing sky window. Korshak nudged
Ronti and indicated a direction with a nod of his
head. The Happy Feet was alive and well, secure in
a new location next to an establishment illuminated
in red and purple but not deigning to announce itself
with a sign.

The Rainbow bar was in a secluded niche on one of

the upper terraces. Inside, small, shadowy booths lined the walls on either side of the door, with a brighter, more open area of tables and chairs taking up the center. The place was moderately busy. Korshak and Ronti barely had time to take two of the bar stools before a voice bellowed, "Well, I'll be! Korshak and his fellow rogue!" A figure who was presumably the proprietor came out from behind a partition dividing off a space at the rear. He was short, balding, and sported an immense mustache covering his lower face in a pair of curving waves. His eyes were brown and beady, and just at this moment glinting with genuine pleasure at seeing them.

"Osgar!" Korshak exclaimed.

"What happened?" Ronti asked him. "Did you get tired of cleaning pipes and raking weeds?" The last they'd known, Osgar had been a maintenance worker on Plantation, the low-tech agricultural and wildlife world.

Osgar shrugged. "You know how it is. Everyone needs a change sometime. I figured it was time to get out of the coveralls and the boots. Anyway, they've got enough younger people coming along now to do that kind of stuff."

"So, how long has it been?" Korshak asked.

"Aw, three months, I'd say. Maybe a little more."

"Different, anyhow," Ronti commented.

"That's true enough. You meet all the characters here. And there are a few stories I could tell you if you're ever stuck for ways to spend your time." Osgar leaned forward, and his voice fell. "There are some names here in Bruso right now who wouldn't like it to be general knowledge. You wouldn't believe how fast news travels in the trade." He straightened up, spreading his arms along the edge of the bar. "Anyway, what can I getcha?"

Korshak ran a curious eye over the display of offerings. "How about a bartender's recommendation?"

"Ever tried Envoy?"

"What's that?"

"A new beer that they brew out on Plantation. That's what they're calling it—to celebrate the star probe. It's supposed to be the way it was done back on Earth, without the synthetics. Getting good ratings. Dark and not too sweet, with a touch of tangy."

"Sure, I'll try it," Korshak said.

Ronti nodded. "Make it two."

Osgar took down two glasses and placed one under a bar tap. "So, what brings you guys here? Somehow I can't see it as recreation or to find out things you don't already know about."

"Business . . . kind of, I suppose you'd call it," Korshak replied.

"Uh-huh."

"To do with the scientist that I work with, who lives in Jakka."

Osgar nodded. "The guy who works with robots?"

"Right. Well, the fact of the matter is, one of them has gone missing."

"A robot," Osgar said, pushing one glass across the bar. Korshak waved for Ronti to take it as Osgar moved the other one under the tap. Somehow, he didn't seem especially surprised.

"Yes," Korshak said.

"And you think it might have been here."

"Now, how would you know that?" Ronti asked.

"It's not exactly the kind of thing I'd expect people to be telling you every day."

"True," Osgar agreed. "But you're not the first. There was a guy in about a week or two ago saying the same thing. He even showed me a picture of it—as if I needed one. He said it was supposed to meet somebody here, but it never showed up." Osgar shrugged as he handed the second glass to Korshak. "That's about all I can tell you."

"And it didn't appear later?" Ronti checked.

"Not earlier, or later, or while whoever the somebody it was supposed to meet was here—assuming he was here. We haven't had any robots." Osgar inclined his head to indicate Korshak's glass as Korshak tried a taste. "What do you think?"

"Not bad. So who was this other person who was in here, wanting to know?"

"I didn't ask him."

"Okay, what did he look like?"

"Like he didn't want anybody to know. Short—about like me, but skinnier. Big black coat, black hat, dark glasses, with a little beard. The beard wasn't real; when you work on Istella, you get to tell. But his face had that kind of yellow-brown color with high cheeks, the way people from Parthesa used to be. You've got a touch of it, Ronti. And he had small hands."

Korshak was smiling to himself, already picturing Masumichi in disguise. Parthesa had been the general name for the eastern half of Asia, over which he had roamed for many years. Korshak caught Ronti's eye and saw he was thinking the same thing.

"So did you ever hear from him again?" Korshak asked, keeping a straight face.

Osgar shook his head. "What would have been the point? All I could tell him was the same as I've just told you. He went away, and that was the last I heard of it." He paused and reflected for a moment, then emitted a snort that bordered on a snigger. "So, what's going on? I wouldn't have thought that much around here would interest robots, if you know what I mean. But anyway, how can you lose one? It's not exactly something that's going to blend into the crowd."

"That's what we're trying to find out, Osgar," Korshak said.

A low *pinggg* sounded somewhere below the level of the bar. Osgar glanced down. "Oh, someone needs service. I'll be back in a moment." He came around the bar and went away to take an order at one of the booths. Korshak tried more of the Envoy. Ronti did likewise.

"Not bad," Korshak pronounced. "Os was right. Almost a taste of the old brews."

"It reminds me of the one you liked in that tavern we used to stay at in Belamon," Ronti said.

"Ah yes, Belamon." Korshak smiled at the recollection.

"One of the most profitable pieces of magic we ever did."

The town's councilors had invited Korshak to put on a show in a festival that they were organizing, and then quibbled over the payment that they had agreed to. Within twenty-four hours of Korshak and Ronti's leaving, the town was hit by a freak storm that devastated the seafront and harbor. The townspeople attributed it to Korshak's powers and insisted on reparation, and an emissary from the council caught up with Korshak's wagon the following day to deliver double the amount owed.

"So Masumichi has already been here," Ronti said. "It would have saved us a lot of trouble if he'd told us."

"Maybe he credits us with greater powers of divination than..." Korshak began, and then stopped as he realized that a girl who had been alone at one of the nearby tables had got up and was coming over to them. She was maybe in her mid-twenties, slimly built, with long dark hair tied back in a clip, and wearing a short, capelike jacket over a sparkly top and tight-fitting pants. Her face had the undecided look of someone not wanting to intrude but needing to say something. Korshak twitched his mouth upward at the corners and raised his eyebrows inquiringly.

"You're the illusionist," she said. "I saw that levitation act with your wife about a month ago, when she was dressed as a princess. They say you'll be doing a show at Beach."

"We hope so, anyway," Korshak replied. "It's still being talked about." Inwardly, he prepared himself for an explanation of how he had done this trick or that trick, or perhaps being solicited to take on an apprentice. It happened all the time.

But the girl continued, "I recognized you, so I was interested, and I couldn't help overhearing a bit. It sounded as if you were asking about a robot."

"That's right," Korshak confirmed. "One was brought to Istella as part of a research program. It was supposed to meet someone here but didn't show up. We're trying to get a lead on it."

"I saw one here," the girl said.

"In the Rainbow?"

"No, but in Bruso, near here."

"When was this?"

"Around a couple of weeks ago."

Korshak shot Ronti a quick glance and looked back. "That sounds like the one. Where did you see it?"

"Do you know the place where the Mediators come and preach?"

Korshak shook his head. "Not really. We only come here once in a while."

The Mediators were a mystical-religious cult that had roots in a variety of practices and belief systems brought from Earth. They had opposed the Istella project but been too small at the time of its inception to change the outcome. Since then, they had grown sufficiently to jointly found their own daughter world, called Etanne, along with several other sects professing a similar need for seclusion and an environment unimpaired by worldly distractions.

"It's just off the Square," the girl told them. "There was a robot there, watching them. It seemed really interested. There are probably Mediators down there today. I can take you there if you like."

— FIFTEEN —

The girl's name was Brel. She lived and worked on Istella, she said, but didn't go into details. Originally from Sofi, she had been brought up to the *Aurora* as a young girl, spent most of the time since then in Jakka, and moved out to be on her own a little over a year ago. Her family back there were "okay, but kind of stifling." She had a twin sister who was "Miss Perfect," she added, making a face, as if that explained everything.

A small crowd had collected in a corner of the Square, where broad steps led down into a sunken rectangular area below a terrace bathed in light from the entrance to a casino and club. A platform with a rostrum was set up at the end opposite the steps, around which several figures in long robes with the hoods thrown back were proffering leaflets. On the platform a bearded man, similarly clad, was speaking below a sign that read: TRANSCEND!

"He's the same one who was talking when the robot was here," Brel said.

"How about the others with him?" Korshak asked.

"I'm . . . not sure."

Korshak glanced at Ronti, who returned a what's-to-lose? look. They descended the few steps and moved closer behind the small crowd of listeners. The expressions and attitudes told mainly of the curiosity that draws people to anything different. An incense-like fragrance pervaded the air, no doubt associated with a bluish smoke arising from a source somewhere at the front.

"Yes, brothers and sisters, on all sides you see man-made wonders. Indeed, the very worlds you live among are wonders, every inch of them the product of human ingenuity that can only be described as breathtaking. It would be foolish to deny that, and Mediators would be the last to belittle achievements of which every one of you has the right to be proud—and should be proud!" The speaker's tone was rich and powerful. He paused and looked around, dark eyes scanning the faces, and then raised a warning finger. "But we must not allow justifiable pride in what we are to turn into the conceit of imagining we are all that can be. The universe that we see, awe inspiring and magnificent though it may be, is merely a shadow of a vaster reality that is not apprehended by the ordinary senses."

"How do you know, then?" somebody near the front challenged.

"Because I have trained my senses to reach beyond the range of the ordinary," the speaker answered.

"That might be fine for you. But how can you convince me?"

"How can I convince a blind man that I can see?"

"That's not the same thing. It's easily proved. Tell him what's across the room, then let him walk over and find out."

"As I am, indeed, inviting you to do. But it requires more application and effort than just walking across a room." Without waiting for a further response, the speaker went on. "In any case, it should be obvious that powers exist which operate on a level beyond anything that we are capable of. Every cell, of the trillions of cells that make up every one of you, is a microscopic, automated factory filled with molecular machinery that dwarfs the complexity of anything ever conceived by the minds of humans." He showed his teeth briefly. "People ask me if I believe in miracles. I tell them, 'Of course I do! You *are* one!'" It drew some smiles.

The finger stabbed upward at the star-filled sky above the Square. "What hidden powers underlie the grandeur of the cosmos? Do you imagine it all happens for no reason, with no plan and no purpose, in the way that some, whose minds are unable to reach beyond the material and the mechanical, would have you believe? On Earth in ancient times—before its decline into the age of material distractions and self-worship that led to the Conflagration—a wisdom once existed that knew and could channel those powers. A level of mental and spiritual advancement that was able to mediate between the vaster reality and the limited realm of experience and perception that we regard as the universe and all that is. . . ." Another pause, ushering in a louder, more strident note. "But out here, a flicker is beginning to arise once again. The retreat we have created at Etanne rejects the excesses of artificiality that make the rest of Constellation a mirror of what Earth became. Amid surroundings that bring back the peace and serenity that Earth once knew, the mind and spirit can reach out and make contact again with . . ."

Korshak knew the line and had no particular need to hear it again. He moved to where he could get a clearer view of the area at the front, beside the speaker's platform. The platform with its rostrum was positioned off-center toward the crowd's right. From it, a narrow carpet of colorful design extended leftward for perhaps seven or eight feet to a small wooden table standing on its far end. A rod projecting upward from the table's center to a little less than shoulder height supported a metal urn in which the incense was burning. To Korshak, the setup told its own story immediately.

Bringing a carpet out for pure ornamentation to a street meeting like this would have been a needless chore and extravagance. The way it was positioned between the speaker's platform and the table effected a superficially logical visual symmetry, but its only evident function was to serve as a totally unnecessary underlay for the table. Which meant that its real purpose had to be something else. It was concealing something. If Korshak's guess was correct, the appearance of the table and the rod standing up from its center was deceptive. They were painted and grained to look like wood, but far from being lightweight and delicate, they were constructed from high-strength metal alloy. The carpet covered a horizontal extension to complete an L-shaped configuration that would resist tipping. The speaker was building up to a demonstration now, before everyone's eyes, of the powers that the Mediators had learned to access. Anyone here could learn it, too. Yes, Korshak thought he had a good idea of where this was leading.

Movement nearby caught his attention. One of the

acolytes was moving among the audience, distributing leaflets. Korshak accepted one obligingly.

"Don't leave just yet," the acolyte murmured. "The Master is about to show one of the wonders."

"What wonder is that?" Korshak asked.

"You will soon see for yourself."

Korshak studied his face curiously. He was young, maybe in his twenties, with yellow hair, gray, opaque eyes that revealed nothing of the person within, and lean features intensified by hollow cheeks and a narrow nose and chin. With the opportunities that abounded in *Aurora*, he could probably have become anything he chose. It had never ceased to amaze Korshak that so many people were enticed by promises of intangible magic that were never fulfilled, when all the time they were surrounded by countless visible proofs of what he still considered to be real magic. Was it just a case of familiarity dulling the senses, and the allure of the strange and the unknown? The acolyte had to know that the wonder he was peddling was faked. So what kind of rationalization did the cult instill to justify such deception and still preserve faith? There were depths to the psychology of this business, Korshak realized, that he still hadn't plumbed.

The audience was primed now, impatient for the show. As the acolyte moved away, a girl who had been sitting out of view at the front rose to her feet. She was thin and wraithlike, dressed in an enveloping white robe secured by a cord at the waist. With the pallor of her features, Korshak's first thought was that it could have been a shroud. Two of the other robed figures came forward, took her by the hands, and led her to the center of the strip of carpet, where she turned to face the audience expressionlessly. At the same time, the bearded Master was stepping down from the platform.

"This is Nyea," he informed the onlookers. "Still a novice, but already attuned to actualizing and focusing energy drawn from a higher plane. In a way, like an antenna, if you will. What you are about to see cannot be explained by ordinary, materialism-based physics. Observe."

One of the attendants had removed the urn from the top of the rod and stepped back. The other drew Nyea a few steps sideways until she was alongside the small table, and then raised her arm to shoulder height, at the same time bending it at the elbow to bring her hand, lightly closed, against the side of her head. This caused the underside of her arm just above the elbow, to where the sleeve of her robe had fallen, to rest on the ring at the top of the rod, in which the urn had rested. The attendant made a show of clasping the rod tightly with both hands, while the Master began making passes in the air, at the same time intoning a rhythmic chant that was taken up by the others, now assembled as a backing group on either side. The wraith's eyes closed, and her face took on a distant look. Her body seemed to stiffen. Korshak glanced at his companions. Brel was watching the performance fixedly, while Ronti looked about at the reactions of the spectators. They were rapt with attention, expectations now at their highest.

Together, the Master, standing behind, and the attendant, to the side, stooped and gripped Nyea's feet, which were adorned with just a pair of string sandals. Slowly, they lifted her feet from the ground, moving them sideways, in the direction away from the table. She remained supported by her upper arm resting on the top of the rod, still being held firmly by the other attendant. Already, there seemed something unnatural about the balance being effected. Her upper body was supported only by the rod, but it seemed stable and firm. A few murmurs of surprise went up among the audience.

They lifted and turned her slowly until she was horizontal, her body remaining impossibly rigid as it lay between the rod under her bent arm at one end, and their two pairs of hands holding her feet at the other. The Master's eyes shone with mystical energy flowing through his being from unknown dimensions of existence. He removed one of his hands; the attendant did likewise, producing gasps of astonishment. They were supporting her now only with the fingertips of their two remaining hands, extended casually as if bearing no weight at all. Then, slowly and carefully, as if not to disrupt the delicate interplay of unseen currents, they withdrew their hands completely. Finally, the attendant who had been holding the rod at the other end let go of it and stepped back. Nyea remained hanging in the air in repose, her only contact with anything now being her upper arm on the rod. The Master snapped his fingers, and her eyes opened. She blinked several times, as if unsure for a moment where she was, then smiled, stretched her leg, and seemed to relax visibly, giving every impression of being perfectly comfortable and at ease.

Exclamations of amazement broke out all around, with some scattered applause. On the terrace above, people outside the casino entrance were stopping and coming across to see what was going on. At the front of the crowd, a man was rubbing the top of his head and looking upward, at the same time proclaiming, "I *feel* it! I can feel the energy!"

The Master put a hand to his brow and signaled weakly with a wave of the other that his strength was fading. As he stood back, mopping his face with a handkerchief, the rest of the troupe converged to catch Nyea and lower her back to the ground before the power expired. In moments the table was dismantled and returned to a stowage space in the platform, and the carpet folded into a stack—not rolled, as would have been more natural—doubtless to accommodate the sections of the concealed metal footing. People were coming forward with questions and comments, which the Master's assistants stepped in to deal with.

Ronti turned to Korshak. "Do you see it?"

"Oh, sure. The setup looked odd from the start."

"Not a bad act, though."

"How do they do it?" Brel asked them.

"That pole and the table aren't what they seem," Korshak said. "You wouldn't bend them with a sledge hammer. There's another part under the carpet. She's strapped to a harness underneath the robe, that supports the side of her body and connects to a ratchet fixing in the top of the pole."

Brel nodded slowly as the principle became clearer, if not in every detail. "Is that why they use someone skinny?"

Ronti grinned. "Well, it probably wouldn't help things much if she were three hundred pounds," he agreed.

"I'm not sure what you mean by a ratchet fixing."

Leaving Ronti to explain, Korshak made his way

around the throng toward the Master, and reached him just as a couple who had been pressing him on some point walked away, nodding and uttering profuse thanks. He stepped in before anyone else could intervene.

"I have a question."

"I am extremely exhausted. If it's about what I just demonstrated, one of my understudies will deal with it."

"No, nothing like that. It's about something that happened around two weeks ago."

Suspicion flickered across the Master's face. "What?"

"It was on another day when you were speaking right here. There was an unusual listener in the crowd. Very unusual. A robot."

"I don't know anything about it."

Korshak saw immediately that he was holding something back. Besides, a robot in the crowd was hardly something that would escape notice, and Brel had said the Master was there on that day.

"That's unfortunate," Korshak said. "Would it help your memory if I talked about leather corsets and a frame that runs under a carpet?"

The Master peered at him more closely, and then glowered. "Korshak! I should have spotted you sooner. So, what's the story? Have you taken to crusading for moral righteousness now?"

"No, I live and let live. I'm here on personal business. But the robot was here, and so were you. You must have seen it. So, you tell me the story."

"There isn't much of a story to tell."

"Then tell me as much as you know."

The Master sighed. "It just appeared. We didn't have anything to do with that, or know where it came from. But it was a believer, all right. Asked me all kinds of questions afterward about how to learn more. Said it wanted to become one of the family."

"What? You mean the Mediators?"

"Uh-huh."

"It wanted to join your sect at Etanne."

"That's right."

And Korshak had thought this couldn't get any stranger. Although, talking with Masumichi had half prepared him for something like this. In terms of its ability to conceptualize, Tek was a precursor of Kog, who had been able to perform the ball-vanishing trick effectively because it had an intuitive grasp of its significance. Unlike their earlier predecessors, who hadn't seen anything remarkable in such illusions at all, Tek would know that what it saw was impossible by the normal rules of how the world worked, but without the analytical ability to do other than accept it at face value. Hence, it had all the makings of a True Believer.

"So what happened?" Korshak asked.

The Master shook his head. "It was too weird. I didn't know what kind of an outfit it belonged to, or what we might have gotten ourselves into. I just wanted it to get lost."

"So what did you say?"

"The usual stuff when someone looks as if they could be trouble: that you have to be properly prepared, which I told it meant getting closer to what's natural. All the dependence on technological stuff that life has become brings the wrong vibes." The corners of the Master's mouth twitched upward for an instant. "I figured that ought to keep a robot busy for a while."

"And that's it?" Korshak asked.

"That's it. It went away. I never saw it again. That's all I know." The Master's body language confirmed it. Korshak nodded. The Master waited for a few seconds, then leaned closer and winked an eye. "So, hey, we're both in the same line, right? Kinda like partners. You meant what you said about live and let live, eh?"

Back at the Rainbow, Brel had bent a flattened drinking straw through two right angles to form three sides of a square. She stood it on the bar and held it with one of the parallel sides resting on the surface, the center part vertical. "That's how I think you're telling me they do it," she said to Ronti. "Nyea is the top part. The pole and the table are the upright. And this is the bit under the carpet. Only the whole thing is rigid." She made motions of trying to tilt the figure. "See, it won't fall over."

Ronti nodded over another Envoy. "You've got the idea."

Osgar, watching from the other side with his elbows resting on the bar, nodded. "I've wondered about that one. It had to be something like that. You wouldn't believe some of the explanations some people come up with, that I've listened to. Magnets, local suppression of the gravity simulators, vortexes in the ether. . . ."

"You get the believers coming in and talking about it?" Korshak said. "Why here? It seems a bit out of the way."

Osgar shook his head. "I didn't mean here. When I was on Plantation."

"What were they doing there?" Ronti asked.

"It's a regular thing for them to spend a bit of time there. Supposedly they need to 'go natural' and get all the technical stuff from the other worlds out of their heads before they move on to Etanne. But what it is really, the cults connive with the farmers to keep them supplied with willing bodies to help out with the work. They do everything the old way, so there's never enough."

"Kind of a spiritual purification," Brel offered. "Before they're admitted to Etanne."

Osgar nodded. "Something like that. And the cults get good deals from the farmers. So I guess everyone's happy."

Aspiring novices seeking preparation for Etanne would find themselves being steered to Plantation. Korshak and Ronti looked at each other as the same obvious thought came to both of them. "Hundreds of people would have seen it going there," Ronti pointed out after a few seconds. "They couldn't miss something like that. Masumichi's been asking around for over a week. How could it have disappeared?"

"Istella has people coming and going all the time who don't want to be noticed," Korshak answered.

It took Ronti a moment to see what Korshak was getting at. "You mean it could have disguised itself? Big coat? Hat and beard?"

"Sure. Why not?"

"A robot? It's too crazy."

"That's why I like it. Anyhow, got any better ideas?" It was clear that Ronti hadn't.

Brel was giving them a puzzled look. "What are you talking about?" she asked.

Korshak grinned at her, then shifted his gaze to Osgar, who was wearing an equally baffled expression. "I think it's time to turn our attention to Plantation," he told them.

- SIXTEEN -

Plantation had been completed a little under three years previously. Its founding was motivated by a growing nostalgia among many of the *Aurora*'s population for the natural environments of Earth, and their desire for a change from artificial vistas. It was inevitable, of course, that whatever might be contrived to convey other impressions would rest totally on underpinnings as synthetic as anything that human ingenuity had ever devised, but the illusion was felt worth the effort by a sufficient number of people to get the project launched. Its subsequent success as a sanctuary where traditional farming skills could be practiced and preserved, and wildlife brought from Earth kept in more natural conditions, along with its popularity as a place for vacations and day trips, seemed to have vindicated the decision.

Sonja and Helmut Goben had moved there from *Aurora* a year after the newly completed miniworld began accepting residents. Their former place in the Evergreen module, set amid plant-conservation zones and recreational parkland, had suited them well through the earlier years of the voyage. But with the mission's population increasing as a new generation began to arrive, more of Evergreen's park space was converted to food production, and its recreational facilities transferred to Plantation. Helmut's work as a microbiologist involved a lot of field time studying microorganisms in their natural habitats, which Evergreen's wildlife preserves had supplied initially, so it was expedient, as well as in keeping with their personal tastes, for them to move, too. Sonja had filled a teaching place in Plantation's junior school, which was located near a village-style community called Huan-ko, huddled together amid the farmscapes and tracts of natural greenery.

Their abode was very different from the ultramodern integrated duplex that they had enjoyed in Evergreen. There were no electronics bringing life and news from other parts of Constellation; no transit tubes or run-abouts; no constant reaffirmation of their dependence on technology by the ubiquitous presence and watchfulness of machines. Instead, they had a two-story house with windows and a roof, that superficially claimed to be of wood, along with an adjoining outbuilding and a patch of land that served as a kitchen garden and supported a mix of chickens, ducks, and several other kinds of animals; no part of Plantation that could be put to use was overlooked. Inspired by Masumichi's layout, they lived in the upper part, and Helmut kept a field laboratory below. And they had finally kept a promise they made to themselves years before by also following Masumichi in having a tree growing up through the center. The children liked it, too. They had friends who came fifty miles from *Aurora* to see the Forest on Plantation. But they could point to their own personal one right here, forming one of the walls of their bedroom.

Sonja stood at the sink by the kitchen window, watching Helmut out in the yard feeding the two goats from a bucket of scraps and peelings. Some friends who had visited them recently while making the obligatory outing to bring the children to Plantation had been astonished to see somebody washing dishes by hand. Sonja hadn't been able to convey the feeling of inner fulfillment that she experienced from doing things in simple, uncomplicated ways. It gave a sense of being in control of her life, of knowing she could get by on her own abilities if she had to—even if it was no more than a fond illusion out here, in an artificial island surrounded by billions of miles of empty vastness from any natural world or star. But beyond that, nobody knew what circumstances might lie in store for that future generation in the years following landfall on Hera. Sonja was one of those who liked to think that she was helping to keep alive the spirit of human self-reliance and resourcefulness that might one day prove indispensable in building the new world that was to be.

Oh, she knew of course that the images that Plantation presented were a facade. But whereas this had never been denied by the high-intensity, nuclear-energized, air-fertilized agricultural levels and manicured surface park of Evergreen, at least Plantation made the effort to pretend at being a natural planet. Even if it did cheat a bit by crowding things together and making the houses too high for their ground plan, it provided a constant reminder that would become more important as years passed by of the origins the human race had sprung from, how far it had progressed, and the qualities that had enabled it to do so.

Sonja could remember her early exhilaration on joining *Aurora* as a teacher, at the prospect of helping to bring about education as it should be: teaching minds how to think and discover their own creative potential, as opposed to indoctrinating them with the destructive prejudices and survival politics that came as part of the cultural legacies on Earth. And in the burgeoning that had taken place since in things like the arts, sciences, and innovative engineering, her expectations had been largely fulfilled.

However, more recent times had seen movement in directions that gave her misgivings. Sonja had always felt unbounded confidence in the power of human creativity to solve its problems of today and continue building better tomorrows. In particular, she believed in the ability of human inventiveness to create new resources out of what hadn't been resources before. A resource wasn't a resource until the knowledge and the means existed to make use of it. At the time of *Aurora*'s departure, large areas of Earth had existed where there was no use for oil or gasoline. Until the development of catalyzed fusion in Sofi, deuterium had been nothing more than a trace curiosity in the oceans. And new discoveries seemed to happen consistently on scales that dwarfed everything that had gone before. There was no principle in Nature that said the process of breaking through into new regimes of understanding and energy control couldn't continue indefinitely, pointing to a future unbounded in terms of what could be known and achieved. The old world's inability to grasp this had driven it to self-destruction in fighting over access to resources that it thought were shrinking and finite, when instead, it could have been creating more on an unlimited scale. *Aurora* represented a distillation of that potential from an environment threatened with being overrun by the weeds of finite thinking, and its concentration into a seed that would one day grow into a world that Earth could probably never become. That her own children and those that she taught would be a part of bringing alive that vision was what brought meaning to her life.

However, while the people that she and Helmut encountered on a day-to-day basis generally echoed similar sentiments—they had moved to Plantation mostly for the same reasons, and tended to be of the same outlook—different ideas were being voiced elsewhere. Although nothing in the present circumstances approached what could be called a problem, some sections of the population were expressing concern over the finiteness of the resources that Constellation commanded, and calling for a policy of restraint on population growth. Recent months had seen protests at the *Envoy* program and demands for it to be reconsidered on the grounds that physical materials constituted the most valuable asset to be had in the present situation, and sending anything away represented the height of irresponsibility. Sonja and others like her were hard put to think of a better way of investing it. Even more disturbing were those advocating a more forceful, centralized authority empowered to impose such standards if judged (by whom was left vague) to be in the common good, which went against the whole principle of renouncing force in favor of trust in rationality and the power of persuasion that *Aurora* had been founded on.

Most people, it was true, accepted the projections showing that the amounts of materials that had been sent ahead to be recovered in the course of the voyage would ensure a sustainable balance with the kind of growth that was expected, and regarded the agitating as a device to build a political power base. But there were those coming of age now who had no memory of such principles or the times that had engendered them. And some of the strange beliefs that were taking hold among the cults that had emerged on Etanne hinted that perhaps the trust in human rationality might have been somewhat misplaced.

Outside, Helmut swilled the empty bucket under the yard faucet at the end of the shed, stowed it inside, and headed back toward the house. He appeared through the kitchen door moments later. "You know, I hope all this work turns out to be worth it," he said, wiping his feet on the mat. "It would be a bit ironic if they find Hera teeming with animal life that's not much different from what we know. Too bad they weren't able to put down any surface landers. . . . Hello, you're looking solemn. Is it meditation hour or something?"

Sonja smiled, shook her head, and returned her attention to the cutlery that she had been wiping and putting away. "It's nothing. I was just thinking about the gloomy things they're teaching children in some places these days—that there's going to be overpopulation, and we'll start running out of everything. Young minds have a right to expect better inspiration than that kind of thing from their elders."

"Oh, it's just a fad that'll pass away. When people start inventing problems to worry about, it's a sure sign that they don't have any real ones. So it's really good news in a way."

"I wish everybody thought like that!"

Helmut looked around. "Speaking of children, where is our own contribution to Hera's future? Isn't Theis back yet?"

"She went off with Uggam, probably on one of their romps. You know what they're like. Sometimes I think she should have been a boy, too." Sonja moved away to make room for Helmut to rinse his hands at the sink.

"What's to eat?" he asked over his shoulder.

"I was going to warm the casserole. There's still about half left."

"Good. It gets better every time it's reheated—like stew. . . . So, you're worried that people might lose confidence in the future."

"It's more the kind of political system that they say we'll have to have to control things—everything planned and universally enforced," Sonja said. "Exactly what *Aurora* was supposed to avoid." She waved a hand as Helmut turned and reached for the towel. "Oh, I know that Ormont would never allow anything like that. But he's not as young as he was, and he won't be there forever. It's some of the ones I see with ambitions to move into his place that bother me. And enough people *are* listening to them."

Helmut was about to reply, when a fit of barking erupted in the yard outside. "What now?" He turned and craned his neck to peer through the window. "Be quiet, Boot." Then a series of raps sounded from the front of the house.

"Someone's at the door," Sonja said. "I'll go."

"If it's Kato again, tell him the seeds should be here tomorrow," Helmut called after her. Then, through the window, "Shut up, you silly animal."

From the indistinct murmuring filtering through to the kitchen, Helmut recognized the voice of Narel, who delivered the mail—usually from an electrically powered cart, sometimes on horseback. One of the things that Plantation's originators had been unanimous about was in wanting a world in which leisurely natural rhythms held sway, decoupled from the real-time torrent of electronic communications and event reporting that drove the rest of Constellation. A consequence was that the message links from *Aurora* and elsewhere terminated at the service hub—which was invisible from the occupied surface parts of Plantation—and the content distributed as mail. Newcomers invariably protested even though they knew what to expect, and tolerated it when they realized that nothing was going to change; then, after a while, a majority came to confess that in some ways they rather liked it. Removing the immediacy of things that were happening in other places, they said, gave more meaning to their own lives and the people around them who were a part of it. Which had been precisely the intention.

The door at the front closed, and Sonja reappeared, opening an envelope. "Narel says that the old fellow on the other side of Huan who was sick is gone. They took him out on the ferry to *Aurora* yesterday. It doesn't sound so good."

"Oh, that's a shame. I liked him. He always had great stories to tell down there in the bar. Still, not exactly unexpected, I suppose.... Who is it? Culia again, asking if her kids can come and stay with us, I bet."

Sonja shook her head as she unfolded the paper from inside. Her face lit up as she read rapidly over it. "No, it's from Korshak. He's coming here again."

"Korshak? It's been a while. What's he doing—bringing Mirsto and Vaydien on another trip?"

"No, alone...to do with something that he's gotten involved in. He'll stop by and see us, of course, he says, but he isn't sure quite when...Oh, and good stars, Helmut! He'll be arriving on Plantation tomorrow!"

~ SEVENTEEN ~

In his days back on Earth, Korshak had observed that virtually everybody had times when they needed to retreat into privacy. Country people enjoyed it naturally anytime they chose, simply by virtue of the distances separating them from neighbors. People in towns, on the other hand, unable to escape the closeness of others, manufactured artificial barriers in the form of subtle codes conveyed through mannerisms and behavior, telling the world when they wanted to be left alone. It naturally followed that urban dwellers were better at reading them, which was perhaps why farmers trying to be sociable found cities to be generally unfriendly places, while town folk tended to see their rural cousins as artless hicks.

Under the conditions of space habitats committed to a voyage that for most would last more than a lifetime, protecting privacy had become one of the most universally respected values. Hence, there would be no point in contacting people involved with administration on Plantation and hoping to get a lead on somebody who might have gone to work there. Not everyone wanted their whereabouts to be bandied around, and their reasons were considered to be their business. All of which meant that the only way for Korshak to pursue things further was to go there in person and see what he could turn up.

Plantation was built as a torus one mile across, formed from a quarter-mile-diameter tube. Since the whole idea had been to create a setting reminiscent of Earth, the outer part of the "wheel" thus formed—corresponding to the tread and adjoining area of walls on an automobile tire—was constructed as a continuous series of window sections, providing all-around visibility of the starfield. This was a consequence of the gravity being synthesized as opposed to simulated by rotation, which enabled the outer periphery of the torus to function as the roof, with the floor and lower parts of the walls forming a valley curving back upon itself below.

A plasma-discharge channel running below the full circle of the roof, fitted with ultraviolet and X-ray filtering, created six localized, albeit peculiarly elongated, "Suns," shining in a pastel sky provided by optically active cells in the roof panels that absorbed red and scattered blue. The moving daytime zone extended a little over halfway around Plantation and completed a circuit every twenty-four hours, while the dark section enjoyed a natural nighttime sky with the roof optics turned off.

Six spokes connected the torus to a hub structure containing the external communications, power generation and support services, docking facilities, and other backstage machinery that the inhabitants did a good job of pretending didn't exist.

Korshak had been there before, as had just about

every parent of young children. Few could resist an unrelenting barrage of entreaties to see the animals and walk through the fabled woodlands (even if the latter were barely a tenth of a square mile in size). Apart from that, not many wanted to. The experience was the nearest the adults would ever come to reliving times that were permanently gone, as well as a bringing to life for a moment the dreams of those who had never known them—and never would.

Dressed in casual working clothes and carrying a bag of personal effects in case he ended up staying over, he emerged from the spoke elevator with other passengers off the same ferry into a subground reception level. The surroundings of metal walls and decking, with girder lattices overhead, and a service desk beside a corridor of doors and windows could have been in any part of Constellation. As was true generally, the support structures for the valley floor above looked light and flimsy to anyone originally native to Earth. Two flights of stairs in which gravity increased progressively led to a vestibule, by which time weight was normal. From there the arrivals passed through a set of double doors and entered a different world.

The reverse sides of the doors were of wood—well, wood-grain veneer over molded plastic—as opposed to the plain lime color on the vestibule side. The doors were in keeping with the woodwork and decor of the lobby Korshak was now in. It was nothing like the fashionably styled interiors of clean lines and blended contours to be found through *Aurora* and elsewhere, but had more the character of Sofi before the onset of its age of widespread mechanization and electricity. There wasn't an illuminated sign or a viewscreen in sight.

Instead, the walls were covered in a repeating pattern of floral and leaf designs—an unusual taste in itself—and adorned with paintings of Earthscapes and rural scenes, and mirrors in ornamental frames set between niches holding statues, pottery, and assorted bric-a-brac. Lamps with ornamental fittings and shades hung from molded ceilings above wooden flooring relieved by carpets, with furnishings carved and finished to suit.

The entrance from outside was at the far end, through which could be seen a covered porch and steps with posts to the sides, and beyond it, glimpses of a building with figures standing outside, and foliage blending into the greenery of what looked like a hillside rising in the background. Several others from the ferry just ahead of Korshak disappeared through a glass-paned door to the side, on the far side of which were tables with people talking and eating. From previous visits, he knew it to be a local meeting place and general store called First Stop situated at the center of the minivillage called Jesson, clustered around the spoke head. He headed toward a door across the lobby, next to stairs leading up, with a frosted window in which were etched the words SERVICES, ACCOMMODATION, INQUIRIES. Inside was a small counter, a message and information board taking up most of the wall to one side, and a door opening to an office space at the rear. Korshak rang the bell provided, and after a short delay punctuated by sounds of papers rustling and the scrape of a chair leg, a woman appeared. She was somewhere in her fifties, short and dumpy, with dark hair cut in bangs across her forehead and makeup applied liberally around her mouth and eyes. She was wearing a loose, robelike dress of purple and lilac with vivid floral designs.

"Hi," she greeted. "Welcome to Plantation."

"Oh, you read minds, too?" Korshak said.

"The morning ferry is just in. It was a pretty safe bet. What can I do for you?"

"I'd like to see what help openings you have here. This is where they're listed, right?"

"Temporary? Time for a change of scene?"

"Exactly."

It was a common enough situation. Despite the efforts to create illusions to the contrary, Constellation living was confined to limited space and constrained within narrow bounds of experience. Just about everybody needed to take periodic breaks from their regular routine in whatever ways presented themselves. A while previously, Mirsto had gone away to a two-week "camp" on Beach devoted to swimming, diving, and the craft of handling small boats, while Vaydien went to work for a spell in an EVA suit on construction of the *Envoy* probe. Although Lois Iles still mainlined in lasers and optics in *Aurora*'s Hub observatory, she spent almost as much time these days rediscovering old-world music and creating virtual Earthscapes. Small wonder that Istella was always bustling. Korshak needed to talk to whoever dealt with the filling of occupational vacancies on Plantation, and posing as somebody seeking a change himself had seemed the most direct way. A bit devious, maybe, but such had been the story of his life.

The woman peered at him more closely. "I know the face from somewhere," she said.

"Small worlds we live in."

"Probably from sometime before, when I was on *Aurora*. Anyway, we can take care of things in the office."

"How long ago was that?" Korshak asked as she waved him around the end of the counter and indicated the door through to the back.

"About six months. I used to manage a laundry on Siden, but it got boring. Back on Earth I always liked gardening, so I figured why not give Plantation a try? I wasn't so sure about the going-primitive part, though. But I had some friends who'd moved here, and they said, 'Dari, you know, when you've gotten used to the pace of things and find you don't need all the junk, and you get to know some of the people, you won't want to go back.' And you know what? They were right. I love it out here."

"That's good," Korshak agreed.

While Dari was talking, she ushered him into a chair in the cluttered office and took her own on the far side of a desk strewn with papers. The surroundings seemed oddly incomplete without datacommunications and other kinds of equipment that would normally be standard in an office—although concession had been made to a text-processing screen and a photocopier, so there were some conveniences that had come to be regarded as indispensable. Korshak remembered realizing with surprise on his first trip to Plantation with Mirsto Junior how much he had come to take *Aurora's* advanced living for granted over the years. There wasn't even a phone service here. The only external communications were from the administrative center located in the hub.

Dari turned to one side and opened a drawer of a small filing unit standing on a side table. She drew several record cards from the indexed sections contained in it, and set them down in front of her.

"What did you have in mind?" she asked. "Anything in particular? The warden for the park areas has a slot, if you know anything about animals. There's always room for field hands, and pick-and-shovel work. Or if you're mechanically inclined, there's a shift available to learn something about climate-control maintenance."

"Actually, I was also looking for some information," Korshak said, coming to the point.

Dari eyed him with immediate suspicion. "Oh?"

"About somebody who we think might have come here about two or three weeks ago, looking for the same kind of thing. I need to find out where he went."

Dari sighed and put down a further card that she had been reading. "Now, you know, Mr. . . ."

"Korshak."

". . . that I can't . . ." Her voice trailed off as the name registered. The look in her eyes softened to a shine of adulation. "*Of course!* But coming here like this?"

"Everyone needs a break and a change sometimes."

"I suppose so. We do get them all. You'd be surprised."

"I doubt it."

"No, I guess probably not." Dari gave a quick laugh, then switched to an apologetic expression. "But I still can't divulge information on individuals we've dealt with—even for you. There are standards. I'm sure you understand."

Korshak had been expecting as much, and he wasn't looking for special treatment. "Okay, never mind individuals. Let me ask you a general question."

"Okay."

"Has anyone unusual been through here in, say, the last two weeks or so?"

"How do you mean, 'unusual'?"

"Distinctly unusual. In fact, not the kind of individual that you've probably got in mind at all. I'm looking for a robot that's gone missing."

"A robot."

"Yes."

Dari's eyelids fluttered for a moment like spinning wheels going nowhere as she strove to process the information. "You mean artificial people? Like the ones we see documentaries about sometimes? You think one might have come *here*, looking for a slot?"

Korshak nodded. "I know it sounds crazy. But that's what we have reason to believe."

Dari shook her head helplessly and showed her hands. "Well, that wouldn't be something it would be exactly easy to miss. All I can tell you is no, we haven't had anybody . . . anything, whatever, like that coming through here. If we had, I'd have notified hub Control and have them check around to see what was going on."

Korshak had been prepared for that, too. He couldn't really see Tek walking in as itself, metal alloys and polymer, and asking for a job. "Well, think of a different kind of unusual," he suggested. He gestured with a thumb at the doorway behind where he was sitting. "The people who got off the ferry with me just now were all out on day trips or come to spend time in outdoor settings—shirts and sandals, sun hats and shorts. Just out of curiosity, have you had anyone through recently who was decidedly different, that you couldn't even see? Muffled up in a coat, with a big hat and a beard, maybe. Possibly talked a little strangely, for example by not making connections that most people wouldn't think twice about."

Even as he spoke, Korshak could tell from the changes in Dari's posture that he was close. All the same, she remained hesitant. "Well, I don't know," she answered dubiously. "Now it's getting individual, isn't it? I can't give out privacy-breaching information. It's code."

"Personal privacy, yes," Korshak tried. "But we're not talking about a person, are we? It's a machine that someone has lost from a lab"—he gestured across the office—"like a copier or a crawler out on one of the construction sites. Privacy is an issue that has to do with humans."

"Well, I don't know," Dari said again. There was a pause. "Even if somebody unusual-looking—in the way you said—*had* been here, I wouldn't have any way of knowing for sure if it was your robot or not, would I? It could just as well have been somebody"—she sought for a word—"unusual. A person. See what I mean?" Dari was clearly torn between not wanting to be obstructive, and upholding professional principles. "Could there be a risk of any danger with this thing running around loose?" she asked finally, offering an easy way out.

"Not that I know of," Korshak replied candidly. He had his principles, too.

Dari thought for a few seconds longer. Then she turned to the file unit again, ruffled among the cards, and drew out another one. She read it over, and her voice changed to a lighter, more casual note, as if she had dismissed the previous topic and moved on to something else. "How about trying something a little different, Mr. Korshak? There's somebody called Melvig Bahoba, who cultivates trees and supplies timber. He's at a place called Highwood, up on the East Ridge. That's just over a quarter of the way around Ringvale going north from here, just past the Forest." Ringvale was the name of Plantation's central valley. "In fact, it's really a part of it."

"Yes, I know the Forest," Korshak said. It was the fanciful name given to Plantation's quarter-mile strip of high-density woodland. "Can't say I've come across Highwood before, though."

"You probably wouldn't unless you were looking for it. It's right at the top of the wall, buried among the trees. You won't get many visitors wandering that far off the circuit, either." She looked at him pointedly over the top of the card. "A good place to pick if you were looking for privacy or wanting to remain anonymous."

Korshak got the message and nodded, keeping a straight face. "It sounds just fine. How do I find it?"

Dari gave him directions, at the same time sketching the details on a slip of paper, and passed it across. "That should get you there. Good luck."

The building Korshak emerged from was the largest of several facing an open space that served as Jesson's central square. They were styled after the fashion of early town housing in Sofi—complete with roofs, since artificially induced rain provided the easiest means for keeping things clean and getting dust out of the air. However, the premium on space resulted in their being limited in expanse and of exaggerated height. Together with the narrowness of the thoroughfares leading away to the open areas a block or so distant in every direction—they could hardly be called streets—the impression was of an oversize toytown. But for now the sky with its peculiar striplight sun was clear and blue, and the people in their summer clothes added to the color of flowers and fruit blossoms visible among the greenery of the valley walls rising on two sides. Korshak set off at a leisurely pace, resolved to make the best of the break that the opportunity offered.

Ringvale was an arresting sight. With its floor facing outward toward the sky, the downward curvature of the torus along which it lay resulted in "horizons" that were unnaturally close in the directions defined as north and south—as if Jesson and its immediate locality were situated atop a domed mountain with the land falling away sharply on two sides. The east-west curvature, by contrast, was in the opposite direction—concave upward—and tighter, forming an immense saddle-shape of walls rising steeply to become vertical at the "ridges" marking the halfway levels where the sky began.

The synthesized gravity could be made to act perpendicularly to the ground everywhere, which meant that someone standing at the top of a ridge, and hence turned ninety degrees with respect to the floor, would see the floor as vertical, while the wall below the ridge on the opposite side would appear and feel overhead, with its inhabitants standing upside down. In practice, the effect of a mild slope was maintained to impart a sense of "naturalness" that conformed to the visual impression, while at the same time facilitating the drainage of water off the valley sides. Interestingly, youngsters like Mirsto, who had grown up among such geometries, saw nothing unusual in them. On the other hand, they found the notion of landscapes without enclosure difficult to visualize, and were unable to comprehend unlimited "flatness" in every direction at all.

Two tracks wound their way northward out of Jesson—straight lines and other echoes of artificiality were avoided wherever possible. Korshak would need to take the eastern one, which was known as Orchard Trail after the plots of fruit trees and shrubs that began immediately past the last houses. The plants represented a small sample of the seed collection carried by the mission and were genetically modified for reduced size yet increased yield, thanks to concealed subsurface hydroponic and aeroponic networks. Intentions were to restore the natural strains on arrival at Hera. In the meantime, what Plantation offered was not a completely accurate reconstruction of how parts of Earth had really been—but it gave an idea.

The next of Plantation's spokes going northward from Jesson joined Ringvale at the local administrative center called Huan-ko. Helmut and Sonja Goben lived just outside it. Since the Forest lay beyond Huan-ko, and Melvig Bahoba's place as Dari had described it was on the far side of that, it seemed that this would be as good a time as any to make good on the promise in his letter to stop by.

~ EIGHTEEN ~

An interesting thing about young humans, Tek had observed, was that they didn't seem to possess inherently any of the judgmental predispositions that caused adult humans to read "good" or "bad" into each other's ways of thinking, when mere thinking couldn't affect the world in any way at all, and to presume motives in others that they had no way of knowing. Its conclusion, therefore, was that they had to be taught such things by the humans who had matured. Why the matured ones should want to do this was still a mystery, since from what Tek had been able to glean of the history of humans in their former world, the consequences had been nothing but trouble. Indeed, if the legend was to be believed, escaping from the specter of all their self-inflicted problems of old arising again had been the reason why *Aurora* was built. The conundrum of it all was how humans could have devised beings in the form of Tek and its kind, that were able to apprehend logic on a level that the humans themselves seemed incapable of applying.

Tek turned over the partly cut board from one of the pines that had been scheduled for felling, tightened the holding clamp, and engaged the screw to feed the board through the rotary saw. A plume of sawdust flew as the pitch rose to a shriek and then fell again. Tek flipped the motor off, released the strips, picked one of them up, and turned to lay it along with the others making up the current quota. The working area at the rear of Melvig Bahoba's house was covered by a roof and open on two sides, the fourth side formed by the tool shed. Beyond the roofed area was a yard stacked with timbers and bounded by the closely spaced trees at the very top of Forest. Two children sat watching, perched on a trestle table by the tool-shed wall. The girl was called Theis, and the boy, Uggam. They were from somewhere near Huan-ko, on the valley floor on the far side of Forest, and had run into Tek in Forest a couple of days previously, when the robot was out recording growth data on a new stand of mixed saplings.

"Was that what you did back on Earth, too?" Theis asked. "Cutting wood and knowing all about trees?"

"I don't think anyone can ever know all about anything," Tek replied. "And I was never on Earth. Why do you assume that I was?"

"Oh. It's just that you're grown up. I thought everyone who was grown up came from Earth."

"That's just because he's big," Uggam said. "Robots are big right from the start. They don't have to grow bigger from being small, the way we do."

"Oh. Is that right?" Theis asked Tek. "So, where were you born?"

"They don't get born," Uggam put in.

"He's right," Tek said, moving back to pick up the other strip from the board. "I was fabricated..."

"What?"

"Put together," Uggam said.

"Oh."

"...on *Aurora*. In a laboratory on Jakka." Voicing an untruth was something that Tek had found he couldn't do, although he was aware that humans sometimes did, for reasons that largely escaped him. He attributed it to the basic programming that his faculties were rooted in. The children had promised not to spread word of his presence at Bahoba's around. The air of mystery and being asked to keep a secret seemed to excite them.

"So, how old are you?" Theis asked. "Do you have a birthday?"

"I suppose you'd say about two," Tek replied.

"*Two?* That's amazing! How can anyone know so much if they're only two?"

But it was evidently perfectly acceptable. Tek felt a fond sense of fellowship with this ability to accept unexpected facts uncritically—something that again seemed to be lost as humans attained adulthood. He had found the same thing with Masumichi's cousin Hori, and Hori's friend Mirsto.

"They only know 'machine' kinds of things," Uggam said. "I read it in a story about them."

"What do you mean, 'machine kinds of things'?" Theis asked him.

"You know, things that machines do. Like solving puzzles, or looking up things, or doing things that have to be worked out with numbers."

"That's not so," Tek objected, registering a sensation that it presumed was mild indignation. "I have a dynamic, self-modifying hierarchical associative net, and am capable of nested abstract cognitive constructions." The looks on the children's faces evaluated distinctly on the negative side of awed. Tek sought back for examples of feats that had impressed Hori and Mirsto. Since Plantation didn't provide access to the general Constellation web, Tek had to rely on its local memory. "I can write songs and poetry, compose pictures, tell jokes." Which wasn't an untruth—it could when it had heard them first. Tek still got into trouble sometimes when trying to invent them, for reasons that were still not clear. "Do magic tricks..."

That got their attention.

Theis's face lit up. "Magic tricks!"

"Show us one," Uggam challenged.

Tek looked around. Several small pine cones were mixed among the sawdust and wood chippings on the ground. "Here." Tek stooped, and reached down before Theis and Uggam had fully realized what was happening. Making a show of picking up one of the cones between finger and thumb, Tek contracted its palm over another that it had covered, and straightened up to exhibit one, keeping the other concealed. Then it turned its other hand palm upward, and rubbing the other finger and thumb together, crushed the cone into dust and fragments, letting them fall into it. "Now watch." The hand holding the pieces closed over them, squeezed for a second, and then opened again to let the other hand assist. In the process, of course, the second hand transferred the intact cone that it had been hiding. Tek held out both hands closed palm-to-palm together and made a play of massaging the contents together. "So!" Suddenly one of the hands opened to produce the undamaged cone.

In the moment for which the children's attention was focused, the other hand surreptitiously disposed of the debris behind Tek's back. The trick came from Hori, who had learned it from Mirsto. Mirsto's father was the entertainer called Korshak, who sometimes worked with Masumichi. How this could be so effective with young humans, Tek had never really understood, since the logic of what must have happened seemed obvious enough. But it never failed.

"Wow!" Theis's eyes widened.

"Let's see your other hand," Uggam said. Tek obliged, at the same time forming an electrical facial pattern corresponding to a smirk. "Not bad," Uggam conceded.

Just then, the back door of the house opened. "Aha! I thought I heard voices," Melvig Bahoba said as he stepped out. "Hello, young fella and miss. Now, what brings ye all the way up here to the top of the valley? I'll bet yer folks don't know where ye's are."

"Just talking to Tek, Mr. Bahoba," Uggam replied. "He's really neat. I've never seen a robot working in Plantation before."

"And he does magic," Theis said.

"Magic, eh?"

"A small amusement that I showed them," Tek explained.

"That's well and good, but it's got its proper time and place. That cuttin' that ye're on is due for collection later today."

"Yes, chief."

"And you two, you're welcome to come an' talk to us when there's no work going on. But there's things around here that ye could get hurt by. So let's call it a day for now, okay?"

198   *James P. Hogan*

They clambered down reluctantly from the trestle table. "We didn't mean to bother you or anything," Uggam said.

"No bother, so long as we understand each other."

"So long for now, Tek," Theis said.

"Melvig gives good advice," Tek told them. "Time to finish work now."

Bahoba turned in the doorway as he was about to go back inside. "And don't you two go climbing into any of the animal reservations, d'ye hear? Some of them are dangerous. That's what the fences are there for."

"We know about that," Uggam assured him. "We won't."

Their direct, uncomplicated way of seeing things felt like a release from grappling with the deceptions manufactured by the world of human adults, Tek thought as it selected another board. Somewhat like Plantation's freshness and closeness to nature after the synthetic artificiality of *Aurora* and the other worlds. It was beginning to understand better why minds that had been steeped in distractions needed a period of solace and purification before they were ready to confront the deeper secrets of the universe. There would be much to learn, it told itself, from the Masters on Etanne.

At the kitchen table, Korshak pushed his empty plate away, sat back, and ruffled the ears of Boot, who was sitting by the chair hopefully. "He reminds me of the dog I used to have. Do you remember him?"

"Sultan? Why, of course we do," Sonja replied.

"Ah, he had a good run. Nothing lives forever."

"Sultan was a magnificent dog," Helmut said. "I

can't imagine why that silly mutt would remind you of him."

"So, why is he called Boot?"

"When he was a puppy, he slept in one of Helmut's shoes," Sonja said. "Wouldn't stay in his box. Boot, stop begging at the table like that. Look at him, Helmut."

"He gets it from the cats. They have no shame."

"Don't criticize my cats. They have charm and dignity."

"Hmph." Helmut looked back at Korshak to change the subject. "So, you're here for a break. What's up at Forest that's of interest?"

"Oh, I mean to be useful while I'm here," Korshak answered. "The woman in the office back at Jesson—Dari. You know her?"

"Oh, yes, of course," Sonja said.

"She gave me a few places to check that could use some help." Korshak didn't want to reveal that Dari had pointed him to anywhere specifically. That way, he could ask about Tek without implicating her. "It's a way to stay in shape, too. Exercise gyms are so boring."

Boot's ears pricked up suddenly. He stood up and moved to the back door from the kitchen, his tail swishing excitedly. A scuffling of feet punctuated by snatches of children's voices came from outside, and then the door opened to admit Theis, Sonja and Helmut's nine-year-old daughter, followed by a boy, maybe slightly older, whom Korshak didn't recognize.

"Well, a fine time this is!" Sonja greeted. "Your lunch will be dried solid, Theis. I was about to give it to Boot." She got up and turned to take a dish from the stove. "Where in heavens have you two been?"

"Oh, just up in Forest," Theis said vaguely.

"What, again? You were there yesterday as well. But I suppose it's the kind of place that children would like. Would you like some of this, Uggam? There's plenty here."

"Um, okay. Thanks."

"Uggam is one of Theis's local partners in mischief," Helmut informed Korshak.

"Hello, Uggam," Korshak said.

"Korshak is an old friend of ours. From when we lived on *Aurora*."

"He's a magician, too," Theis put in as Sonja deposited a plate in front of her.

"What do you mean, 'too'?" Sonja asked her.

"Oh, nothing. . . ." Theis hurriedly busied herself with breaking and buttering a piece of bread. "How long is Korshak here for?"

"He's just stopping by for a while today. But it seems as if he's going to be on Plantation for a little while. I'm sure he'll be back again soon."

Helmut started to rise. "We can go into the other room," he said to Korshak. "I have a drop of something that I think you'll appreciate. Just the thing to send you on your way."

"Sounds like a good idea to me." Korshak got up and followed him to the door.

"That's the only kind I have," Helmut said as they went through.

"Will you show us some magic before you go, Korshak?" Theis called after them.

"You never know your luck," Korshak returned.

Sonja spooned some casserole onto another plate and set it down. "Have some bread, Uggam. There's butter there. Or oil."

"Thank you, Mrs. Goben."

The men's voices came through the open doorway over the clinking of a bottle and glasses. "So, you'll be looking to see what work's going, eh?" Helmut said. There was a short pause. Then Korshak spoke, sounding serious.

"To tell you the truth, that's just an excuse for me to talk to some of the people here and move around. The real reason I'm here is to try and get some information."

"Anything we can help with?" Helmut asked.

"Maybe. Do you know of any robots being on the loose around here? On Plantation?"

In the kitchen, Sonja looked around in surprise and didn't see Uggam almost choke in the act of swallowing. "Robots?" Helmut's voice repeated.

"One's gone missing from a research project in *Aurora*," Korshak said. "There's reason to suppose it might have come here. Have you seen one? Or heard talk about anything like that?"

"Nothing," Helmut replied. Then, a little louder, "Did you hear that, you kids in there? Have you seen a wandering robot in your travels?"

"It could be disguised. Maybe a person who looks out of place. All covered up," Korshak added.

Theis and Uggam shook their heads together in short, jolting movements. "No," Theis managed in a tiny voice.

Still holding the cloth that she had used to pick up the dish, Sonja moved away from the table and into the kitchen doorway. "This wouldn't be one of Masumichi's, would it?" she asked into the other room.

"Yes, as a matter of fact," Korshak said. "He took it

on one of his world-knowledge-expanding expeditions, and it disappeared. He doesn't want it advertised—especially at a time like this, when questions about the reliability of the robots could cause *Envoy* to be put on hold."

"Doesn't it mean that there might be a good reason for doing just that, though?" Sonja queried.

"Not really," Korshak answered. "But it's exactly what a lot of people are likely to think. Masumichi says the models developed for *Envoy* are a hundred percent. The one that's gone missing was a special-purpose prototype connected with his private research. More sophisticated but less predictable."

"Why would it come to Plantation?" Helmut asked, still sounding mystified.

"In transit. We think it wants to join one of the cults."

"You're kidding!" Sonja disappeared from sight into the next room. "On Etanne?"

"Yes."

"Whoever heard the like of it?"

At the table in the kitchen, the two children looked at each other with horrified faces. "They're trying to catch Tek and make him go back," Theis whispered. "They can't! He's our very own secret robot."

"Korshak is going to Forest," Uggam whispered back. "You heard him. He'll find Tek for sure."

"You have to go back up there and warn him."

"Why me?"

"I'm home already. If I go out again now, there'll be all kinds of questions. Just say you have to go, and run back up."

Uggam frowned desperately as if searching for a

way out, but finally nodded. He looked down at his half-filled plate and then around. Boot, cued by some uncanny instinct, unfolded from the floor and stared up. Uggam slid his plate off the table to hold it out, and it was clean in two slurps and a licking. Uggam replaced the plate, got down off the chair, and moved toward the back door. "I have to go now, Mrs. Goben," he called. "Thanks. Nice meeting you, Mr. Korshak."

Sonja came back in, looking surprised. "So soon?"

Theis played her part dutifully. "Aren't you going to wait and see some magic, Uggam?"

"I have to get back. I didn't realize it was so late."

"Aren't you even going to—" Sonja began, then checked herself. "Great stars! It's all gone! You must have been hungry!"

~ NINETEEN ~

From Helmut and Sonja's, the trail continued northward between mixed horticultural and crop cultivations extending across Ringvale's floor to the left, and a simulation of open heath and hill slopes with a variety of domesticated animals roaming loose on the right, where the slope curved upward to become the East Ridge. Numerous paths crisscrossed the lower parts of Ringvale, and Korshak passed a scattered traffic of people, mostly visitors from their appearance.

Trees began appearing after a short distance, closing together quickly and consolidating into the band known as Forest, which extended the full width of Ringvale from the crest of one bounding ridge to the other. Here, Korshak veered rightward and began climbing; or at least, he followed an angled line to ascend what had been a rising valley side when seen from the floor. But because of the localized vertical effect, he experienced the peculiar sensation of the ground beneath his feet sloping only mildly upward, while the vista of Ringvale on his left opened out and rose higher to become an impossibly concave sweep of landscape arching overhead like an immense wave of green frozen at the moment of being about to break. Many people—especially those whose perceptual norms had been formed on Earth—confessed that they had never been able to get used to this. Maybe for this reason, and also because the growths of vegetation became coarser and denser, and the trails harder and sparser, the numbers of people to be seen dwindled rapidly until Korshak was able to enjoy for a brief while the illusion of actually picking his way through a real wilderness forest, far from human habitation. It brought back fond but at the same time, in some ways, sad memories of land that stretched endlessly from horizon to horizon, day after day. He sometimes wondered if he would make the same decision again, with the better understanding he now had of the "magic" that had created *Aurora*. But it was not to be changed now, and he thrust the thought from his mind. The high extremes of Forest were one of Mirsto's favorite places, too. Vaydien had promised to bring him out to Plantation for a visit if Korshak found that he needed to stay on for a while.

Guided by the sketch that Dari had given him, he came to what had to be Highwood on the far side of Forest, right at the ridge crest. From here, the West Ridge forming the opposite side of Ringvale had rotated to a position almost directly overhead, while beyond the nearer ridgeline that Korshak had almost reached, a blue expanse of what would be seen from below as sky curved away and upward, giving the impression from where he stood of a crazily tilted ocean rising from a shore hidden by the final line of trees.

By this time the trail had shrunk to a path barely

wide enough for one person. From what Korshak could see of the rooftops, Melvig Bahoba's place consisted of a typically narrow-plan two-level house with outbuildings and an attached shed of some kind at the rear. Behind that was an area which from the absence of treetops seemed to be cleared. The trail approached the house from the side, and a short distance ahead, came out onto a wider track from the front, pointing straight downward toward the valley floor—or from Korshak's distorted perspective, "upward." The breeze generated by air recirculators located behind the ridgeline carried a hint of horse manure. Might as well get some practical return from the animal types that were being preserved, Korshak supposed.

After studying the layout for a few minutes, Korshak left the trail, having decided to circle around to learn what more he could before approaching the house directly. He might even spot Tek if Tek were there, which would at once make the whole business of having to ask questions of Bahoba unnecessary. But maybe because Korshak had fallen out of practice at judging such things over the years, the going was heavier than he had expected. Trees and undergrowth closed together into a thicket that quickly had him struggling to find a way through, in the process making all kinds of noise that was the last thing he needed. He had just stopped and given up, with the intention of returning to the trail, when an irascible voice called out from somewhere nearby.

"Tek, is that you? What in the name of whatever's holy are you doin' out 'ere? I've been looking all over— Oh." A man who must have been at least in his sixties had appeared from among the trunks and brush a few yards away. He had a full, bushy beard, grizzled but still with traces of coppery hue, and was wearing a floppy-brimmed hat with a leather vest, work pants, and calf-length boots. He peered at Korshak as if unsure for a moment if he might be seeing things. "Who the Earth are you?"

Well, at least that had saved a lot of care and questions, Korshak reflected. He grinned awkwardly. "Is it Melvig Bahoba?"

"I am."

"The name's Korshak. I was told by Dari in Jesson that you might have a slot for some short-term help here." Korshak had seen no reason to complicate anything further by using an alias. He was used to people recognizing his name, but if that was so of Bahoba, he didn't show it.

"What kind of work d'ye think you can do if ye can't even find the front door?"

"I thought I saw a shortcut through the trees, but it wasn't. Maybe I'd have been better coming up the direct way." A brown and black dog had materialized alongside Bahoba, having made no noise although it must have long known that Korshak was there.

"Hm. Well, let's talk about it inside. You'll be better off this way than trying to go back, in any case." Bahoba turned and began leading back the way he had come, with the dog falling in at his heels, positioning itself between the stranger and its master. The brush thinned as they approached the rear of the house. They emerged into a yard stacked with various cuts of timber, and crossed it to a work area covered by the roof that Korshak had seen from the trail. A wall of the house bounded the far side of it. They entered via a door into a small scullery and storage room that led through to the kitchen.

More than anything, it suggested an interior of the cottages that Korshak had known in his years of traveling among countries like Arigane. A bare wooden table cluttered with an unwashed plate and bowl, and some items of food yet to be put away took up the center of the room, augmented by a couple of upright chairs, an open-fronted dresser with shelves of dishware and knick-knacks, several cupboards, one of which looked like a pantry, and a sturdy cooking range. A door to one side opened through to the rest of the house. In the center of the far wall behind it was a hearth with an open fire—the first that Korshak had seen since leaving Earth. He had never heard of such a thing anywhere across Constellation. Yet there had been no chimney visible outside. If there were, he would surely have noticed it.

Bahoba must have followed his surprised gaze. "Some contraption up above there takes care of the smoke," he supplied. "If it were up to me, I'd let it blow free. That's nature's way of cycling nutrients back into the soil. Instead, they go to all kinds of palaver doing it with chemicals an' such. Do they think anything would 'ave grown back on Earth if the rain were sterile?" He closed the door that they had come through and hung his hat on a hook behind it, alongside a coat and a device with a long handle and straps that looked like a tool of some kind. The brown and black dog remained outside. "Anyroad, it's 'andy enough for getting rid of the trash." So saying, he scraped the leftovers from the plate into a bowl on a side table and deposited the plate in the metal sink below the window. "'Ave y' eaten yet, yerself? There's fresh stew in the pot, still warm."

At Bahoba's waved invitation, Korshak sat down on one of the chairs at the table. Bahoba took a pipe from a jug on the mantle above the hearth, along with a tin that was lying alongside it, and pulled up a worn, upholstered fireside chair for himself. "Thanks, but I just ate with some friends down just this side of Huan-ko," Korshak said.

"Oh. Anyone I know?"

"Helmut Goben and his wife, Sonja. I knew them when they lived on *Aurora*."

"Yes, I know of 'em. She teaches at the school down below. He's into bugs and bacteria and whatnot. Their little girl comes up 'ere sometimes with 'er friends. You know—exploring around, the way kids do."

"Theis?"

"Aye, that's 'er. There's more mischief in that one than looks would tell." Bahoba finished packing the bowl of his pipe, applied a flame from a spill that he lit from the fire, and sat back to regard Korshak as he puffed it into life. "So, ye're thinkin' ye might want to come an' 'elp out 'ere, eh?"

"Just looking around at this point," Korshak replied. "Dari gave me a list of possibilities."

"D'ye know much about trees and timber?"

"A bit about woods and woodcraft, anyway. I could turn a pretty good hand to carpentry at one time—in the days back on Earth."

"Is that right? And what else did ye do?"

"I suppose you could say I was a kind of traveling entertainer."

Bahoba nodded. "Aye, I thought mebbe so. It's in

the eyes. They've got their own kind o' life with folk like that, and they miss nothing."

"You don't seem to miss much yourself," Korshak returned.

"Ah, well... I 'ave me moments, I suppose, like everyone else." Bahoba puffed some more. "It's a case of keepin' the mind exercised and active, in't it? Learnin' to trust yer own opinions. If ye're just goin' to soak up what comes from outside, ye might as well be a sponge." He sank back and contemplated the kitchen contentedly through rising wreaths of smoke, then after a pause remarked distantly, "I still need to fix the 'andle on that drawer."

The first question that had brought Korshak here was already answered. He pondered for a few seconds on the best way of using this knowledge to press things further, and decided, with somebody like Bahoba, on the direct approach. At the same time, he couldn't come straight out and say he was here looking for Tek, since that would implicate Dari, who had trusted in his discretion.

"That name you were calling, that you thought was me when I was thrashing about out there," he said. "Tek."

Bahoba's eyes shifted instantly, but his expression remained neutral. "Yes?"

"I work with a scientist on *Aurora* who does research into machine intelligence and builds robots," Korshak said. "One them was called Tek. It's not a name you hear every day. It couldn't be the same one, could it?"

"Would you expect to find 'is robots working in places like this?" Bahoba asked.

"You never know. One of the big problems they

still haven't really solved is giving them the knowledge of everyday life that people start absorbing from the moment they're born. So they get sent to all kinds of places to widen their experiences." Korshak gestured vaguely, indicating the surroundings outside. "Frankly, it wouldn't surprise me. I was just curious."

Bahoba emitted a single reflective puff from his pipe and nodded. "Yep. 'E's the one. Been 'ere about two weeks or so, I'd reckon. Doesn't do a bad job, either. Follows just what ye tell 'im, which is more than I can say about some people that I've known. Mind you, that can 'ave its drawbacks, too, on occasion. You learn to be real careful about exactly what you do tell 'im. Gets some strange meanings into his 'ead sometimes, does Tek. Like, if I was to ask you to put the fire out, you'd know what I meant, wouldn't yer? But ask 'im the same thing, and he'd likely chuck it through t' window, heeh-heeh-heeh!" Bahoba cackled wheezily.

"So, how did it get here?" Korshak asked.

"Come knockin' on t' door, askin' fer a job, same as you did—except at least 'e were able to find it. 'T were Dari who sent 'im up as well. She probably didn't know what 'e was, though. All wrapped up in a big cloak, with an 'at, an' a beard the size of an 'orse's tail—like some kind of villain from those horror movies that the kids like."

"Did it say why? Where it was from? What it was doing here?"

"Didn't figure it was any o' my business. Two 'ands is two 'ands. And to tell you the truth, I were a bit intrigued meself." Bahoba watched and waited awhile. "Will you 'ave something to drink, anyroad?" he asked at last. "There's good coffee on the stove. Grown right 'ere, just down a little ways."

"Sure . . . thanks," Korshak replied, grateful for the break while he digested the information. Bahoba got up, took two mugs down from the dresser, and turned to fill them from a pot standing on the range.

"I just take mine black with nothin', the way the Maker intended," he said over his shoulder. " 'Ow does yours go?"

"What? Oh, the same will be fine."

Bahoba turned back, handed one of the mugs across, and sat down again with his own. He treated Korshak to a long, thoughtful stare while he tasted it. "That weren't no coincidence, you working with the scientist who built Tek," he said. "You came 'ere lookin' fer 'im, didn't yer? That's why ye were prowlin' around at back an' gettin' all tangled up out there."

Korshak sighed and nodded. "Yes. Tek went missing on a trip from *Aurora*, and nobody knows why. They asked me to try and find it."

Bahoba picked up his pipe again and considered the statement. "From the way 'e were all dressed up, I'd say 'e didn't want to be found. Anyroad, what right does anybody 'ave to say 'e can't go where 'e wants, the same as you and I can? I mean, it's not as if 'e were the same kind o' thing as a gearbox or an 'arvesting machine over in Evergreen, is it?"

AI's rights was a subject that Masumichi talked about frequently, and as far as Korshak was aware there seemed to be as many opinions as specialists. It wasn't something that he especially wanted to get hung up on now. He replied, "Some people argue that they're like children, and you can't let them just go wandering all over the place. It's not really a side that I get involved in. I was just trying to do a favor for a friend." And then, to change the subject, "Do you have any idea what it's up to?"

"Tek's future plans, you mean?"

"Yes."

"Well, I'm not sure. 'E asks a lot o' questions about funny things ... you know, them strange groups they've got goin' all over Etanne, and the daft things they believe."

"The cults and churches."

"Aye. Only Tek takes it all seriously. I don't mind so much when it's things like thinking that dead people or aliens out there somewhere can talk to you inside yer 'ead. That's their lives and their business as far as I'm concerned. But it's the ones who make other people's lives their business that I worry about. You know what I mean? The kind who think the world would be a better place if more people were like them, an' they're so sure of themselves that they want their own likes and dislikes to be forced on everyone else. That's what they call fanatics, in't it?"

Bahoba took his pipe from his mouth for a moment and gestured with it. "If some of 'em 'ad their way, I wouldn't be allowed to do this. Fer me own good, mind you. Bad fer me 'ealth, they say. Shortens yer life. So what if it is? It's my 'ealth and my life, in't it? I'd rather live a shorter life that's me own than one where other people 'ave more say over it than me. And there's others with ideas about drugs and medical stuff that they think everyone should be made to take—'fer their own good. Then you've got the scares going around about 'ow there's goin' to be too many people, an' everythin's goin' to run out, an' we 'ave to be told 'ow much we can use, an' what way to live. I mean, where would it stop if people like that ever got in charge of things?"

"You seem to know quite a bit about them, Mr. Bahoba," Korshak remarked.

"Aye, well, we get a lot of 'em coming though 'ere, on Plantation. Some kind of ritual they go through, to do with getting free from the influences of artificial places like *Aurora* and the rest before their minds can open to whatever great wisdom it is they think they're goin' to find. I think it's more a case of gettin' 'em away from anyone who might talk some sense into their 'eads." Bahoba sucked at his pipe reflectively. "There's some crowd over on Etanne that calls 'emselves the Dollarians. Them's the ones that Tek asks the most about. They're to do with some kind of mad god that was worshipped all over the old world before it blew itself up. From some o' the things I've 'eard, that 'ad a lot to do with why it 'appened."

"I've heard of them, but I don't know much about them," Korshak said.

"Me, neither. I've got better things to do than worry meself about them kind o' carryin's on." Bahoba took his pipe from his mouth and gestured with the stem. "But if ye go about 'alf a mile north from 'ere along the ridge, ye'll come to an animal reserve with a fence around it, because there's some there that can be dangerous. The warden's name there is Jor-Ling. 'E's got a feller workin' there who'd be able to tell you more about the Dollarians than I can. My understandin' is that 'e's meanin' ter join 'em before very much longer."

"Do you think that's what Tek's doing, too?" Korshak asked.

"Well, I wouldn't really know. I've never 'eard of a robot doin' anythin' like that before. Ye'd be better off askin' Tek."

Which they didn't appear any closer to being able to do. Korshak braced a hand on his knee, looked behind him first to one side, then the other, then turned back. "I'd like to. So, where is it?"

Bahoba frowned and rubbed the back of his neck. "Ee, it's right funny, that. 'E were 'ere, workin' away one, maybe a couple o' hour ago. Then I realized it 'ad all gone quiet out there, and when I went out, there were no sign of 'im. I 'aven't seen 'im since. The only thing I can think of is, 'e might be up in 'is room."

"The robot has a room?"

"I know, it sounds funny, don't it? But I just let 'im 'ave the same one that all the others who come to 'elp 'ere use. Didn't seem right, somehow, not to. Better than 'avin 'im 'anging around down 'ere all the time, too. Anyroad, come on. We'd better go up and 'ave a look."

Bahoba set his mug down on the table and got up to lead the way through to the house. "That's a fine dog you have," Korshak said as he followed into a small hallway at the foot of a flight of stairs. "Interesting that he didn't make any noise when I was out there."

Bahoba began climbing with slow, heavy steps. "Well, 'e likes to see what people are up to before 'e lets 'em know 'e's there. No good yappin' an' makin' a fuss an' scarin' 'em off, is there? That way yer never find out what's goin' on. I've known a few people who could learn from that. I think every animal's there for a reason. They've all got something to teach, if we'd only take the time to get to know 'em. . . . Whew. When I was a young lad, runnin' up t' stairs was as easy as runnin' down. These days it's as 'ard to go down as it is to go up."

They had reached a landing with a hall stand and a couple of doors, and a short passage leading away to more doors. Bahoba stopped outside one, rapped on it a couple of times, and waited. There was no response. He rapped again, louder. "Are you in there, Tek? Ye've someone 'ere who wants to talk to yer." No answer. Bahoba and Korshak exchanged questioning looks. Then Bahoba shrugged, turned back to the door, and pushed it open.

Inside was a small room with—incongruously, considering its present occupant—a bed, an upright chair and table by a window looking down over the wider track at the front of the house, an easy chair, a free-standing closet, and a few other basic furnishings. The walls were of board painted cream, and bare except for some pictures, a mirror, and a set of shelves in an alcove. There was no sign of Tek.

Bahoba stood in the middle of the room, looking around for several seconds. Then he pushed the door closed to reveal some hanging hooks on the back of it, which were empty. Frowning, he moved to the closet and opened it to inspect inside.

"It's gone—all 'is stuff," he announced. "That cloak that 'e wore when 'e come 'ere, 'is 'at and the big coat—all of it."

"You mean Tek doesn't wear any of it around here?" Korshak said, surprised. The thought hadn't crossed his mind. "It goes around openly as a robot?"

"There's nobody to mind up 'ere. Wouldn't be able to work in that lot, anyroad. See fer yourself."

Korshak moved forward and peered inside. The closet was empty apart from some pillows, linens, and other oddments that obviously belonged to the house. He looked at Bahoba questioningly.

"I suppose there's a place for you 'ere if you decide you want it," Bahoba said. "But I don't think that's what ye really came for, is it? It looks as if Tek's gone, Mr. Korshak. And if you want my opinion, don't ask me 'ow, but I'd say 'e knew you were comin'."

- TWENTY -

Korshak had nothing to gain by staying longer, and Bahoba had as good as said that he didn't expect him to do so. Korshak left shortly afterward, carrying his bag slung across a shoulder. At this point he had formed no clear plan of what he intended to do next. His guess was that if Tek didn't want to be found, as seemed to be the case, its first move would be to try and leave Plantation, which would mean getting to the ferry dock at the hub. However, six spokes connected the torus to the hub, three of which provided general access for anyone wishing to travel. Hence, the only way to keep a watch on who was leaving—assuming he could get there before the next ferry departure— would be to find somewhere suitable to wait at the dock itself. The next spoke continuing northward was now the nearest with a public-transit service to the hub, so instead of angling back through Forest the way he had come, Korshak took the wider track leading directly down to the valley floor.

His thoughts had progressed that far, and he had gone only a short distance from the house, when, not far ahead of him, a figure who had been sitting on one of several cut stumps by the side of the track straightened up, looking in his direction. It was a woman in a light jacket and tan shirt worn open over casual pants. She gave every indication of having expected him and having been waiting. As Korshak drew closer, he recognized her as Lois Iles, the optical physicist from the Hub observatory on *Aurora*. Years previously, in the time leading up to *Aurora*'s launch, she had also been involved in identifying and recruiting likely candidates for the mission.

It had been a while now since their paths had crossed. He had last seen Lois at a reception that Masumichi had held celebrating the first child to be born to one of his innumerable relatives. She was somewhere in her forties now, her shoulder-length hair still blond and wavy. The firm set to her mouth and features was relieved from harshness by a rounding of the nose and chin, and just at this moment softened further by an expression of amusement at Korshak's obvious perplexity.

"Hello, Korshak," she said.

It was a day of one weird thing after another. "I don't believe in coincidences," Korshak replied simply.

"I waited a little way farther up, nearer the house, where I thought I'd be able to catch you before you reached it, whichever way you came," she said, as if that explained anything at all. "But I missed you somehow. The first thing I knew was when you and Bahoba were crossing the yard at the back. So I waited here. I had a feeling you'd probably come down this way—but it was close enough to see if you went back the same way you came." She paused. Korshak just stared at her. "Did you talk to Tek? What have you told it?" she asked.

Korshak's mental gears began turning again and gradually came back up to speed. Since he hadn't mentioned Tek by name to anyone other than Bahoba, Lois must have known about it already. And there was only one way she could have learned about his being directed here. "You've been talking to Dari," he said. "I thought it wasn't the done thing to broadcast other people's business. What's going on?"

Lois's manner lost the flippancy that she had been effecting. "There's more going on than you're probably aware of," she said. "Really, Korshak, I need to know what was said. It's important that Tek's intentions not be interfered with. I was sent here to keep an eye on it."

Korshak could only show an empty hand. "I didn't talk to it at all. I haven't even seen it. It's taken off. Gone. Sometime in the last hour or so."

Lois bit her lip, thinking rapidly for several seconds, then reached inside her jacket and produced a phone. Her gaze flickered over Korshak's face, taking in his astonished expression while she spoke. "Priority bypass, code seven, seven three . . . nine-two . . . Message forward to Op C-Two. Subject has departed from last known location within last one to two hours. Whereabouts and destination unknown. Need to instigate immediate exit-port surveillance. Description remains as previously reported, as far as is known. Out." She returned the phone to her pocket and turned her face fully toward Korshak for the inevitable gesture of protest at the phone. "Official business," she told him before he could say anything. "We've got a lot to talk about. This isn't the best place. There's a spot lower down, off the track, by a waterfall. We can go there."

❖   ❖   ❖

In the normal course of events, an individual's movements were considered a matter of personal privacy. However, exceptions were made in cases involving the public interest. Lois's help had been enlisted by Andri Lubanov, who, although not bestowed with any formal title to that effect, acted in one of his loosely defined capacities as Director in Chief Ormont's political intelligence officer. Among other things, this meant being aware of undercurrents and developments likely to affect the stability of the governing executive. His office was taking a great interest in the activities of some of the cults that had established themselves on Etanne.

"Most of them are as crazy as they seem, and nothing more," Lois explained. "But some have political motives that go deeper."

They were sitting on corner bench seats in an open-fronted hut built as a rain shelter below the waterfall that Lois had mentioned. The gravity synthesizers beneath the creek bed were adjusted to enhance the flow downward from the ridge. Weather around Plantation changed in response to data from sensors monitoring air and soil conditions, which meant it was unpredictable—hence the usefulness of a shelter. A group of chattering day-trippers had been in occupation when Korshak and Lois arrived, but left soon afterward.

"I thought you did lasers and optics, and played old-world music," Korshak said. "How did you get mixed up with Lubanov's people? That doesn't sound like your kind of world."

"Back in the recruiting days, I brought Marney Clure out of Tranth," Lois replied. Korshak nodded.

Clure's name was generally known. He had a reputation for dynamism, directness, and radical views. Some even tipped him as a likely successor to Ormont in years to come. Lois continued, "He stuck around me as a kind of mentor while he was finding his legs on *Aurora*, and we've stayed in touch ever since. He still comes to me for opinions and advice."

"Okay."

"One of the cults on Etanne is called the Dollarians. Do you know much about them?"

Korshak decided to play dumb and see where this was leading. He shrugged. "I've heard of them. It's supposed to be based on some old-world religion or something, isn't it?"

"Not strictly a religion. More of a fanatical ideology that elevated buying, selling, and owning property above everything else in life. It was obsessed with numbers. People were judged on the basis of their possessions, and tried to measure the comparative worth of everything to ridiculous extremes."

"What they were and what they did weren't important?" Korshak queried. Evaluating people by the worth of their contribution had become so taken for granted in Constellation that it was difficult to visualize any other way of doing it.

Lois shook her head. "That didn't matter. Business dominated just about all aspects of everyone's lives." She leaned down from the seat and used her finger to trace a wavy line in the sandy floor, and then drew two lines through it: $. "That was their sign—a sort of sacred symbol. You've probably seen it before."

"Is that what it means? I never knew. So, what does it have to do with Marney?"

"The Dollarians are behind scares about resource depletion and the population getting out of control, stop *Envoy*, and things like that. The aim is to undermine confidence in Ormont's administration and prepare the ground for an opposition movement to eventually challenge it. Spreading irrationality helps the cause by making people suggestible and manipulable. But underneath, there's a hardcore agenda to get their people into the Directorate and eventually dominate it. The plan is to have things run their way."

Korshak raised his eyebrows. "And what's their way?"

"Well, as far as the general picture goes, you can see where they're coming from already. Scares to make people feel insecure about the future and lose confidence in the present system. More planning and control as the only sure protection. Which, of course, means power in the hands of whoever can come off looking as if they have the answers."

"Uh-huh. So?"

"They were putting out feelers for likely candidates to groom for a future leader figure—probably also a fall guy who would be expendable if things went wrong. For whatever reasons, they picked Marney as a possible. Some of their people made contact inconspicuously and started to sound him out. But that was where they miscalculated. Marney may have ideas that challenge accepted ways of thinking, but he's straight. If he ends up heading the Directorate one day, it will be legitimately, through the system, not via anything underhanded." Lois made a throwing-away motion with a hand, as if the rest shouldn't really need spelling out. "Marney came to me and asked what he should do. I took it to Lubanov. It turned out that Lubanov had been watching the Dollarians for some time—I don't know exactly how; he has his ways. He seems to think they're planning something big, sometime soon, but he's not sure what.... Or else it isn't considered to be something that I need to know. But that was how I got involved, and how I learned most of what I've just told you."

Outside the shelter, a deer and a large breed of goat had appeared and were drinking at the pool beneath the waterfall, at the same time keeping a wary eye on the humans. The foraging area available in Plantation could never have supported its animal population naturally, and was supplemented by force-grown fodder from Evergreen. An elaborate underground industry kept things looking the way they did above the surface.

"Okay," Korshak said again when he had absorbed that much. "So where does Tek come into it?"

"The cults are always sending their people to Istella. It's almost funny in a way. They're either sermonizing against debauchery and the libertine goings-on, or they're proselytizing for new recruits."

"I know. We've all been there."

Lois sighed. "This might sound wild, and I don't know how it happened, but Tek showed up there a couple of weeks ago—on its own, like one of the crowd. It got interested in a line that one of the cults was pushing, and said it wanted to join!" Lois looked at Korshak expectantly. He reacted neutrally, neither pretending surprise nor giving anything away. Lois seemed surprised and mildly deflated. She interrogated him silently with her eyes for a few seconds. "You knew that already."

Korshak nodded. "It's one of Masumichi's."

"Of course. You work with him, don't you?"

"Masumichi took Tek to Istella as one of his mind-broadening exercises."

Lois couldn't suppress a smirk. "Istella would do that, all right."

"They got separated, and Tek went astray. I agreed to help Masumichi try and find it."

"So how did you track it to Plantation?" Lois asked.

"I didn't. That was just a hunch. A lot of neophytes who join the cults come here first as a soul-purifying experience. Tek talked to the bunch called the Mediators. Their guru told him to do just that."

"How come you know that much?" Lois asked curiously.

Korshak smiled mysteriously. "I've got my ways, too. But that's about all I do know. I'm guessing that's what happened."

Lois shook her head. "Not quite. The Dollarians got to Tek after that. They probably had someone around when he talked to the ones you just mentioned. I really don't know. But we think it was they who organized getting him here."

"Are they going to recruit Tek?"

"That's something Lubanov would very much like to know, which is why he put Tek under surveillance. But it had to be in a low-profile way. The Dollarians could have eyes around here, too."

Korshak sat back to think over what had been said. Now the picture was starting to make sense. Lubanov had identified the Dollarians as the political base of a scheme to subvert the existing governing system as part of a move toward an eventual bid to overthrow it. They were planning something significant and imminent, that he needed to know more about. At the same time, a robot shows up wanting to become a disciple on Etanne, and the Dollarians—for whatever reason—intercede to steer it into their own recruitment path. Lubanov arranges to have Tek watched and its movements followed, which explained how Dari came to be involved. With Tek's looking likely to remain at Bahoba's, it would only seem necessary to station someone like Lois in the vicinity on some pretext to wait for developments. Keeping a place like Bahoba's under continual surveillance without attracting attention wouldn't be practicable in any case.

Korshak stretched his legs out and rested them on his bag. "So Lubanov's got you tangled up in his line of tricks, eh? I assume Dari must have been under orders to alert you to anyone asking about Tek."

"You catch on quickly," Lois said, nodding.

"Magicians are like that."

"How did I miss you? I figured I'd catch you this side of Huan-ko before you got to Bahoba's, but you disappeared."

"I stopped to visit some friends on the way. Sonja and Helmut."

"Yes, from way back. I haven't seen them for a while. Are they here now? How are they doing?"

"Just fine. Helmut's turning into a farmer. Theis— their little girl..."

"Yes, I met her when she was small."

"She's shooting up like a beanstalk."

"How old is she now?"

"Nine or ten, going on twenty."

"Seriously? I can't imagine! It doesn't seem possible."

A short silence ensued. Lois felt in another pocket

and produced a bag of glazed nuts. She tipped several into her hand and offered the bag across. "Plantation home produce. They're good."

"So, what happens next?" Korshak asked as he accepted. "The docking port is where I was heading. Tek won't be able to get off Plantation without being picked up again—assuming that whoever you talked to just now manages to get it covered in time."

"They will. There isn't another ferry due out for several hours."

Korshak had already concluded as much. If there were any doubt, they would hardly still be sitting here talking like this. "Okay," he agreed. "Then let's suppose Tek does go on to Etanne. What's the plan?"

"I'm not sure that there's been time to work out anything detailed yet," Lois replied. "It's only a guess at this stage that the Dollarians are recruiting it. The main concern was to stop you from getting to Tek and persuading it to go back. Lubanov wanted to get one of his people here to talk to it first, before it moves on."

"Talk to it about what?" Korshak asked.

Lois drew a long breath before replying, at the same time giving Korshak a look that seemed to say, *This wasn't my idea. I'm just telling it.* "Lubanov has been wanting to put a plant inside the Dollarian Academy on Etanne to find out just what's going on there. But people like that are suspicious of everyone, and getting caught would mean all kinds of trouble. But who would be suspicious of a crazy robot—especially one they'd invited in there themselves?"

Out of habit, Korshak had been about to make one of the nuts vanish before her eyes from between his fingers. In his surprise he dropped it instead, and it fell into his lap. "You mean Lubanov wants to turn it around? To have it working for him instead?"

Lois nodded. "Yes, exactly, Korshak. It was pure opportunism—when he learned that the Dollarians were interested in Tek. And the even nicer part about it all is, if Tek can be persuaded to cooperate, everything it sees and hears when it's in there can be monitored remotely. A robot as an inside spy. Isn't that the wildest thing you've ever heard?"

– TWENTY-ONE –

There was little more that Korshak and Lois could do until they heard back from whomever Lois had contacted earlier. Korshak had formed no plans beyond heading for the docking port and hoping he would get there before the next ferry left, and the purpose of that had now been overtaken by events. Until they received some news, he didn't even know how long he might need to remain on Plantation. More animals appeared at the pool in front of the shelter. A goat wandered in and began jostling Korshak inquisitively with its nose—probably as a result of being fed by visitors. Korshak felt that there had to be a better place to wait things out. Lois suggested going back to where she was staying. It was easy to get to, on account of the need to keep a watch on Bahoba's place.

"Where is it?" Korshak asked. "Down in Jesson? Or maybe somewhere this side of Forest?" In reply, Lois just smiled mysteriously and got up from the bench. Korshak picked up his bag and followed, leaving the goat staring after them indignantly from outside the shelter.

Instead of returning to the track they had followed down from Bahoba's, they threaded between the rocks around the pool and through a gap opening to a narrow path that Korshak wouldn't have known was there. It wound its way amid thickets of brush, trees, and formations of boulders that were probably shell forms, to what appeared to be a rocky crag, ten feet or so high, covered with bushes and shrubs, its sides broken into flowery ledges, sloping upward to a flat top. Korshak had seen structures like this high up on the valley sides before. Beneath its screen of greenery, the top was actually the inlet to one of a system of extractor grilles, where air rising from the lower valley was drawn off for processing and recycling. The extractors were popular congregating places for birds, who brought seeds, and the air currents carried spores and microfaunae, accounting for the richness of the plant life.

Hidden somewhere nearby would be a monitor panel that enabled maintenance engineers making their inspection rounds to check the local environmental conditions and adjust the unit's operating parameters as required. Lois located it at once behind a dummy rock in a crevice, obviously knowing it was there. Then she did something that Korshak had never seen before. After a cursory glance around to make sure they were alone, she entered a code into the touchpad to one side of the panel, responded to a query of some kind that appeared on the screen, and then looked expectantly at a slab or rock alongside. It stood almost vertically, two feet or so wide at the base and tapering toward the top, with a web of cracks choked with flora and mosses patterning its surface. As Korshak watched, it swung inward to reveal itself as a concealed door. He should have been prepared for anything by this time, but even so looked at Lois in amazement. She grinned, obviously enjoying herself, ushered him on through with a wave, and turned to close the monitor panel. Korshak stepped in over the sill running across the base of the door, and found himself in a different world.

Lighting had come on automatically to show the top of a ladder going down a metal-walled shaft. Korshak stepped onto it and descended perhaps twenty feet to emerge from a recess onto a railed walkway running above a gallery maybe twelve feet wide, lined with pipes, cables, and ducting, and curving away out of sight in either direction. Lois joined him several seconds later and took her phone out to enter something before pocketing it again and looking at him.

"It's just a day of surprises," he told her.

"Well, it's a change to see you on the receiving end of them, Korshak," she replied. Then, indicating the surroundings with a motion of her head, "Beats tramping all the way back down into Jesson."

"Taxi service?" Korshak guessed.

"Being here on Directorate work can have its advantages."

They walked a short distance to where stairs led down to the gallery floor. A general-purpose personnel runabout of the kind used all over Constellation arrived minutes later. They ran automatically, directed by buried sensors and transmitters, and carried up to six people. Lois had already given the destination. Korshak settled back and lapsed into thought as the runabout took off smoothly with a low electric whine.

"You know, I can't say I'm totally comfortable about this idea," he announced after a while. "You're right. I've worked with Masumichi and his robots on and off ever since we left Earth. The research models are still not reliable enough for what you're talking about, Lois. You can never be sure what one of them might do next. You don't know what you could be getting into."

She made an empty-handed gesture. "As I said, it was a question of seizing the opportunity while it was there. There's no clear plan yet as to how to exploit the situation. If we can get a hookup into Tek, the direction might be handled remotely."

"If it will let you," Korshak replied. "They have an override that lets them shut down external links. That was why Masumichi couldn't find it on Istella."

"And that's why we need to talk to it before it gets to Etanne," Lois said.

They seemed to be heading generally downward, toward the valley floor. The gallery terminated in a large, brightly lit space of machinery, tanks, and pipework extending through several levels, where technicians in white coveralls and hard hats were attending to various tasks. The runabout halted by a door on one side, and they disembarked to enter a short corridor flanked by instrumentation bays and a control room full of screens and consoles. This brought them to another door, and beyond it, a further change of scenery yet again.

It felt like the crew quarters in some of the large ships that Korshak remembered in the port of Belamon, or some kind of hostel. From the small hall that they were now in, two passages led away on one side, with doors at intervals, while the sounds of kitchen clatter came from somewhere nearby on the other. "Plantation probably has as many people down here as on the surface," Lois explained. "Maybe more, for all I know. I have a cabin for however long I'm here. We can go there for now. Or maybe you'd like to eat?"

"I had something at Sonja and Helmut's," Korshak said. "But after trekking up to Bahoba's and developments since, a coffee would go down well.... And maybe a sandwich or something, sure."

Lois indicated a set of double doors ahead. "We could probably find you a place down here, too, if you need one. Will you be wanting to stay on?"

"I don't know yet."

The double doors brought them into a cafeteria area, with long tables by the walls, several smaller ones in the center, and a serving counter at one end. Maybe a dozen people were scattered around, eating and talking, one or two reading. Lois went to the counter, while Korshak headed for an empty corner where they would be able to talk. Lois joined him minutes later with two coffees and a cheese sandwich on a tray, along with a small salad for herself. "Plantation grown," she explained as she sat down. "There is a difference."

"Enjoy it while you can," Korshak told her. He had been looking around while he waited. "It's like one of my illusions, only more elaborate. Nothing you see up there is what it seems. I've been coming to Plantation for years, and even then I never really realized."

Lois drank from her cup, set it down, and began eating. "Well, the people who built it evidently thought it was worth the effort. And a lot of others must have supported them. I guess a one-way ticket from Earth can do strange things."

"Mirsto would love it," Korshak said. "He's fascinated by things like this."

"You mean the underworlds that you don't see?"

"Exactly. We have to use the deep-level maintenance tubes when we go anywhere on *Aurora*."

"So, is he going to be an illusionist, too?"

"I don't think he knows yet. He's into robotics as well. His closest friend is one of Masumichi's tribe. Masumichi is working on a way of tapping straight into the operator's sensory system for controlling his robots, instead of going through regular interface channels the way they do with telebots."

"Direct neural coupling?" Lois nodded. "Yes, I've heard about it. It's not exactly new as a concept. But it'll be neat if he can do it."

"Mirsto has a new sister, too. Did you know?"

"*Really?* Well, congratulations! No, I didn't."

"Kilea. Coming up to three months."

"Is she doing okay?"

"Just fine."

"And Vaydien?"

Korshak sighed but returned a smile. "It's a very different life from being a princess in Arigane. But she makes the best of what it offers."

"Do you think she misses her old life?"

"Oh, parts of it, I'm sure. Don't most people? But she wouldn't go back. She's every bit an *Auroran* now. She even did a spell of EVA work out on *Envoy*—earlier on, before the pregnancy slowed her down." Korshak was about to bite into his sandwich again, when another thought struck him. "I suppose they have regular communications down here below the surface?"

"Yes, they do."

"I'll have to give them a call, sometime.... Shouldn't we have heard something back from your people by now?"

"I guess they have nothing to say yet."

They fell quiet for a while. On the screen above, the view had changed to a telescopic view of *Aurora*, fifty miles away, moving slowly against a background of glowing cosmic-plasma filaments. Two men in green coveralls who had been talking over their empty plates at a nearby table got up, sent them a couple of cheerful nods, and left.

"So what is it about the way Ormont's administration runs things that these people don't agree with?" Korshak asked. "Or is it simply a case of craving for power?" The background politics of things had never really interested him, and he tried to stay out of it. But as with everything else, he was curious.

Lois toyed with her salad and thought before answering. "It goes deeper than that. What's at stake is the world view and belief system that the society we build is going to be governed by. The choices we make here will shape the future world on Hera. Will it be a world where people are free to become all the things that human potential is capable of? Or one where they tie themselves down by artificial constraints to what amounts to little better than an animal level of existence? Which was what happened to Earth."

Korshak hadn't expected anything quite so profound. "You'd better explain," he invited.

"What led to the old world destroying itself, more

than anything, was its failure to grasp that human creativity is effectively unlimited," Lois replied. "In particular, they were fixated on the belief that their resources were finite, and a growing population would simply use them up faster. So they lived in perpetual conflict with a dilemma. They needed technology to create the wealth that enables a better quality of living. But greater wealth results in greater numbers of people, which to their way of thinking meant simply hastening the day when everything would run out." Lois gestured with her fork and made a face that said things could only go downhill from there. "The result was insane competition backed by organized violence as everyone scrambled to grab what they could. The wealth ended up in the hands of a small minority who controlled the power to defend it, and anything beyond subsistence level was denied the rest, because it would just have the effect of making more of them."

"But Sofi didn't think that way," Korshak said.

Lois nodded emphatically. "Which is exactly the point. When people need something, and there's only so much of it, there are two ways they can respond. They can either fight over what there is, and then lose anyway when it's all gone. Or they can learn to make more. That's where humans are different from animals. Animals react passively to the situation they're in, and consume resources. So, they can only exist in numbers that are consistent with the natural replacement rate. Humans create resources. And if you look at Sofi's experience, it happens as a series of breakthroughs into higher domains of knowledge and control over physical reality that expand to greater limits all the time. So there aren't any real limits."

Korshak had heard that kind of argument advanced before. He had also heard others disputing it. "And do you think that can continue indefinitely?" he queried. The suggestion was implicit, but it seemed counterintuitive.

"Yes," Lois affirmed. "That's what the universe outside is there for. There are no limits to how many we can become, how far we can expand, or how much we can achieve. That was what I meant by human potential. The old world didn't even come close to understanding it."

"That's a pretty sweeping assertion," Korshak commented. "It sounds more like a declaration of faith."

"It is," Lois agreed without hesitation.

"What if it's wrong?"

"Every age of human culture has a unique soul that animates it and defines its nature," Lois replied. "Like any other living organism, which it is, it can only live according to that nature. Our beliefs are an expression of what we are. The old world was blind to its own potential, and its belief in its own finiteness was what destroyed it. Sofi was a rejection of that belief. But when Sofi started to become divided within itself, the soul that it expressed was threatened. Preserving that soul is what *Aurora* was really all about."

‑ TWENTY‑TWO ‑

At the table in her workroom at the rear of the apartment on Astropolis, Vaydien smoothed out the tapestry that she had been composing on and off for the past couple of months, and tilted her head to one side as she inspected it critically. It showed, as best she could remember it, a view looking down over the city of Escalos from the hills lying to the south. It was to go on a wall in Mirsto Junior's room, and so she had included numerous animals in the foreground. She was pleased with the way it was coming along, she decided. An earlier one depicting islands set in an ocean—which, if truth were known, she had considered no more than a practice effort—had impressed one of the organizers of the swimming camp that Mirsto had attended, and now graced their club rooms on Beach. She had based it on images from the *Aurora*'s archives. Her previous life had never taken her beyond Arigane and the adjoining parts of central Asia, and she had never actually seen a real ocean—but there had been no need to go into that. Most of the animals in the present work had never been native to Arigane, either, for that matter.

She was happy in the existence that was now to be the rest of her life. While there were moments when she found herself dreaming wistfully of the places that had seen her childhood days, she would think then of Shandrahl's cruelties and treachery, her stepmother Doriet's scheming, what life would have been like with Zileg, and tell herself that Leetha was welcome to all of it. Vaydien had become a new person—or was it more a case of discovering the person she had always been and never known?

In this wondrous world that moved between the stars, she was finding a universe so vast and awe-inspiring as to make Arigane seem like an insignificant speck of desert. One day a new world would be born that would compare in the same way to the whole of Earth; and through Mirsto and Kilea—and maybe more to follow, for she and Korshak were far from old yet—and their descendants, they would be a part of it. The thought prompted her to turn her head unconsciously to the doorway through to the living area, which Mirsto and Hori were in the process of taking over in the course of a game they had invented using an assembly kit of plastic blocks and shapes. She was about to get up and go through to ask if they were getting hungry yet, when the room sounded a tone indicating an incoming call. "Voice on," she acknowledged aloud. "Accept visual, direct to workroom." Moments later, Korshak's face with its generous mane of dark, curly hair and straggly mustache to match appeared on the wall screen.

"Surprise!" he greeted.

Vaydien's face lit up with delight. "Hey! Well, it is indeed. Where are you?"

"On Plantation."

"I thought there were no communications from Plantation."

"There aren't from the parts most people go to. But I'm in the underworld that you don't see, where the backstage machinery is. Here, it's different."

"Trust you to find any secret tunnels. So, how is everything going?" Korshak had been somewhat reticent on what was taking him to Plantation. Vaydien gathered that it was a sensitive matter that had to do with an awkward situation that Masumichi was in, and hadn't pressed him for details.

"Moving along," Korshak said. "Nothing much to report at this point. I just called to say hello while the chance was there."

"Do you know yet if you'll be staying over?"

"I'm not sure. We're waiting for some news at the moment."

"Who's 'we'?"

"It turns out that Lois is involved, too. She's got a cabin in the crew section here. That's where I'm calling from."

"Lois the astronomer?"

"Right."

"How's she doing?"

"Just fine." Korshak glanced away over a shoulder. "She's on another call right now."

"Say hello for me."

"I will. How's Junior?"

"He's next door with Hori, building another *Aurora*, I think. Want to say hello?"

"Sure."

"Hey, Mirsto. Your father's on the screen. Want to come and say hello?"

Mirsto came running in through the doorway moments later and halted beside Vaydien, facing the screen. "Dad! Mom said she didn't think you'd be able to call for a while. Where are you?"

"Across on Plantation."

"How come I didn't get to go?"

"It's business this time. The kind of thing people can't talk about too much. I'll tell you about it some time later."

"Are there animals around there, where you are?"

"Not right here. I'm down underground, in the part that you don't see. But I saw some earlier—by a waterfall. They came right up."

"A waterfall! I didn't know they had those there."

"Neither did I. I'll bring you up to see it the next time we take a trip. It's up on one of the ridges."

"Are there robots, too? Mom said that what you were there for has something to do with Masumichi. Hori's here. We're making space constructions with the fabricator set. And assemblers that crawl over them—just like real ones."

"Sounds neat.... No, there aren't any robots here right now."

"Masumichi's neural coupler is cool," Mirsto said. "You think that you really are the robot."

"Yes, I know. I've tried it."

Mirsto's nose wrinkled. "I think it's more fun being a robot. *People* have to be stuck inside places like Astropolis and Jakka all the time, where there's air, and it's warm enough. *They* can go outside, and over, and under, and anywhere. Why do we have to have air and stuff?"

"Questions!" Vaydien murmured to herself.

"Because people had to be able to stay alive long before there were any robots," Korshak answered. "It's a complicated story. We can go into it when I get back."

"When will that be?"

Just then, a woman's voice that sounded like Lois's issued from somewhere in the background. "Korshak, there's news."

Korshak looked to the side for a moment, and then back. "Sorry, look, I have to cut this short. Something's happening here."

"Your father's busy," Vaydien said to Mirsto.

"'Bye, Dad," Mirsto acknowledged, and waved a hand reluctantly.

"See you soon, promise," Korshak told him.

"Take care, Korshak," Vaydien said as the image vanished.

Korshak swung away from the screen to face Lois, who was holding her hand phone toward him. "This came from Lubanov's surveillance team," she said. "See who went through the docking port less than five minutes ago." Korshak took the unit and peered at the image frozen on its tiny screen. It was centered on a figure standing in what appeared to be a short line of people. But nothing of its appearance could be made out. It was wrapped in a voluminous cloak that left just the bottom parts of its long boots uncovered below, while a full beard, turned-up collar, and a floppy, wide-brimmed hat pulled low obscured everything of the face. It all matched the descriptions that Dari and Bahoba had given.

"That's Tek," Korshak confirmed. But he was puzzled.

"Did you say it went through the port? They didn't stop it? I thought the whole idea was to get to it first, before it arrived at Etanne."

"It isn't going to Etanne," Lois told him. "It arrived at the hub port to catch the ferry that's leaving for Sarc. Lubanov's people think there would be a better chance of talking to it there without advertising themselves to the wrong people. So the plan is to let it carry on, and they'll have something set up at the other end."

- TWENTY-THREE -

S arc was the most recent of the Constellation worlds to open itself to occupancy. Physically, it was rather small, and there was nothing remarkable or exciting about its form, which was a sphere without adornments. In fact, there was little that was remarkable or exciting about Sarc in any way at all. That was the idea. It had been built by conservative-minded elements of the populace appalled by the decadence and licentiousness of Istella, who in response decided to establish a haven for what they considered to be the proper standards for a society to maintain, and in particular, a source of correct moral guidance and example for the young.

Dress was sober and subdued; surroundings tended to be plain and utilitarian; strongly expressed social pressures produced behavior that was restrained, with an emphasis on propriety and manners. And yet, few things were expressly prohibited. One could buy a drink, or even stronger narcotics if anybody willing to sell them were found, but it was rapidly learned that becoming incapable through one's own actions wasn't a good way to impress friends, make new ones, or be welcomed back in future. Such violations of

rights as theft or resorting to violence in the course
of a dispute were regarded as manifestations of low
breeding and ignorance rather than criminality. In any
case, they were almost invariably counterproductive,
since the normal practice of the inhabitants was to go
armed—mainly as a precaution against visitors, so they
said, although it was more the assertion of a principle
than from any real need—and onlookers were quick
to side actively with a victim. People were expected
not to confuse manliness with rudeness, nor polite-
ness with servility. Nobody questioned that humans
living together in a community couldn't be free to
behave in any way they chose, and some restraint on
excesses was essential. The aim, however, was to create an environment in which those restraints would be
cultivated consciously from within, rather than having
to be imposed forcibly from without.

To the surprise of many, the response in terms of
the number of people electing to move there was not
insignificant. Even more so, the resistance encountered
among the younger members of families considering
such a move turned out to be far less than the divin-
ers of popular sentiment had predicted, and many
appeared to welcome the prospect. It seemed that
devoting oneself to scientific questions and technological innovations, or striving for things like athletic or
artistic prowess for their own sake could be rewarding
enough for a while, but without their serving some
overriding ideal or purpose, true satisfaction in life
remained elusive. In a similar kind of way, Istella's
playgrounds, while continuing to provide an endless
source of distraction for some, eventually became
facile and boring for others, while the philosophies

dispensed on Etanne began to sound shallow and less convincing. All of which would provide ample and welcome material for the social psychologists, counselors, and therapists to study and debate for years. Others called it growing up.

If that were the case, Fuji Warco conceded that he hadn't fully grown up yet. He found the place stern and exacting—a bit like being in the house of the austere maiden aunt he remembered as a child, with endless incomprehensible rules of etiquette and decorum that he was in constant terror of transgressing. He'd take a fling on Istella with an anything-goes orgy thrown in for good measure, or even a hick-style Plantation dance party with fiddles and farm boots anytime, he decided.

He was on Sarc for a week or two, supervising the fitting out of a new School of Traditional Literature & Arts that they would be opening shortly. His other function, which he didn't advertise openly, was that of an unofficial agent for Lubanov's office. The message addressing him in the latter capacity had come without warning and given him such short notice that he had no real idea what was happening. It said that a mysterious passenger, referred to as "Traveler," would be arriving from Plantation on the next ferry.

"Blue," another of Lubanov's people, would approach Traveler at the docking bay and bring him via a roundabout route to be handed over to Warco. How Blue would accomplish this wasn't clear, but the message implied that Blue had been furnished with information that would get Traveler's attention. The use of a roundabout route would be to verify that Traveler wasn't being followed—by whom, the message didn't say. Warco's task would be to stay with Traveler and keep him out of sight until somebody from Lubanov's staff got there from *Aurora*, who presumably would know what was going on. Blue called Warco on audio to confirm the arrangements shortly after the message arrived. The voice hadn't been one that Warco recognized.

He watched as Kelerosk, the electrical foreman, finished checking connections in the power-and-air-distribution cabinet at the end of a partly finished corridor on Level 3, and set aside the drawing he had been consulting. On Kelerosk's far side, an indicator light on the maintenance robot that was undergoing training and had been observing came on to signal that it had gone into "rest" mode while it indexed and cross-referenced the actions it had learned and would be required to reproduce.

"All tested and correct, sir," Kelerosk announced. "Would you be so kind?"

Warco accepted the proffered viewpad showing the certification sheet where Kelerosk had already signed off for the job, and added his own name in the box provided. One thing he had come to respect about Sarc was that things got done right, and people were reliable. "About time for your break, isn't it?" he said as he keyed in his confirmation. He didn't think he sounded gruff, but being around Sarcans always made him feel that he did.

"If it's convenient."

"Sure. Afterward, we need to talk about the main lighting and ring system in the theater. I think it's going to need higher ratings on the cutouts." He waved a hand toward the drawing that Kelerosk was holding. "Here, I'll take that. I'm going back that way."

"Much appreciated, indeed."

Warco almost said "My pleasure," but changed it to "See you later." These things could be catching.

He returned to the room that was being used as a site office. Nobody else was there at the moment. Just as Warco closed the door, his phone emitted its audio call tone. He pulled it from his pocket and answered.

"Warco."

"This is Blue."

"Okay."

"Traveler has agreed to meet you and is on his way. I have been observing from a distance, and there is no sign of anyone tailing him. It seems clear to go ahead."

"Okay." Warco had suggested that the best place to keep Traveler out of sight until the person or persons being sent from Lubanov's office showed up would be the lower rooms at the rear of the site, which were just being used for storage at the moment.

"He's almost there now. He is expecting you to be at the door from the service corridor at the rear, the one you described."

"Okay."

"Just one other thing, so that you are suitably prepared. I should tell you that Traveler is a robot."

It took a second or two for the words to register. Warco blinked. *"What?"*

"Not the kind that you're used to working with," Blue said hastily. "Apparently, it's a research type, far more advanced. That's really all I know."

Warco was still trying to collect his jumbled thoughts together. "I was under the impression that they're

trying to keep this low-profile—whatever's going on.
I mean . . . having a robot walking around loose isn't
exactly the best way to do that. Isn't it attracting
attention out there?"

"It's disguised," Blue said. "Very effectively, too. I
talked to it at some length, and even then I couldn't tell."

Crazier and crazier, Warco thought. "Well, I'd better
get on down there. Is there anything else?"

"That's all I have. Just keep it out of sight there
until you're contacted again. They should have somebody there in under an hour."

"Okay. Checking out."

Warco left the office and made his way down
through the rear classroom section, which was still
under construction, through the meeting hall and what
would be the dining facility behind, to the area at the
rear. At least, a robot ought to be easier to hide, he
told himself. Just walk it into a closet and tell it to
switch itself off.

The door that he had specified opened out into
the maintenance corridor and was on the far side of
a space being used to store materials. He had barely
arrived there, when a couple of raps sounded softly
from the other side. Warco checked around to make
sure there was nobody in sight, then unlatched the
door and opened it. A heavily muffled figure, its face
hidden by a hat, dark glasses, and a beard, was waiting on the other side. Warco ushered it inside quickly
and poked his head out to look around. A man who
had been watching from the corner of a side corridor
some distance away sent a quick wave and vanished.
Warco turned back inside, closing the door. Even
close up, he could have been fooled. It was uncanny.

"I was told that you have important matters to discuss concerning the Dollarians," Traveler said. "The subject is of extreme interest to me, as you are no doubt aware." The voice was amazingly realistic, too. It even had a hint of throatiness.

"I don't know anything about it," Warco replied. "My job is just to keep you here and out of the way until somebody arrives who does know. It shouldn't be more than an hour."

"Very well." Traveler lapsed into immobility and seemed prepared to remain so for the duration. This really wasn't the best of places to hope to remain unnoticed for any length of time. Warco realized that telling somebody to walk into a closet didn't come so easily after all.

"We shouldn't stay here," he said. "It gets too much traffic. There's a place farther along that's more out-of-the-way."

"Very well."

Warco led the way to a little-visited room where drums of sealants, adhesives, and coatings, and lengths of pipes and conduit were stacked. Inside, the air had the sharp tang of a type of solvent that somebody had been working with recently. "This should be okay at this time. . . ." Warco started to speak, then stopped as he saw that Traveler was making strange twitching motions with its head. Then, suddenly, it sneezed explosively, clutching a hand to its nose and in the process dislodging the glasses. Warco gaped in bewilderment. What the hell kind of robot was this? He peered more closely. If that beard was false, then so was Warco's own head of hair; and the face and eyes were as human as his were.

"So, who are you?" he demanded. "I was told to expect some kind of robot. And excuse me if I sound a bit out of place on Sarc. But just exactly what in hell is going on around here?"

Traveler pulled off his hat and straightened up to reveal himself fully. "I do what I do, in the sacred cause of the Dollarians," he announced. "It is not my place to question. I merely follow the instructions of ones who are more gifted than I."

"Oh gods," Warco breathed. "One of those." At that moment, his phone announced another call.

"I'm the person that you're expecting from head-quarters," the voice informed him. "Just to let you know, we've commissioned a private hopper since the regular ferry has been delayed, so I might even be there sooner. Is there any sign of Traveler yet?"

Warco gazed at the latest complication to his life and sighed. "Yes, he's here," he said into the phone. "So, sure, come on over as soon as you like. But I don't think you're going to like what you find here."

— TWENTY-FOUR —

A few agitated steps took Korshak across the tiny living area and to the wall of Lois's cabin on Plantation. He wheeled around and threw up his hands. "We were set up! They figured somebody might be watching Tek, and sent one of their believers to Sarc as a decoy. The real Tek is probably on Etanne already."

At the seat behind the fold-down table, Lois finished relaying pieces of the news from her contact on *Aurora* and set down the phone. Korshak had heard enough to get the gist without her needing to elaborate further. "Lubanov's furious. I guess it all happened too quickly." She sighed. "He probably isn't used to losing out."

Korshak knew the story of Lubanov's involvement in the *Aurora*'s hurried departure from Earth, of course. He quelled his restlessness sufficiently to stop pacing and sat down on the stool by the breakfast bar in front of the kitchen space. "It was a chance we'll never get again."

"A body inside the Dollarian Academy that nobody would have suspected," Lois agreed. "I'd like to know why Lubanov is so concerned about them. Do you think..." She saw that Korshak was only half listening, and got up to retrieve their coffees from the autochef, which she had ordered just before her phone rang. "What are you thinking?"

Korshak accepted the mug absently and took a long sip before answering. "If Tek is on Etanne already, maybe there's still a chance. If we could just get the right message to it somehow."

Lois waited.

"The Dollarians have done half the work for us already.... There was that other aspiring miracle-worker up at the animal reserve, that Bahoba talked about. What did he say the name of the warden there was? Jor-Ling, that was it."

"Korshak, what are you talking about?"

Korshak returned gradually to the present. "When I was at Bahoba's, he told me there's an animal reservation not far away along the ridge, managed by somebody called Jor-Ling. Apparently there's another Dollarian hopeful there, waiting for the call to move on to Etanne, just as Tek was."

"So, what about him?"

"We can't talk to Tek directly, because it's shut off its communications. But another Dollarian rookie who was in there with it could."

"To get Tek to agree to being an inside spy for Lubanov?"

"Yes."

Lois shook her head perplexedly. "I'm not with you. Why would a rookie hopeful want to do that?"

"*He* wouldn't. But someone else taking his place, who got brought into the Dollarian Academy instead, might."

"An impersonator, you mean? But who..." Lois's voice trailed off as she realized what Korshak was driving at. "You mean *you*?"

"Why not? I've done worse in my time."

"How do you even know you look like him?"

"I don't. But how do we know that whoever's expecting him on Etanne knows what he looks like? In any case, there's only one way to find out, isn't there?"

Lois ran through it in her mind again and shook her head firmly. "It's got too many unknowns, Korshak. The people on Etanne might not have met him yet, but he has to have some kind of contact here on Plantation. Even if you managed to do a credible job with makeup and disguise, you still wouldn't know enough background to pass yourself off—things they'd talked about, what the arrangement is."

"Unless he filled me in on all that," Korshak said, but the enthusiasm was already fading from his voice.

Lois pressed the point. "But why should he? Why would he agree to step down, when this is probably a big moment in his life? All it's likely to do is raise questions and make things difficult for him to get back in line again afterward. I can't see what line you're going to take that will persuade him."

She was right, Korshak told himself. He'd spoken before thinking it through. He drank from his mug and frowned as he searched for a different angle. "Okay," he announced finally. "I agree. There's no good reason why he should make way for a substitute. But it doesn't have to be either him or me, does it? Why can't we both go?" New light crept into his eyes as he warmed to the idea. "I turn up as another Dollarian wannabe who's heard that he's got a ticket to

Etanne, and figured maybe I could string along, too. All I'd need is for him to point me to whoever the contact is here, and I can play it myself from there. What do you think?"

Lois faltered. "Shouldn't we clear this with Lubanov's people first?" she suggested.

"I don't see why. What are they going to contribute? How long would it take, and how long have we got? We've already seen what happens when too many coordinators get involved. I say we handle it ourselves. Contrition is easier than permission."

"But do you know enough about the Dollarians to come across as a believable believer?" Lois persisted.

Korshak grinned, his normal level of self-assurance now restored. "That's the next thing we have to work on," he told her. "You've got a screen over there, and I assume it can access the general Constellation web. Do you feel like being a research assistant for the next few hours, Lois? It's time for me to take a crash course in the ancient world religion of the sacred Dollar."

- TWENTY-FIVE -

A long time had gone by since Andri Lubanov walked out of the Sofian military's Internal Security Office and drove south to the launch base at Yaquinta to shuttle up to the *Aurora*. In the years since, he had never changed the name of the vaguely delineated "Research Section," adopted as a provisional measure to accommodate him into Ormont's Command Directorate staff. The nebulous title could conveniently cover virtually any activity that might be expedient to preserving the smooth running of the complex web of conflicting human perceptions and interests that the *Aurora* mission was turning into, without need to seek formal approval.

Disagreement was mounting over interpretations of the degree of autonomy the offspring worlds should expect to enjoy, and what say they should have in the allocation of resources. Scarcity and desirability were what determined value, and in the present condition the commodity in greatest demand was structural material and the support engineering needed to turn it into habitable space. Some of the demands that were being voiced amounted to aspirations to sovereignty, which in effect made some of the activities engaged in by

Lubanov's office exercises in foreign intelligence. While this had the familiar feel of working on home ground as far as Lubanov was concerned, "foreign" wasn't a word that the *Aurora*'s original founding charter had used.

He sat in his office in the Directorate center on Astropolis, contemplating the latest message from Lois Iles—referred to by Lubanov's office as "Pixie"—still on Plantation, displayed on the main screen. The "Magician"—although most of his serious work these days seemed to be with psychologists of both human and artificially intelligent nature—who had gone there in search of the crazy robot had missed it too. The inescapable conclusion was that it had been spirited away to Etanne while everyone's attention was focused on Sarc. Score one for the opposition, Lubanov conceded grudgingly. Characteristically, he had written the setback off to experience without wasting time on chafing or recriminations. The thing to do when these things happened was learn what one could from them and move on. And the intriguing question raised in this instance was, *why*? What was so important to the Dollarians about getting Tek to Etanne?

Lubanov had learned enough to know that the Dollarians had political ambitions that went a lot further than dedication to rediscovering a secular old-world doctrine of acquisition and competition—which Lubanov saw as contrived to isolate individuals by setting each against all, thereby empowering a controlling élite who acted very much in concert to promote *their* common interests. And from the energy they were expending on helping to spread the overpopulation scare and denounce as irresponsible a program that could be invaluable to future generations by informing them on the right preparations for arrival at Hera, he suspected that their design was to delay or disrupt the *Envoy* program—possibly with a view to gaining control of its resources for their own advantage.

The possibility that he feared most was some kind of physical sabotage. But proving something like that was another matter. If Lubanov could have had his way, he would send in a force from *Aurora*'s Police Arm, put the whole of Etanne under martial lockdown until *Envoy* was launched, and put an end right there to all the guessing and the risk. But Ormont was adamant that such heavy-handedness would not be in keeping with the principles that *Aurora* had been conceived to uphold. In any case, it wasn't Ormont's style.

Accordingly, some time previously, Lubanov had persuaded the engineering managers and supervisors involved with *Envoy* to introduce a system of security precautions—the first time such a thing had been known since *Aurora*'s departure. These required tighter restrictions on the personnel authorized to work outside on *Envoy* or as remote telebot controllers, and permanent logs of all telebot operations. In addition, he had quietly instituted a series of background checks on new applicants for work on the construction and modification program.

Beyond that, he could do little without a better idea of what was afoot. He had tried infiltrating two plants of his own among the Dollarians without Ormont's knowledge—one didn't involve a superior in matters that would compromise him if they went sour; being prepared to take the bullet was what Lubanov understood by loyalty. Both the plants had been uncovered, the second meeting with a nasty accident shortly after being evicted from Etanne. Whether it had been just that or a message, Lubanov didn't know, but his suspicions inclined toward the latter. Either way, his enthusiasm for attempting a repeat had been dampened.

Then he learned that fortuity had provided another set of eyes and ears—not to mention various other types of senses that could all prove useful—in the form of Tek, undergoing preparation on Plantation to be sent to exactly where Lubanov wanted them. And if Tek got into some kind of trouble, it wouldn't be at the risk of any human cost that Lubanov might lose sleep over. He had just needed some way to communicate with it first, convince it that the Dollarians were selling a line, and recruit it to a better cause. But Tek disappeared abruptly before anything could be organized. Either because Pixie or another of Lubanov's people on Plantation had been spotted, or as a general precaution, the ruse was set up on Sarc, and Lubanov had fallen for it.

But now it appeared that maybe the chance Lubanov had tried to seize might not have been lost after all. Before Tek vanished, Pixie had revealed her involvement to Korshak and explained the reasons for Lubanov's interest—to the extent that she was aware of them herself, anyway—to prevent him from unwittingly derailing Lubanov's plans. Now, Korshak had volunteered to help, and concocted an outlandish scheme to follow it. He would pose as an aspiring Dollarian who had exiled himself on Plantation for a period as a means of self-preparation, and in that role introduce himself to another Dollarian inductee that he had identified there. His plan was in this way to meet whoever the inductee's contact on Plantation was, and thence obtain an interview for himself at the Dollarian Academy on Etanne, which hopefully would result in his admission. Korshak's appearance would have to be altered to some extent, of course, but his stage experience would enable him to take care of that. Korshak knew Tek from his work with Masumichi. If he did manage to get himself accepted into the Academy, and if he could find Tek and talk to it, there could be a chance of saving what had seemed to be a lost cause.

Lubanov didn't put the odds of success at anywhere near what he would normally bet on. But had he believed in any of the old-world gods, he'd have to accept now, he concluded, that they were telling him something. This wasn't the kind of situation that people like him let go to waste.

"Voice on," he instructed. "Connect to Hala Vogol." A window opened on the screen he was using, showing the face of the assistant who was coordinating with Lois.

"Yes, chief?"

"I've just read the latest from Pixie. We go with it, no question. But the next part depends on how Magician gets along with this Dollarian newbie that he's found out about. Now that he'll be visible, we can't have him going down to the subsurface anymore. How are you planning on keeping tabs on where he goes from here?"

"He is aware of that, and has arranged to stay with his friends at Jesson," Vogol replied. "Pixie is an old acquaintance of theirs who'd be expected to visit, so she'll have no trouble staying in contact."

Lubanov nodded. "That's good. Look, if Magician does manage to get himself into the Academy, we'll need a way of communicating with him. If they take him on board there, it will be as a novice. The novices aren't permitted to carry regular phones." Lubanov knew that from the reports of the people he'd tried to insert there. "Can you send some equipment to Plantation for Pixie to pass on to him? Make sure that Pixie can brief him on how to use it." Various devices existed that enabled surreptitious communications. Lubanov would leave it to Vogol to pick something suitable. "Also, it's important that we know of anything that occurs there or that he comes across relating to *Envoy*. The same goes for the robot, if the Magician can recruit him. Make sure that Pixie alerts him to be looking out for the word."

"I'll take care of it," Vogol promised.

~ TWENTY-SIX ~

The bear paused in its rummaging beneath a felled log and watched as Rikku moved closer. Rikku moved carefully through the undergrowth, following the line of the fence, which in places was barely visible. Deer, pigs, a few bison, apes, and other kinds of animals that could mix together shared this section of the reserve, but with the restricted space they tended to become intensely territorial. The rule was to keep them well fed, which allayed aggressive instincts. All the same, Rikku kept a firm hold on the stunstick that he carried, and drew reassurance from the solid feel of the firearm holstered at his hip as a backup. The carnivores that couldn't coexist had to be segregated, which was why it was important to be sure the fences were kept in good repair.

He stopped to clear aside a growth of vines and creeper, and tested one of the support posts. It yielded enough to reveal loosened flanges where the horizontal struts joined. Rikku grunted and moved on to try the next one. "The section here needs looking at," he called to Yonen, who was following several yards behind. People always worked in twos, minimum, on these duties. "Looks like it'll need half a dozen brackets with fastenings."

"Got it." Yonen made a note in his pad. "That brown fella up there seems to be taking an interest in you."

"I'm keeping my eye on it."

Yonen was about the same age as Rikku, which meant they would both have been boys when the *Aurora* left Earth. But unlike Rikku, Yonen was here just as a break from his normal existence on Siden, where he was training in some kind of engineering.

The original plan had been to carry a broad representation of Earth's animal and vegetable life-forms almost entirely in the form of frozen fertilized ova, seeds, and clonable DNA. However, when Plantation was conceived, the restriction was relaxed to allow some selected types to be raised and to reproduce for a period, the idea being to maintain a limited but rotating population that would provide a changing variety through the years and generations of the voyage ahead.

Rikku was glad that the decision had gone the way it had. The mystery of how organisms came to be alive had long fascinated him, and it was a source of profound cognitive stimulation for him, as well as a psychic satisfaction in itself, to work among living things. In some ways, he would be sorry to have to leave it all when the time came, which would not be long now, for him to move to Etanne.

He was familiar with the studies that Sofian astronomers had made of Earth's Solar System, and had seen the images returned by probes during the years of early space exploration that had preceded *Aurora*. All in all, lifeless bodies were pretty dull and repetitive places of dust, rock, ice, and sometimes a few gases, where nothing very interesting happened. An alien arriving on Earth, whose only prior knowledge had been of such examples, would immediately be struck by the presence of two classes of objects that absolutely didn't fit in or belong. First, there would be all the artifacts created by humans, such as clothes, buildings, vehicles, and tools, which natural forces left to themselves could never produce. And second, the even more astonishing complexity and abnormality of living things, which in addition to exhibiting forms that violated all the rules of chance, were able to extract whatever materials they needed directly from their raw environment, and reproduce themselves by purely self-contained processes without external assistance. If it took all the ingenuity and resourcefulness of human minds to conceive and create the former, then what kind of incomparably more powerful mind had been necessary to bring about the latter?

The sages of the old world had understood such things, and their wisdom was being resurrected again on Etanne. Most powerful of all had been the sect that had inspired the Dollarians, which had become universal in commanding a worldwide following. It was singularly apt that Rikku should be destined to join them now, because the principle that the Dollarian creed embodied had been that of survival and growth in the face of competition, thereby epitomizing the processes that shaped and guided living things. Hence, mastering the mysteries and disciplines of the Dollarians would provide the necessary grounding and insights for eventually comprehending the forces that drove life itself.

A bell sounded from the direction of the warden's station. One . . . two . . . three peals. It was a signal that Rikku and Yonen were wanted back there. They looked at each other questioningly. "What have we done now?" Yonen said.

Rikku raised his shoulders in a sustained shrug. "Nothing that I can think of. Did you finish with that pump that Jor-Ling said he wanted to use?"

"All back together and working."

"Well, there's only one way to find out, I suppose."

They turned, and keeping a distance of a few yards between them, began retracing their path in the direction they had come. As any conscientious scholar would, Rikku had tried to arouse Yonen's awareness to the wondrousness of it all, too. But Yonen didn't think there was anything especially remarkable about life, and that it could arise of itself, spontaneously from nonliving matter. Rikku decided that familiarity from childhood could dull a person's sensibilities and render them blind to the obvious.

Behind them, the bear looked away and returned to its rummaging.

"Yonen, I need help loading feed bags to haul out to the Little Gully," Jor-Lin said when they returned.

"Sure thing."

"And Rikku, you have a visitor. He's waiting in the clinic."

"Oh? Who?"

"I didn't ask. He says that Melvig Bahoba sent him here. I think he's interested in that outfit that you're waiting to hear from."

Jor-Ling and Yonen disappeared around the corner of

the station's lab annex, and Rikku went the other way to the veterinary wing. Gallier, the resident animal clinician who ran the wing, was away attending to something on the far side of Ringvale that day, which meant that Rikku and the visitor would have it to themselves. Doubtless, that was why Jor-Ling had put the visitor there.

The visitor got up from the stool by the dispensary counter as Rikku entered. Around forty, at a guess, he was a little older than Rikku had expected for some reason, of medium height, clean-shaven with a head showing a shadow of dark stubble, and dressed in a rough cloak over a plain rustic tunic. There was a light suppleness in his movement, and his eyes were dark and alert, giving Rikku the feeling of having taken in all there was to know of him from the outside even in those few seconds.

"I take it you are Rikku," he said. Rikku nodded. "My name is Shakor. Melvig Bahoba directed me here. I presume you know him?"

Rikku closed the door and moved into the room. "Yes. The forester south along the ridge."

Shakor inclined his head to direct Rikku's attention to Gallier's wall board, on which he had scrawled a $ sign with one of the pens from the tray below, and smiled faintly. "I'm interested in the Dollarians," he said. He didn't push himself by insisting on shaking hands, but settled back on the stool after the courtesy of standing. "I was intending to go to Etanne to try and join them, but I don't know anybody there. I'm told that you are already in touch with them and on your way there. I wondered if maybe I could join you—a way of introducing myself to them, as it were."

His voice was quiet and pleasant, but projected

a strange quality of confidence that intrigued Rikku, while at the same time putting him more at ease. Rikku moved away from the door and propped himself against the edge of Gallier's desk, facing the wall in one corner, and folded his arms across his chest. "People don't normally just walk in there," he said. "A period of detachment and preparation is necessary first, to free the mind from dependency on artificiality and distractions. That's why I've been working here."

"I'm aware of that," Shakor replied. "And to that end I have been living the life of a solitary itinerant here on Plantation, with no fixed lodgement. I'm hoping that would qualify me."

Rikku uncovered his hands enough to make an empty gesture. "Something like that wouldn't be for me to say. They make the rules."

"I know. But I assume they have someone here on Plantation that they make contact through."

"Mm . . . yes," Rikku conceded, giving nothing away.

"Then that's all I ask—to meet this person and put my case directly. A better way of going about things than knocking at doors on Etanne."

"I don't have a way of initiating anything," Rikku cautioned. "They always contact me."

"That's all right. I've been waiting long enough. If you could just let me know when you hear from them, so that I can be there, too, that would be sufficient."

Shakor seemed personable enough, and his manner was open and direct. Rikku could see no reason why he should refuse. If the irregularity of the situation violated some rule that the Dollarians operated by, that would be between them and Shakor. His willingness to bring them another potential recruit could surely only count to his credit. "How will I let you know if you don't have a fixed place?" he asked.

"Can you get a message to Melvig Bahoba?"

"Yes, that's no problem."

"I'll pick it up from there. And thanks for agreeing to help. It means a lot."

"I'm happy to help a spiritual brother." Rikku eased himself back to sit more comfortably on the edge of the desk and regarded Shakor curiously for a few seconds. "What took you to Bahoba's?"

"Oh, as I said . . . I've been all over."

"So how did you hear about me?"

"Melvig told me. I guess he and Jor-Ling talk to each other."

"I thought maybe it was from that robot he's got working there," Rikku said. Bahoba's robot wasn't especially a secret among people up on the ridge. But they tended not to talk about it outside their own circle to avoid drawing hordes of visitors up there. There seemed little point in not mentioning it now, since Shakor could hardly have been there and gotten to know Bahoba without coming across it.

"You mean Tek," Shakor answered.

"It just appeared there, on some kind of research field trial or something, didn't it?"

"I couldn't say. Melvig isn't exactly the kind of person who minds other people's business."

"Jor-Ling says that it's got an interest in the Dollarians, too, for some crazy reason."

"So Melvig told me. But I never talked to it. It isn't there anymore."

Rikku's eyebrows rose. "I didn't know that. Where did it go?"

"I'm not sure. I don't think Melvig knows, either. It seems to have been sudden."

"To Etanne, do you think?"

Shakor shrugged. "I really don't know." He seemed about to say something else, when a new thought struck him. "Do you have any idea when you'll be going there, Rikku?"

"It should be anytime now. In fact, when Jor-Ling told me there was someone here just now, I thought that might be it."

Shakor seemed pleased at that. He nodded in a way that said the important things had been covered, and the talk could turn to lighter matters. Rikku was still intrigued by this strange character who had appeared out of nowhere, and what had led him to seek such a path at what was usually a settled stage of life.

"What attracts you to the Dollarians?" he asked.

"Oh, many things. . . ." Shakor's eyes roamed over the room, as if he were collecting his thoughts. "It all gets to seem so shallow and trivial after a while, doesn't it? Machines; these tiny islands of ours in the middle of nowhere; the pointlessness of this day-in, day-out existence. . . . I suppose it's the thought of having the chance to glimpse a bit of what they knew back then, in the old world."

"Yes!" Rikku agreed with enthusiasm. "That's it! The deeper reality! To know the universal principle of life."

Shakor eyed him penetratingly, seemingly evaluating his reaction. "And then I've heard it said that they are involved with much of the criticism that's going around of the way things are being run now. That interests me, too. All our futures are at stake."

Rikku knew of the concerns that were being voiced,

of course, and they seemed to make sense. If the Dollarians had any connection, he wasn't aware of it. No doubt they had their reasons. As Shakor had just said, everyone's future was at stake. The politics didn't interest Rikku.

"I don't know anything about that," he said. "But I'd say they were right anyway. How can you let the population grow without imposing some limits in our finite situation? And right now, we have new material assets sitting out there that are priceless, and they're sending them to Hera! That doesn't sound to me like the kind of leadership whose rationality we should be entrusting ourselves to."

Rikku realized belatedly that the other might not see things that way and regretted having committed himself to a view one way or the other. It wasn't his main preoccupation, after all. He hoped that they weren't going to get into an ideological dispute at this stage of a relationship which only a moment ago had felt so amiable and comfortable, and braced himself to be challenged to defend his position.

But Shakor merely smiled acquiescently and seemed happy not to take it further.

"Interesting," he replied.

~ TWENTY-SEVEN ~

By the time *Aurora* and its daughter miniworlds caught up with the first materials and supplies raft, the raft had drifted approximately a quarter of a million miles from its planned course. Representing an angular error in the order of a half arc-second at this distance, it amounted to a phenomenal success in navigational precision. The raft had been programmed to cut out leaving a reserve of power in hand, and the first action as the Constellation formation drew close had been to send a signal reactivating its drive to accelerate it up to a velocity matching *Aurora*'s. The fusion drive employed by the raft had been an early Sofian design—the first to be used for a major, long-range mission—and its mounting platform had been retained to serve as a base for the replacement baryonic-annihilation system that would power *Envoy*. The smaller mass of *Envoy*, coupled with the high thrust of the newer drive, would give it the performance capability needed to boost itself ahead to Hera.

Currently, work was almost complete on fitting the upgraded probe with a complement of instrumentation and robotics to carry out the desired tasks of reconnaissance and reporting back from Hera. To avoid excessive trafficking back and forth to Constellation, which despite the raft's accurate positioning was still several hours' flight time away, the remainder of the raft's structural members and a portion of its cargo had been used to construct a local station from which the conversion of *Envoy* could be carried out, and where the equipment produced for it could be assembled and tested. The station was called *Outmark*. Future intentions were to incorporate the discarded fusion drive from the raft to enable *Outmark* to be maneuvered closer in to Constellation, and expand it into a technological research, education, and manufacturing center, where much of the existing industrial activity would be relocated. Also—as would eventually be required for each of the other progeny worlds, too—the drive would provide the necessary means of braking when the flotilla entered the final leg of its approach to Hera.

Occupancy of *Outmark* had commenced as soon as the external hull was pressurized. With the amount of work involved in both the completion of the station itself and the conversion of *Envoy*, the shifts were soon busy around the clock and had abated little since. Launching of *Envoy* was now due in just under two weeks, and Lund Ormont decided that a show of recognition in the form of an official visit from the Directorate would be in order to acknowledge the efforts of the troops. His other, less-advertised reason was a desire to make a personal contribution to boosting morale by countering the negative press that *Envoy* had been receiving from some quarters.

Several voices within the Directorate had called for an information campaign to refute the more extreme of the claims that were going around, but Ormont had vetoed the suggestion. The facts and figures were readily available for anyone with enough serious interest and who was capable of understanding them, he insisted. The Directorate's business was making policy decisions according to the dictates of evidence and rationality, not staging a public-relations circus.

Despite the length of time for which it had now been operational, *Outmark* still had a bare and unfinished look about it, Ormont thought as he and his party of a half-dozen came out of the Final Assembly & Test Shop, where they had seen some of the subsatellites that would be deployed from the *Envoy* orbiter. Escorting them were Vad Cereta, *Envoy* project coordinator, and Wesl Inchow, the chief instrumentation engineer. In the final stage of their shuttle flight from *Aurora*, the visitors had seen the cache of cargo from the raft that hadn't been used for *Outmark* floating in space, along with the dismantled fusion drive. The proportion of the total that had gone into *Envoy* really wasn't that great, belying the exaggerations that were being made and substantiating further that the underlying motives were political.

They followed a lane marked by tape showing the path where the floor was gravitationally activated. On either side, piles of tied-down stores stood beside unlaid plates and open sections where the synthesizers were waiting to be installed. From the beginning, priority had been given to work directly related to *Envoy*. Tidying up *Outmark* could wait until later. An opening through the wall brought them into a brightly lit space of fitting bays and bench areas where figures in white coveralls and lab smocks were busy at assorted tasks. Here and there, faces turned, and people nudged and murmured to each other as the director in chief and his party entered.

Cereta led the way over to a corner where a jumble of desks, work tables, and viewscreens stood crammed together beside an open space. As the party approached, one of the dozen or so people working in the vicinity got up from a screen and came forward to greet them. Several yards away, a stepladder six feet or so high with steps on both sides had been positioned in the center of the aisle running beside the desks and worktables. Metal panels blocked the space between the desks and the ladder on one side, beneath the ladder itself, and between the ladder and the rear of some electronics racks on the other side, with the result that anyone wanting to go in that direction would have to climb over. But that wouldn't have been so easy, either, for another panel was clamped above the platform at the top of the ladder, leaving a space below it no more than six inches high. Several among the group stared at it with puzzled expressions as they drew up around Cereta in front of the open area.

Several rows of upright metal crates of lightweight frame construction took up most of the space. The crates stood a little higher than a man and measured on the order of three feet along a side. They were divided into tiers of cubical cells, each about large enough to accommodate a clenched fist, giving a capacity that worked out to 1944 cells in a crate. It wasn't that Ormont was some kind of calculating prodigy who could assess such things by eye. But knowing what the itinerary for the tour would be, he had done his homework.

The crates at the back, by the wall, were lined closely together and filled; those around the open part of the floor, partly so. The occupied cells contained intricate electromechanical assemblies of chips, actuators, and appendages built around shells in several colors. More were stacked on shelves at the rear. The ones inside the cells and on the shelves were retracted into a compact configuration for storage. Others, complete or in various stages of dismemberment, with their sensing probes and attachment latches extended, lay scattered on the work benches. They suggested some strange kind of alien arthropod, and were known, appropriately, as "spiders."

Cereta turned and extended an arm to indicate the crates. "If you don't know what these are, you shouldn't be working in the Directorate," he told the group. He was short in stature, with two remaining patches of hair fringing a smooth head, but bright-eyed and ever-alert with the kind of energy that gave the impression of somebody who devoured problems for breakfast. The transformation of an inert stockpile of materials into a functioning habitat in what had seemed an impossible timescale to most people had in no small part been Cereta's doing. If he had agreed to mount an official publicity campaign, Ormont reflected, Cereta would be the kind of person he'd want running it.

"Modular robots," Poli Pamimendes, from *Aurora*'s Housing Department, responded.

Cereta nodded and went on to explain anyway. "With traditional kinds of robots like the ones that crawl around welding space structures or checking pipelines, different types come specialized for each kind of task. If a particular task isn't needed anywhere today, the robots that are specialized for it sit around with nothing to do." He shrugged and looked from side to side. "Something tells us we ought to be able to do better. Well, we can. . . . But why don't I let Wesl take it from here, because these are his people's creation."

"And Shikoba's," Wesl Inchow said, smiling. He had moved over to the nearest bench while Cereta was speaking, and picked up one of the intact spiders.

"Oh, right. Mustn't forget Masumichi Shikoba," Cereta agreed.

"And this is Zake, who runs the section here," Inchow informed the visitors. The man who had risen from the workstation nodded a grin of acknowledgment. He was holding a remote-control unit in one hand. Behind him, the rest of the team had stopped what they were doing and were watching with interest.

Inchow held the spider up for everyone to see. He was a stockily built Asiatic, from the same islands as Shikoba. "Instead of designing a different robot for each task, you build many copies of one simple module. A module can't do much by itself, but they can assemble together to form a system able to do complicated things. The same collection of modules can reconfigure itself for different tasks or different working environments. An analog in nature would be the thousands of different specialized proteins that make up living things, all formed from the same assembly kit of twenty amino acids. Here's an example of a mobile configuration that might be used for terrain exploration."

Inchow stepped aside and gestured to draw attention to a composite structure formed from maybe

fifty or sixty spiders that had been standing farther
back beside some boxes. It was about knee-high and
consisted of a knobby body supported on six multi-
ply jointed legs, with a turretlike head at one end,
bristling with sensor stalks, lens housings, and other
protuberances. Such an assembly might carry out
reconnaissance work on Hera. The crates from which
the spiders deployed would be carried down to the
surface by *Envoy's* landers.

He nodded to Zake, who thumbed a code into the
remote unit that he was holding, and the assembly
of spiders stirred into life. Moving with a surprisingly
smooth, flowing gait, it circled the open space of floor
as if scanning its environment, and then darted forward suddenly, causing the nearest of the visitors to
draw back in alarm. As they opened to allow a path,
it came out into the aisle and turned in the direction
where the stepladder and the panels to the sides of
it stood blocking the way.

"Zake's just giving it broad goals of which way to go,
as a strategy-formulating program might in a remote,
self-directing operation," Inchow commented. "How
it gets there is something it figures out for itself."

The walker reached the bottom of the steps and
paused for several seconds. Then a series of movements
occurred among the spiders at the front, in which the
first pair of limbs transformed from legs attached at the
underside to arms extending from what had become
shoulders. The spiders forming the ends of the arms
transformed their manipulators into grasping claws that
it used to begin pulling itself up. As it proceeded to
ascend, the other limbs modified themselves similarly,
turning the walker into a climbing caterpillar. At the

top it paused again at the low opening beneath the upper panel, and after more agitation among the modules assumed a snakelike form to wriggle its way through, and then reverted to a variant of the caterpillar, which could be seen descending the steps on the reverse side. Inchow strolled forward and lifted one of the blocking panels at the side away, allowing it to return now reformed as the original walker to exclamations of approval and a scattering of applause from the watchers.

Ormont delivered some words of appreciation to Zake and the team, who were looking pleased, and reminded them that he would be addressing the full staff of *Outmark* after the lunch that had been organized in the cafeteria. Since that was the next item on the day's schedule and there was some time to spare, he let the party break up at that point to continue talking with Zake and his people, and left with Cereta.

"This visit was a good idea," Cereta said as they walked away. "The guys have had a tough time meeting the deadlines—especially in more recent times with Lubanov's restrictions."

"Yes, I'm aware of that."

"How much of it could be imagination, do you think?"

"Oh, over the years I've come to learn that Andri is someone to be listened to. He has good instincts."

"They needed some uplift anyway, Lund. Some of the stuff that's being said around Constellation can get people down, even if they don't buy it. It gets me down at times."

"That was the main reason we did it," Ormont replied.

Cereta was quiet until they came to the stairs leading down to the level where the cafeteria was situated. Then he said, "A lot of people are saying we should be running our own line of counterpropaganda. No punches pulled. Show it all as it is. Discredit them enough in public, and they wouldn't dare try anything." His tone said that he was far from sure that they weren't right.

"The trouble with that is that if you have to imitate your opponent and adopt his methods, all you've done is turn into another version of what you were trying to beat. So it really doesn't matter which side prevails. He wins either way."

"Hm.... Let me think about that."

At the bottom of the stairs was a foyer area with doors into the cafeteria on the far side. A knot of people heading that way sent Ormont looks of recognition, which he acknowledged with a nod. One side of the foyer consisted of a window wall that extended beyond the partition to run the full length of the cafeteria. Lubanov was standing alone at the guardrail along the wall, staring out at the starfield and *Envoy* riding several miles off.

"I need to talk to Andri about a couple of things," Ormont said in a low voice. "I'll catch up with you inside." Cereta nodded and went on through.

Envoy resembled a mushroom with a flared stalk, with a head in the form of a hexagon rather than a dome. The propulsion system formed the stalk, which along with the command module constituting the core of the hexagon would remain above Hera as the Orbiter. The faces of the hexagon carried shells covering the stowage bays for the landers, which would deploy to selected spots on the surface. Just at the moment, it was at the center of a clutter of hardware and umbilicals hanging around it in space, looking as if it had been frozen in the act of exploding.

"The drive would be the obvious target," Lubanov said without turning his head. "A big enough explosion there would make sure of things. If it were concentrated near the tail, there would be minimum destruction of hardware that would be recoverable and usable."

Ormont looked away from Lubanov's reflection in the window and followed his gaze. "And with expectations suitably prepared in advance, you'd stand a good chance of getting away with it," he remarked. *Envoy's* baryonic-annihilation drive was a high-performance design, stressed close to maximum to achieve the required boost to Hera. There had been a spate of warnings of late from alleged authorities about possible accidents. Engineering management had issued statements demonstrating that the risk had been wildly overstated, but once such ideas had taken root it was never possible to eradicate them completely.

"Exactly." Lubanov turned to face Ormont and leaned against the rail behind him. "We have just two weeks to go. If it were up to me, I would break out weapons from the armory, equip a special force from the Police Arm, and put them on Etanne to lock the whole place down until after the launch so that a mouse wouldn't be able to move in there without our knowing about it."

Ormont nodded. "I know you would, Andri. And you know it isn't my way. Start that kind of thing now, and we'll be on our way to creating old Earth all over again before anyone even arrives on Hera.

But show me some solid evidence, and then, sure, you have your green light."

"Very well. But can I have your approval to form such a unit, and have them standing by ready for fast response?"

"Do you really think such melodramatics are necessary? For over a month we've kept tight control over everyone who's in a position to interfere with things—EVA work and telebot operators. There are full logs of every move they make. And no independent vehicle could make it out here from Constellation without being detected."

"I know that's how it seems," Lubanov replied. "But one thing I've learned is that the most predictable certainty in life is that unpredictable things will happen. I'd like a team at the ready and standing by out here until the launch is over. If an emergency develops, they won't be any use four hours away back home."

It made sense. Ormont nodded reluctantly. "To be stood down on successful launch," he agreed.

"Naturally."

More people were coming through and disappearing into the cafeteria, which from the rising noise level was evidently filling up. Ormont motioned with his head to indicate that they should follow. Lubanov unfolded from the guardrail and straightened up.

Ormont sighed as they began moving toward the cafeteria entrance. "You know, Andri, maybe I should have listened more when you said you wanted to put someone on the inside among the Dollarians. How much difference it might have made to have some idea what they're up to. Deceitful, I know, but sometimes necessary. Too late now, I suppose."

Lubanov gave him a sharp sideways look as they walked. "Well, not necessarily, maybe.... How would we stand if I could come up with something?"

"Why? What do you have in mind?"

"Oh...nothing specific for now. But let me look into it some more." Lubanov's voice had a curiously vague note to it, Ormont thought.

– TWENTY-EIGHT –

In terms of surroundings and the mood that they inspired, Etanne was about as different from Plantation as it was possible to get. Whereas Plantation brought together natural vistas designed to recapture—even if as caricatures—the feeling of open skies and unspoiled Earth, Etanne was compact and enclosed, focusing inwardly upon itself in solemn introspection. While Plantation exulted in sunny hamlets hidden among forested slopes, Etanne brooded in windowless cells and somber halls. Plantation echoed and preserved life that had been; Etanne peered forward to life that some said was to come.

A half-dozen founder groups had organized the original construction between them, since none had been large enough to justify a daughter world of its own or be capable of managing such a project unaided. The design philosophy that resulted called for a modular structure to afford each sect the isolation and seclusion it desired, along with a measure of autonomy consistent with having to share essential supporting services. It was implemented as a wheel consisting of a core zone surrounded by a ring of segments separated by radial segregation and communications corridors, each segment devoted to one of the member groups and sized according to the number to be accommodated. The geometry allowed for future growth by the addition of a second and possibly further rings, which might be occasioned either by increases in the size of the existing groups or the introduction of new ones. The modules making up the peripheral ring were rectangular in section, giving the wheel an overall flat cylindrical form, with square edges.

Korshak had not been to Etanne before. His first impressions as he and Rikku came out of the docking port and passed through a circular viewing gallery of sky windows to the core zone service area were of starkness and utility after the bright faces presented by the modules and Hub facilities of *Aurora*. Its main structural members were of bare metal, with the wall panels between coated in plain, subdued colors, and floors of a uniform gray woven-mesh composite. The architecture was styled to produce an exaggerated impression of height by emphasizing verticality, which it achieved by means of tall, narrow doorways and closely spaced, fluted uprights. In a way, appropriately, it reminded him of some of the monasteries and retreats he had visited during his former travels across Asia.

Rikku was enraptured by it all. "I feel as if the meaningful part of my life is just about to begin, Shakor," he said as they approached a line of figures who seemed to be awaiting the arrivals. "It's all so symbolic—as if the times of shallow distractions are behind now. That must be why it was built this way."

"True, brother! How true!" Faithful to the role he was playing, Korshak's voice shook slightly with awe and emotion. He would explain his changed appearance to Vaydien later.

One of those waiting was a youth of about twenty, wearing a plain brown robe with a $ embroidered in yellow on one side of the chest, which Korshak picked out immediately. But he gave no indication of the fact and waited until the youth identified them and stepped forward, smiling enigmatically. He announced himself as Furch, another Dollarian novice, who had been sent to meet them. He would conduct them to the Dollarian sector of Etanne, where they would first have lunch. Afterward, Rikku, whose entry was already approved, would begin the precursory formalities. For Shakor, an introductory interview had been arranged with a superior called "Banker" Lareda. Judging by Furch's reverent tone, the title signified a rank of considerable standing within the Dollarian order.

A pair of imposing doors emblazoned with $ signs and set in a rounded arch gave admission to the Dollarian sector of Etanne, which they called their Academy. On the far side was a lobby area, sober in furnishings and decor, with a desk attended by a gray-haired disciple attired in a plain brown tunic. Furch cleared them through, and they deposited their bags in a side room, to be collected later. Korshak's bag was not the one he had taken with him to Plantation, but another that Lois Iles had given him when they met at Sonja and Helmut's house before Korshak left.

From the lobby they entered a larger space that seemed to be a central concourse, with doors on all sides and corridors leading away in several directions.

Numerous people were in evidence going about their business, clad in a variety of styles ranging from simple tunics to long, enveloping robes. Furch led the way along a corridor flanked by what appeared to be meeting rooms or classrooms to another concourse, smaller this time, on the far side of which was a door into a communal dining area that he announced as the "refectory hall." Its paneled walls boasted some ornamentation in the form of statuary and pictures, mostly portraits, and it held a dozen or so long tables seating six on a side, along with a larger one extending almost the width of the room that looked like a head table for formal occasions, but which was unoccupied at present. The rest all had some people seated at them, it being the period for the midday meal.

Following Furch's example, they joined a short line at a serving table staffed by kitchen helpers to receive helpings of soup and bread, a fish-and-pasta casserole with vegetables, and sliced fruit with cream, and found a table with a group talking among themselves at the far end. The styles of dress seemed to fall into distinct categories, which presumably denoted various kinds of specialty, or perhaps levels of proficiency. Korshak was surprised to see that besides the robes and tunics, there were some patterned more along the lines of the uniforms worn by *Aurora's* Police Arm, and in pictures he had seen of the military services that had existed in Sofi, Tranth, and other parts of Earth. He remarked on it as they sat down and started eating.

"It reflects the two aspects of the Dollarian movement," Furch informed them. "The spiritual and ideological aspect is necessary to chart the course that is to be taken. But ideals alone are no use without a capacity for action to turn them into reality. In the same way, *Aurora* needs both a destination and propulsion to get there. Neither is of any use without the other."

"I see!" Rikku sounded intrigued, as if the revelations he had come to receive had already begun.

"That's what the two bars on the dollar sign stand for," Furch said.

Korshak had been looking around while he listened. In a far corner, four figures in dark gray robes with deep cowls that concealed their faces even while they ate were sitting apart from the general company. "Who are they?" he inquired, inclining his head in that direction.

Furch turned to follow his gaze. "They're called the Genhedrin," he replied. "An inner sect of adepts who have attained the highest level of spiritual insight. The source of the deeper wisdom that guides the movement."

"I see."

"Fascinating!" Rikku breathed. He stared at Furch curiously. "How did you find the path that led you here yourself? What part of Earth did you come from originally?"

"Those are things we're taught not to discuss," Furch told him. Rikku checked himself and nodded that he understood. Well, at least that would save him the bother of having to explain a lot of things, Korshak thought to himself.

The conversation turned to the philosophy of Dollarism, serving Rikku's impatience to hear more and giving Furch the opportunity to air his own further-advanced insights. Basically, what had made it a force capable of sweeping across the world was its recognition of the universal law that the key to advancement lies in competition, and progress results from selectively accentuating the positive and eliminating the negative. The idealization of cooperation and equality that had been enshrined into *Aurora*'s charter was misguided and could only result in the misdirection of resources to ends that were unworthy. It was early days yet, and the beginnings were small. But correction of the error by whatever means it entailed would eventually be unavoidable if the system failed to reform itself.

Korshak listened while Furch elaborated, and said little. Whether he was backward-looking and unenlightened he didn't know, for he had never been able to relate much to the machinations of power politics, let alone the more sophisticated intellectual environment of Sofi, which was outside his direct experience. But it all sounded to him like a recipe for generating the kind of conflict and divisiveness that would be the last thing that an extended space mission like this needed. On the other hand, he saw what could be the basis for dividing opponents among themselves as a means of clearing the way for a focused group to move in to a controlling position.

At any rate, it gave him a better idea of the kind of answers that would be in order at his interview.

Banker Lareda had a pugnacious, darkish countenance, with a full head of black hair, a shaggy beard setting off a set of powerful white teeth, and immense eyebrows that hovered over his eyes like bat wings, contrasting with the whites to intensify their stare. He sat with his hands clasped on the heavy desk in the office where Korshak had been brought, the hood of his dark gray robe thrown back on his shoulders, and the front open to show a black shirt with $ insignias imprinted on the breasts, over a barrel chest. Seated to one side of him was a younger man with fair hair and a clear face, wearing a brown cloak over a tan, two-piece tunic, whom he had introduced as "Broker" Ningen without elaborating further. "Broker" was seemingly an inferior rank to "Banker."

"So, Mr. Shakor, you are interested in joining us," Lareda said, running his eyes over the screen of the viewpad lying in front of him. His voice was deep in the bass register, with a trace of an edge that had a crisping effect. "From the central part of Asia originally, I believe."

"More to the east, the Parthesa region," Korshak replied.

"Where specifically?"

"A city called Escalos, in the Arigane country of Parthesa. My father was a maker of clocks and mechanisms, which I apprenticed in." A factor that worked in Korshak's favor was that as part of the policy according the highest value to personal privacy, it had been decided early on not to keep records of individuals' previous lives. The life ahead was deemed to be what mattered, and that had begun with *Aurora*.

"How did you come to be recruited to the mission?" Lareda asked.

"My father was widowed, and when he died, I was put under the care of an uncle called Mirsto, who was physician to the royal court at Arigane." Lareda and Ningen exchanged meaningful glances at the mention of the name. Korshak continued, "Later, when I grew up, I became a traveling vendor and repairer of mechanisms. But I ended up on the wrong side of the prince of a neighboring realm, who had a reputation for malignity and violence. I went to my uncle for advice and protection. He told me about Sofi and *Aurora*, and that people from there that he was in communication with had offered him a place, which he'd accepted. He felt that my life might be in danger after he was gone, and was able to arrange for me to go too."

"Who was this prince that you were in trouble with?"

"His name was Zileg. He was heir to the throne of Urst."

Lareda looked at Ningen, who returned a faint affirming nod. "And what kind of trouble was it?" Lareda asked.

Korshak summoned a sheepish look and spread his hands in an attitude of candor. "One of those romantic affairs that young men are prone to fall into. But what I was unaware of was that the maid in question was also a favorite of Zileg's." Korshak shrugged. "He wasn't the kind to take such a slight lightly."

Lareda snorted in a way that dismissed the matter. "Where does your uncle live now?"

"He died about a year after the voyage commenced."

Lareda nodded. Korshak got the feeling that he had known that. "And so, tell us what you've been doing since."

Korshak took a moment, as if to organize his thoughts. "In the early years, I was entranced by all that I saw. I had several residences on Astropolis and Jakka, all the time devoting myself to the study of Sofian science and technology. Nothing had prepared me for the like of it. In return, my contribution was to work as a technical assistant to Masumichi Shikoba, who did research into machine cognition and robotics. As far as I know, he still does."

"Yes, we're aware of him."

Korshak spread his hands briefly. "But as I learned more about Sofi and its history, it seemed that something was missing. With their lead over everywhere else, the Sofians should have dominated the world. Instead, they isolated themselves behind mountains and deserts, and when the spirit to build a new world became uncontainable, they left Earth to go elsewhere. I remembered the holy men and the orders of priests that I had known on Earth, and I thought that perhaps the problem with Sofi had been that it became too fixated on material things, and had lost touch with a higher reality. That was the time when people were talking about building a retreat for the pursuit of such matters, which became Etanne." Korshak indicated the surroundings with a gesture. "So I discontinued my technical studies and went to work in various mundane positions on Beach and Evergreen, while I meditated upon such things and discussed them with others, many of whom became involved with the sects that now exist here."

"But you didn't join any of them yourself?" Lareda queried.

Korshak shook his head. "I may have been missing something, but I couldn't escape the conclusion that much of what they were saying was wishful thinking . . ." He hesitated. "And, I have to say, in many cases the masters that they followed were deceiving them with trickery."

Lareda gave the impression that that didn't come as a surprise, either. "And then?"

"I was confused and disappointed, and needed to be by myself to think. Many aspirants to Etanne go through a preparatory period on Plantation. I decided I would do that, too. And from some of the people that I met there, I learned about the Dollarians. *This* was what I had been searching for! Not a fantasy built on supernatural imaginings and daydreams, but a secular, pragmatic philosophy that related to the real world. The formula for expansion and universality that the Sofians had missed. I spent many months as an itinerant on Plantation, studying the lessons and practicing the disciplines that were required. When I felt I was ready, I made inquiries and was directed to Rikku."

"And what made you decide you were ready?"

"That is for you to decide, not I."

Lareda gave Korshak a final long, searching look, and then turned to Ningen and sat back in a manner that said it was his turn.

Ningen studied the back of a hand while he massaged it with the other, and then looked up. "You were from Arigane originally, you said? You grew up in Escalos."

"That's right."

"And traveled extensively in the region."

"Yes."

"Hm. A fortuitous coincidence. It turns out that I'm from that part of the world myself. A place called Belamon. You might have heard of it."

"The seaport in Shengsho. Yes, I was there a few times. They sailed the big ships."

"I had occasion to visit Arigane, too. Can you tell us who the ruler there was at the time?"

"That would have been Shandrahl." It was clear now why Ningen was present.

"He had a hunting lodge about twenty miles out

from the city, that I stayed in once—in the hills to the north."

"Er, the hills were to the south," Korshak corrected. Good try, he thought.

"Ah yes, quite so. If your uncle was the court physician, do you also happen to know the name of the princess there, Shandrahl's daughter?"

"There were two. Vaydien was the elder. Her half-sister was Leetha."

"Anything else about them?" Ningen asked in a curiously suggestive voice.

Korshak had seen where this was going. "Vaydien is here, on *Aurora*," he replied. "She was one of the party that escaped from Escalon, that included Mirsto."

"And not yourself?"

"I joined them later, with a group of Masumichi Shikoba's relatives. That was how I first became acquainted with him."

"But the party that escaped from Escalon did include another person, who is quite well known," Ningen prompted.

"The entertainer and magician, Korshak. He had come to Shikoba's attention somehow. I don't know the details. He and Vaydien later married. I have visited them on Astropolis, where they live—although not for some time now." Korshak paused, then allowed a faint smile as if a thought had just struck him. "It was probably things I saw of Korshak that made me suspicious of the wonders I was shown by some of the other sects that you share space with, here on Etanne."

A short silence ensued. Lareda and Ningen looked at each other, but neither of them had anything further to ask at that point. Lareda stared down at his hands for a moment, then raised his head in a way that said he was satisfied. At least, for now.

"Very well, Mr. Shakor," he pronounced. "We approve your acceptance as a provisional member of the order as a novice with the rank of junior clerk. Since you have technical aptitude and experience, I'm also assigning you to the workshops, where I'm sure the supervisor will find many useful things that you can help us with. Accountant Furch, whom you've met, will acquaint you with the entry procedure. We will expect to see you, Junior Clerk Shakor, at the daily General Meeting, first thing tomorrow morning."

– TWENTY-NINE –

The General Meeting took place every morning as a pep talk and recitation of faith to spur the troops, but also with trappings of ceremony and symbolism that carried undertones of a religion. It was held in a large auditorium known as the Assembly Hall, where rows of seats faced a raised dais with a pulpitlike speaker's rostrum. Korshak had been told that all members of the sect were required to attend. They were seated in groups according to the part of the order they belonged to, with rank descending from front to back within each section and the various classes denoted by the attire worn. The major division, reflected by a central aisle dividing the right and left sides of the hall, was between the robes and the military-style uniforms, which Furch had described the day before as representing the "spiritual" and "action" sides of the order. Korshak had learned since that these were the "Speculative" and "Executive" branches respectively, both terms apparently being derived from the old-world system that had inspired the movement.

Korshak and Rikku, clad in the white tunics without cloaks of the junior-clerk rank, sat with the other novices at the back, several rows behind a block of darker robes that included Furch. The hall was almost full, permeated by a murmur of voices in subdued tones. However, a line of maybe a dozen or more seats was still empty, right at the front on the left-hand side. Korshak touched Rikku's shoulder and indicated them with a nod of his head. "Who are those seats for? Any idea?"

"No, I haven't. Must be a special category of some kind."

"There don't seem to be many in it."

But even as Korshak spoke, a side door opened, and a line of robed figures with cowls covering their faces filed silently out and took their places in the empty row. He recognized them as the Genhedrin caste that he had seen in the refectory at lunch the day before.

Then a burly, bearded figure in a dark gray robe with the hood thrown back—Banker Lareda, no less— appeared from the wings and mounted the rostrum steps to commence the proceedings. He extended his arms, and with the exception of the row of Genehdrin, who continued to sit solemn and motionless, the hall rose. Korshak's briefing the day before had prepared him for what to expect. The first item, led by Lareda in his resounding bass-baritone, was the Dollarian anthem, "Prevail and Prosper," in keeping with the general spirit, somewhere between a hymn and a march, delivered by the entire company with full-throated fervor. Memorizing the words had been one of Korshak's initial tasks, and he sang along with all the vigor and expression of an earnest believer and seeker at last finding his element. The chances had to be pretty good, he figured, that the place was monitored by recording cameras. Everyone then sat, and Lareda proceeded into a series of inspirational messages and announcements for the day that turned out to be the buildup for the principal dignitary to be appearing that morning, who had materialized from the rear and moved forward to the rostrum side of the stage as the introduction was made. Lareda then descended the steps and stood aside deferentially to make way for Archbanker Sorba. Applause was evidently not in order. The hall sat in rapt and expectant silence.

Sorba wore an ankle-length cope richly embroidered in gold and yellow, with a red cassock and skullcap. He had a white, flowing beard that reached to the top of his chest, and a pink, yet delicately formed face in which his eyes caught the hall lights to gleam like pinpoints of metal as he turned his head this way and that to emphasize a point or underline a pause, every move and tone studied and calculated. As one who had devoted many years of his life to mastering the arts of communication, persuasion, and suggestion, Korshak was impressed—and mindful of the effect it was having on those around him.

The first part of Sorba's address reaffirmed some of the key articles of party doctrine, most of which Korshak was familiar with by now. The importance that the present administration was giving to unity and cooperativeness conflicted with the ideal of diversity stressed by the mission's founders. The idea of people wanting to live in harmony sounded nice, but it stultified the spirit of aggressive self-reliance that the descendants on Hera would have to preserve if they were to have a viable future. The way to preserve it was through the dynamic of robust competition and the accompanying cultivation of excellence that had prevailed across the old world. From the Dollarian movement that would protect the vision of *Aurora* today would grow the power capable of building the new world tomorrow. That was the first time Korshak had heard it openly declared that the aim was to gain political power over the mission. He noted also that all the way through, Sorba made constant references to ancient Earth and its peoples, stressing their cultural and genetic heritage, and kinship to those present. It was an effective ploy for winning the sympathies of people in the present circumstances, alone in the vastness of space with only memories and records to link them them with their ancestral home.

At that point Sorba paused portentously and swept his eyes around the auditorium. His voice lightened to a more conversational tone. "Yesterday evening, I was talking with Banker Lareda, and he told me about a newcomer among us that he interviewed recently, who was drawn to the movement by a desire to learn more of the power that ruled over the old world. And this was very good. It's a sign that our word is spreading and being listened to. However, this newcomer saw it purely as a secular technique, effective in attaining material accumulation and physical superiority in the battles of human affairs. He dismissed the reality of any higher source of inspiration and guidance because some of the other . . . shall we say 'bodies'? . . . that we are obliged to share space with here on Etanne have professed simplistic beliefs, and used elementary deceptions in their attempts to promote them. I have heard this kind of thing before, and it disturbs me."

Sorba paused to let the hall reflect on this, his

arms braced, hands gripping the edges of the lectern at the front of the rostrum. "It disturbs me greatly, and I want to say a few words for the benefit of any others who may be harboring similar inclinations toward such a mistaken impression. . . . Can anyone really believe that a force with the potency to win over an entire planet, finally triumphing over all its adversaries and rivals, drew its strength from nothing more than ambitions of avarice and domination? Yes, it had the effect of satisfying such desires, but these were *effects*, not *causes*! In the same way, the fact of being alive gives rise to needs for us to eat and breathe, and the needs manifest themselves as desires that prompt us to appropriate action. Eating and breathing are not the causes of life, but serve the needs that are in its nature. And so it is in the nature of human cultures to expand and prevail, and it is this nature that derives from a higher plane of life that calls forth the actions that are appropriate to those ends."

The whole audience was tense and silent as it took in the message. Sorba raised his hand and extended a finger for emphasis. "Let no one here be mistaken. The universe consists of more than the stars and nebulas and galaxies that we see extending away in whatever direction we look—however far into the unprobed depths of physical space they may extend! Because there is a realm that transcends physical space, from which flows powers that defy the limits that physical dimensions impose, and *this* is the source from which life and growth are driven. And here lie the roots of who and what we are."

Rikku, who had an open viewpad on his knee and

was making notes with a stylus, gave Korshak a quiet nudge, as if to say *I told you*.

On the rostrum, Sorba continued, "I will remind you of some of the things you have heard that you may have forgotten. The fiscal sages of the old order knew and were in communication with this reality. That was what gave them mastery over a whole world. Sofi, despite its material achievements, could never equal them. There are some of us today, who are rediscovering that reality. In our day-to-day routine—and especially in our dealings with others outside of the order—we tend not to discuss this side of our activities. This is partly because the time is not ripe yet for a proper understanding and acceptance of what we have to offer. And not least, to avoid our being thought guilty of the kinds of trickery resorted to by our neighbors, that I alluded to a moment ago."

Sorba's voice fell, drawing the last iotas of attention like a receding light. "But I will now share something with you that I would not normally divulge, even in a gathering such as this, because it is pertinent to what I have been saying. Those among us who have attained, shall we say, a deeper level of contact with the reality that lies beyond the senses, are sometimes privileged with knowledge that is not explainable within the framework of the perceived one-way cause-and-effect relationship that the nature of physical reality imposes. In short, events that have yet to come to pass can reveal themselves to us." Sorba shrugged dismissively. "Among certain religious systems that I remember from past years on Earth, that entertained aspirations or pretenses of that nature, it was known as prophecy. We choose not to glorify ourselves with any such appellations, but accept it simply as a fact of the condition to which our explorations have led us." He turned his head for a moment to gaze at the row of cowled Genhedrin.

"I'm sure I don't have to remind anyone here of the serious situation we face as a result of our growing numbers and the finiteness of our material resources—a situation that will persist far into the future, beyond the lifetimes of any of us. Nor do I need to comment on the irresponsibility of the *Envoy* project, which intends to send an invaluable portion of those resources away to where they can be of no tangible use or benefit in helping to alleviate the situation. Many voices are being raised across Constellation to contest the decision. And yes, we add ours to them because it gains us sympathy and visibility, which advances our cause."

A thoughtful expression came over Korshak's face as his eyes followed Sorba's to look again at the Genhedrin. The first problem he faced was determining the whereabouts of Tek. All members of the order were required to attend the daily General Meeting, he had been told. *All?* Right there, just a matter of yards away, was a perfect means for concealing a member of the company that might otherwise have trouble passing muster visually. Interesting.

Sorba continued, "But let me tell you now that, useful as they may be in elevating the public consciousness, the fears are ungrounded. So you may all sleep easily and devote your energies to other things. Why do I say this? Because the vision of the future that I have seen reveals that *Envoy* will not become a reality. Can I prove it to you? No, because demands for proof are applicable to the mechanical reality of matter and forces that we have risen beyond. It is something that I *know* with a certainty based on faith, which I am asking you to share. The same faith that gave the Dollar"—Sorba half turned and raised an arm to indicate the large $ sign suspended above the stage—"hegemony over Earth. And the faith that will see it rise again one day, over Hera! I leave this message with you, so that when the reality unfolds as has been foreseen, then all of you, too, will believe."

Sorba straightened up at the rostrum and looked squarely out at the hall. *"Prosper and Prevail!"*

"AMEN!" came the mass response.

Furch came up to Korshak and Rikku afterward, amid the figures milling and dispersing in the foyer outside the Assembly Hall doors. "What did you think?" he asked eagerly. His face was still radiant after the revelations.

"It exceeds all my dreams!" Rikku enthused. "I've truly arrived at my destiny."

"Well, you did pick a somewhat exceptional day to begin."

"No, I mean it."

"And you, Shakor?"

"Can I wait until we see what happens with *Envoy*?" Korshak replied. He knew it wasn't the right answer to give but said it anyway.

Furch looked at him reproachfully. "You know, you only erect your own barriers to advancement with such an attitude," he said.

"I'm sure the company and support here will change it," Rikku put in. "Remember, Shakor has had an unusual, solitary situation to contend with."

"I'm glad that you understand," Korshak acknowledged.

Furch was looking at him strangely, his head inclined to one side. "I wouldn't be surprised if you were the newcomer that Archbanker Sorba was talking about just now," he said. Korshak grinned faintly, shrugged, and said nothing.

"Well, Rikku and I have things to do this morning," Furch told him. "Is there anything you need me to help you with?"

"No. I think that Banker Lareda has arranged for me to introduce myself in the workshops. My past experience should make me useful there."

"Do you know the way?"

"I'm sure I can find it, thanks. And I have to collect some things from my cell first."

"Very well, then. We'll see you later, Shakor. Possibly at lunch."

Korshak was tempted to say that he wasn't up to prophesying things like that yet, but thought better of it.

He made his way through to the dormitory section of narrow passages and doors, and ascended two levels to the tiny cell he had been given, designed to accommodate two but with no other occupant at present. It contained two cots, chairs, closets, and standard viewpads for use as study terminals, a shared table and set of shelves, and a washbasin. Inside, he closed the door, made sure it was secure, and then retrieved his bag from inside the closet he was using and set it down on one of the cots. Lois had obtained it from Lubanov's people somehow and shown him how to use it.

It had the look of being well used, and was of a

modest-size backpack design, as would be appropriate
for anyone spending time on a place like Plantation.
One of the things that was unusual about it, however,
was the adjustment slide on the right-hand strap,
which, when pressed the right way, opened out on
one edge and came away as a flat box-shape with one
of its sides open—like a pair of square, parallel jaws.
Korshak detached it and turned to the table where
the two viewpads were lying. Taking one of them, he
turned it around and located the quartz aperture at
the rear that the unit's infrared signals passed through
to communicate with equipment built into the room.
He slipped the jaws around the edge of the viewpad,
positioning it such that the aperture aligned with the
interface disk on the inside of the hinge piece, and
clipped the attachment tight.

One of the first things Korshak had discovered was
that novices were not permitted regular phones—he
wasn't sure yet how far this might be the case with
other ranks also. Lubanov's people must have known
it, too, which made Korshak suspect that more had
transpired than Lubanov's merely "wanting" to put
somebody inside the Academy as Lois had been told.
But the inmates needed to study, and if life was not
to be made impossibly restricted, that would mean
having access to the general Constellation web and
the resources that it served. The model of viewpad
provided in the novices' cells didn't include regular
communications capability. However, to be usable it
had to send command information into the web as
well as return desired information from it. The attachment that Korshak had fitted over its input-output
port enabled information from a chip built into the

backpack slide to be multiplexed into the outgoing signal. Equipment operated by Lubanov's office would detect an identifying header in the signal and extract whatever message had been piggybacked on it. The only thing needed now was a means of creating and inserting such a message, and of retrieving whatever came back the other way.

Korshak turned to his bag again and took out a handheld reader of the kind used for perusing documents and other information stored in removable chips. Such devices provided a convenient way of carrying many books around, and again would be a normal possession for somebody of an intellectual bent leading a reclusive existence. Except that Korshak's reader wasn't normal. One of the books in its stored library contained a page that looked innocent, but which had been contrived to include every character and mark of the language somewhere at least once. Touching the appropriate sequence with the point of a pen caused the message thus spelled out to be written into a location on the reader's removable chip. Inserting the chip into the viewpad attachment would then impress it onto the next outgoing signal, using Etanne's own communications infrastructure to convey it to its destination. Incoming messages worked the other way, and became viewable on the reader.

Korshak activated the viewpad, and using its symbolic repertoire composed a command for access to the web archives. When the requested page appeared, he extracted the chip from the viewpad attachment and inserted it into the handheld reader. Interrogating it produced a code signifying that a message had been received. He had been expecting a response to the one he had sent the previous evening to test the channel and confirm his arrival. The screen displayed:

Your test received. Please acknowledge.
Nothing further here for now. Standing by.

Korshak grunted, cleared the screen, and brought up the composition page to prepare a reply. It seemed they were in business. The corners of his mouth twitched upward at the aptness of the term.

~ THIRTY ~

Masumichi Shikoba had been growing increasingly nervous while he waited, with the result that when the house computer finally chimed and announced the callers at the door, he practically leapt up from the stool where he had been fiddling with a piece of circuitry on the bench. A shot on the wall screen showed Andri Lubanov standing outside as expected, along with another man that Masumichi didn't know. Leaving Kog standing switched off in a corner, he went through to the hallway to receive them himself. Lubanov's manner of cool, dispassionate efficiency had always unnerved him to some degree. Now, on top of that, Masumichi's mind had been conjuring up all kinds of visions of the trouble that his deviousness, compounded by the theatrical attempt to cover it up, might have gotten him into. Why else would the head of the bureau that handled the more sensitive of Ormont's dealings want to come here in person, with the reason being given that it had to do with Tek?

Lubanov was of lean build but comparatively broad across the shoulders, with a straight mouth, austere, hollow-cheeked features, and pale blue eyes set beneath a broad, round brow and hair that was close-cropped even though thinning. He slipped off a light topcoat as he entered, revealing a gray two-piece suit and a straight-neck shirt of the same hue. The man with him was younger, with a somewhat fleshy face and full head of straight yellow hair, combed to one side.

"We were slightly delayed," Lubanov said. "This is Hala Vogol, who works with me. And Hala, Masumichi Shikoba—the key person behind the next generation of robots that we can expect to see." Masumichi acknowledged the introduction with a slight bow. Vogol returned a nod.

Masumichi turned to the doorway opening into the lab, but at the same time indicated the spiral staircase. "We can go up to the apartment if you prefer. It's more comfortable up there."

"Down here will be fine. We won't keep you long," Lubanov returned.

"As you wish." Masumichi led the way into the lab, with Vogol following at the rear, turning his head in bewilderment at the tree growing up through its hole in the ceiling. Then his expression changed to one of interest and curiosity as he took in the profusion of immobile robots, partly assembled robots, countertops with bits of robots, and racks of electronic equipment filling the room. Masumichi moved the stool that he had been using across to his desk, which was wedged in a corner beneath loaded bookshelves and a graphics station, and moved a box to clear space on another. Vogol sat down, but Lubanov paused to study the exposed wiring and crystal-matrix arrays of an opened head. Masumichi lowered himself into the chair facing them.

"Integral telescopic and microscopic vision," Masumichi supplied. "At least, that's the idea. So far we've only tried out bench simulations."

"Hm. Interesting." Lubanov turned away and moved forward to prop himself loosely on the unoccupied lab stool, his weight still supported by his legs. "About a month ago, Tek went with you on a visit to Istella," he said without preliminaries.

Here it comes, Masumichi thought. He swallowed and struggled to maintain a neutral face, which he felt was radiating his thoughts like a neon sign regardless. "An essential part of equipping artificial intelligences is to give them exposure to as wide a range of experiences as possible," he replied. "It emulates the world knowledge that humans acquire in the course of living. Istella seemed to offer a suitable extreme."

Lubanov's eyebrows rose. "So I would imagine. But he went astray there, and you asked Korshak if he'd try and track him down for you."

Masumichi licked his lips and nodded, at the same time interlacing his fingers to prevent his hands from shaking. He was overreacting even in his own eyes, but found he couldn't prevent it. "Korshak has worked with me over the years. He knew Tek."

"Yes, he'd owe you, too, wouldn't he," Lubanov said. "You arranged his escape from Arigane, along with his wife."

"That's right." Was there anything Lubanov didn't already know? Masumichi had gone over the questions that he anticipated and tried to rehearse answers. *How did Tek come to be alone? Where were you when he disappeared?* But already it seemed futile. Lubanov could probably tell him. He braced himself.

But instead, Lubanov asked casually, "Have you seen or heard anything of Tek since?"

Masumichi shook his head.

"So you don't know where he is?"

"No."

"I thought they had electronic communications access. Can't you locate them through that?"

"They have the ability to close it down. It's a bit complicated to explain, but it has to do with the internal psychology that we're trying to develop."

Lubanov nodded that there was no need to go into it. He looked at Masumichi for a few seconds longer, and then said, "Actually, Tek is on Etanne. So is Korshak. They're both inside the Dollarian Academy there. We have a means of communicating with Korshak. But for reasons that needn't concern us for now, we would also very much like to gain access to Tek. But that's not possible at the moment, for the reason you've just given. We're hoping that Korshak will be able to persuade Tek to cooperate in changing that. What we'd like is your help in setting up whatever would be needed at this end. That's why we're here."

As Lubanov spoke, Vogol produced a notepad and pen from his pocket. Masumichi blinked. That was it? All they wanted was some technical help? His personal life had nothing to do with it? He found himself wanting almost to laugh out loud in relief. He opened his hands expansively. "Well, of course.... What do you wish to know?"

"What kind of communications does Tek have?" Lubanov asked. "Regular web video and data pickup? Some kind of special interfacing? Or what?"

"Regular Grade 3 two-way web capability," Masum-ichi replied.

Vogol scribbled a note. "So you can talk to it via standard web devices: phone, viewpad...."

"Correct—provided Tek has it enabled."

"So Tek can hook into Etanne's grid?"

"The internal local-distribution grid, yes. But not the interworld trunk beams. We never had any need for something like that."

Vogol wrote some more and looked up. "Isn't there something called a neural interface, too? How does that work?"

Masumichi was momentarily surprised that they knew about that; but then, if they were in touch with Korshak it made sense, he supposed. "It's a technique for bypassing the conventional interface devices—touchpads, screens, helmets, bodysuits—and coupling the robot's senses directly into the operator's brain," he replied. "Likewise, motor commands from the operator go the other way and drive the robot's actuators. To a limited degree, it creates the illusion of actually being the robot." Masumichi grinned, restored to his normal self now. "It's an interesting experience, and quite an ingenious technical feat, even if I do say so myself. Kog, over there in the corner, is equipped with the current version. Tek had an experimental prototype fitted as an add-on."

Lubanov was looking interested. "Are you saying that the remote operator can see and hear what's going on where the robot is?" he checked.

"Exactly."

"And take over its movements, again as if he were there himself? Look for things? Examine things?"

"Well . . . yes." Masumichi was at a loss to guess what might be the point of this.

"What kind of interface does the operator use?" Vogol asked.

In answer, Masumichi got up, walked around to some shelves, and came back holding an intricate head harness made up of metallized straps, stretch panels, and tapes thick with pickups and microwiring. It extended down over the ears as two side pieces to join a collar that hinged into two halves, from which a cable terminating in a jumble of connectors protruded toward what would be the rear of the wearer.

"This connects to an antenna unit that beams to the robot," he said.

"Beams?" Vogol repeated. "Are you saying it needs line of sight?"

"Correct."

Lubanov took the harness and turned it over in his hands curiously. "Does that mean you couldn't connect to Tek, with Tek inside Etanne?" he asked.

"You couldn't use the neural coupler," Masumichi replied. "It's too high a bandwidth. As Mr. Vogol says, that needs a line-of-sight beam."

"There's no way around that?"

Masumichi wrinkled his face up and thought about it. "Not anytime soon. These things are always possible. But you'd be talking about some extensive development and testing. I get the impression you are looking for something sooner."

Lubanov passed the harness to Vogol. "Tomorrow. Two days at most," Lubanov said.

"Oh, great galaxies!" Masumichi shook his head. "No way, I'm afraid."

Lubanov stared at him for a second or two, then nodded resignedly. "So we could use this neural interface when the robot is where the beam can see it. But with it inside Etanne or otherwise out of sight, we're limited to a regular web channel."

"That's about it," Masumichi confirmed.

"But we'd still be able to monitor the robot's vision and audio via a regular channel," Vogol pointed out. "And if it can be induced to cooperate, we could direct it by voice."

Lubanov nodded. "That should be sufficient," he agreed.

"It's our only choice," Vogol said.

Lubanov turned back to Masumichi. "One more thing. I should tell you that this is a sensitive matter that relates to the highest level of general security. Nothing of what we have said here is to be repeated. Confine any discussions strictly to technical issues."

"I understand," Masumichi said.

"Interesting?" Lubanov asked Vogol, who was examining the harness.

"Very," Vogol replied. "I've read things about the concept but never actually seen it implemented. I'd be very interested to try it out while we're here. It would give me a better idea of what it can do."

"Would it be possible for us to see a demonstration?" Lubanov asked Masumichi.

"Oh, I think that could be arranged," Masumichi said, rising and rubbing his hands together briskly.

It seemed that this wasn't working out to be such a bad day after all.

~ THIRTY-ONE ~

For reasons that Tek had been told would become clear in due course, the leadership did not wish it to be generally known that a robot had joined the order. Some among them had therefore been opposed to its attending the General Meetings because of the entailed risk of revealing the fact. Tek wasn't supposed to know this, but something that humans who were inexperienced in robotics seemed unaware of was that, at the cost of reducing attentiveness elsewhere, Tek was able to switch its hearing to a higher sensitivity than that which humans possessed. Consequently, they sometimes failed to make appropriate allowances for range and volume when they thought they were speaking privately. Banker Lareda, however, who had championed Tek's interest in the Dollarians from the beginning, had considered it important for Tek to experience the same motivation and sense of belonging as any other inductee, and had overruled the objection.

Lareda's insight had been profound indeed. Tek's daily excursions from the rooms where it remained out of sight, meeting only representatives of the few who knew of its existence, were like an inflow of vigor and inspiration enabling it to feel as one with the movement. The high point had come three days previously, when Archbanker Sorba had spoken. The Illustrious One's revelations had borne out all the things that Tek had been intuiting and connecting together in its studies. The headiness of the discoveries came again now, as Tek pulled the cowl forward around its head, drew the thin face piece down inside, and joined the Genhedrin in the side room off the Assembly Hall, lining up to make their customary entry. They didn't speak or otherwise identify themselves to each other. Tek had full trust that the leaders knew best in not wishing to advertise its presence, and this cover provided the ideal means. Banker Lareda had confided that Tek had been selected to carry out a special mission that was of crucial importance to the future of the order and would ensure Tek's immortalization as a sainted figure. To be accorded such an honor after being introduced so recently was almost frightening in the status that it implied. Tek only hoped it would prove worthy when the time came. The decision not to draw attention to it was very likely to avoid arousing envy among others in the order, the robot surmised.

The precise nature of Almighty Dollar, the supreme god worshiped across the ancient human world, was something that Tek hadn't yet worked out. But already the picture it had assembled of the universal Church, encompassing all nations, races, politics, and lands, that had arisen in acknowledgment of its supremacy evoked wonder and reverence. The major cities of old had vied with one another in erecting soaring temples dedicated to its glorification. Their main purpose had been to attract Dollar into choosing them as places to reside in, for it had been an itinerant god that moved from place to place to favor the most deserving followers. Sins of laxity and complacency would bring retribution in the form of the Flight of Dollar, while diligence and fortitude earned maximized blessings in its Returns.

For the citizens who existed in those times, their religion had dominated every aspect of life. No transaction was made, nor sphere of activity proposed, without a consecration ritual submitting it to the valuation and approval of the Supreme Arbiter. To be judged unworthy of a Credit blessing was one of the gravest failings, a condition deemed to be insoluble. Many sects of specialized priesthoods, some of whose orders were recalled in the titles of the Dollarian ecclesiastical hierarchy, devoted their lives to mastering the Church's secret rites and counseling the faithful.

The door ahead was opened, and the file of solemn figures emerged to walk to their accustomed seats. Tek could almost feel the eyes and attention of the hall palpably as it faced the stage, and couldn't resist turning up its hearing sensitivity and performing a quick scan of the surroundings to pick up what others might be remarking on the entrance of itself and the Genhedrin. Surely they would be overcome by awe and reverence.

"Are you serious? My grandmother could have thrown a shotball farther than him. Three to one, you say? You're on. . . ."

"And you left it on Plantation? Sure, I know someone there who'd be interested. How much are you asking for it?"

"We both saw him coming out of her place on Istella. But for Dollar's sake don't tell anyone. . . ."

Ah well, Tek thought, it was probably early days yet for some when it came to inner advancement, even if their formal ranks might suggest otherwise. In time they would rise beyond such shallowness and awaken to the enlightenment that comes from within.

Tek felt bodings of great events soon to unfold as Banker Lareda mounted the rostrum steps to lead the hall in the Dollarian anthem. Exhilaration surged through the robot as it stood, soaking up the atmosphere, for the Genhedrin didn't sing. When the last chorus had subsided, they all sat for Lareda to begin the day's address and lesson. There was nothing really new this time; the topics were all either ones Tek had heard before or come across in the course of its studies since arriving on Etanne. Nevertheless, the feeling of participating along with the entire company of the movement was sufficiently intoxicating and uplifting in itself—as it always was.

And then a strange thing happened. A data flag in Tek's imaging system registered a strong input outside the normal optical-frequency band. The robot identified its source as a patch on the rear wall of the stage, behind the rostrum where Lareda was speaking, that was emitting or reflecting in the infrared. The patch moved even as Tek registered it, and then came into focus as the sacred sign of the Dollar. The design traversed the wall slowly until it was almost at one side of the stage, and then reversed direction to trace an arc upward and over, and then down again toward the other side.

What did it mean? It couldn't have been intended for the audience in general, because humans couldn't see in the infrared. Tek glanced from side to side, just to be sure. Not a head was turning or showing any sign of awareness of the phenomenon. So could it be?

Surely not.

A sign from Almighty Dollar meant for Tek alone? A portent bespeaking the importance of the special task that was to be assigned to it?

Tek raised its head almost fearfully to follow as the $ symbol climbed the wall again to move out over the stage and hover on the ceiling above the front of the auditorium. It halted there, and for a fraction of a second its brightness fluctuated in a rapid series of pulsations, then steadied again. This repeated twice more. Tek compared the short-term retention records and determined that the sequence of pulses had been identical in each case. Analysis quickly identified the pattern of fluctuations as a standard communications code. The plaintext rendering read:

I speak only to you, Tek. A messenger has been sent and will reveal himself. Watch for further signs.

And the vision was gone.

Tek was still in too much of a daze to function coherently when the Genhedrin rose and left the Hall, thirty minutes later.

Rikku, sitting next to Korshak, making notes on his viewpad during the Meeting on the first day, had given him the idea. Working some time into his assigned hours in the workshops over the next few days, he had contrived a small infrared projector and oscillator that fitted inside the case of a regular stylus that he took, along with his own viewpad, to the Meeting the following morning. As he had observed previously, numerous members of the audience were similarly equipped, and his idle toying with the stylus while he listened to the speaker had attracted no attention. The single head among the seated Genhedrin that had reacted when he flashed the image on the rear wall of the stage, and then followed it on its side-to-side excursions and up overhead, had told Korshak all he needed to know.

His next objective was to establish some form of two-way dialog. He hadn't determined yet how he would go about this. In his three days since joining the Academy, he had seen Genhedrin from time to time, moving silently among the normal traffic of people in the concourses and corridors, so the most straightforward approach seemed to be to set up a rendezvous with Tek somewhere. But Korshak hadn't settled on a way to do this without revealing himself, which would give the game away since Tek knew him from his work with Masumichi. The purpose of persuading Tek to spy for Lubanov would be served more effectively if Tek continued believing that it was being guided by a supernatural, almighty power.

"I suppose you think this makes you exceptional in some way." Broker Morgal, the supervisor of the workshops, sniffed and straightened up from peering critically at the water line booster pump running on the bench.

"I was just showing that it seems to be fixed," Korshak said. The pump fed the showers and other plumbing in the senior washroom. Banker Lareda had complained that instead of turning off when it was supposed to, it would go into a "hunting" cycle of switching itself off and on indefinitely. After Morgal dismissed it as a design flaw that couldn't be fixed,

Korshak had fitted a couple of nonreturn valves to the hot and cold outputs, which rectified matters.

Morgal had been picking on anything Korshak did since the first day. Whether it was simply his nature, or because he felt threatened by a show of competence in another, Korshak didn't know—or especially care. "There's more to being an effective competitor that just showing how smart you think you are," Morgal griped. "Who do novices think they are, coming in here and trying to show *me* my job?" Korshak looked aside and sent a helpless look to Accountant Trewany, another workshop artisan, of the same rank as Furch, who was turning a bearing liner on a lathe a short distance away and trying not to look as if he was overhearing. Trewany shrugged, shook his head, and bent to his work. "How much was the time worth that you spent fooling with this, eh?" Morgal demanded. "You never thought about that, did you? You wouldn't even have known how to put a figure to it. But you think you're a Dollarian adept already. If I'd wanted it done this way, I'd have said so, wouldn't I?" He stalked away toward his cubicle at the end of the room, at the same time throwing back over his shoulder, "Since you've wasted the time on it, you might as well go ahead and reinstall it."

Korshak waited until Morgal had disappeared, then moved over to stand watching Trewany. "Is he always like this, or did I just pick a bad week?"

"He takes Dollarian principles very seriously. Competing and winning dominate his life. He says that's how things were in the old world."

"Surely they couldn't have been like that everywhere, all the time."

"Oh, probably not," Trewany agreed. "I'm sure they had to stand together against outsiders. But in their internal dealings with each other, everyone needs to ease up."

"Well, I'm relieved to hear that," Korshak said. "But it would be nice to see more evidence of it."

Trewany stopped the lathe and reached for a laser micrometer to check a dimension. His mouth curved upward briefly. "How long have you been here, Shakor? Three days? That makes you an outsider in the eyes of most people. Give them time. Maybe after you see one of the Phantasmians' shows you'll find we're not all so bad."

"Who are the Phantasmians?" Korshak asked.

"You see. You haven't even heard of them, and you rush to judge us already. Our week is mostly a sober affair of business and study. But every weekend we have a performance of mixed acts and entertainments in the Assembly Hall to relax and appreciate some artistry. The Phantasmians are the group who organize it, but anyone can enter."

Korshak was intrigued. "What kind of entertainments do they have?" he asked.

Trewany shrugged. "Anything, really. Dramatic pieces, recitations, music, juggling and balancing acts, even a dash of buffoonery to lighten things up. You probably won't believe it, but Banker Lareda did a comic magic act not long ago, lampooning the antics of the Mediators next door on Etanne. I take it you know of them?"

"I've heard of them," Korshak said. "I can't say I was really sold, though."

"Cheap trickery," Trewany pronounced. "I'm amazed

that anyone could fall for it. You know, Shakor, I sometimes wonder if it was a good thing, trying to make
the original *Aurora* population a reflection of human
diversity. It could have been a wonderful opportunity
to select what was brightest and best, and have that
as the seed that would shape the world that is to
come on Hera. Don't you think?"

"By concentrating more on people like us, you
mean," Korshak said.

Trewany looked surprised as he replaced the micrometer and opened the jaws of the lathe chuck to release
the workpiece. "Why, yes. What else?"

Korshak smiled affably but said nothing. It had
never ceased to amaze him how so many seemed to
think that the world would be a better place, and all
its problems go away if only everyone else could be
more like them. He returned to the bench where he
had been working and turned off the pump prior to
disconnecting it.

A deeply thoughtful mood had overtaken him by
the time he left, carrying the pump and a toolbox,
ten minutes or so later.

The Repository on the basement level kept stocks of
just about all things used in the Academy, from robes
and viewpads to pieces of furniture and kitchenware.
Xaien lifted a bundle of bedsheets fresh from the
laundry off of the cart and stowed them in a space on
one of the linen shelves. "I know it was part of the
gospel, but I could never see how it could work," he
said to Nerissa, who had delivered the load and was
airing some views on doctrine before she returned.
She argued compulsively about anything, seemingly

from need of constant reassurance that she could always come out on top. "So you had this ideal of a free market. Very well, let's suppose that it existed. Now, just because of the way the world is, some people, either because they're smarter, work harder, are just lucky, or for whatever reason, will do better than others. Right? So they have more dollar power to command laws that will benefit themselves and penalize everyone else, at which point a free system ceases to exist. So it's inherently unstable."

"Not at all. Because the point you're missing is that—" Nerissa's voice broke off as another figure appeared in the open doorway of the store room. He peered around, saw them, and stepped inside. He was in his later thirties, maybe, lithely built, with dark eyes, close-cropped hair, barely more than stubble, and dressed in the white tunic of a junior clerk–grade novice.

"Yes?" Xaien asked, moving out from the aisle between the shelves. "Can we help you?"

In response, the newcomer produced a yellow ball from his pocket. Saying nothing, he held it out at arm's length for a moment, and then turned his hand over so that the ball rolled into the back of it. Raising his hand slightly, he caused the ball to roll the length of his arm to the shoulder, then by hunching his back, across behind his neck to the other shoulder, and finally all the way out to the back of his other hand, where in seeming defiance of gravity it continued over the tips of his fingers to settle into his waiting palm.

Xaien was about to say something, and then realized that the act wasn't finished yet. The novice showed the ball again, passed it to the other hand, showed it once more, then brought his two hands together in a mutual massaging motion, slowly compressing the space between them until they were rubbing palm to palm. He then turned them outward and open to reveal them empty. Xaien heard Nerissa gasp behind him. The novice pointed into the air, moving his arm as if he were following an object around the room. Suddenly he snatched at something and made a throwing motion toward his other hand, which he then opened to reveal not one, but two balls. The novice grinned expectantly.

"Wow!" Nerissa breathed.

"*That* was cool," Xaien pronounced.

"My name is Shakor," the novice said. "I've been told about the weekly program that the Phantasmians put on, and I thought I might be able to contribute something to it."

"If you've got more acts like that, you could have the whole show," Xaien said.

"Really? I'm glad you think so. Look, I was thinking of making it a kind of comic routine, with a Genhedrin character. What do you think? Would that go down well?"

Xaien's face creased with mirth. "A Genhedrin as a comic magician? I love it!"

"I'd need to borrow a Genhedrin robe, then. This seemed to be the place to ask."

"Oh, I think we can help you out with that." Xaien began walking back toward some other shelves piled with robes, tunics, and various kinds of other garb. "It's a pity they don't let you talk much about yourself. It sounds as if it would make an interesting story. How long have you been here now ... ?"

❖   ❖   ❖

A plan that would allow him to confront Tek without being recognized had started to form in Korshak's mind, but he still needed to work out the details. Masumichi's research had focused on forms of robot intelligence to interact with a world that would be perceived primarily through vision—as was the case with humans. Although it would have been technically straightforward, he hadn't equipped them with a faculty for identifying voiceprints. Hence, all Korshak would need to do was disguise his appearance. The Genhedrin robe could have been designed for the purpose.

– THIRTY-TWO –

It was called the "Warhorse." Measuring approximately twelve feet in length overall, it took the form of two cylinders three feet across, set end to end and joined by a narrower waist to accommodate the rider. The front part constituted the bomb, a low-yield fission device salted with a mix of elements selected to produce a detonation signature resembling that of a baryonic-annihilation reaction, along with a grappling mechanism for attachment. The rear part of the Warhorse contained a thermally dark pressured-gas propulsion unit suitable for low-speed local maneuvering. The exterior surfaces were finished in a black matted-woven-fiber compound virtually invisible to regular local-surveillance-and-approach radars.

Banker Lareda pushed against the struts of its supporting cradle and the taut securing lines to propel himself slowly around it, inspecting the device from one end to the other and then back again. Broker Seesilan, who had supervised the engineering, watched from an anchor point at a support stanchion to one side, while two technicians from the Dollarian uniformed Executive branch looked on from farther back. It was early morning, before Lareda's appearance at the daily Meeting. They were in a service bay forming part of a warren of repair and maintenance shops located at the periphery of Etanne's wheel, in the outermost parts of the Dollarian sector. This area was off-limits to all but the highest ranking, and a select few organizers and technical specialists involved in the plan. The gravity synthesizers had been turned off to facilitate hauling the cradle over to the exterior-access lock chamber, through which the Warhorse would be moved outside.

Lareda paused at the waist to check over the rider's indicator panel and controls. In the course of the past few weeks they had been modified from their original layout to one that would suit a more humanoid form. He indicated a small display screen on the panel and turned his head. "This wasn't here before, was it? What's it for?"

"A visual numeric readout of position coordinates, velocity vector, status indicators, and a couple of other things," Seesilan replied. "The way we had it before, they would have been superposed on the operator's visual field." Lareda nodded and went through the controls, testing them for range and smoothness of movement. Satisfied, he moved on. It was appearing that the elaborately conceived, carefully implemented scheme would not have to be abandoned after all. Just when all had seemed irrevocably lost, a quirk of fate in a form that no one could have dreamed of had offered a bizarre solution.

The Warhorse had originally been equipped to carry the standard general-manipulator telebot acquired from one of the construction projects. The far side of the access lock from the bay they were in opened into a maze of housings and protrusions making up Etanne's exterior "tread." Directed by a human operator inside Etanne, the telebot was to have guided the Warhorse inward across the wheel to the main docking port in the hub complex, where it would attach to the outside of a ferry departing for *Aurora*. The telebot operating range was sufficient for the same operator in Etanne, when the next opportunity presented itself, to move the Warhorse to one of the long-distance shuttles leaving for *Outmark*. At the far end, another Dollarian operator, inserted in among the telebot controller crews at *Outmark*, would detach the Warhorse from the shuttle and move it out to *Envoy* using its own propulsion. Detonation would be remotely triggered to coincide with the launch fire command. It had all seemed so straightforward, yet ingenious. The program of agitation and publicity to prepare the public went ahead vigorously as planned.

But then, around a month previously, just when it had seemed that they would have a clear run, Lubanov had suddenly imposed security checks and supervisory rules that made any prospect of using the local telebot controllers at *Outmark* unthinkable. The telebots had nowhere near the range to operate over the quarter million miles from Constellation. There wasn't the time to come up with a radical alternative. In one crushing move, the entire plan was undone.

That was when word came back from Dollarians on Istella that a robot had appeared from somewhere and made approaches to the Mediators as a would-be recruit. Looking back, Lareda couldn't honestly recall who had first come up with it, but amid the banter of laughs and jokes among the upper hierarchy, the realization emerged that here could be a solution to the problem. With the right encouragement, here, perhaps, was a substitute rider that would be capable of operating autonomously in a space environment without need of any human controller or telebot link at all.

But obviously it had come from somewhere—it turned out to be a research program in Astropolis, and the robot was called Tek—and its owners would be missing it, which meant that people would be looking for it. So the first thing they had done was spirit it away to Plantation before one of the other cults, or anyone else, could get their hands on it, while the crazy idea was scrutinized and debated—and eventually adopted.

While the changes to the Warhorse were being rushed through, the question then arose of moving Tek to Etanne. Since the chances were that many eyes would be on the lookout by that time, a volunteer wearing the garb that had been used to bring Tek to Plantation took the ferry to Sarc. It was evidently as well that the precaution had been taken. The decoy was intercepted on arrival and directed to a rendezvous with some people who sounded like anything but research scientists. Almost certainly, they had been agents of Lubanov, who had been taking a disturbing interest in the Dollarians for some time, and even attempted on two occasions to infiltrate spies into the Academy. But by that time it didn't matter too much, since Tek had already made an inconspicuous exit from Plantation on the next ferry to Etanne.

Trying to fathom what went on in a robot's brain was a strange and frequently perplexing experience. Words didn't always communicate what one thought they were

communicating. The Dollarians who made the first proselytizing approach to Tek on Istella got into immediate
difficulties when Tek interpreted "stock dealing" and
"sharp practices"—relating to the old world—as having
something to do with the manipulation of gaming cards.
For some strange reason, Tek had a fixation on stage
magic and conjuring illusions, and could find meanings
for the most innocuous things in those terms. Probably
it was a result of being exposed to the Mediators and
their stunts before the Dollarians intervened.

Then events had taken a more fortuitous turn,
when Tek, after arriving on Plantation in disguise and
posing as an arrival looking for work, found its way
to the abode of an eccentric recluse forester. The
forester thought that the Dollarians were resurrecting
an old-world theistic religion, which led Tek to make
one of its inexplicable jumps of logic by concluding
that Dollar had been the name of the omnipotent
supernatural god that the old world had worshiped
universally. And this suited the Dollarians very well,
for it gave them not only the perfect operative for
the mission, physically and temperamentally, but one
who believed with the passion that only the divinely
inspired could command that in carrying it out, it would
be directly serving the ultimate Power that ruled the
universe and everything going on in it.

Envoy would launch in three days' time. The schedule
of ferries to *Aurora* and the frequency of shuttles going
out to *Outmark* gave a comfortable margin of time in
which to move the Warhorse into position. Everything
seemed to be working out very satisfactorily indeed.

"We'll plan on moving it out to *Aurora* tonight,"
Lareda said to Seesilan. "Later on today, I'll have Tek

brought here for a run-through and briefing. When can you have everything operational?"

"We've got some final adjustments and checks to go through," Seesilan replied. "Say, first thing this afternoon?" He sent an inquiring look at the two technicians, who returned nods.

"Have things ready by then. But now I must get ready for the Meeting."

"There is one other thing," Seesilan said.

"Oh?"

Seesilan gestured at the Warhorse. "The surface finish is about as nonreflective as it's possible to get. But what about this rider that you're talking about? It sounds to me as if we'll need some provision there, too. Some kind of covering with a hood, of the same material."

He had a point. Lareda reproached himself inwardly for not having thought of it. He nodded curtly. "I'll talk to Morgal in the workshops after the meeting and have them put something together right away. Carry on."

Launching himself with a light push, Lareda floated to the doorway, where his trajectory became a curve under the influence of the synthesizers, and landed him on his feet. He negotiated a series of passages and shafts that brought him to a chamber opening out through a secured door into the main part of the Academy. The spectacular failure of *Envoy* would add credence to everything the Dollarians had warned about, he thought to himself as he emerged. And then their numbers would grow.

Stressing competition and survival was a good recruiting tool that appealed to the human instinct to excel and seek recognition from peers. The emphasis on that side of human nature in the old world had been due to a commercial doctrine called capitalism, that divided enterprise among many privately directed interests and pitted them against each other. Such a system was effective in keeping everyone else divided against each other, while a cohesive controlling elite who excelled at working together to protect their common interests remained unchallenged and did very well. The same strategy would divide the population of Constellation, and with appropriate direction lead to the subtle and gradual accumulation of power in a way that would be invisible to the majority, with the few who were awake to what was happening being dismissed as cranks.

Where the old world had come undone was in the legacy it had no control over, of existing as a planetwide agglomeration of many powers whose mutual destruction had been as good as assured as soon as they acquired the technical means of bringing it about. That would not happen on Hera. By the time the mission's descendants made planetfall, they would do so as a single coherent society, schooled and disciplined to an idealized social design that would maximize efficiency and stability. The big problem with the old world had been that those who possessed the vision had never had the opportunity to take rightful command from the beginning. It would not be allowed to happen again.

Lareda's phone sounded just as he was entering the central concourse, heading for the Assembly Hall. The tone told him it was on a secure channel. He stepped into a recess behind a support column to be out of the general flow, and answered in a lowered voice. The caller was Archbanker Sorba.

"Are you alone?" he demanded.

"I'm just outside the Hall, but you can speak."

"Did you check on the horse?"

"I did, and all seems well. The rider will be briefed on it this afternoon for departure tomorrow, as planned."

"We need to bring it forward," Sorba said. "I have reports that a special-duty Police Arm unit has arrived at *Outmark*, equipped with heavy weapons. It's Lubanov's doing. I don't like it. There's talk that he's tightening up the checks on the shuttles leaving for *Outmark*. Get the horse to *Aurora* now."

"I'll get back to the techs and see what they can do," Lareda said.

"No. Don't ask them anything. Tell them. Call me back." The line cleared.

Lareda thought rapidly as he thumbed in the code for Seesilan. It would mean having the Warhorse sitting there for three days. If the launch engineers decided to run a thorough last-minute inspection of *Envoy*, it would all be over. But he could see no alternative. It was a risk they would just have to take.

"Seesilan."

"Lareda again. Look, I've just been told there's a change of plan. We're moving the horse out right away. Expect the rider there after the Meeting. You and the other two are excused attendance today. Get moving on things immediately."

- THIRTY-THREE -

Having a Genhedrin robe was like being given a passport to anywhere in the Academy. Korshak was able to wander at leisure among places where a novice's tunic would surely have attracted attention. And since it was customary not to engage the Genhedrin in talk unless they initiated it, nobody asked questions.

The door at the side of the Assembly Hall that the Genhedrin used opened into a passage that led to a landing serving a set of back stairs and an elevator, which was also where several other corridors met. It thus provided a convenient means for bringing them together from various locations before making their entrance to the morning meetings—more impressively done as a body, which was doubtless the intention. The passage entered the landing through a bulkhead door that was normally open, but which could be closed in the event of an emergency. An indicator panel mounted above the doorway gave information on pressure differential, locking status, and alert level when the door was closed.

The elevator, located across the landing from the bulkhead, was of a design that dispensed with doors and the chore of waiting. Two openings side by side gave direct access to a continuously moving chain of compartments, each large enough to take a person, one side going up, the other going down at a speed that permitted stepping on and off with comfort. On reaching the top of the ascending chain, a compartment shuttled sideways to become part of the descending chain. The design was used around Etanne but hadn't caught on among the other miniworlds of Constellation. Some said it was because the style blended in with Etanne's general image of utility and austerity. It was called a "grandfather train." Nobody knew why.

Ideally, everyone was supposed to attend the morning General Meetings as a psychological preparation for the day. In the real world, occasions arose when some other matter demanded priority, and this could happen to the Genhedrin as well as anyone else. It was therefore no cause for concern when, two days after Korshak's performance in the Repository, the line of figures in cowled gray robes filing through after the morning's ceremony to go their separate ways passed a similarly garbed form already stationed a few yards past the bulkhead doorway. Since none of them had reason to look back and up, they didn't notice the small device taped to the underside of the indicator panel, attached to a thin wire extending a short distance down the side of the doorway; and even if they had, the chances of their reading anything amiss into it would have been as good as nonexistent. But the tiny white reed flexing momentarily as Number Eleven in line passed by below told Korshak all he needed to know.

While others went off in different directions along

the corridors and up or down the stairs, Eleven joined several who were disappearing into the elevator, standing back to wait his turn. Korshak drew up behind moments later, brushing lightly against Eleven as he did so. In the process, he surreptitiously pressed a flake of congealed white paint on the back of Eleven's robe. Eleven stepped into the next empty compartment going up, and Korshak did likewise with the one following, which was also empty. As the floor of the compartment came level with the deck three stories up, a robed figure with a white smudge on its back was walking away along the corridor to one side. Korshak stepped out and followed.

The part of the complex that they were now in consisted mainly of small private rooms used by senior members of the order, not generally frequented by the rank and file. Eleven walked a short distance and stopped outside one of the doors. He seemed about to voice a command to open it, and then turned its head questioningly, as if just becoming aware of Korshak's presence. The Genhedrin cowl contained a face piece of thin muslin, effectively transparent to the wearer but masking his features from anyone else.

"You are the one who is known as Tek, who is not of flesh," Korshak intoned. "And I am the Messenger who you were told would reveal himself."

Tek turned slowly. The two face pieces enclosed by their cowls regarded each other. "Is it time?" the robot asked.

"No, but the time approaches," Korshak answered, not having a clue what they were talking about.

"How long do I have to prepare for the task?"

"We must always be prepared, Tek, for the call can come at any moment of any day."

"Yes. Of course." Tek inclined its head to take in Korshak fully. "And are you of human form, O Messenger?"

"I am. For those whose minds are newly opening, word given through a simple channel speaks more effectively. Inspired revelations can be mistaken for imaginings and delusions. But Masters who have risen above doubts can safely communicate directly."

"What name do you go by?" Tek asked.

"The form I have assumed for this errand is that of the humble novice who is known as Shakor."

A door opened a short distance away, and a man wearing the brown cloak of a broker emerged. He acknowledged their presence with a respectful nod and disappeared in the other direction. "The room here is private and at our disposal," Tek said, indicating the door. "I have exclusive use of it. . . . But you probably know that already."

This was going to be tricky, Korshak realized. He needed a lot of information from Tek. But the robot believed him to be the emissary of a supernatural intelligence that already knew everything. Asking too many questions, or asking them in the wrong way, could sound odd enough to arouse suspicion. He would have to tread carefully. First, however, there were the latest instructions from Lubanov's office to comply with.

"One selected to serve Almighty Dollar does not retreat to a dungeon like a mouse in hiding," he replied. "We will commune from where the mind and the soul can open out to the universe and the greatness of His creation."

"Lead, and I will follow."

Somehow, the grandfather elevator didn't seem an appropriate means of conveyance for a Messenger sent

on a divine errand. Shunning it for the stairs, Korshak
moved ahead with quiet dignity, yet at the same time
maintaining a noble and erect poise, his arms clasped
together in the deep sleeves of his robe. On reaching
the level of the central concourse, they passed through
it to the front lobby area, and without a glance in the
direction of the reception desk, carried on through the
main entrance to exit the Dollarian Academy. Korshak
had discovered in the course of his explorations that
Genhedrin, presumably along with other senior grades of
the hierarchy, were free to come and go without being
required to check in and out or offer any explanation.

They were now in the central part of Etanne's wheel,
where the communal facilities and supporting infrastructure were concentrated. The people about them
included figures in the assorted garbs of the other
Etanne-based cults, as well as some in the regular attire
of visitors there out of curiosity or just to spend a few
hours somewhere different. It was the first time that
Korshak had been out of the Dollarian sector since his
arrival, and he had to concentrate on remembering how
to get back to the service zone at the core, where he
had come through with Rikku. It wouldn't do for one
sent by Almighty Dollar to be seen losing his way.

The docking port was located at the wheel's center,
where ferries attached to a tapered cupola protruding as an extension of the axis. A glass-walled gallery
encircled the base of the cupola, forming a viewing
deck with an all-around vista of stars, and providing
catering facilities along with a shop, information desk,
and waiting areas for incoming and departing passengers. Korshak drew Tek around to a point where
Aurora, twenty miles off, was close to center in the

view above. They were between the times for scheduled ferry stops and there were not many people around, which made things easier. He stopped and turned his head upward, gesturing with a raised arm.

"Behold, Tek, the grandeur that speaks to us. You have wondered in the past at the knowledge of the humans who created you. But what are they or all their works, compared to this? And what power brought forth them?"

"You voice my innermost thoughts and memories," Tek murmured, following Korshak's gaze.

Not difficult, since they had talked about it in Masumichi's lab. "You must now open your mind and soul to the forces that will inspire," Korshak went on. This was the awkward bit. He needed Tek to reactivate the communications link that had been turned off since it went astray on Istella. But simply telling it to do so in so many words would risk shattering the whole illusion. Why would the Power that ran the universe have to depend on a human-made piece of electronics to convey what it had to say? Korshak was gambling that Tek would react automatically by unblocking all its sensory channels of its own accord. Tek stood waiting, immobile and enraptured.

Korshak retreated slowly, as if fearful that his proximity might intrude. Beneath his cowl, he was wearing a lightweight audio headset and pickup, also on loan from the Repository, courtesy of Xaien, and wanted to be sure he was out of range of the robot's high-sensitivity level of hearing. Since he didn't know what kind of monitoring the Dollarian internal-communications system might be subject to, he had refrained from using it inside the Academy. But out here he would be accessing the general Constellation web directly. According to the directions he'd been given, Lubanov's office should be standing by. He activated the circuit and spoke in little more than a whisper.

"Magician calling Wizardry. Testing. Do you read?"

Several anxious seconds passed; then a voice came through in Korshak's earpiece. "Wizardry reading you, Magician. What's the story?" The voice wasn't one that he recognized—presumably an operator on Lubanov's staff. They were aiming a beam at Etanne to try and connect with Tek's neural coupler.

"I'm on location as specified and have subject with me," Korshak replied. "We have a line of sight to *Aurora*. Have attempted reenable. You're clear for trial transmission now."

"Okay. . . . Let's give this a shot."

"You're working that end yourself?" Korshak was surprised. He had expected them to bring in Masumichi to operate the link.

"We'd rather handle this ourselves. I got some practice in with younger brother." A reference to Kog, Korshak presumed. A small child appeared in his field of vision and stood gawking up at him. Korshak tried to ignore him, but this just wasn't the time.

"Get lost," he hissed through the face-piece inside the cowl.

"Huh?" the voice said in his ear.

"Oh, sorry. Just something that's going on here."

A couple talking to a woman at a service desk a short distance away called, and the boy went trotting back.

Then: "Hey, I think we're in business. I'm seeing *Aurora* from where you are. We're also connected to Tek over a regular web voice channel. Since you're the one who knows the score there, you may have to tell me some of the things I need to say."

"How come I can still hear you now if you're on NC?" Korshak queried.

"Father is here, directing the technical side. He's doing some I/O juggling that I'm not sure I follow."

Father had to be Masumichi—which explained why he wasn't operating the neural coupler. It sounded as if he had set up some irregular Input-Output connections. Normally, if an operator was neurally connected, anything he said would be uttered by Tek, which was obviously not happening. Korshak moved closer to a support column with a noisy air-extraction grille, which he hoped would mask his voice more.

Tek's arms opened out and rose slowly, as if in a gesture of appeal toward the heavens. The robot's voice came through in Korshak's earpiece. *Aurora* had evidently patched him into the circuit. "An irresistible force invades my being! I am possessed!"

Normally, the robot's conscious awareness was suppressed when an NC operator took over—as if the robot were asleep for the duration—so it wouldn't be able to vocalize. It seemed that in this case Masumichi was leaving that faculty functioning for effect.

A man who had been passing by stopped to stare curiously. Hopefully he would just accept Tek's melodramatics as some kind of cult ritual to be expected on Etanne.

"The servant awaits," Tek announced.

"Okay, who am I?" the operator on *Aurora* asked.

"Since you're with Wizardry, I assume you're familiar with the Dollarian pitch," Korshak replied.

"Pretty much."

"Tek has gotten it confounded with old-world super-natural religion. You're Almighty Dollar, the ultimate spirit power that runs the universe. Tek thinks you've singled it out as a chosen agent. I'm the Messenger who confirmed it. Over to you. It's waiting for orders."

Korshak wondered how whoever was hooked into the NC interface would play this. The object of the exercise was to get Tek to agree to being a roving set of eyes and ears inside the Academy. But why would the almighty power that ran the universe need to depend on anyone's eyes or ears anywhere?

"You hear me as a voice in your mind, Tek. I am the one who was known across all of Earth long ago, and when the times are right there, I will appear again."

"Yes! I hear! I hear!" Tek acknowledged.

"But the errors that were made there will not be allowed to happen again on the world that is to be. Hera shall grow in the spirit of the true faith from its beginnings. That was why I caused the Academy to be founded, and why you were brought there. The time has come for the word to be spread and the people prepared."

Tek lowered its arms and turned to survey its surroundings. It took a few experimental steps, then began moving on a slow tour to take in more of the gallery. It seemed that the operator was enjoying himself.

"My soul surrenders!" Tek's voice exulted. "My body is possessed. The greater will asserts itself. What must I do?"

The robot identified Korshak and came closer to look him up and down.

"The Messenger you see before you is the first of many who will come forward. You, Tek, are to be the

*Medium by which I will communicate my bidding,
and through which each will share his intelligence,
one with another. Thus will many minds and many
bodies work as one in my service."*

"Does the Messenger hear us?" Tek asked.

*"The Messenger has not yet reached the plane that
connects you and I, Tek. He will require the physical methods of humans to communicate. As will the
others also."*

"So I should reopen the electronic ears that listen
to the voices of Constellation?"

"Yes."

Neat, Korshak thought to himself. "Does Almighty
Dollar speak to you?" he asked aloud, figuring that
he was expected to say something.

"Oh, yes, indeed, Messenger," Tek replied. "A Great
Design has been revealed to me. You are privileged
to be the first of others who will follow."

"Already, your horizons exceed my own," Korshak
said. "Of what nature is this design, and what will
be our part in it?"

The *Aurora* operator cut in, addressing Tek over
the NC beam and copied to Korshak. *"It is good that
the Messenger is eager, but he must be patient yet."*

"Your ardor commends you, Messenger," Tek relayed.
"But the time for you to know has not yet come. All
will be revealed as Dollar in His wisdom decides."

"So let it be," Korshak conceded.

*"You have done well, Tek. I leave you for now. Be
vigilant for the signs."*

"I shall do as commanded."

Korshak continued to regard Tek impassively while
the NC beam disconnected. The robot lowered its

head and relaxed its posture, seemingly contracting in stature and uncannily showing all the signs of someone coming out of a trance. "It is done?" Korshak inquired.

"For now, Messenger. But much work lies ahead. Meanwhile, let us return. I have meditations and preparations to attend to."

Korshak was amazed at how quickly their roles had reversed, with Tek now assuming primacy. But if Tek believed itself to be under divine inspiration and protection, so much the better. It would be that much more determined in whatever tasks it was assigned. Letting Tek set the pace now, striding firmly and purposefully, Korshak fell in a step behind as they headed back toward the core zone.

A little farther away along the gallery, a man who had been standing with a woman, contemplating the universe outside, turned his head to follow them and gave a slight nod when Korshak looked his way. It was reassuring to know that Lubanov had some of his people here on station, in case they were needed.

– THIRTY-FOUR –

On an observation deck surmounted by a transparent dome, located in the outer part of *Aurora*'s Hub observatory, Hala Vogol opened his eyes and touched a panel on the table in front of him to disconnect. "That's it," he announced. "They've gone back inside. We've lost him on NC." He leaned forward in the chair to loosen the head harness that he had been using, while Masumichi stepped closer behind to help unfasten the collar. At a bench nearby, Lois Iles checked a reading on the beam controller where the cable from the collar connected, and switched off the antenna unit aimed upward to train on the distant light of Etanne. Lubanov, who had been watching silently throughout the proceedings, moved forward to follow events on the main screen of the console beside Vogol, which was monitoring the output from Tek's visual system—hazy as a result of the muslin face piece that the robot was wearing. From here on, the only contact would be via the regular Constellation web communications. In addition they had a separate channel to Korshak, but at present he was refraining from using it because of the robot's acute hearing mode.

"It is done?" The voice of Korshak, walking alongside Tek, came through on audio.

"For now, Messenger. But much work lies ahead. Meanwhile, let us return. I have meditations and preparations to attend to."

"I'm amazed that such concepts can take root this easily in an artificial mind," Lois said as she moved back around to join them.

"I'm amazed myself," Masumichi confessed. "Trying to understand what's happening will take a lot of work."

Lubanov said nothing. He had got what he wanted—a potential observer and listener inside the Dollarian Academy. But the loss of the NC connection meant that they no longer had direct control over Tek, and as yet there hadn't been an opportunity to spell out to Tek what was required. And even if that could be accomplished and Tek's cooperation assured, it was by no means certain that anything significant would be learned in the few days they had available.

Lubanov had visited Etanne before, as part of the normal practice he followed of keeping aware of what was going on. Familiar images appeared on the screen of plain, unadorned surroundings with lines of accentuated perpendicularity. Several of the passing figures paused to stare at the two dourly garbed ascetics walking from the core zone; Vogol had obtained a good shot of Korshak rigged out as a Dollarian while he was directing Tek. Lubanov still marveled at the audacity of the scheme Korshak had devised to get himself into the Academy. But it had worked. What else could one say?

Korshak's voice came again. "The time is close when I must relinquish association with this body that I have used as a vehicle. But I have more yet to say."

"Yes, Messenger?" Tek replied.

"I have served before as herald to prepare minds inside which Almighty Dollar would choose to speak."

"Other minds in Etanne?"

"Oh . . . other places; other ages. Times that once were."

"The sages of the old world! You knew them!"

The view on the screen showed Korshak as Tek stared at him for a moment, and then shifted to an archway framing a pair of lofty doors bearing $ signs. Lubanov had seen the entrance to the Dollarian Academy before from the outside but never entered.

A hand that in close-up could be seen to be a painted, flesh-colored glove pushed one side open to reveal a lobby area, somber in appearance, with a glimpse of a desk to one side. The arrivals evidently paid no heed to it, but proceeded through into a larger space that seemed to be a concourse of some kind.

Korshak's voice continued, "The experience can be overpowering until a certain familiarity is acquired— even for those of aptitude. Hence, Dollar will not unduly tax the endurance of one who is newly awakened. Therefore, Tek, expect that He will more often communicate His further desires through me until your time of adjustment is completed."

"I understand."

"Good move!" Vogol exclaimed. "That guy thinks fast. He's telling Tek to keep its webcom circuits open."

"Excellent," Lubanov breathed to himself.

"And now I must leave," Korshak said. "But I am directed to charge you with a task that pertains to your further development. Very soon now, the enterprise is due to depart that is known as *Envoy*. Avail yourself of opportunities to become knowledgeable of all aspects of this venture. The reason will become apparent in due course."

"Shrewd," Lois complimented.

"I will set myself to the task," Tek promised.

"Be alert for my calls."

"How will I know you?" Tek asked.

"By the name of the novice that I have given."

The view on the screen followed Korshak moving away among the people in the concourse and then disappearing along one of the corridors. Then the field moved to center on the end of another corridor, which began enlarging as Tek moved toward it. Figures flowed off the left and right of the screen. One could almost feel the newfound buoyancy in the robot's tread as it marched confidently forward to wherever its destination was now. The four people on the observatory deck twenty miles away watched and waited curiously.

"*Shakor, where have you been?* You were due here half an hour ago. What kind of behavior is this? You'll never make it past novice if this is your idea of developing self-discipline."

Morgal was on him the moment he appeared inside the workshop. "I'm sorry," Korshak mumbled. He had stowed the Genhedrin gear in a place he had found to conceal it, and was back in the white tunic that he had been wearing underneath. Not knowing what might take place in his absence, he didn't risk leaving it in his cell. "I had some affairs to attend to after the meeting. I can stay late to make up."

"Never mind that for now." Morgal turned and

spoke over his shoulder as he led the way across to Korshak's workbench. "I have an urgent job for you that's just come up. Banker Lareda has asked for it personally. It must be done immediately. Forget everything else for now."

At his own bench nearby, Accountant Trewany was cutting and trimming pieces from a roll of some black matted-fiber material. Morgal picked up the ones that were done and brought them over to Korshak. Along with them he had a piece of paper with the roughly sketched outline of what looked like a riding cape with sleeves, extending far enough above the shoulders to sit over the head like a hood, but without need of accurate shaping—all the signs of a rush job dreamed up at the last moment.

"Needed by the first thing this afternoon," Morgal said. "Nothing fancy. It's not meant to last. You can use fast-bonding adhesive for the seams. And we need ties to close the front and a pull-cord around the face. Okay? The edge is to seal down all the way around onto a surface of similar material. Accountant Trewany will make up cling patches to take care of that. Any questions?"

"It seems straightforward enough," Korshak said. He knew better than to ask Morgal what this was for.

"Get to it, then," Morgal told him.

In the observatory deck on *Aurora*, Vogol leaned back in his chair, and the others relaxed their attention from the screen where they had been following Tek's progress. After entering the Dollarian Academy, the robot had made its way to the rear part, used a peculiar form of open, moving-belt elevator to ascend several levels, and retired to a room that appeared to be its quarters. From Korshak's communications, it seemed that the presence of a robot had not been made general knowledge. The image on the screen was fixed unmovingly on the opposite wall and had gone out of focus. What might be going on in the circuits that constituted Tek's mind—if that was the correct term—was anybody's guess.

Masumichi had been following the succession of views with interest. "A solemn sort of place, by the look of it," he remarked. "Not where I'd choose to go to take a break. What is it, exactly? An attempt at resurrecting some kind of old-world religion? A political indoctrination center? An educational college? Or what?"

"You could probably say all of the above," Lubanov replied. "It's designed to be all things to all people. You see in it what you want."

"Based on a worldwide economic doctrine or something, wasn't it?" Masumichi said. "I confess I've never spent much time studying these things."

"I can't say that surprises me," Vogol threw in. "Where would you find the time?"

"It empowered an elite by pitting everyone else against each other," Lubanov said. "So they were prevented from organizing to defend their common interests. Thus, at root the system was inherently destructive."

"How so?" Masumichi asked.

"They advanced themselves by eliminating their rivals, but that meant they were also destroying each other's customers and business. So what seemed good for each one considering only its own interests was disastrous for the whole."

"They've gotten it the wrong way around," Lois Iles said. She had picked up the NC harness that Vogol had set aside and was studying it curiously.

"Who?" Lubanov asked.

"The Dollarians. They're confusing cause with effect."

"How do you mean?"

"Yes, the obsession with conflict and competition spread worldwide—exactly why, we'll probably never know. But it led to the discovery of what organized human labor and inventiveness is capable of achieving— the transformation of an entire planet, *despite* the system's inherent destructiveness. But the Dollarians confuse the power with the belief system that stumbled on it." She laid the harness back down and turned to face the others fully. "Imagine what that power could have achieved if it had been directed differently. They could have made Earth an idyllic place for everyone. A planet with its natural qualities preserved and the toil taken out of life; a setting for what human existence ought to be, instead of a rat race that consumes lives in pointless strife."

Lubanov was about to comment, when a chime sounded over the audio channel connected to Tek. The image on the screen cleared and moved to center on the door. A small screen set into it showed the head and shoulders of a formidable-looking, bearded, black-haired man with huge eyebrows.

"Voice on. Open," Tek's voice instructed.

"Something's happening," Vogol said, straightening up again in his chair. The others converged around him again to follow on the screen.

The door opened, and the visitor entered. He was wearing a gray robe over a dark shirtlike garment.

"Where have you been?" he demanded. "I've been looking for you since the end of the Meeting."

"Ambulating and communing with inner voices," Tek replied.

"We are recording?" Lubanov queried.

"Check," Vogol confirmed.

"Get all of this."

The bearded man closed the door behind him and assumed a magisterial pose, arms clasped horizontally inside his sleeves. "The time has come for your mission to be revealed, Tek," he announced.

"So the revelations from Dollar have informed me," Tek answered.

Lubanov rested an arm on the back of Vogol's chair and leaned closer. So, finally, maybe they would learn the reason why Tek had been brought to Etanne.

The man went on, "You have attended well and learned much since joining us. In choosing you for this task, we were indeed guided."

"It is not my place to question," Tek replied.

"It is the design of Almighty Dollar that the world which is one day to be on Hera shall be founded from its beginnings on principles that will avoid the tragedy suffered by Earth. But in the years since our departure from Earth, other ambitions have come into play that would cause us to stray from the path that was intended. Our future rests in the hands of ones whose policies are not wisely decided. The ineptness of those who are exalted by being accepted as leaders is exposed by the folly of the venture known as *Envoy*. It is now my honor to reveal to you the role that has been assigned."

Lubanov could hardly believe his good luck. Only

minutes ago he had been doubting if there might be time to brief Tek on what they wanted him to look and listen for on Etanne—the Dollarians' plans concerning *Envoy*. Now, all of a sudden, it seemed that the information was about to be volunteered. It was too good an opportunity to just leave Tek there to relay passively whatever the visitor chose to divulge. They needed to be able to prompt him for more. "Get the line open to Korshak," he told Vogol. "This wants an input channel, too."

"Korshak had reservations about that," Masumichi reminded them. Whether the Dollarians were tapping communications from inside the Academy was unknown.

"We'll risk it," Lubanov said. "This could tell us everything we need to know." Vogol reached to the side to draw a viewpad closer. On the screen, the dialog on Etanne continued.

"You say you have communicated with Dollar directly?"

"I have."

The other's eyebrows rose momentarily in a flicker of disbelief. It was moot whether Tek would have registered the significance. "Which would imply that your knowledge of the more-enduring realm that lies beyond this transient one is affirmed."

"I have no doubt of it."

"So, you would accept the end of your service here on this material plane as an entry into the greater reality?"

"Indeed, I would welcome it gladly!"

Vogol looked up. "I'm not getting through. Korshak isn't answering."

Lubanov cursed inwardly. "We can't let this pass without having any control," he declared. "Connect through to Tek yourself. Korshak set him up to expect more inputs from the Messenger. It will just have to be you. Try to get this guy's name."

Vogol turned back to the panel.

Tek was overcome with admiration for the alacrity with which the plan was unfolding. It had barely returned from its mystical theophany, and already Banker Lareda had appeared.

"I will take you now to a place that you have not been to before, where the preparations have been made," Lareda said. "There you will be shown the means by which your task is to be accomplished, and undergo instruction in its execution."

Just then, an interrupt occurred in the web channel that Tek had been told to keep open. The robot acknowledged with a flip of a mental switch.

"This is the Messenger," a voice in its head informed it.

Tek injected a silent vocalization into the circuit. "The servant hears."

"It is the desire of Dollar to follow you through your task. I shall be His witness."

"I obey as commanded," Tek responded. Although the robot did find it mildly surprising. Why would Dollar have to depend on the feeble senses of one such as Tek to follow anything?

Lareda turned to open the door again, and ushered Tek through into the corridor from which he had entered. "Your name will be immortalized through ages to come, until the time of Hera and long afterward," he promised.

"The Banker's words cause me to rejoice," Tek said.

"They are not mine, but Sorba's. I merely convey them."

They came back to the elevator. Lareda stepped into the next compartment on the side going down, and Tek took the following one. As soon as Tek was alone, the Messenger spoke again. *"Almighty Dollar has directed that I am to learn through you, for the instruction of those who will come after."*

"I understand," Tek sent back.

"Does this task of which the banker speaks involve action concerning Envoy?"

"It would seem that this will soon be revealed."

"Has there been mention of Envoy before, since you were brought to Etanne?"

"Only of the folly that it demonstrates."

"What of the task that you are to perform?"

"Only that I have been chosen for a special mission."

Openings to successive levels moved upward outside the compartment. The landing off the side of the Assembly Hall, from which Tek had entered earlier, came and went. The figure of Lareda appeared several levels below that, standing and waiting a few feet back after stepping out. Tek did likewise and joined him.

The surroundings had a different feel from the communal parts of the Academy above that Tek was familiar with. The floor was of metallic mesh, and the ceiling lined with pipework and cabling. To one side, a metal ladder led up to a railed platform that disappeared between pieces of machinery. They followed a corridor past equipment bays filled with valves and electrical gear to a door bearing a sign saying AUTHO-RIZED ADMITTANCE ONLY, which Lareda opened by entering a code. The far side was noisy, and the air smelled of hot oil.

"I share your eyes but not your memories," the Messenger said. *"Where does this lead now?"*

"I know not," Tek replied. "The grandfather has never brought me to this place before."

"Who is Sorba, of whom the grandfather speaks?"

Confusion tinted with an undertone of alarm resonated in Tek's circuits. While its senses continued registering the surroundings as it followed Lareda, the focus of the robot's attention shifted inwardly. The Messenger's questions had been sounding progressively more strange for one in contact with supernatural powers. The query about *Envoy* had carried a distinct implication of concern. But Tek's education since being brought to Etanne had left no doubt that sending *Envoy* was a grave error of judgment and principle. Hence, the voice that claimed to be the Messenger's appeared to represent a position in conflict with that of Almighty Dollar's true intermediaries. And now he who called himself the Messenger was using "grandfather" as if it pertained to Lareda. But the real Messenger was from Etanne and would have known that it referred to the elevator—he had even traveled on it with Tek less than an hour before.

"Speak the name by which I would know you," Tek challenged.

The silence that followed was unnaturally long. Then, "I have already said, I am the Messenger."

It was clear that the voice Tek was hearing now was that of an imposter from the forces of Evil that had subverted Dollar's plans on Earth, and had reappeared again to frustrate the Design for Hera.

Tek was not schooled with the knowledge to deal with this. It would have to be placed in the hands of those whose understanding was far beyond the robot's. In the meantime, Tek had to protect itself from exposure to any risk of corruption. It deactivated the circuit and set itself resolutely to concentrating on the task that was to be revealed. Tek's faith told it that Almighty Dollar would communicate when the time was right.

"What's happened?" Lubanov snapped—although he thought he had a pretty good idea. The screen had blanked out, and Vogol was not getting a response.

"He's killed the channel," Vogol replied. "It's disconnected. There was some code name between them that we didn't know about."

"The questions were too pointed," Lois said. "He suspected you weren't the Messenger."

Lubanov nodded bitterly. It had been a calculated risk. The chance was there to find out everything they needed to know, and he'd had seconds to make the decision. There was nothing to be done about it now.

"Try raising Korshak one more time," he said. "It looks as if he's going to have to make contact physically again."

Several hours elapsed before Korshak responded. He explained that he had been given a rush job in the workshops where he had been assigned, and unable to get away.

He reported back later that he had gone to the room that Tek had occupied, but obtained no response. Neither had he managed to locate Tek anywhere else. It seemed that the robot had vanished again.

- THIRTY-FIVE -

It was early afternoon when Lareda returned to the workshops to collect the rider cape that he had sketched for Morgal that morning. Tek was with Seesilan, being instructed on the operation of the Warhorse. Lareda didn't know what to make of its insistence that Dollar had spoken to it and confirmed its calling as the Chosen One for the mission, but something seemed to have affected it, intensifying its dedication beyond even the fervor that it had exhibited previously. And that was just as well. The horse had been designed to carry an expendable construction-type telebot remote-directed by a human safely ensconced at a console miles away. Since the modus operandi hadn't changed, Tek's stated eagerness to depart the material plane in pursuit of a higher spiritual reality would be spectacularly gratified.

When Lubanov restricted access to the telebot controllers at *Outmark*, Lareda and Sorba had debated at great length the arguments for and against seeking a volunteer martyr. Although some could almost certainly have been found among the ranks of the believers, the option was a messy one, with risks of all kinds of backlash that could tarnish the leadership's image and set everything back years. And then, out of nowhere, a solution had appeared that avoided all of it. Sometimes, when things like that happened, Lareda was tempted to wonder if there might really be an Almighty Dollar at work somewhere after all.

Morgal had the cape ready in the cubicle that he used for office space at the end of the workshop. Lareda held it up and looked it over. "Not a bad job, considering the rush," he commented. "Did you do it yourself?"

Morgal shook his head. "Seesilan had another problem that needed some work in a hurry. I gave it to that new novice, Shakor."

"Oh, yes.... He's signed it with his name in the corner here. Hm. He seems to have a good hand when it comes to workmanship, anyway," Lareda said. He caught the dark look on Morgal's face. "You don't think so?"

"Oh, he's good," Morgal agreed. "Too good."

"How do you mean?"

Morgal moved to the door and closed it. "There's something not right about him. He's made of more than the stuff of a dreamer who wanders about on Plantation trying to get in touch with nature. There's a competence there that he tries to hide, but I can tell. And he's always watching—doesn't miss a thing."

Lareda folded the cape up slowly and wedged it under an arm. He did recall noting the unusual charisma that Shakor had projected at the interview, but he had been under pressure from too many other things to dwell unduly on it at the time. Already an instinct was telling him that he had erred. "Do you think he could be another one?" he asked. He meant another attempted plant by Lubanov.

"That's what I'm saying," Morgal replied. "He was over half an hour late after the Meeting this morning. Now he's gone again. Something's going on."

Lareda tugged at his beard, scowling. That was also the time that Tek had gone missing. And the incident on Sarc showed that somebody was trying to get to Tek. They couldn't take any risks at a time like this. The first thing to do was have Shakor detained and kept under observation until the operation was over. The explanations and any necessary apologies could wait until then. . . . And if it turned out that no apology was called for, they would have to make sure that the message back to Lubanov was spelled out more clearly this time.

Sending Morgal a silent nod of agreement, he reached inside his robe for his phone.

"Voice on. Connect Archbanker Sorba," he instructed.

Beneath the sinks in the men's washroom along a side corridor from the central concourse was a removable floor plate that gave maintenance access to the plumbing. The space beneath provided a convenient hiding place for Korshak's Genhedrin robe and audio headset. Transformed once more into the white tunic of a raw novice, he waited until all was still and emerged from one of the stalls with the bundle wrapped in a piece of plastic sheet. Stowing it out of sight and replacing the floor plate took no more than a few seconds, and moments later Korshak emerged into the corridor and headed for the dormitory area to go up to his cell.

He needed to send a message updating Lubanov's people on the still-negative result of his attempt to locate Tek before getting back to the workshop. Morgal was getting suspicious over his absences, and at this stage in all that was happening, he didn't want to complicate things further by creating a confrontation. Tek had gone incommunicado again when Lubanov's operator got too pushy, and then vanished once more. Any plan to sabotage the launch would have to be implemented through *Outmark*, and the Dollarians had already shown themselves adept in smuggling the robot aboard ferries. But maybe it was there that they had gone too far and given their method away.

He ascended two levels in the dormitory section and came into the corridor where his cell was located, automatically slowing his pace and casting an eye around for anything unusual. If there was a camera covering the corridor, he had never managed to spot it. At the door, he paused to inspect the strand of waxy compound, setting hard and brittle in a minute or so, that he always stuck across the crack after leaving— not on the latching side, where some intruders might think to check, but on the hinge side, where nobody ever did. The strand was broken. Someone or ones had entered, and might well still be inside, waiting for him. Just at the moment, Korshak didn't want to know why. He turned silently about and departed back the way he had come. His sojourn on Etanne might be about to come to an abrupt end, he decided as he took the stairs down. But if Tek was in the process of being sent elsewhere, there was little more that Korshak could accomplish here anyway.

His senses were on full alert as he came into the

central concourse. He hadn't proceeded more than three paces, when he spotted the two figures in Dollarian Executive-branch uniforms away on the far side. Their manner was not that of persons going anywhere, but prowling—looking this way and that, searching the faces of the people who passed. Korshak melted into a gaggle of novices and lower ranks moving in the general direction of the Assembly Hall, intending to take a roundabout route back to the washroom. But as he appeared at the side of the foyer in front of the Hall, he saw two more a short distance away in one of the doorways. They appeared to be interrogating somebody wearing the plain brown robe of an Accountant. Korshak recognized Furch, and Furch saw him at the same instant. Furch must have said something, for the two heads swung around in unison to follow his gaze. One of the figures pulled something from a pocket and began talking into it. Korshak was already retreating back toward the concourse. Without waiting to see what happened next, he quickened his pace and disappeared into a side corridor.

He heard their footsteps rush by outside the washroom as he was releasing the catches of the floor plate, and figured that he had ten seconds before they met others coming in the opposite direction who had seen nothing. The robe came out of its wrappings, and the floor plate clicked back into place. As if on cue, the door burst open and four Executive uniforms charged in, only to moderate themselves to a respectful pace at the sight of the Genhedrin calmly wiping his hands under the dryer by the sinks. A stall door was closed. One of the four moved over, tested it, and nodded quietly to the others. There was nobody in there, but the wadded tissue jammed between the top part of the frame and the door was tight enough to give a first impression of its being locked.

"We can wait a few minutes," another said in a low voice.

The Genhedrin finished his ablutions without hurry and left. There was no reason why any of the four should have noticed the plastic wrapping stuffed into the waste bin below the sink, covering the headset that there had been no time for Korshak to put on.

Uniformed Dollarians were still about, watching in the viewing gallery around the docking port, when Korshak, still in his robe, rematerialized several hours later to board the ferry for *Aurora*. However, it wasn't they who stopped him, but the couple he had seen that morning on his way back into the core zone with Tek.

"Pardon me," the man said. "But I'm from the Directorate. We have a small security issue that we have to check on. Could I ask your cooperation?"

"What do you wish?" Korshak asked.

"May I see one of your hands, please?"

Korshak extended an arm. The man pushed the sleeve back far enough to uncover the wrist, checked around it lightly with a fingertip, evidently looking for a glove, and then produced a small metal wand which he touched against Korshak's shoulder.

"No, I'm not a robot," Korshak murmured in a low voice. "It's Magician. You saw me this morning. Time to leave town. Notify Wizardry for me."

"Will do."

"So, should I take it that Tek hasn't come through?"

"Not that we've seen. And there's no other way off Etanne."

So Lubanov had arrived at the same conclusion. Korshak had always liked working with professionals.

When Korshak came out of the arrival gate on *Aurora* less than an hour later, two of the "Research Section" staff were waiting to take him straight to a debriefing session with Lubanov.

Meanwhile, in the dark recesses of the *Aurora*'s docking bays, the Warhorse detached from its lodgement between the engine-mounting spars of the ferry that Korshak had arrived on, and hugging closely to the lines of the Hub structure, made its way stealthily toward the larger port where the shuttles to *Outmark* docked.

- THIRTY-SIX -

I t was good to be home again. After the cramped, windowless crew cabin in Plantation's underworld, followed by an ascetic's cell on Etanne, the familiar surroundings of Astropolis gave Korshak the reassuring feeling of a return to reality.

He stood just inside Mirsto Junior's room, where he had been insistently conducted within minutes of arriving. Mirsto turned back from reaching to the shelves above the bed and presented his latest creation, a wooden box with a hinged lid, about big enough to hold an orange, finished and polished with a simple but neatly worked pattern of marquetry inlay. "I made it in the carpentry class at school," he announced.

Korshak opened the lid and inspected the inside. "Not a bad piece of work," he complimented.

"Now, who does he take after, I wonder?" Vaydien said from the doorway. Korshak had materialized without warning. Even though she had become accustomed to surprises over the years, she was still getting over the shock of seeing him with a shaved head and no mustache. "He goes away, saying he may need to stay over for a night or two, and comes back two weeks

373

later looking like some kind of monk from a monastery back on Earth," she had commented to Mirsto. Wandering had always been in his blood, Korshak had told them. The explaining could wait until after they had eaten.

Mirsto took the box back, picked up one of the pieces from a board game that he and Hori played, placed it inside, and closed the lid. "I guess you know the rest," he said, offering the box back.

"Can I look?" Korshak asked cautiously.

"Sure."

Korshak lifted the lid. The box was empty. Mirsto opened a hand to reveal the game piece. "What do you think, Dad?"

"Good."

"Could you spot it?"

"Well, that wouldn't have been fair, would it? I know what to look for." The box would have a false bottom with a section that opened when the lid was closed to deliver the contents into the holder's palm. As Mirsto put the box and the piece back, Korshak noticed the tapestry adorning the opposite wall. "Hey, you finished it," he said to Vaydien.

"Finally. Like it?"

"It certainly brightens the room up. Escalos from the hills. . . . Now, doesn't that bring back some memories!"

"I cheated a bit with the animals, though," Vaydien confessed. "Half of those were never within a thousand miles of Arigane."

"Well, I like them," Mirsto said. "And it's my room."

"Then that's all that matters," Vaydien agreed.

"What animals did you see on Plantation?" Mirsto asked as they followed Vaydien back toward the hallway.

"Shh." Vaydien nodded toward another of the doors. "Kilea's sleeping."

"Oh, lots of kinds. I'll tell you about them over dinner," Korshak murmured.

"You sound hungry," Vaydien said as they came into the kitchen.

"Famished."

"Didn't you have anything while you were at the Directorate?"

"Could have, but I decided to come straight back. What do we have?"

"Oh... Hori was here yesterday, and we had a steak pie. There's still about half of it left. I could throw something together to go with that."

"Sounds perfect."

"What's this, Dad?" Korshak looked back. Mirsto was investigating the open-top carrier bag that Korshak had set down in the hall. Korshak had obtained some regular clothes on arriving at Astropolis, but he still had his Dollarian garb from Etanne with him.

"That's okay. You can look at it," Korshak said.

Mirsto drew out the gray Genhedrin robe. Still inside the bag was the white novice's tunic that Korshak had worn under it. "Is this yours?" Mirsto asked, holding the robe up in the kitchen doorway and looking puzzled.

Vaydien couldn't suppress a chuckle. "It goes with the haircut and the shave. But seriously, what are you doing with it?"

"I ended up on Etanne," Korshak replied, pulling a chair up to the table and sitting down. "The crack about the monk wasn't far off."

"Etanne?" Vaydien repeated. This was the first she

had heard of it. Nobody had said anything to alter her impression that Korshak had been on Plantation the whole time. It had been a case of the fewer who knew otherwise, the better. "I thought you were looking for Masumichi's robot." She produced a beer from the refrigerator along with the pie dish and set it down on the table with a glass. "You said it had gotten interested in the cults. I'd never heard anything so crazy. So, is that where it went?"

Korshak nodded. "We were pretty sure, anyway. But the only way to find out for sure was to get inside. An opportunity presented itself...." He shrugged and filled his glass, leaving it at that.

Vaydien waited for a moment, then turned and looked at him questioningly, her expression asking to know more.

"It's a bit of a sensitive issue," Korshak said. "I'm not sure that I can say any more right now." He motioned with his eyes to indicate Mirsto, who was still investigating the robe through the open doorway.

"Political? Is that why you were at the Directorate?"

"Exactly. Later?"

Vaydien nodded that she understood.

Korshak turned the bottle around and inspected the Envoy label. "Ah, the good stuff," he remarked.

"You said you liked it after you and Ronti came back from Istella, so I got some in. Everybody's drinking it—except the doomsayers. The launch is in two days."

Korshak had temporarily put *Envoy* out of his mind. Lubanov seemed to have done all that could reasonably be expected. Korshak had personally experienced the promptly instituted checking of suspicious-looking travelers leaving Etanne, and on arriving at *Aurora* he had learned that shuttles leaving for *Outmark* were being subjected to more stringent procedures. The only way Tek could have avoided detection would have been by getting through as a passenger before Lubanov acted, but reconstruction of the time scale from the information Korshak had provided showed this to be impossible. Nevertheless, Lubanov's people were conducting diligent searches all through *Outmark* and would continue doing so until the launch was completed.

"Did I tell you that Ronti and I ran into Osgar when we were on Istella?" Korshak asked.

"Yes. He's running a bar there now. That was the first place you went, looking for the robot."

"Heard anything from Ronti?"

"He seems to be spending a lot of time at Beach lately. I think he's found a new ladyfriend there."

"There's a surprise. Have you heard anything more about the show there that he was supposed to be organizing?"

"I'm afraid not.... How about some warmed-up mash and corn with this? I can make some fresh gravy."

"Great. I'll need to give him a call to find out what's happening."

As was inevitable, Mirsto had put on the robe and came in through the doorway trailing it behind him like a blown-down tent. The cowl turned toward Korshak as Mirsto peered at him through the muslin face piece.

"Oh, are you going to Etanne, too, now?" Korshak asked him. "That's a robe from one of the sects there. They've rediscovered an all-powerful god from the old world who was called Dollar."

"No," Mirsto said. "It's my invisibility cloak—like the one that Cosmic Man wears. Can you make it work for me?"

"What do you mean, make it work?"

"To get it to make people invisible. *You* could figure out a way."

Korshak took another swig of beer. "Well, now, that's something we'll have to talk about. There's what you and I call magic, and there's..." His voice trailed away as the implication sank in of what Mirsto had said.

"Yes?" Mirsto's muffled voice said from the cowl after several seconds.

Invisibility cloak. The cape that Morgal had wanted made in a hurry that morning had been of an unusual black matted-fiber material that Korshak had wondered about at the time. It would be ideal as a nonreflector of radiation—maybe to conceal a small object approaching something like *Envoy* amid the bustle of activity going on around it.

And there was something else. When Korshak had called Vaydien briefly from Lois Iles's cabin on Plantation and talked to Mirsto, Mirsto had described how he and Hori had tried out Masumichi's neural coupler. It was cool, Mirsto had said. "You think that you really are the robot." It was more fun being a robot. People had to be stuck inside places like Astropolis and Jakka all the time, where there was air, and temperatures were warm enough. Robots could go outside—over, and under, and anywhere....

Outside.

"Dad?"

"Korshak, are you all right?" Vaydien looked around from the counter.

Korshak felt a sudden cold wetness on his thigh. He had sat back unthinkingly in the chair and let his glass tilt. A slow, sickening sensation was rising somewhere in his stomach.

"It doesn't matter," he murmured distantly. "None of it matters. Lubanov's people aren't going to find anything. It's not going through the internal system at all. It's going around the outside somehow. It could even be there already."

"Korshak, what are you talking about?"

Korshak was already rising from the table. "Sorry... I'll explain everything later," he said. "But you're going to have to put that away again for now. I have to get back to the Directorate right now. I think we may have an emergency."

– THIRTY-SEVEN –

They met in the outer room to Ormont's office in the Directorate, which he used as a mini–conference facility. Vad Cereta was the last to arrive, having come from the Hub docking ports. It was fortuitous that events had caught him in a quick visit to *Aurora* and not at *Outmark*, where he spent most of his time. He had been about to board a return shuttle but postponed it until a later one. Korshak filled in the background from his chair at one end of the large table taking up the center of the room, opposite Ormont, and then came to the point.

"Checking the passengers leaving Etanne, and controlling traffic from here to *Outmark* isn't going to do any good. Tek isn't using the regular routes. They've got some means of moving it outside." A silence fell while those present digested the information. Cereta shuffled his feet and fidgeted. Masumichi was looking out of his depth and crestfallen, as if all of this were somehow his doing.

"Maybe across Constellation," Cereta said finally. "But all the way to *Outmark*? Two hundred fifty thousand miles? How? I can't buy it."

"They don't need an independent vehicle," Lubanov pointed out. "We supply those already. The robot functions outside. It can hitch rides—from Etanne to here, and from here to *Outmark*. All it would need is a device for local maneuvering when it got there. A simple pressurized thruster. What little thermal there was would be lost against the background. With the absorbent surface that Korshak's talking about, you'd never spot it."

Cereta was already nodding to concede that he had spoken too hastily. "Then we mobilize full external checks of the ferries and shuttles right away," he said.

"That wouldn't be sufficient," Lubanov replied. "The robot could be out there already. It's had enough time. We have to go over every inch of *Envoy*, too."

Cereta made a conciliatory gesture. "Okay. If that's what we have to do, it's what we—" He left the sentence unfinished as he saw that Masumichi was still looking worried and shaking his head. "What's the problem?"

Masumichi wrinkled his face up and bit his lip while he sought to put it into words. "Consider the situation. *Envoy* is a large, complex structure with all kinds of external niches and recesses. You say, we go over every inch of it. So how do we do this? Maybe with something like the mobile cradles that the construction crews use. You put some people in suits, send them outside in cradles, and they deploy around *Envoy* with spotlights and glasses, trying to find where Tek, and whatever the device is that it's using, are hiding."

"Well, something like that, I suppose," Lubanov agreed. He looked at Cereta, who shrugged and nodded.

"How else?" Cereta asked Masumichi.

"I can't think of anything else. And that's the trouble. You have these platforms nosing around, shining lights into here and there. Obviously, Tek is going to see them before they see it. Now, from what we've surmised, Tek has accepted to go on what we assume is a suicide mission involving some kind of bomb, which to fit in with the propaganda we've been hearing would ideally be detonated to coincide with the launch." Masumichi glanced around briefly. Nobody interrupted. "That's if all goes according to plan. But how would a robot like Tek react to realizing that it was about to be discovered? It could sit there and let its mission be thwarted. Or it could decide to act prematurely on the grounds that less effect is better than no effect at all."

A few second passed before Cereta voiced the obvious. "Well, you tell us. You're the one who made it."

"That's the problem. I can't. It's a dynamic, self-modifying, associative system developed specifically for research into making autonomous inferences. Being predictable would defeat the whole purpose." Masumichi shook his head. "I can't tell you what it would do. If it's in the grip of some kind of religious zeal, it might well opt for martyrdom and glory. And with all those search parties out there, we'd be risking a lot more than just an unmanned probe and a lot of work that's gone into it."

"Oh gods." Cereta sat back heavily in his chair.

"Do we know for sure that it's acting autonomously?" Ormont asked. He had been following intently but so far said little. "Isn't it possible that the final fire command would come from Etanne? It could presumably link into the web wavelengths operating around *Outmark*."

Vogol, who had accompanied Lubanov from the Research Section, looked dubious. "We've been scanning continuously to detect any open channel. But it's been switched off ever since it shut down on Etanne."

"Having it depend on a remote authorization would be inefficient in any case," Lubanov put in. "Its capacity to act autonomously is precisely what makes it ideal for this kind of operation." He thought for a moment longer and then added with a growl, "I wouldn't trust those people to hold back, anyway, even with the search parties out there."

"Then we have to find some way of getting it to switch its communications on again and try and reason with it remotely," Cereta said.

"How?" Vogol asked.

Cereta looked appealingly to Masumichi, but Masumichi could only show his empty hands.

Korshak had remained silent, letting the others talk the ramifications out for themselves to see if anyone else might come to any conclusions different from the ones he had while riding the capsule across Astropolis to the Directorate. Nobody had. He hadn't been driven to agree with Cereta's last statement, however. There was another way he had thought of, that might work.

"Nothing you attempt remotely will persuade Tek to switch on again," he said simply. "I'm the only one here who has dealt with it face-to-face. It won't trust any voice that tries to talk to it over a communications link anymore. The only entity it will believe now is Almighty Dollar."

"Same question," Cereta said. "How is Dollar or someone pretending to be Dollar supposed to get through to it if it's not listening?"

"They won't—not over a com link, anyway," Korshak answered. "But it will listen to Dollar's Messenger."

Uncertain looks flickered from one to another among the others around the table. Each seemed to be looking for something they had missed. "Then how is the Messenger supposed to talk to it?" Vogol asked.

"The same way as before," Korshak replied. "Face-to-face."

"But that was you, dressed up in that mystic's outfit that you were wearing when you arrived on *Aurora*," Lubanov said.

"So why shouldn't it be me again? I've still got the robe back home. It could be here in half an hour."

"Then what?" Lubanov asked.

"I take a shuttle to *Outmark*," Korshak answered. "We've still got the best part of two days. It doesn't need a circus of search parties. I'm betting I could find it in that time."

"Even without the circus, how could you be certain of getting close enough for it to recognize you before it panics?"

"That's my trade," Korshak replied confidently.

"We're talking about *outside*," Vogol reminded him. "You were inside Etanne last time."

"So you put me in a suit. That's what they're for."

"Do you even know your way around the outside of *Envoy*?" Cereta queried. "Masumichi said a minute ago, it's a large and complex structure. He wasn't kidding."

"*I* don't," Korshak replied. "But Vaydien does. She worked on it for a while. I can have her direct me remotely. Or we could use one of your own people out there if you like."

"Have you had any previous EVA experience?" Cereta asked dubiously. "Or training with suits?"

"No," Korshak admitted. The point had occurred

to him, too, but he'd assumed it was something that could be taken care of. Cereta didn't seem so sanguine.

"It takes time and practice," he said. "Especially if you want to come across as a messenger from the gods and not some kind of slapstick act. And even the light-duty models are pretty bulky, and with a pack. Just how big is this robe?"

That had bothered Korshak, too. "You've got a point there, Vad," he agreed. "The only thing I can think of is that if we have to, we do a rush job of enlarging it."

"It would need to be more like a tarp."

Lubanov, who had been steepling his fingers under his chin while he listened, sighed and shook his head. "Korshak, I respect your nerve and your initiative," he said. "But in all honesty, I can't see that it would have a chance. Adept as you are, it's an environment that you have no working knowledge of. Vad knows what he's talking about."

"Could somebody from a trained EVA crew pull it off, do you think?" Ormont asked.

"It would take too long to fill a new person in on all the background," Korshak said.

"And that's assuming you could find someone suitable in the time we've got," Cereta threw in.

That seemed to kill it. The room became still. Korshak had nothing further left to offer. It was one of those rare moments when he felt himself sliding into despondency. Then Masumichi, who had been staring distantly through the table, said, "You don't need a person in a space suit at all." He looked up. "Why are we talking about all this? To send this Messenger from Dollar to a place where he can communicate with an entity that functions perfectly comfortably outside because it happens to be a robot. Well, the answer is simple: make the Messenger the same thing."

"Same thing?" Vogol repeated.

"Yes." Masumichi waved a hand in the general direction that indicated the next of *Aurora's* modules around the Ring. "Over in Jakka. You've worked with it yourself. We send another robot. Let Kog be the Messenger."

Korshak blinked, and then stared. The suggestion was so audacious that he felt himself drawn to it irresistibly already. Another robot. It answered everything.

But Vogol was frowning and not seeming so happy. "We'd still run into the same problem as before," he said. "Tek saw through it when I tried to pretend I was Korshak. How can we expect Kog to get away with it? If Tek smells another rat at this stage, it'll guarantee he blows the whole works."

Masumichi was smiling, as if he had been anticipating the objection. "You're forgetting the neural coupler. We put Korhsak at the other end. So for all intents and purposes, that means he *is* Kog."

Vogol's frown deepened. He shook his head. "No. That won't work. There's only regular web communications out there at *Outmark*. They can't handle NC. Even if you shipped the antenna out there, it would just give you a narrow beam from *Outmark*. *Envoy* has too many shadows and dead spots—and the entire reverse side would be blind anyway. Korshak had to take Tek out to the viewing gallery for it to work on Etanne. We're not going to have that kind of cooperation this time."

Masumichi continued smiling and nodded his agreement. "All the same, I think there's a way we could make it work," he said.

- THIRTY-EIGHT -

The movie was about shooting wars between private corporate armies in the old world, and was just building up to the climax where the champions of two rival energy suppliers were about to settle things by facing each other on an avenue lined by spectators in one of the fabulous skyscraper cities. Historians had expressed doubts that things had really been like that, but it made good entertainment and helped foster a healthy spirit among young people of standing up for themselves when it was called for.

What had always mystified Vaydien about the old world was the enormous number of automobiles. Even around Arigane, which had never been one of the major population centers, she had seen excavations that had turned up the remains of thousands. Where, she asked herself, had they ever managed to find enough trained drivers? A woman who did research for one of the libraries had told her that there weren't any as such; everybody drove themselves—from schoolchildren not much older than Mirsto to octogenarians in their dotage. Vaydien didn't believe it. Vehicles capable of a hundred miles an hour, strung together along strips of roadway twenty feet wide? The idea was ridiculous. Half of them would have been dead within a day.

"Is Dad going away again already?" Mirsto asked from the other chair.

"Not this time. He just had some unfinished business that he remembered across in the Directorate. He hasn't even left Astropolis. He'll be back later tonight."

"That's good to know, anyway. He was only just back. What was he doing with those funny clothes?"

"You know, I'm not really sure myself. He'll tell us all about it in good time."

Mirsto's attention drifted back to the movie. "I think the one from the nuclear empire will win. You can always tell, because they wear white hats. Is it true that they had to fight, otherwise they lost their jobs? I'm not sure I'd have liked that."

An incoming-call tone sounded. Vaydien's viewpad told her it was from Korshak. She directed it to the kitchen and went through to take it there.

"A change of plan," he announced.

"Change? I didn't even know we had one."

"Lots of urgent things are going on. You know that gray robe with the cowl that I brought back with me in the bag?"

"You mean Mirsto's invisibility cloak?"

"Yes. Look, can you bring it over here right away?"

Vaydien realized that after years of being married to a magician, nothing ever really came as a surprise. "Where are you? Still at the Directorate?"

"Yes. Ormont's office."

"Ormont? I'm impressed. I take it he's not going to wear it."

"Not his style. We need it for something at *Outmark*."

Vaydien sighed to herself inwardly. "Does that mean you'll be going there?"

"We are. You're needed there, too. You can drop Mirsto and Kilea off at Hori's place on the way. Tell them it might be for a day or two."

"I'm on my way," Vaydien said resignedly.

The only coasts that Ronti had seen back on Earth had been bleak, windswept expanses of muddy flats, rocky headlands, and gray seas. If this was the fake, artificial substitute, he was all for it.

He lay on a towel spread out on the warm sands of Beach, his back propped against an ice chest well stocked with Envoys and assorted other delicacies, watching the surf roll in from the offshore wave maker. A few feet away, Ginaya rubbed oil over the parts of her body not covered by a swimsuit that was more suggestion than actuality. In fact, Beach's "sun" was designed not to emit potentially harmful wavelengths, but Ginaya had grown up in Sofi and insisted that being on a beach wasn't the same without going through the oiling ritual.

"But if you were the king's bodyguard, why did you leave the palace?" she asked. "It sounds to me more as if you should have been trying to stop the others."

Ronti shook his head. "He was a wicked man. I had decided long before that I couldn't remain in his service. So when I found out that the magician and the physician were planning an escape, instead of turning them in, I threw my lot in with them and helped them organize it."

"A man of principle and integrity," Ginaya said admiringly.

"That's how I like to think of it," Ronti agreed.

"Okay. So where were we? The prince and his cavalry were charging across the bridge. But you couldn't take off until the others were inside, and the physician was slowing them down. What did you do?"

"The situation was desperate. Arrows were already falling around us. The horsemen would be upon us in moments. It was obvious that the physician would never make it in time."

"You didn't leave him?"

"No, of course not. Suddenly I had an inspiration!"

"What?" Ginaya asked breathlessly.

"Just inside the door of the lander was one of those flare pistols that they have for emergencies. I grabbed it off the wall, ran down the lander's steps and out into the road, and fired it head-on into them. They had never seen anything like it before and had no idea what it was. It burst right in among the thick of them, in the middle of the bridge. You've never seen such a rout. Bodies and horses falling off both sides into the water. It was complete panic...."

At that moment, a call sounded from Ronti's phone, in the pocket of the shirt slung over the ice chest behind him. Frowning, he sat up, reached back, and fumbled for it.

"I told you to turn it off," Ginaya said.

"I should have." He flipped it to audio. "Hello? Ronti here."

"Ronti, it's Korshak."

"Well, hey! How's Plantation?"

"Oh, that's history. I'm back on *Aurora*, in Astropolis. Long story. No time to go into it now."

"Okay."

"I need your help. Urgent. Where are you?"

"Relaxing on Beach—or was. What's up?" Ronti cupped a hand over the mouthpiece and whispered, "Just a little bit of business." Ginaya nodded.

Korshak went on, "The mirror for the Teleporting Man." It was a prop for a new trick that they were working on—a high-quality, one-way reflecting sheet large enough to cover a person, at present in their workshop on Jakka.

"Right," Ronti acknowledged.

"Can you get over to Jakka for it? I need it as soon as you can manage."

"Well, I guess so. Where are you, exactly?"

"Right now I'm in the Directorate. But the mirror needs to go to the Hub docking area. Take it to the shuttle port for *Outmark*. The people there will be expecting you."

"Can do."

Ginaya read the glum look on Ronti's face. "What is it?" she hissed.

"I have to go to Jakka and then the Hub. Right now. Sorry. Something urgent has just come up."

"You will still be coming back later?"

"Oh, yeah—I'm pretty sure, anyway. But if anything changes, I'll call you. It's just that there are times when certain things have to come first." He finished the beer he had been drinking and stood up. "You know, Gin, sometimes I feel as if I've never stopped being a bodyguard."

Hera, of course, met all the criteria for a habitable world, such as size, temperature range, surface and atmospheric chemistry, and data returned from the old-world probe confirmed that life had established itself there. The question that couldn't be answered was whether it included some form of intelligence, and if so, the degree to which its culture had progressed. The mixture of gases that enveloped the planet carried the unmistakable signature of living things; images captured from orbit showed areas that varied in color and extent with the seasons; but beyond that, little more could be said. Answering the question was one of *Envoy's* principal objectives.

In *Aurora's* Hub observatory, Lois Iles was finally catching up with her own work after being drafted into helping Lubanov out and ending up on Plantation. Marney Clure had never lost interest in her work and was in the lab on one of his periodic visits. A screen by the chair where he was sitting showed a transmission from *Outmark* of the last-minute activity going on around *Envoy* as the final items of equipment were absorbed inside before the auxiliary craft and service platforms were pulled back to clear the launch zone. Shortly before, there had been a news item on a protest demonstration staged outside the Directorate offices.

"Ormont did the right thing in not letting it become the subject of a popularity circus," he said to Lois, who was reviewing her backlog of technical papers from the archives. "The whole business is being engineered to create a political following. They're cherry-picking whatever can be twisted to fit a preconceived agenda. That isn't science at all."

"That's right. But most people wouldn't see it," Lois agreed.

"And yet it was how governments were formed in

the old world," Marney said. "Everybody had a say, and what the majority went for decided. So everything was reduced to the lowest common denominator. It would be wide open to corruption and manipulation. I can't think of a worse system."

"Lubanov says the same thing."

"It's not going to happen here, because we're in a space environment, and everything else has to be subordinated to surviving in it," Marney said. "So the necessity of having the Directorate forces a form of government comparable to what you had in Sofi. But what will perform a parallel function after we get to Hera? You see my point? What will stop it going the same way as Earth?"

The ruling power in Sofi had been held by members of an elite class, defined not by birth or wealth but by achievement, that appointed its own successors. Not everyone was happy with the institution, and disagreements over its merits had been a factor in bringing about the division that led to *Aurora*. Lois didn't really want to be sidetracked by getting into it right now, and sought for a tactful way of replying without seeming disinterested. She was saved by an incoming call at the console where she was working.

"Excuse me, Marney." A screen to one side of the one she was using activated to show the features of Masumichi Shikoba. "Hello again, Mas," Lois greeted. "What can I do for you?"

"I have an unusual technical requirement and am hoping you can help."

Lois sighed inwardly and turned her chair to face him fully. It seemed the world was determined. "What's up?" she inquired.

"Are you alone?"

"Just a second." Lois looked across toward Marney. "Marney, sorry, but this could be kind of sensitive. How about getting us a couple of coffees from the pot next door? Mine's black with nothing."

"Sure." Marney unfolded from the chair and ambled away. Lois turned back to the screen showing Masumichi.

"Okay, go ahead."

"It's about the NC beam that you set up for us to connect to Tek when he was on Etanne."

"Yes?"

"Could some of the equipment you've got there be hooked up to give us a wider-spreading beam? I want to flood an area, say, five miles across from a distance of fifty miles."

Lois sent him a puzzled smile while she thought about it. A slightly defocused dish antenna setup ought to do it, she thought. Or possibly a phased pair. "Yes, I think so," she said finally. "When would you want it?"

"Right away. . . . Oh, and something that's fixed on *Aurora* won't work. We'd need to be able to ship it out."

"That shouldn't be a problem," Lois said. "What's happening?"

"We want to cover *Envoy* from *Outmark*. Briefly, we think Tek's hiding out on *Envoy* somewhere, and up to no good. The idea is to send another robot out there after it. 'Why' will make a great story that I'll tell you sometime, but not now."

Maybe they didn't need to ship anything to *Outmark*, Lois mused as she turned it over. Some of the higher-power equipment would probably be able to operate direct from *Aurora*. She was about to suggest it, when it occurred to her that the two-seconds-plus

round-trip signal delay over that kind of distance
would make coordinated NC operation impractical.
Masumichi would know it, too. Scratch that idea. But
then another drawback crossed her mind.

"When you say hiding out on *Envoy*, what do you
mean?" she asked.

"Somewhere on the outside, among all the booms
and pylons and nooks and crannies. Or maybe in the
drive nozzle."

"You're still going to be stuck with line-of-sight
contact," Lois pointed out. "The connection's going
to be very erratic if you send another robot in there.
You could easily lose it altogether. Have you thought
about that?"

"Yes, we have," Masumichi replied. "And we think
there's an answer."

Site operations around *Envoy* were directed from
a transparent-domed tower jutting up out of *Outmark*
above a clutter of superstructures, radar housings, and
antennas. The Traffic Control Section was at its busiest,
screens and status summaries glowing on all sides, and
all stations manned. Installation of the probe's orbital
and surface instrumentation, deployment systems, and
robotics was complete. Propulsion and navigation had
passed manual triple-inspection, and the crews were
pulling back while a final round of remote testing was
being conducted from *Outmark*.

Cyblic Heshtar, operations director, had come up
from his office on the level below to be present on the
floor during this final and crucial phase. A distant glow
in the starfield visible through the dome marked where
Envoy hung in space, illuminated by an entourage of

arc lamps. A few yards away from where Heshtar was standing, Wesl Inchow, the instrumentation engineering chief, turned away from a console where he had been watching over the operator's shoulder, and came over. Although his face showed the strain of being on the go virtually nonstop for the last forty-eight hours, beneath it he looked relaxed and happy.

"Well, Cyb, that's the last of our guys out and accounted for. Speaking for me, I'm as good as on stand down. How's it going overall?"

"Smooth as can be expected. We're on the easy straight."

"I think we're going to see some partying around Constellation when this is over."

Heshtar grinned. "I'd say Istella's in for a busy run, too." He was about to say more, when he caught the duty controller trying to attract his attention from the supervisory console up on the dais in the middle of the floor area. "Excuse me for a moment, Wes." He moved over, at the same time tilting his chin inquiringly.

"I've got Cereta through from *Aurora*. He's asking for you personally."

Heshtar climbed the couple of steps up to the dais and moved around into the view angle of the controller's screen, where the image of Cereta was waiting. "Vad. How's things?"

Cereta answered characteristically, without preliminaries. "Hi, Cyb. Look, this is right from the top—Ormont. We need to schedule a whole new movement schedule out there. The stuff that's being pulled back toward *Outmark* all wants to be sent back the other way and fanned out to stations on the far side of *Envoy* from where you are. Got that?"

"Far side?" It didn't make any sense.

"And get some thrusters attached to the old raft fusion drive and the materials stacks and move them back there as well."

Heshtar's jaw dropped. "What do *they* have to do with this operation?" They'd had a schedule that had stood for months. Until a minute ago they'd been ahead of it with almost a day to spare. Now, all of a sudden, this was panic city already, all over again.

"Believe me, Cyb, you don't have time to hear it all now. I want to create a backdrop of objects behind *Envoy* that will form a screen about ten miles out. We want to illuminate the area with radiation from *Outmark* and have it reflected back so that just about every spot on the far side of *Envoy* will see it from some angle or another. You can break into those stacks of materials and spread the contents out to fill in the gaps. I'll be on a shuttle that's leaving *Aurora* less than an hour from now."

"What kind of craziness are we into now?" Heshtar demanded.

"You think that's crazy? I'll be arriving with a party that includes Lubanov and one of his spooks, a magician, an astronomer, a computer scientist, and a robot. Tell you the rest when we get there."

- THIRTY-NINE -

T he humans with their machines and their vehicles were withdrawing to leave *Envoy*'s flared stalk with its hexagon mushroom head floating seemingly motionless among the stars. Stillness and serenity descended. From a recess formed by a diverter-fluting inside the nozzle of the main baryonic-annihilation drive, Tek gazed out and contemplated the vastness of the universe.

In his final revelation of the full gravity and significance of the mission, Banker Lareda had explained how the *Envoy* program went beyond being simply an irresponsible squandering of priceless resources that would better serve the need of ensuring survival in the immediate term. By preoccupying people's minds with dreams and fantasies of a future that was still generations away, it diverted their attention from the essential business now of setting the foundations for the social order that Almighty Dollar had decreed as the governing force that would shape that future. The functional destruction of *Envoy*—while preserving most of its material assets—would bring focus upon the realities of the present and help create the receptiveness toward the Dollarian message that would be a sounder guarantee of the future. Now that Tek understood this more clearly, its awe at the intricacy of the Plan it could see unfolding was reinforced, and its resolve to carry through its assigned part in fulfilling it, redoubled.

Since its inspiration on Etanne and further demonstration of worthiness in rejecting the False Voice, Tek's insight had deepened to the wondrous way in which the truths that had been known on Earth long ago echoed the life principle of struggle and the striving for excellence. The holy formula for compound interest that it had found quoted universally in the ancient financial scriptures quantified the process of exponential growth that was the expression of all life. Yet the connection extended even more deeply to reflect in its message the fundamentals of physical reality. Whether this was a manifestation of the expanding awareness that Banker Lareda and Archbanker Sorba had prepared Tek for, or an anticipation granted by Dollar of the revelations to be experienced on the transmaterial plane, it didn't know, but even the glimmerings that it was beginning to grasp were overpowering. Small wonder the Messenger had cautioned Tek to expect that Dollar would limit direct communications in the early stages.

Tek had known from its researches that the universal Dollarian faith of ancient Earth had related its measures of the worth of all things to the accumulation of rare and heavy metals, but it had never understood the reason for their being conferred with such sacred status. But in a flash of comprehension the robot had realized that these elements represented the culmination of the

chain of nuclear transmutations that began with the
first synthesis from primordial energy, and their eleva-
tion to sacramental objects symbolized the unification
of the sacred dollar with the cosmic forces responsible
for the creation of the universe itself. While at the
other extreme, the concept of credit, which applied
projected but as yet unrealized dollars to future commercial undertakings, mirrored the potentials awaiting
actualization that were inherent in the superposition of
quantum states. From the largest to the smallest scales
governing expression of the cosmos, the parallel was
complete. Tek could only bow in humble reverence
before the Mind that had conceived it all. The robot's
one ambition now was that at some time in a future
yet to be, it would grasp the Purpose.

A sudden change of illumination inside the tail
nozzle where the Warhorse was attached broke through
Tek's ruminations. From somewhere beyond the black-
silhouetted parts of the *Envoy*'s tail structure framing
the robot's view of the universe—whether near or
far, it had no way of telling—a radiation source had
come on, registering more in the heat band of Tek's
visual spectrum, directed at the vessel. Tek assumed
it to be some kind of beacon or signaling system
connected with the launch preparations. But then
it began fluctuating rapidly in intensity. The pattern
conformed to the same communications code as that
exhibited by the $ sign that had appeared on the wall
at the Morning Meeting on Etanne, when Almighty
Dollar first initiated contact.

Tek straightened up in its position astride the center
of the Warhorse. *"Tek,"* the message said. *"Dollar's
Messenger brings tidings."*

Then Tek remembered the last contact, and the awe that had begun to rise reflexively inside it gave way to a more cautious skepticism. Insulating itself from the possible influence of unwanted inputs, the robot activated only the transmitter side of its communications faculty to respond. "I hear."

"Your rejection of the impostor that tried to deceive you on Etanne is recognized and to be commended."

And for all I know, I could be hearing it still, Tek thought to itself. "Yes?" he replied neutrally.

"Almighty Dollar desires a final communion before you carry out the mission that has been assigned."

"Then by all means let Almighty Dollar initiate it. Far would it be from me to question the divine will."

"This means is too restricted, as your own experience will testify. When Dollar speaks, it is directly to the mind."

In other words, whoever or whatever it was that was talking via a modulated radiation signal was asking Tek to turn its communications reception capability back on. And that told Tek just about all it needed to know. The meaning of it all was clear now. From the beginning, the conceiving and implementation of the entire *Aurora* project had been inspired by Dollar to replant on another world the seed of the Plan whose growth to fruition had been foiled on Earth. The same Evil Powers that had been responsible then desired *Envoy* to be launched, since the false hopes and fond delusions following its success would obstruct introduction of the proper system of authority and social discipline that preparation for Hera demanded. Their way to achieve that would be by possessing Tek with a malign spirit that would prevent it from accomplishing its task. But first they would have to induce Tek to open up its mind to them.

"If it is indeed Dollar who would speak with me, what need has He of techniques that serve the limits of mortals?" it said.

"Would you question His methods and His judgment?"

"I would not. But I do question *your* veracity."

All of which was pretty much the way Korshak had expected things would go. Lubanov had predicted that the target zone would be the tail section, and Vaydien had been able to provide information about the details and geometry of that part of the craft, along with some suggestions as to likely places of concealment. But that still left a lot of territory and hardware to be covered within the main drive nozzle's quarter-mile-diameter aperture. The illumination of the interior by a pulsed-code signal from a wide-angle source floating a couple of miles off the stern had been to draw Tek into revealing its position, which its transmissions had pinpointed.

Korshak had spent a good part of the shuttle flight out from *Aurora* practicing with one of Masumichi's neural couplers, and by now he felt comfortable with it. Although he knew intellectually that he was sitting back in repose at a console aboard *Outmark*, with everything he thought he was seeing and doing entering his brain via an antenna trained in the direction of *Envoy*, the sensation of actually being there, with the cavernous recesses of the drive ducts and their reaction fairings disappearing away into blackness ahead, the stark outlines of ancillary structures around him, and the void of space opening out behind, was uncanny. Guided by computed updates that appeared as a cross icon superposed on his visual field, he had been getting steadily closer and could now discern Tek's outline through the image intensifier.

"Okay, I've got it," he said—the audio-vocal from his head harness was switched through to a speaker in the room.

"There, upper right of center," he heard Vaydien's voice say to the others, who were following on a screen copying Korshak's visual input.

"The rounded bulge?" Masumichi's voice checked.

"Yes—in the recess behind that diverter fluting."

"That's Tek? It seems to be wearing some kind of shroud. It must be the cape that Korshak described."

"Yes, I see it." The last voice belonged to Vogol, who was also fitted out with a harness and collar at another console.

Korshak moved a hand to adjust a control of the personal-mobility unit that Kog was clipped to—a compact device that suited individuals used for moving themselves around outside at the construction sites.

"Okay, I'm moving in," he told them. "Are we ready with the special effects?"

"Check," Lois Iles confirmed.

Something nearby caught Tek's attention. A strange, radiant glow had appeared and was approaching. As it drew closer, the robot saw that it was more than just a glow: a glowing shape standing out among the shadows, getting larger. The shape was in the form of the sacred $ sign. But even as the sensation of shock reverberated through the reactive level of Tek's circuits, the cognizant part reminded the robot that it was facing a resourceful opponent.

Before it had accommodated to this new development, the sign exploded in a flash of light that faded rapidly to be replaced by a familiar figure in a dark robe with a deep cowl. Or at least, it was a figure in a familiar form. On Etanne, the Messenger from Almighty Dollar had taken over a human vehicle, but this could be no human body, unprotected in the vacuum of space. The pulsating illumination from outside had ceased, but the Messenger was holding a lamp which Tek's optical analyzer showed to be flickering to the same code.

"Am I not the Messenger who revealed himself to you as was foretold, and stood with you before the stars when Dollar spoke?" the lamp asked.

"You are indeed of that form," Tek sent back. "But why would the power that could usurp your voice on Etanne not be capable of usurping your appearance, too? If Dollar's will were to speak with me, I would know. But I do not know. To grant you credit of belief would constitute an unsecured loan, which violates sound business principles. I have studied the scriptures." Tek had moved its hand to the detonator button on the horse's control panel and unlocked the safety latch. It feared a trick, and if anything sudden happened was resolved that its last action would be to carry out the mission.

"Dollar's Messenger seeks no loan. Is he not currency backed by gold of the highest standard?"

"Certainly is the Messenger of Dollar so. But I say he whom I see before me is a counterfeit of base metal. Dollar's message has been paid in full and the receipt issued. No more is owed. Nothing further needs to be said."

Korshak had been bracing the mirror in front of Kog at a forty-five-degree angle to Tek's line of sight, which meant that it had reflected a portion of the outside starfield before Kog entered the drive nozzle, and of the internal shadows and structures afterward. In either case it would have been invisible against the surroundings without minute examination. The principle was the same as that of the mirrors in the cabinet that Korshak had used to contrive Vaydien and Mirsto's escape from Shandrahl's palace in Arigane long ago. The dollar sign affixed to the back of it, formed from a modestly heated electrical conductor that would be sufficient to register in Tek's infrared range, had been added as an afterthought at Lois's suggestion. The flash of light out of which Kog in his Genhedrin robe had magically appeared had overloaded Tek's visual sensors long enough for Korshak to send the mirror and mobility unit out of sight behind a flow divider in one direction, while the reaction propelled him to an anchorage at the base of a strut in the other—both of which features he had carefully steered toward before igniting it. Using a surreptitiously wedged foot to prevent himself from gyrating feet over head while he spoke with the lamp—a distinctly undignified spectacle to have presented for a Messenger from the Almighty—he now confronted Tek from a distance of twenty or so feet.

"We've got an intensified close-up from one of the drones," Lois's voice said in Korshak's ear. A number of self-mobile camera units had floated inconspicuously in under the rim since Tek's location was identified, and had been moving to obtain the best viewing angles. "He's on something that looks like a dumbbell, with a narrow center section. The cape was probably more to cover his movements outside. He has it thrown back now. There's what looks like a panel in front of him, and he has one hand clasping something on it. His posture looks suspicious and wary."

"Got it," Korshak acknowledged. It told him that Tek was right on the edge. Trying to talk Tek out of the task it was committed to by concocting some line that Dollar did want *Envoy* to fly after all wouldn't be the way to go, Korshak decided. The contrary was too deeply rooted in Tek's mind, and the confusion that would result from arguing otherwise would very likely be enough to send him past the tipping point. The only way was to get Tek to open up its NC link and seize control before it could act. There was one card left to play that might do it.

"I gave you a name by which you would know me," he sent to Tek. *"Would that be sufficient to convince you?"* Vogol's inability to supply the name was where his attempt to impersonate the Messenger had fallen down last time.

"You offer yourself as your own guarantor?" Tek retorted. "What kind of fund manager would accept that? There has been ample time for you to probe the mind of the novice who was used, and your powers to do so, I do not doubt. Your bond is worthless on my balance sheet."

"Wisely said, Tek. But it is not my pledge that I offer. Would you accept the word of Banker Lareda, who speaks in turn for the Archbanker Sorba?"

The pause before Tek answered was noticeable

enough for Korshak to know he had made an impact. "The banker himself? Indeed, that would be a certification of authenticity that could not be ignored—if it were the signed original. But I see the trick. You will tell me I have to activate my receiver circuit for the banker. Thus would I be undone."

Korshak flipped his audio to local long enough to murmur at Vogol. "This is it."

"Ready and primed. We have the beam locked on him," Vogol confirmed.

Korshak switched back to Tek. *"Remote communication is not necessary. The eventuality was anticipated, and the proof that you desire is already there with you now."*

The tilting of the head beneath the hooded cape captured the human mannerism perfectly. "How so?"

"Was it not Banker Lareda personally who provided you with the cape of concealment that you wear?"

"It was."

"And did Banker Lareda himself not arrange for it to be made in the workshops on Etanne?"

"To my knowledge, it was so."

"Then I will reveal to you now, Tek, that Dollar, in His wisdom, even then inspired the banker to have written into that creation the confirmation that it was known you would require."

Tek's befuddlement again resulted in a hesitation that was palpable. "I do not comprehend the terms of this contract," it returned finally.

"The name that it was agreed would be the sign of Dollar's true Messenger is still known to you, is it not?" Korshak sent.

"It is."

"Look then carefully among the folds of the garment that Banker Lareda commanded be made. And there you will find the proof that cannot be denied."

"Thus you would distract my attention while you move to thwart my design."

"Your hand is poised, and no move could be swift enough. But the moment is not yet." Korshak opened his arms out and then folded them stolidly on his chest. *"Search for the sign, Tek."*

The robot looked down hesitantly, then quickly up again for a moment as if to check. It loosened a side of the cape from its attachment, turned it over, and began examining along the edge, glancing up every few seconds—but the robed figure of Kog continued watching and waiting impassively. And then Tek came to a corner, opened a fold to examine something more closely, finally raising it before its face and staring at it wonderingly.

In accordance with his lifelong custom of endorsing his creations, Korshak had signed his name at a place where two of the seams came together. But it wouldn't have done to leave evidence of his true identity lying around, so he had signed it SHAKOR.

"I, who was chosen, doubted! Can it ever be absolved?"

"Ask not me, but He who awaits your answer."

Vogol came through. "The beam's registering! He's opening up."

"Go for it!" Lubanov snapped.

Tek felt the same overpowering sense of possession that had come over it in the viewing gallery on Etanne. The robot just had time to surrender to the blissful sensation of ecstasy sweeping through its being before commands coming in over the NC beam overrode its internal functions, and the consciousness that it had been experiencing ceased.

– FORTY –

A site tug carrying a dozen suited engineers and technical specialists arrived less than a half hour later to retrieve the two robots and haul the bomb and its conveyance away for examination and disposal. The operation was performed surreptitiously, without any public announcement. Before the tug had returned to *Outmark*, Lubanov's fast-response force was quietly embarked on an unscheduled shuttle departure. Not long after its arrival at *Aurora*, an unremarkable transporter appeared off the hub at Etanne, requesting docking permission. The important thing had been to get them there before *Envoy* was launched. The Dollarian Academy was overrun and occupied before anyone there realized that something had gone seriously amiss and had time to start thinking about removing evidence.

Tek's self-initiated communications blackout turned out to have had its advantages too. A message to Lubanov from the unit's commander reported that the viewing gallery at Etanne was filled with cult members from the various sects, waiting to see the launch, including a large contingent of Dollarians who had been brought out to witness the fulfillment of Archbanker Sorba's prophecy that it would end disastrously.

At Cereta's invitation, Korshak and the others stayed at *Outmark* to watch the launch from the dome of the site operations tower, which was being used to direct the event. Although the construction and traffic-movement control that had been going on for months was over and most of the associated work stations shut down, the crews were back almost to a man to see their effort and dedication brought to its culmination. Virtually all of Constellation would be following the live transmission on screens, although the flash—even from that distance—would easily be visible to the naked eye. The latest news was that much of the protest movement seemed to be wilting in the tide of excitement and enthusiasm that was taking over, with some of its proponents showing signs of last-minute defection.

"T-minus-five and counting. Fine attitude correction effected. Ignition sequencer is go." Cyblic Heshtar, who had directed site operations and was assisting the launch team, reported from a console. Cereta was not actively involved in this phase but stood looking on from the center of a group to one side that included Wesl Inchow, head of the probe instrumentation program, whose part was also over. Korshak was with Vaydien and Masumichi, taking in the views of *Envoy* from numerous screens around the floor, being sent by remote cameras positioned close in. Outside, it was visible to the eye as a bright spot in the starfield, dimly discernible through the dome wall darkened to protect against the light and radiation glare when the drive fired.

It hung serenely, drifting almost imperceptibly against the cosmic background, like a coiled spring or a pent-up racehorse at the starting line, its very stillness and tranquility seemingly a portent of the awesome power lying within it, waiting to be unleashed. Watching it on the large display dominating the floor, Korshak felt that finally his coming of age in the new world of wonders to which his life had led was complete. Twelve years ago he had been a wandering illusionist with a talent for mechanisms, to whom such a creation would have been as inconceivable as the true nature of the heavens would have been to any inhabitant of Arigane. But he had studied and he had learned, and his understanding had grown until he was able to contribute to such work as Masumichi's. And now, with *Envoy*, he had become a part of something that would once have seemed impossible.

It was Real Magic.

He felt fulfilled.

"T-minus-three. Primary holding," Heshtar anounced.

The launch director came in from an adjacent station. "Release inhibitor shield interlocks. Confirm annihilator alignments."

"Interlocks released. Annihilator alignments confirmed at zero-zero, zero-point-one, and zero-zero," another voice replied.

"I remember watching *Aurora* as a light crossing the sky back on Earth," Vaydien said. "The light became a world that my children will live in. And now we have another light that will go ahead of us to another world that their children will live in. *Aurora* was the bringer of a new kind of life."

"More than just that," Lois Iles said. She was

James P. Hogan

standing with Lubanov, Vogol, and a few more from Lubanov's office, in front of a screen showing Ormont, who was following from the Directorate on *Aurora*. "It symbolizes a new way of life."

"The potential that was always there but not free to express itself." Marney Clure, who was standing with her, spoke without turning his head. He had matured into a deep thinker and influential political figure since the day Lois brought him from Tranth. Opinions were that he would lead a powerful movement one day, if not the entire mission. "What *Aurora* symbolizes is the triumph of the human mind and spirit over the unreason and passions that destroyed the first attempt. Hera will become that way of life."

"Is that why *Aurora* was conceived?" Lois asked him.

"*Aurora* wasn't conceived. It was an imperative that had to express itself." News from Earth had come through intermittently. In recent years it had told of a deteriorating situation in Sofi, faced by rising opposition and threats from without, and deepening political divisions at home over how to respond to them. Yes, in the shorter term it possessed the ability to maintain its superiority by imposing a worldwide tyranny of force, which would be a betrayal of all the principles that it professed to believe in. But even then, how could it hope to prevail indefinitely against the universal hostility that such a course would engender from numbers that an entire planet would eventually command? Most of those who had debated the issue felt that there was no ready answer, and eventually the same forces that had consumed Earth before would do so again.

"Into the last minute." A glowing numeric display

of the countdown appeared across the bottoms of the screens. Views from *Aurora* showed crowds out in the urban plazas and smaller numbers in places like Evergreen and Plantation, staring up at the sky windows. Even on Istella, the gaudy lights and signs had been turned down, and the squares between the darkened arcades and show palaces filled with hushed, upturned faces.

"Disengage primary hold. Enable igniter trigger."

"Primary hold is off. Trigger enabled. We have go on all."

The launch director addressed a screen on his panel. "Over to you on zero?" Ormont nodded on the screen showing him. It had been agreed at Cereta's suggestion that Ormont should have the privilege of issuing the final command.

At Korshak's side, Vaydien pressed closer. He slipped a reassuring arm around her. Lois smiled encouragingly.

"It would be ironic if the alarmists' fears come true after everything we've put into this," Lubanov commented. Only he could have thought of it.

Three . . . two . . . one . . .

"Launch," Ormont commanded.

Even through the electronically attenuated wall of the dome, the whole of the control floor lit up like day as, fifty miles away, a jet of blue-white plasma lanced across space, its length such that through some peculiar trick of optics it appeared to be curved. *Envoy* itself was invisible, but already the source of the jet was moving visibly, extending a line in the opposite direction that was already beginning to take on a curvature of its own. Korshak thought of the replays he'd seen of the *Aurora*'s departure as captured from

Earth and sent on after the ship. Like the protestors against *Envoy* who had relented as the magnificence of the achievement of the species they belonged to at last burst upon them, many who had opposed *Aurora* had subsequently beamed well-wishes for its future, as if Earth were sending its farewell.

Earth was a living organism, Korshak realized as he stared at the screens and thought of the images he had seen of it progressively receding. It had struggled and grown to bloom to the limits that its potential was capable of. When the final convulsions set in that would lead to decline and decay, it had mustered its dying strength to hurl a seed of itself out to take root among fresh, uncontaminated beginnings. And then it would die, as every organism had to. The older Mirsto had understood that within the first year out, before he died. Korshak was beginning to grasp it only now.

The line of radiance burning across the sky pointed in two directions. Behind lay the world that once was and could never be again. Ahead was the world that would be, that could become all that it was capable of.

And in the vastness of the empty void between the two, the tiny fleet of miniature artificial worlds hurtled onward to whatever its destiny would be.

The following is an excerpt from:

RING OF FIRE III

EDITED BY
ERIC FLINT

Available from Baen Books
July 2011
hardcover

Birds of a Feather

Charles E. Gannon

Owen Roe O'Neill started at the burst of gunfire, not because—as a veteran of the Lowlands Campaigns—he was unaccustomed to the sounds of combat, but because such sounds were now out of place near Brussels in 1635. Old habit had him reaching toward his sabre, but the pickets at the gate leading into the combined field camps of the *tercios* Tyrconnell and Preston seemed utterly unconcerned by the reports. As O'Neill let his hand slip away from the hilt, his executive officer, Felix O'Brian, jutted a chin forward: never at ease atop a horse, O'Brian didn't dare take either of his hands from the reins to point. "So what would all that be, then?"

Ahead and to the right, a score of the men of *tercio* Tyrconnell were skulking about in the trenchworks surrounding the commander's blockhouse. So far as Owen could make out, they seemed to be engaged in some perverse, savage game of hide-and-seek with an almost equal number of troopers from *tercio* Preston. As he approached, the soldiers of the Tyrconnell regiment repeatedly bobbed and weaved around a sequence of corners, usually in pairs. One stayed low, training a handgun or musketoon on the next bend in the trenchworks while the other dodged forward. If one of Preston's men popped his head around that far corner, the man with the gun fired, immediately reaching back for another weapon. If the approach was unopposed, the advancing trooper finished his short charge by sliding up to the corner and—without even checking first—lobbing a grenade around it.

Of course, these "dummy" grenades simply made a kind of ragged belching sound as they emitted puffs of thin grey smoke: rather anticlimactic. But the training and the tactics were startlingly new. And quite insane.

"This is what comes of O'Donnell's visit to the up-timers," Owen grumbled to O'Brian. "Thank God he's given over his command."

"It's only *rumored* that he's resigned his command," amended O'Brian carefully.

"Well, yes," Owen consented. "Too much to hope for until we see the truth of it, eh?" But as soon as he'd uttered the saucy gibe, Owen regretted it: Hugh O'Donnell, Earl of Tyrconnell, was hardly a poor commander. Quite the contrary. And humble enough, for all his many admitted talents. Maybe that's what made him so damned annoying—

"Seems we've picked up an escort," observed O'Brian, glancing behind.

Sure enough, close to a dozen monks—Franciscans, judging from the hooded brown habits—had swung in behind their guards, who remained tightly clustered around the *tercio* banners of Tyrone and O'Neill. One of the monks was pushing a handcart through the May mud, prompting Owen to wonder: *had someone died en camp?* Or maybe the brown robes had come to seek used clothes for the poor? If the latter, then the monks were in for a rude surprise: the Irish *tercios* were no longer a good source of that kind of easy charity. They were in dire want of it themselves, these days.

As he approached the *tercios'* staff tents, Owen noticed that, in addition to the pennants of the staff officers, a small banner of the Earl of Tyrconnell's own colors were flying. As he gave the day's camp countersign to the interior perimeter guards, he pondered the fluttering outline of the O'Donnell coat of arms. Strange: did this mean that Hugh was actually here—?

A lean fellow, sabre at his side, came bolting down the horse-track from the much larger commander's tent, perched atop a small rise. The approaching trooper was an ensign: probably Nugent, O'Neill conjectured, or maybe the younger of the Plunkett brothers. No matter, though: they were all cut from the same cloth and class. New families, all half-Sassenach; all lip-service Catholics. Some allies, those.

But Nugent or Plunkett or whoever it was had stopped, staring at the banners carried by O'Neill's oncoming entourage. Then he turned about and sprinted back up toward the commander's tent without even making a sign of greeting.

"Seems we've got their attention," muttered O'Neill through a controlled smile.

"See what you've done now?" O'Brian's voice was tinged with careful remonstrance. "They seen the Earl of Tyrone's colors. They'll think John is wid' us! They'll think—"

"Let 'em think. They do so much of it as it is, a little more can't hurt. Aye, and let 'em worry a bit, too."

"But—"

"But nothing. Here's the Great Man himself."

Thomas Preston had emerged from the commander's tent. He was an older man, one of the oldest of the Irish Wild Geese that had flocked to Flanders after the disaster at Kinsale, thirty-four years before. And Irish soldiery been flying to Flanders ever since: leaving behind increasing oppression and poverty, they had swelled the ranks of their four *tercios* now in the Lowlands. Mustering at slightly more than twelve thousand men, many of the newer recruits had been born here, grown here, learned the trade of the soldier here. And all knew that the recent consolidation of the Netherlands, and the consequent divisiveness amongst their Hapsburg employers, made their own future the most uncertain of all.

Preston did not look approving—or happy. After a few sharp phrases, he sent the runner back down the hill; he waited, arms akimbo, a dark scowl following the young ensign's return to O'Neill's honor-guard.

"Colonel O'Neill," the ensign panted before he'd come to a full stop, "Colonel Preston would have the commander's password from you."

O'Neill looked over the thin fellow's head—he was not much more than a *gossoon*, really—and stared at Preston. "Oh, he would, would he?"

"Yes, sir." A second group of pickets had come to flank the youngster. "Apologies, but Colonel Preston is most insistent. New security protocols, sir."

"Is that right? And those are his fine ideas, are they?"

"No, sir; they are Hugh O'Donn—I mean, the Earl of Tyrconnell's, sir."

Ah, but of course. The ever-innovative Earl of Tyrconnell's legacy lived on in the camp he had abandoned almost a month ago, in the first week of April. O'Neill's gaze flicked briefly to the small O'Donnell coat of arms fluttering just behind him. Or, maybe he had *not* abandoned it, after all...

O'Neill urged his mount forward. "The commander's day-sign is 'Boru.'"

"Very good, sir, you may—"

But Owen Roe O'Neill had already passed, his entourage—including two officers from John O'Neill's Tyrone *tercio*—following closely behind. The monks, however, were detained by the guards at the staff tents.

O'Neill said nothing, gave no sign of recognition as he approached the commander's tent, with Preston's pennant snapping fitfully before it. Preston was equally undemonstrative. O'Neill stayed atop his mount, looked down at the older man and thought, *Sassenach bastard*, but said, with a shallow nod "Colonel."

Preston was not even that gracious. "Where is the Earl of Tyrone?"

"I expect he's enjoying a nap about now."

Preston's mustache seemed to prickle like a live creature. "Yet you fly his colors."

"I received your instructions to come without the earl. I have done so. But he is symbolically here with us in spirit—very *insulted* spirit—Colonel Preston."

"Damn it, O'Neill: the whole point of excluding him was so that you *wouldn't* be carrying his colors."

Owen, bristling reflexively at the profanity, found his anger suddenly defused by puzzlement: "You were worried about his—his colors?"

"Yes, blast it. And why did you bring those bloody Franciscans with you?"

O'Neill looked back down the low rise: most of

the monks had moved past the first checkpoint, were drawing close to the second, where the commander's day-sign was to be given. Two lagged behind with the handcart, near the staff tents. "I assure you," muttered O'Neill," they're not my Franciscans. I'd not bring—"

The flap of Preston's tent ripped open. O'Neill gaped: Hugh Albert O'Donnell, in cuirass, was staring up at him, blue eyes bright and angry. "The Franciscans who came in with you—do you know them? Personally?"

"No, but—"

Hugh wasn't looking at him anymore. His strong neck corded as he shouted: "First platoon, down the hill! Guards: take hold of those monks. Immediately!"

Owen Roe O'Neill was, by all accounts and opinions—including his own—excellent at adapting to rapid changes on the battlefield. But this was not a battlefield, or rather, had not been one but a slim second ago. And that change—from common space to combat space—was not one he easily processed.

Stunned, he saw the nearest monks pull wheel locks from beneath their robes and discharge them into the second set of pickets at murderously close range. Further down the slope, one monk pushed the handcart into Tyrconnell's staff tent while his partner drew a pistol on the guards there.

—end excerpt—

from *Ring of Fire III*
available in hardcover,
July 2011, from Baen Books